THE WEDDING NIGHT

"Come along, honey," Kane whispered, his voice rough
and unsteady. "I've waited a long time for this night."

When he released her and took her hand, D'lise allowed
him to lead her to the bed. A pretty nightgown of sheer
muslin had been laid across the foot of the bed, a gift from
Ellen. She reached for it as Kane turned down the covers,
but he caught her hand.

"Leave it, D'lise. I want nothin' between us. I want to feel
every inch of your soft, bare body against mine."

"But, Kane." D'lise shrank from the idea of his seeing her
naked.

"But, nothin', wife." Kane's fingers were already working
at the small buttons on her bodice. "Didn't you promise the
preacher that you'd obey me?" He quirked a teasing eyebrow
at her. "Are you going to disobey my first order?"

Other *Love Spell* and *Leisure* books by Norah Hess:
WILLOW
MOUNTAIN ROSE
JADE
BLAZE
KENTUCKY WOMAN
HAWKE'S PRIDE
TENNESSEE MOON
LACEY
DEVIL IN SPURS
WINTER LOVE
FANCY
FOREVER THE FLAME
WILDFIRE
STORM
SAGE

KENTUCKY BRIDE

NORAH HESS

LOVE SPELL BOOKS   NEW YORK CITY

To Raeanne, Bob, and Tony

LOVE SPELL®

July 1998

Published by

Dorchester Publishing Co., Inc.
276 Fifth Avenue
New York, NY 10001

ISBN 0-505-52270-5

The name "Love Spell" and its logo are trademarks of Dorchester Publishing Co., Inc.

Printed in the United States of America.

Chapter One

Kentucky, 1781.

The girl, almost gaunt in her thinness, moved across the hard-packed dirt floor to the rudely constructed fireplace. Her mass of curly black hair fell almost to her waist as she tilted her head back to reach a hand to the mantelpiece and start the clock that had been stopped two days ago—that terrible day when her aunt could no longer endure the abuse she received from her brutish husband and had thrown herself off a tall bluff, crushing the life from her tired and worn body.

D'lise Alexander shivered, remembering the sound of hard clay clods rattling onto the rough, hurriedly thrown-together coffin. Her aunt's husband had made the coffin from scraps of warped, knotted-pine planks that had been tossed into the barn years ago, unfit to be used around the farm. They had, however, been good enough to bury his wife in.

She carefully moved the hands of the old clock to what she figured the time was, at least near enough. After giving the pendulum a swing, she stepped back, her deep blue eyes staring blindly at the fire that was almost out. Aunt Anna had escaped her husband's cruelty, but what about the rest of them? The two bound-boys and herself?

She laughed bitterly. She might as well be a bond slave herself. She was treated no better than fifteen-year-old David and ten-year-old Johnny. Actually she was treated worse than they were. Rufus Enger had never wanted his wife's eight-year-old niece to come and live with them. "Another blasted mouth to feed," he'd raged when she arrived at the flat-roof shack, frightened and still grieving for her parents, who had died of influenza within two weeks of each other.

But Auntie's husband had known that his neighbors would frown on him if he refused to take the orphan in, and he craved their good opinion. D'lise shook her head, her eyes brimming with unshed tears. The very first day of her arrival in the Kentucky hills, the man had shown what a cruel and amoral person he was.

She and Aunt Anna had been taking her clothes from her bag and placing them on a narrow shelf—there was no dresser or chest of drawers in the two-room shack—when Rufus slammed open the door and stamped inside. She and Auntie had looked up with startled eyes; then her tiny relative had begun to whimper.

Her husband was coming toward them, his fat fingers undoing the belt that circled his large belly. Her aunt had backed away from him, shaking her head, her eyes dread-filled. "No!" she cried out as he freed the broad strip of leather from its loops.

"Why ain't supper on the table, bitch?" he rasped and swung the buckle end of the belt toward her cowering aunt.

D'lise had screamed and jumped aside as the first swipe of the belt across her narrow back brought her aunt to her knees. She stared with horrified eyes, crying hysterically as the belt continued to rise and fall on the thin, bent back. She learned later that Rufus was always careful to ply the belt where the welts and broken skin wouldn't be visible to his neighbors.

Finally, when it looked as if her aunt was ready to faint, her husband tossed the belt to the floor. When D'lise rushed to her aunt and knelt beside her, his beefy hand lashed out, striking her on the side of the head, knocking her onto the floor. She lay there, stunned, until Anna whispered, "Go into the other room, child."

D'lise pulled herself up, shaking her head to clear it. Her eyes widened in confusion. The uncle she hated already, would hate for the rest of her life, had dropped his homespuns down around his ankles, and as she watched, grabbed her aunt by the shoulder, shoved her onto the bed, and climbed in beside her. Again her aunt called out for her to leave the room, and the horrified eight-year-old, who didn't understand what was happening but knew somehow that it was wrong, left the room.

Crouched under the kitchen table, tears running down her cheeks, she listened and wondered at the thumping noises coming from the bedroom. In her young mind she knew that her aunt was still being punished in some way, and she wondered fearfully if her terrible uncle would punish her in the same way should she anger him.

It finally grew quiet in the other room and, wiping her eyes, D'lise crawled from under the table and with held breath, opened the bedroom door a crack and peered inside.

Rufus had pulled on his homespuns and was strapping his belt back on. As her aunt struggled her worn dress down over her hips, he drew back a foot and kicked her in the leg. "Get supper on the table, bitch," he growled and left the cabin.

D'lise continued to stare blindly into the now dead ashes of the fire, hatred for Rufus Enger turning the blue of her eyes almost black with the force of it.

The despicable man had gotten his wife in a family way numerous times, but none of the pregnancies had gone full-term. The beatings and lust visited on her already weak body had always brought on miscarriages. Each time Anna lost a baby, the more dear her niece had become to her.

Only one time had the aunt gathered the courage to stand up to her husband.

D'lise had been around thirteen years old the day he grabbed one of her budding breasts and squeezed. She had let out a pained and surprised cry. Aunt Anna had slammed a cook pot on the table and, her eyes fierce, hissed in a deadly voice, "If you ever again lay a hand on that girl with lust in your mind, I'll kill you if I have to wait until you're asleep."

Rufus had known his wife meant every word of her threat and he had never touched D'lise again—not in that manner. She still got her share of beatings. In fact, after Auntie's standing up to him, she seemed to get the belt more often.

D'lise pulled herself back to the present when she heard Rufus swearing at one of the bound-boys. He had bought their papers two years ago. David was fourteen, tall and rail thin, and Johnny, at eight years old, was frail and small for his age.

Johnny had cried a lot the first couple of weeks, as he was forced to do work that would tire a grown man. But after receiving several beatings for his tears, he had learned to swallow them and suffer in silence. She and Auntie had longed to go to the child, console him, but hadn't dared. Not only would Johnny have received more lashings, she and Auntie would have as well.

They had hoped that with the boy's arrival their work load would lessen. How foolish the thought. D'lise grimaced. Nothing had changed. Rufus had set them all to clearing more land, planting more crops. She had thought that the hatred she bore the man could get no worse. But when night after night she could barely drag herself to bed, she knew a hatred for him that was all-consuming. Many times a day she found herself scheming ways to kill him, or at least to get away from his brutality. She would take her aunt with her, of course.

Her plotting always came to nothing. She could think of no way to kill Rufus. He always had his Kentucky rifle with him, even slept with it. She would never be able to get her hands on it. And even if she did, she had no idea how to use a firearm.

If she did manage to run away, now that Auntie was gone, where would she go? There was no nearby village where she could seek safety or find a job that would support her. There was a fur post about five miles away, but the only women the owner hired were whores and tavern wenches. She could never bring herself to be that sort of woman. She hated men too much, would be unable to bear their touch. She'd throw herself off a bluff also before submitting to male abuse.

The clock on the mantel, the only object in the shack

11

worth anything, struck four times. With a heavy sigh, D'lise turned from the fireplace. There was milking to be done and supper to be made. Auntie's passing had barely made a ripple in the scheme of things on the homestead. Even as she had lain in the ugly coffin, waiting to be put into the ground, the usual work had gone on; the usual beatings were delivered.

Yesterday D'lise and the boys had worked from dawn to dusk cutting stalks of withered corn and carrying them to the barn. During the winter months the dried husks would be fed to the livestock. She looked down at her palms, full of broken blisters and old calluses. This morning, up until an hour before the funeral, Rufus had kept her and the boys chopping wood and stacking it between the trees standing about in the weed-choked yard. It took a lot of fuel to keep the drafty old shack even halfway warm when the winter winds blew and the cold and dampness seeped through the cracks between the log walls.

But there had been a short period of rest last evening. Their neighbors had come to view Auntie's remains, to sit with the grieving family for a while. She, D'lise, had been the only one truly grieving. The boys had never been allowed to know the gentle woman, to feel her goodness. To them she was just another body who worked for Rufus and received beatings as regularly as they did. Rufus, of course, pretended a great grief.

There had been no viewing of Aunt Anna's body. Her husband had nailed the lid on the coffin as soon as he placed her inside the wooden box. He hadn't even bothered to straighten out her limbs or cross her hands over her chest. At the neighbors' surprised looks, he had explained that when poor Anna slipped and fell over the bluff, she had smashed her face. When he said, "I didn't want the poor children to see her all disfigured," it had been all D'lise could do not to stand up and yell out that Auntie's death had been no accident, that she had deliberately killed herself to escape the hell she lived in.

As though Rufus could read the intent on her face, he gave her a black scowl that promised she would pay dearly if she uttered the words. She had quietly accepted her neighbors' condolences with a nod of her head.

The men and women were leaving then, and were barely out of sight of the cabin when Rufus blew out the candle that sat on the coffin. ''I'm not wastin' a candle on that stupid bitch,'' he muttered and went off to bed. Within seconds his loud snoring rumbled through the cabin. David and Johnny sought their hard pallets on the floor, lying close together, their faces turned to the wall as they, too, fell into an exhausted sleep.

She had sat alone through the long night with Auntie, sometimes crying, other times thankful that at last her tiny relative was at rest. There would be no more beatings for her, no more lust visited on her tired body.

D'lise's head ached from her sleepless night, and she was bone tired as she picked up the two milk pails from the table and made her way to the barn. She chewed nervously at her lower lip as she stepped into the dim interior of the building. There was a gnawing fear inside her that was stronger than her dread of beatings. Twice today she had caught Rufus looking at her with that same leering look he used to have just before he came at Auntie, his fingers undoing his fly. That small person was gone now, and who would protect her niece from her husband?

D'lise had known for some time that it bothered the loathsome man that there was an eighteen-year-old female under his roof that he didn't dare touch.

A shiver ran down her spine. He'd dare now. Even if David and Johnny had the courage to try to help her, their puny strength would be as nothing compared to his. Rufus was strong. He rode to the fur post every day and ate a hearty meal of meat while the rest of them got along on salt pork and cornmeal mush.

The meat from the beeves and hogs that were butchered every year after the first frost never got to their table. It was taken to the post and sold. D'lise often wondered where Rufus kept his money hidden. He spent very little of it, so he must have a good amount stowed away somewhere.

However, she and Auntie and the boys ate fairly well in the warm weather. They had the use of the garden then. Of course all the bigger and better vegetables went to the post, as did the jams and jellies she and Aunt Anna put up each summer and the bushels of apples and pears they picked in the fall.

A grim smile curved D'lise's lips. Rufus didn't know it, but she and the boys had always managed to hide a bushel or so of the fruit in a cave about a mile from the shack. Eating an apple and a pear each day during the winter had kept them from having scurvy at least. Of course, Auntie had shared their little hoard.

One of the cows lowed, letting D'lise know that her full udders were becoming uncomfortable. But before starting the milking, she walked about the barn looking for something she could defend herself with should Rufus sneak up on her and try to attack her.

She finally picked up a piece of broken board about two feet long and as thick as her wrist. She hefted the hard oak in her hand, judging its weight. One good clout to the side of his head should slow the fat man down considerably.

D'lise took a step toward the waiting cow and almost stepped on the scraggly cat that hung around the barn, wise enough to keep out of Rufus's way. When the tom came and rubbed against her leg, she took the time to bend over and scratch his rough ears.

"You're waiting for some milk, aren't you, Scrag?" she said gently to her pet. "But we must be careful *he* doesn't see you drinking his precious milk. What doesn't go to the post is fed to the hogs, you know."

Grim humor flashed in D'lise's eyes. She and the boys had managed to outwit the fat man in another way. David had secretly sliced a long-necked gourd in half, scraped out the seeds, then dried it in the sun. It made a fine dipper. Whenever Rufus wasn't around, it was taken from its hiding place under the chicken house and dipped into the pail of fresh, warm milk. After each boy had drunk a gourdful, she would drink hers. They were always careful to add that amount of water to the pail, though. Auntie had warned them that Rufus had a habit of checking the amount of milk occasionally.

The cat, Scrag, got his milk straight from the cow's teat. He'd sit beside D'lise, his mouth open, waiting for her to squirt the milk into it until he had his fill.

"I guess the boys won't get theirs tonight, Scrag," D'lise said as she pulled up a stool and placed the pail under a full udder. Laying the stick down beside her, she added, "He's got them splitting fence rails."

The cat mewed, and with a grin D'lise squirted a stream of milk into his mouth. When he turned away and began washing his face, she pressed her head against the cow's warm body, and using both hands made the milk hit the bottom of the pail with a rhythmic ringing sound.

She had finished with one cow and had started on the other when she sensed that she was being watched. A trembling took hold of her body. It was *him,* she knew, and wondered fearfully if Rufus had seen her give Scrag

15

the milk. If he had, he would be furious and she would be in for a beating—or worse.

Dread-filled, she continued to coax the milk from the cow, wondering where the fat man was and what he was planning to do to her. There was no sound in the barn except that of the cows munching at the pile of hay one of the boys had tossed down from the loft earlier.

D'lise's uneasiness increased with each passing second. She waited in dull misery, wondering when Rufus would make his move. Finally she could coax no more milk from the deflated udder and knew that she must face whatever awaited her.

With a resigned sigh she rose to her feet, her eyes scanning the barn, peering into the dark corners. In the tension that gripped her entire body, she forgot the club she had so carefully searched out. Trying to keep her face blank of the terror she could almost taste, she picked up the two pails and walked toward the barn door.

She saw him then, at first only the shadowy outline of his large bulk. Her body grew tight as he stepped out of the corner where he'd hidden himself, his belt already in his hand. He stalked toward her, slapping the broad strip of leather against his leg.

"I seen you give that flea-bitten cat that milk, missy," he growled. "What do you think I'm gonna do to you for that?"

D'lise could only mutely shake her head.

"You know." The fat lips leered. "You're gonna take your precious aunt's place from now on. You're gonna get what she always got when she displeased me."

D'lise shook her head again, this time in vehement denial.

"No use shakin' your head." Rufus's beady eyes skimmed over her slender body in its worn dress. "After

16

I give you a taste of the belt, I'm gonna ride the hell out of you. When I'm finished takin' my pleasure, you'll stop lookin' at me like I'm some kind of slimy slug that's crawled out from under a rock. I broke that stupid wife of mine, and I'll break you.''

D'lise was suddenly calm, and as cagey as a wild animal trapped in a corner. If she could somehow get past Rufus, make it to the door, she could outrun him. She could hide in one of the many caves that dotted the area and stay there until she figured out a solution to her dilemma.

Keeping her eyes steady on the man who was sure he had her in his power, she made as though to set the pails of milk on the floor. When he was almost upon her, grinning wolfishly, she straightened up and flung one pail of milk at his face. Even as he bellowed his rage and swiped at the milk that blinded him, she was through the door and running for the dense stand of maple and cedar dotting the gentle slope in back of the shack.

D'lise heard Rufus's heavy footsteps pounding behind her, but she wasn't worried. She was fleet of foot and he would never catch her.

She was only a yard or so from the small forest when one of her feet stepped in a hole. She let out a sharp cry of pain as her ankle twisted and she was on her knees. She tried to stand, but could not. Her left ankle would not hold her weight. It was either badly sprained or broken.

With frustrated tears running down her cheeks, she began to crawl toward the cover of trees. If she could make it to their shelter she might still elude the monster coming up behind her.

Pebbles bit into her palms and knees as she tried to crawl faster, her ankle throbbing from her exertion. But even as her own breath came in gasps, she could hear

17

Rufus panting behind her and knew with a sinking heart that he was gaining on her.

D'lise was finally at the edge of the woods and was looking around frantically, trying to decide which way to crawl, where best to hide. The decision was taken away from her as Rufus's heavy weight landed on her, flattening her sidewise on the ground. When she regained the breath that had been knocked out of her, she began to fight silently, biting, scratching, and kicking. This hellish man was not going to violate her.

Although she put all her strength and determination into warding off her hated relation, D'lise knew despairingly that she was slowly losing the battle. She was weak as a kitten and fighting for breath when his fat fingers reached under her dress and tore at her bloomers.

In panic, and in dread of this panting fat man implanting himself inside her, she let out a piercing scream. In one last bid to be free of the weight pressing her down, she managed to rake her nails across the fat, sweating face, gouging them deep into his flesh. After a howl of pain, Rufus swore an ugly oath and drew back a fist to strike her in the temple to render her unconscious.

D'lise stared up at the fist, waiting for it to descend, thankful that she wouldn't be aware of the rape that was about to be visited on her.

The fist never landed. From behind them, a hard, gravelly voice spoke. "I wouldn't do that if I were you, mister."

Chapter Two

The snow-white stallion lunged to the top of a hill, snorting his displeasure at the lean coon-hound keeping pace with him.

"You might as well get used to him, Snowy," the broad-shouldered, slim-hipped rider said. "I think Hound has adopted us."

The thick mustache above the heavy blond beard hid the firm lips that settled in grim lines. Kane Devlin was remembering how a week ago he had come upon a homesteader beating the half-starved dog with a heavy stick.

"Hey, mister," he'd shouted, riding Snowy almost on top of the tall, raw-boned man, "what in the hell are you doin', beatin' that animal?"

"What's it to you?" The farmer spun around, a dark frown on his face.

It was comical how his features lost their threatening look when he gazed into the coldest eyes he'd ever seen.

19

He tossed the stick to the ground and whined, "I can't get this lazy son of a bitch to go huntin'."

Kane continued to glare at the man until he stirred nervously and broke eye contact. He gave a startled jerk when Kane ordered, "Fetch the animal some food and water. And I mean proper food. Meat!" he called after the homesteader hurrying toward his cabin.

Kane was stroking the cringing dog's head when its owner returned and placed on the ground a pan of venison stew and a pail of water. When the dog only looked at it longingly, Kane gave the man a black look.

"Stand back," he ordered. "He's too afraid of you to eat. You've damn near beat and starved the spirit out of a fine hound."

While the tall, thin man looked on sullenly, Kane watched as the dog licked the pan clean in less than a minute. There was no doubt in Kane's mind that, had he ridden off immediately, the mean-eyed bastard would have taken back the stew. Kane gave the hound a pat on the head as it lapped up water, wondering how long the poor devil would live in that man's care. When he swung back into the saddle, he felt the homesteader's eyes boring into his back as he rode away.

That night, cooking his supper over a campfire, he had looked up at a stirring of underbrush. He hadn't been too surprised to see the hound belly-crawling toward him, a short length of rope hanging from around his neck. Where had the half-dead animal gotten the strength to break away?

"Come on, boy," he called softly, snapping his fingers. "You're welcome."

The abused dog stood up on all fours at the gentle coaxing and came to him, his whole rear end wagging at the sound of kind words. Kane pushed him away as the dog's long tongue tried to lick his face in happy greeting. "Lie down." Kane patted the ground and smiled when he was obeyed immediately.

Later he had shared the roasted rabbit with Hound, the name he had given the dog, and Hound had been his constant companion ever since. With nourishing food in his belly every day, his big-boned frame was filling out and he was becoming a magnificent-looking animal. Kane had no doubt that the dog would fight to the death for him.

Kane reined the stallion in, his eyes raking the hills. For the past couple of hours he had been coming across occasional spots that were familiar to him—a lightning-blasted tree, a spring tumbling from deep inside a cave. It wasn't his old stamping ground, but he had traveled through this part of the country at one time or another. He wasn't more than a day or so away from his place. And if he wasn't mistaken, there was a small fur post in this neck of the woods.

Kane had been away from his beloved Kentucky hills for four years fighting in the War for Freedom. He had spent a hellish winter with Washington at Valley Forge, a time he didn't think he'd ever forget. There had been little food, and the shacks the men lived in gave scant protection from the freezing wind and cold. The horses had starved to death, and the men had been forced to pull the wagons that brought in the meager supplies.

But finally he was going home, sick to death of killing, of seeing a man's lifeblood spreading on his bayonet's blade. October 18, 1781. Cornwallis had surrendered and the fighting was over. If he never had to take another man's life he would be a happy man. He only wanted to get back to his traps, his cabin, and his friends, and resume his old, carefree life.

But violence had always played a big part in his life,

Kane remembered, nudging Snowy down the hill. Almost since he could recall, actually. When he was ten years old, cholera had spread through the town where his family lived. It had killed half the population, including his parents and young sister.

And though by some miracle he had escaped the disease, there had been times when he wasn't so sure that he had been one of the lucky ones.

He hadn't been allowed to live alone in his home, but he hadn't been told where he could go. Everyone was in such a state of fear and worry that no one paid any attention to the score or more frightened children who roamed the streets.

Like a wild little animal, he had fought other children for crusts of bread tossed into the street. He had defended his sleeping place in an outdoor privy, and ventured to the kitchens of the wealthy where sometimes he was given food, but more often was chased away.

Then one day his uncle Buck had found him, and he had been thrown into another world.

Uncle Buck. Kane's eyes softened. His father's brother, a huge man with a genial smile and a reckless disregard for anything that smacked of convention. He was a law unto himself and thumbed his nose at the rest of the world.

"I'm takin' you to God's country, boy," he'd said that night after a hearty meal in an inn several miles into the country, where the plague hadn't reached. "Your Uncle Buck is a trapper, and he's gonna turn you into a fine one too."

The big man had stood up then and, giving his roguish grin, said, "Our room is at the end of the hall. You take the cot that has been set up next to the window. Leave the bed for me." He had given him a broad wink before adding, "I'll most likely have company when I retire."

Kane's lips curled in a grin as he continued to remember. His big, handsome relative did have company when, around ten o'clock, he had stumbled into the room, a giggling barmaid hanging on to his arm.

His voice slurred from drink, he hushed the woman as they fumbled their way to the bed. "Don't wake my nephew. He ain't ready to see what we're gonna get up to."

But the nephew was already awake, and wildly curious as to what Uncle Buck and the woman were going to *get up to*. He had gotten an education that night as he lay quiet as a mouse watching the performance on the bed.

And while he was trying to make sense of what was happening between the couple on the bed, sleep had overtaken him.

The next morning, only Buck lay sleeping on the bed and Kane had half thought that he had dreamed it all. But the other half of his brain told him it was no dream. However, when his uncle asked him later if he had awakened him when he came in last night, something warned him to say no.

After a breakfast of bacon and eggs, biscuits and gravy, they had ridden away, heading for the Kentucky hills, Kane seated proudly on the old nag his uncle had bought from the man who ran the inn.

Over the years until he was fourteen, he had learned all there was to know about trapping, and had loved every minute of it. On his sixteenth birthday, his uncle had decided that it was time he learned about women and had taken him to a brothel. There he learned all the ways a woman could please a man. When the next trapping season came around, and thereafter, he and Buck had shared whatever whore or squaw his relative brought home for the winter. The woman got a good workout each night, but she had plenty to eat, lived in a warm cabin, and was never brutalized by either him or his uncle.

Then Buck had met, fallen in love with, and married Lottie. A dance-hall girl, beautiful on the outside, rotten on the inside. As young as he was, he had known that she would bring nothing but pain and grief into their lives. When he tried to explain his fears to his love-sotted uncle, he was knocked to the ground for his trouble.

Lottie had been faithful to Buck for four or five months, then had begun to entertain men while he was gone running his traps. The marriage was less than nine months old when one day his uncle caught Lottie and another trapper in bed together.

Sick to his soul with rage and unbearable pain, the disillusioned man had raised his musket to his shoulder and blown them apart. He had then put the barrel of his handgun into his mouth and squeezed the trigger.

After making arrangements to have his uncle put to rest, Kane had struck out on his own, ever after avoiding pretty women like the plague.

Snowy topped another hill and Kane reined him in. He had caught sight of a young girl sprinting along like a graceful deer. He frowned when he saw an obese man trying to catch up to her. A mass of curly black hair streamed from the small head, and as he watched, he silently cheered her on. He saw that she was making for a distant stand of trees, easily outstripping the lumbering man who chased her. He watched the long, flashing slim legs and knew that she was going to make it.

He was lifting the reins, ready to move on, when suddenly the girl was on the ground. ''Hell, she's twisted her ankle.'' He frowned when she tried to stand and couldn't. ''She'll never make it now,'' he muttered as she began to crawl toward the shelter of the trees. "The fat man is gainin' on her."

He swore softly when the man caught up with her and threw his heavy weight onto her slight figure, mashing it into the ground. His eyes gleamed with admiration when she began to fight like a wildcat. He wondered what she had done to make her father so angry.

"Wait a minute!" he exclaimed. "That's not her father. A father wouldn't try to tear the underwear off her."

He sent the stallion thundering down the hill as the girl raised a hand and scratched the fat face looming over her. He was close enough then to see the open fly, the fat appendage sticking out of it. The bastard meant to rape the girl.

He pulled Snowy to a plunging stop just as the man raised a fist to strike the girl. "I wouldn't do that, mister," he called, sliding from the saddle.

Rufus looked up, startled, then hurriedly stuffed himself back into his homespuns. He rose to his knees and turned an angry face to the man standing over him. "Look, stranger," he warned, "keep your nose out of somethin' that don't concern you. This girl needs a hidin' and I'm gonna give it to her."

"A hidin', huh? Do you punish your daughter by rapin' her?"

"She ain't my daughter," Rufus answered sullenly. "She's my niece by marriage. And I wasn't tryin' to rape her. She likes her pleasurin' rough."

He grinned unpleasantly. "Would you like to join me? Won't be no trouble for her to take care of us both."

"Do you make a habit of that, fat man?" Kane asked contemptuously. "How much do you charge for the use of her body?"

"I ain't never done it before." Rufus's face was beginning to turn white beneath the dirt. "We aim to get married tomorrow."

D'lise gave an audible gasp of outrage, and Kane looked at her face for the first time. He kept on looking. Never had he seen a woman more beautiful. The deep blue eyes in the exquisite face blazed with blue fire, the lovely red lips pulled back over small white teeth in a feral snarl. She reminded him of the wildcats that roamed the hills, spitting and scratching at everything that came near.

His eyes fastened on her heaving breasts, one half bared from her struggling. His hot gaze moved down to the long legs that could wrap around a man's waist and make him think of heaven. He moved his eyes back to her face and blushed for the first time in his life. She had seen his perusal of her and she didn't like it one bit.

He gave her a cold look, then turned to the man who still straddled her. He had no time for beautiful women. They brought a man nothing but pain and misery. Nevertheless, she was female and deserved his protection. Uncle Buck had drummed that into his head.

"It sounds to me marryin' you is news to the young lady," he said to the man who watched him narrowly. "I don't believe she'd marry you to save her soul from hell." The toe he nudged the fat rump with wasn't gentle. "What do you have to say about that? Do you think she wants to marry you?"

"It don't make a whit of difference what she wants," Rufus said defiantly, rising to his feet. "We're gettin' married tomorrow whether she likes it or not. It wouldn't look fittin' to the neighbors if she stayed on with me, her aunt dead and buried now. And she ain't got nowhere to go," he added complacently. "There ain't much she can do about it."

Kane looked back at the girl, his hard eyes searching her face. He saw loathing and dread in the blue eyes and was reminded of the hound he had saved from the beating. That same beaten look had been in his eyes too. "Is that what you want?" he asked quietly. "Are you willin' to marry this poor excuse of a man?"

"Never!" Her eyes spat fire. "I wouldn't marry him in a fit."

A slow, amused smile changed the hardness of Kane's face. "I thought not," he said.

"Now listen here, mister," Rufus bellowed belligerently, "you just be on your way and mind your own business." He took a step toward Kane, and Hound, standing on braced feet, growled deep in his throat while the hair on his neck bristled.

"Don't be foolish, homesteader," Kane drawled. "If I give the word he'll tear your throat out."

Rufus stepped back, a sickly pallor spreading over his face. "What are you meanin' to do?" he finally croaked.

Kane bent over and scooped D'lise up in his arms. "First we're goin' to wherever you live. Then the girl is gonna pack her duds and I'm takin' her with me."

"You can't do that!" Rufus yelled, almost jumping up and down in his fury. "It ain't right! It's sinful! You're makin' a whore out of her!"

"Shut up and walk ahead of me," Kane ordered, "before I cut your tongue out. She'll be better off as my whore than she would be as your wife."

D'lise started at the flatly spoken words and peered at the man who was stepping along as though she didn't weigh more than a peck of potatoes. His face was lean and hard—what she could see of it above the bushy beard—and if there was any softness in it, she couldn't see it. His eyes looked as if he'd never been young, and she was just a little afraid of him. Oddly enough, she felt safe in his arms. However, if he thought she was going to act the whore for him he had better give it more thought. There wasn't a man alive who was going to use her. If he even looked like he expected to bed her, she'd slip away from him. She'd take her chances with the wild animals in the woods before submitting to him.

They arrived at the cabin, and as Kane turned sidewise to get D'lise through the door she saw David and Johnny peeking around the corner of the shack, their eyes full of dread. She felt a coldness around her heart. Rufus would take his rage out on them. It would be the belt for the poor boys, and probably no supper.

But nothing would change for them even if she stayed on. The beatings would continue, and there wouldn't be any more food on the table.

The stranger was setting her on her feet then, asking if she could manage to get her clothes together. She nodded that she could. Then, her eyes widening, she yelled a warning to him.

Rufus, in a grip of smoldering rage, had grabbed a butcher knife off the table and was preparing to plunge it into the broad back turned to him. Kane whipped around as she shouted, "Watch your back!" and the knife at his waist seemed to jump into his hand. With a flick of his wrist, he sent it winging through the air, plowing into Rufus's right shoulder blade. From the way the handle quivered when it hit, Kane knew the bone was smashed.

Blood spewed forth, and D'lise whispered, half hopefully, "Will he die?"

Kane walked over to the howling man and jerked the knife from the bone and flesh. "Naw," he answered, wiping the blade on Rufus's pant leg. "He'll live, but the arm will be useless the rest of his life. He won't be beatin'

28

any more young'uns and women with it.''

"I need a doctor," Rufus yelped. "I'm gonna bleed to death.''

Ignoring the hysterical man as though he hadn't opened his mouth, Kane gave his attention to D'lise. "Get your clothes together, and bring a blanket along. The nights are cold now.''

Where is he taking me? D'lise wondered as she limped across the floor toward the bedroom. It sounded like some distance away if they were going to be camping out. "A hundred miles wouldn't be too far away as far as I'm concerned," she muttered under her breath.

As she passed into the room where her aunt had known such degrading pain, the anguish of losing so many babies on the sagging bed, her eyes fell on the only chair in the place. A rocker. A rocker that only Rufus used. Everyone else sat on either the two hard benches flanking the table or the straw-filled pallets she and the boys slept on.

An unpleasant smile, filled with hatred and resentment, shaped D'lise's lips. She walked over to the chair, snatched it up, and carried it back out to the fireplace. As the flames licked at it greedily, Rufus roared, "What in the hell did you do that for? Where am I gonna sit now?''

"You can sit on the floor with the boys," she said carelessly as she swept aside the ragged fustian bag that separated the two rooms.

D'lise stood in front of the shelf that had held her pitiful supply of clothing for the past ten years. She choked back a sob, seeing her aunt's two worn dresses and one petticoat folded neatly alongside her own clothing. The only difference between the two piles was that hers had a pair of bloomers. Auntie hadn't been allowed to wear them.

Forcing herself not to dwell on what she couldn't change, D'lise took up the few articles of clothing, then

29

laid them back down to go over to the bed and rummage beneath it until her fingers came in contact with a book. She pulled four of them out and placed them on top of her other belongings. Holding them to her chest, she hobbled back into the other room.

Rufus was still bellowing that he needed a doctor as she found a haversack and shoved her belongings into it. Ignoring Rufus, as did Kane, who sat playing with his knife, she pulled the thin blanket off her pallet, unaware that two pair of eyes watched her fold it, then shove it into the sack. Fat squinted eyes shot revenge at her, while slate-gray ones turned slumberous, studying her. Kane was wondering if he wasn't making the worst mistake of his life, taking her away with him.

Clutching the sack to her chest, eager to leave Rufus Enger for all time, D'lise cast her eyes on David and Johnny, who had ventured to the door and now stood gaping at Rufus and his bloody shoulder. Would the stranger take them away also?

She looked away from the boys to the bearded man with the hard eyes. He met her gaze straight on and shook his head. "I can't take the boys with me," he said, sympathy in the gaze he turned on the thin faces that watched him hopefully.

"You're damn right you can't take them," Rufus stopped groaning long enough to growl. "Them two boys are bounded over to me until they're twenty-one. I know my rights."

Kane's eyes narrowed as he studied the fat man. "Do you also know it's against the law to abuse a bound-person, to overwork them, to not give them nourishing food? Those two boys and this girl don't look to me like they've had a square meal in a long time."

When Rufus made no response, only glaring at Kane,

he said, "I'm going to write a letter to a friend of mine who works for the man in charge of placing unfortunates like these two. You can be sure that your case will be investigated." He turned his gaze on David and Johnny then. "In the meantime, you boys keep a watch on your backs. Don't let this bastard sneak up on you with a club. Things shouldn't be too hard for you now. Remember, he only has the use of one hand."

When he took D'lise's arm and steered her toward the door, Rufus yelled after them, "Damn your rotten heart, I'm gonna bleed to death. I need a doctor."

Kane paused long enough to grab a dish towel off the table and toss it into the frightened man's lap. "Hold this to your shoulder. If I run across a doctor I'll send him out to look at you."

"There's one at a post a few miles from here," D'lise said reluctantly. As far as she was concerned, Rufus Enger deserved to bleed to death. The world would be a better place without him.

"Let's go then," Kane said and, taking her arm, helped her hobble out of the shack.

He couldn't believe how light she was as he grasped her waist and lifted her onto the stallion's back. He'd bet she didn't weigh a hundred pounds. "Thanks to that fat bastard I should have killed," he muttered angrily to himself. "Anyone with half an eye can see it's been short rations for her and those two boys."

Kane lifted a hand to David and Johnny, who stood in the door watching with sorrowful eyes, then swung up behind D'lise. Picking up the reins, he said, "Hang on and direct me to that fur post."

D'lise pointed the way as the stallion set off at a brisk walk. A picture of Rufus clutching his shoulder came to D'lise. This man taking her away could be quite cruel, she realized. Had she whistled up the devil in her desire to get away from her aunt's husband?

Her knowledge of men, other than Rufus, was slight. Single men had never been allowed to come around the shack, and on the few occasions Rufus had allowed her to accompany him to the small post, she hadn't dared lift her gaze from her lap.

But this stranger couldn't be worse than Rufus Enger, D'lise told herself. He looked hard, acted hard, but he didn't appear to be evil. Also, he was capable of affection. It had showed in the way he had patted his hound's head when he ordered it to stay outside.

She decided that she would be very careful not to stir him up, and over the clip-clop of the stallion's hooves, she said, "My name is D'lise. D'lise Alexander."

"That's a pretty name," Kane said. "Different, but pretty." After a moment he said, "I'm Kane Devlin."

D'lise smiled to herself. What an apt name for the cold-eyed man.

"What do you do for a living, Kane Devlin?" she asked timidly, half afraid of what his answer might be, half afraid that her question might displease him. But she had a right to know what lay in store for her, she told herself. For all she knew, he might also own a farm, maybe bigger than the one they were riding away from. If that were the case, her work load would be heavier than ever.

Her shoulders sagged. It didn't bear thinking that she must slave the rest of her days. She thought of her aunt, aging too fast from hard work and abuse. Then a soft breath of relief feathered through her lips.

"I'm a trapper," Kane had answered her.

She smiled. She didn't know much about trapping, but she'd never heard of a woman doing it. Maybe it wouldn't

32

be too bad, living with this Kane Devlin. Just as long as he didn't get any ideas of sharing her bed.

D'lise had just relaxed a bit when the air was split with a yowl that was half angry, half entreating. "What in the hell was that?" Kane pulled in the startled stallion, patting his neck, calming him down with soothing words. D'lise looked back over his shoulder and saw what she had expected to see.

Scrag, his tail standing straight up, was running along behind them. Poor fellow, she thought, how could I have forgotten him? He was the only friend she had left in the world. So many times his soft purring had been her only consolation after one of Rufus's beatings.

A sadness in her voice, she said, "It's my cat, Scrag."

Kane looked behind him and thought he had never seen a sorrier-looking animal. "I hope Hound doesn't see him. He'll tear him apart."

"I doubt that." D'lise laughed softly, confidently. "Scrag has mostly lived in the woods all his life. He can pretty well take care of himself."

Kane heard the affection in her voice, the pride she felt for her raggedy-looking pet. She would miss him. Before he knew it, he was asking, "Do you want to take him with you?"

"Oh, may I?" D'lise's eyes shone their happiness.

"I don't know why not. If you think he can hold his own with my dog."

D'lise hesitated. "How far are we traveling? I wouldn't want to wear the poor thing out."

Kane's lean fingers scratched his heavy beard thoughtfully. "Around twenty miles or so, I judge."

D'lise sighed. Scrag's short legs would never be able to keep pace with the stallion's long stride. His paws would become sore and bleeding from trying to do the impossible. "I guess we'd better leave him behind," she said, a slight quiver in her voice.

Kane remembered a time when he was a youngster. He'd had to leave behind a puppy once when Uncle Buck had decided to move on to new territory. The boy had kept his tears hidden as he handed the dog to another trapper, but he had grieved for that small ball of fur for a long time.

"Do you think he'd let you hold him?" he asked gruffly, disconcerted that he should show concern over a skinny girl and her rag-tailed cat.

"Oh yes," D'lise answered eagerly. "He loves to be close to me."

"Well, here he is. Get him up in your lap." Kane held the stallion steady, thinking there weren't many males who wouldn't love being near D'lise.

"Scrag, come on, boy, jump." D'lise patted her thigh.

The cat sat down, his sides heaving, his green eyes studying the white horse, the hard-faced man on its back.

"Come on, Scrag," D'lise coaxed, alerted by the impatient stirring of Kane's body that he wasn't going to waste too much time for her pet to make up his mind. Then suddenly, as though he had decided the man could be trusted, the tomcat gave a leap that landed him in his mistress's arms. "You silly fellow," D'lise scolded as he settled down in her lap, purring so loudly Kane chuckled. "Why are you so stubborn?" She scratched him under the chin. "We were about to go off and leave you."

"Where did you learn that fancy talk?" Kane asked as he jiggled the reins, moving Snowy out. "Not from old Rufus, I'll wager."

"Fancy?" D'lise asked in surprise. "I never thought of my speech being fancy. My aunt was a schoolteacher before she got married. She always insisted that I talk what she called the King's English. She used to tell me that she could give me very little of the material things of life, but she could give me a good education.

"Nights when Rufus passed out in a drunken stupor, which was almost every night, she'd drag the school books from under the bed where she kept them hidden from Rufus. We'd pore over them then as long as we dared."

"So, you know how to read and write, do you?"

"Yes, and do figures too. Can you read and write and do sums?"

"Yeah, I'm fair at it. I went to school until my parents died. Once in a while my uncle Buck, the man who raised me, would have me do a few lessons." Kane smiled as he remembered. That had happened seldom. His relative was usually too occupied with running his traps or being pleasured by whatever woman might be sharing their cabin at the time.

"Your aunt sounds like she was a lady," Kane said. "How'd she ever get tangled up with that low-life back there?"

"Aunt Anna was a lady in every sense of the word. You can bet Rufus didn't show his true nature until after they were married. She told me once that she soon learned that it was the property left to her by her parents that he really wanted.

"He gave her her first beating on their wedding night when she refused to sell her home. He used his fists on her, then brutally raped her . . . and continued to do so until she gave in." D'lise sighed raggedly. "That was the beginning of the hellish life she was to lead until the day she died. Two days ago she took her own life. We buried her today."

35

Kane ground out an oath. "Maybe I ought to go back there and kill the varmint."

"No," D'lise disagreed. "The way he'll have to live from now on will be worse than death to him. With his useless right arm, he won't be able to vent his spleen on anyone anymore. You've taken away the weapon he used to use so freely."

Kane gave a rumbling laugh, making Scrag hiss. "It's gonna get worse for him too as time passes. A couple years from now that kid, David, will be able to beat hell out of him. If he's smart, he'll cripple Rufus's other arm."

There was a pause in their conversation; then Kane said, "Why don't you lean back against me? You'll be more comfortable. You're gonna get awfully tired, sittin' so straight and stiff."

D'lise wished that she could do just that, for her body was tiring. Her rigid seat in the saddle was jarringly uncomfortable, but it would be more so if she leaned her back against anything. It was raw from the beating she had received the morning just before her aunt jumped to her death. It had been healing, but the tussle with Rufus had opened up some of the belt wounds.

There was also another reason. She shrank from the idea of being so close to a man. It was bad enough that his arms encircled her waist as he handled the reins. When she said shortly, "I'm fine," Kane shrugged his shoulders.

It was just as well she kept her distance from him, he thought. As it was he was having a hell of a time controlling an arousal. If she did settle back in his arms she would discover that fact right away.

They reached a stretch of forest, and silence settled between them as Kane pulled Snowy into a restful walk. Yellow and red maple leaves drifted in the still air, falling softly on their heads and shoulders. There was a fall chill in the air of the dense woods and D'lise shivered, her arms full of goose bumps.

Kane felt the slight tremor that went over her and broke the silence. "Shouldn't we be comin' to that fur post pretty soon? It feels like it may rain anytime."

D'lise looked up at a patch of dark sky. It looked as though the rain she had feared would fall on Auntie's coffin had held off as long as it intended to.

"I think we're getting close to it," she answered, peering through the trees. "I've only been there a few times."

"I guess that polecat kept you folks pretty close to home."

"We were never allowed to go out of sight of the shack unless he was with us. When Aunt Anna asked to go with him to the post to do some shopping, his answer was always 'make do with what you've got or do without.' Needless to say, we did without."

"Are you sure you don't want me to go back there and kill the bastard?" Kane asked, half jokingly, half seriously.

"No." D'lise laughed. "Anyhow," she said, pointing to her right, "there's the post."

Just at the edge of a line of cedars was a rudely constructed log building, low in height but quite long. There were several horses tied to a hitching rack just off a narrow porch running the length of the post. Kane frowned when he saw the mounts. He'd have to keep a close eye on D'lise. She was prettier than any woman had a right to be, and those hill men in there would eye her like vultures. And he had no doubt that she, like all beautiful women, would encourage their attention.

The thing to do, he told himself, was to get the supplies he needed, then get the hell out of there. Although he knew it would rain sometime tonight, it wouldn't hurt either of them to get a little damp. The alternative could be much worse if they lingered at the post.

Kane halted the stallion and slid to the ground. He lifted D'lise out of the saddle, the cat held close to her breasts. As he tied the fractious stallion to a tree, well away from the other horses, the maudlin laughter of women, mingling with that of drunken men, rang out. He wondered uneasily what kind of hellhole he'd brought the girl to.

"Stay by Snowy," he ordered the dog when it came panting up to him. When Hound trotted over to the white horse and sat down on his haunches, D'lise looked at Kane uneasily.

"What about Scrag? He's not going to like being around all those strangers in there."

Kane stood a moment, looking down at the ground. "Do you think he'll stay up in a tree until we're ready to leave?" He looked up at D'lise.

"I guess he might." D'lise nodded. "If he sees me go through the door I think he'll wait . . . for a little while. He might decide to come looking for me if I'm gone too long."

"Well, boost him up in that oak over there and we won't take any longer than necessary. I need to buy a few items for tomorrow morning's breakfast, and I thought we might as well eat our supper here if meals can be had."

"They can," D'lise said, walking toward the tree. "Rufus eats here every day." She stretched up on her toes to set Scrag on a limb, warning him to stay put until she came for him. His green eyes stared back at her, unblinking.

With a sigh that came all the way from the soles of his feet, Kane took D'lise's arm and pushed open the slab-board door.

The drunken hilarity inside faltered, then stopped altogether when the man and woman were noticed. As Kane had guessed, the men gaped at D'lise. And though it annoyed him, he could not blame the rough-looking hill men. Her rare beauty would make a statue stare. And he had no doubt she was enjoying every hungry look.

With one hand firm on her arm, the other hovering over the broad-bladed knife at his waist, Kane started elbowing his way toward a long bar. A low murmuring rose behind him, and he heard snatches of talk. "That's that woods-queer girl of . . . How'd that stranger get hold . . . Ole Rufus never lets a man get near . . ." He felt D'lise stiffen and realized she'd heard herself called woods-queer before.

"Are you hungry?" he asked, to put her mind on something else.

An odor of roasting meat wafted to D'lise, making her mouth water. She hadn't eaten since early that morning and the cornmeal mush had been digested hours ago. "I could eat a bite," she said off-handedly, not about to let the trapper know she was starving.

"Good," Kane said, and a moment later they stood in front of the whiskey-stained bar made of rough planks placed on three tall barrels, one on each end and one in the middle to take up the sag. A tall, thin man walked the length of the bar on the other side and stood before them.

"Howdy," he said, mopping at the bar with a rag that looked as if it had just been used on the floor, all the time looking at D'lise with admiring eyes. When Kane cleared his throat to get his attention, the middle-aged man looked at him and asked, "What'll you have, stranger?"

There was no lust in the eyes that had been bent on D'lise, so Kane answered in a civil manner. "I need a few supplies, but first we'd like something to eat. It sure

39

smells good back there in your kitchen.''

The bartender's grin widened proudly. ''My son does the cookin' here. The kid can cook better than any woman in these hills. He'll be proud to feed you.'' He jerked a thumb toward the wall opposite them. ''Take a seat over there and I'll bring it to you when it's ready.''

Kane nodded and led D'lise back through the press of a dozen or more men who grudgingly parted to let them through. Once they were clear of the rough-looking lot and had arrived at the plank table, its only support another barrel, Kane motioned D'lise to sit down on the split-log bench drawn up to it. When she gingerly sat down on its splintered surface, he placed one moccasined foot on the bench near her and leaned one elbow on his bent knee, as he kept his eyes on the men who continued to stare at D'lise. The cold hardness in his eyes and his protective stance warned the men to keep their distance.

He spared a glance at D'lise, to see if she was enjoying all the attention, but she sat quietly, her gaze on her lap. Consequently, he did not know how uneasy she was, feeling the men's eyes on her person.

If the whole bunch of them should come at Kane at once, could he fight them off? D'lise was asking herself. She remembered how adept he was with that wicked-looking knife at his waist, and thought that he was probably just as proficient with the gun strapped around his hips.

She relaxed a bit and watched the tavern slatterns move noiselessly about the room, their faces haggard and drawn. Poor Aunt Anna had always gone around like that, ever trying to avoid her husband's attention.

D'lise thought of David and Johnny. How were they faring? Certainly they had received no beatings from Rufus since she left them. But had they the gumption to make themselves some supper?

And had Rufus stopped bleeding by now?

Her eyes lifted to Kane. "You forgot to send a doctor out to the shack. If Rufus bleeds to death, the law will be after you."

Kane's lips twitched in amusement. "There's not much law out here, mostly the law of might." He dropped his foot to the floor and straightened up. "But I'll go talk to the proprietor about sendin' someone to take a look at the fat hog."

He then turned to face the men who watched them, his hand firmly on his knife. His eyes like glacial ice, he warned, "Any man who messes with what's mine has got himself a whole lot of trouble."

"Think you're a big bad man, do you?" a gimlet-eyed man asked, placing his hand on his own knife, which was shoved into his belt.

"Mister, you ain't seen bad yet, but it's comin', you lay a hand on this girl while my back is turned."

The hill man tried to stare Kane down, but the dire threat in his eyes soon made him look away. A tittering went through the audience of men and women, and the man's face darkened with rage. He turned to his squaw and took his anger out on her by catching her across the mouth with the back of his hand. She uttered a sharp cry of pain as she fell to the floor, then closed her lips stoically.

God, men are brutal, D'lise thought as Kane walked away from her. She gripped her hands together until the knuckles turned white. Would these men pounce on her now, drag her off into some dark corner, make her endure what her aunt had lived with all her married life?

She relaxed a bit when it appeared the men weren't going to come any closer to her. Apparently they were

41

heeding Kane's warning. A long sigh of relief escaped her, however, when Kane returned and sat down beside her.

"See that old fellow tryin' to put on his jacket?" Kane directed her attention to an elderly man struggling to get his arm into a sleeve that was minus an elbow. "That's the doctor. He's gonna go take a look at Rufus now."

A moment later, when the old gent fumbled open the door, Kane swore under his breath as a slash of rain hit the doctor in the face. It had come sooner and harder than he had figured. This was no fall sprinkle, but a hard, cold downpour coming out of the north. He slid a glance at D'lise's worried face. He couldn't make the girl camp out in such weather. As thin and undernourished as she was, she was bound to come down with pneumonia. Was there a room to be had in this place? He frowned.

Kane's thoughts were interrupted when D'lise looked up at him anxiously and said, "Poor Scrag. Cats hate to get wet."

The words were hardly out of her mouth when a wet, bedraggled Scrag shot past the doctor just before he closed the door behind him. The animal stopped in the middle of the floor, his back arched, his tail twice its normal size, hissing and spitting. While everyone gaped in amazement, D'lise jumped to her feet, calling, "Scrag! Here I am, boy."

With a nerve-shattering yowl, the half-drowned feline streaked across the room toward her. She picked him up and stroked his head, soothing him with softly spoken words. She looked up at Kane then, a helpless query in her eyes.

Kane gazed at the thin, beautiful girl with traces of grief still in her eyes, then at the equally thin, mean-looking tomcat in her arms. What had he saddled himself with?

he wondered, for the first time realizing the seriousness of his involvement with D'lise Alexander. In taking her away from fat Rufus, he was now responsible for her welfare. If he didn't watch it, his whole way of life was in danger of being changed by this slender little female.

His voice was gruff when he spoke. "I'll speak to the owner about a room. There's no two ways about it. We've got to spend the night here."

As if to make his statement more positive, the rain began to beat against the shake-covered roof, sending rivulets of water down the two small windows.

"Come along, let's go talk to the man," Kane muttered, taking D'lise by the arm and causing Scrag to hiss at him. "Shut up, you ugly piece of fur," he snarled. "You're not out there in that downpour like my stallion and hound are."

Scrag's answer was another hiss.

"Kinda wet out there, huh?" the bartender remarked when Kane and D'lise stood in front of him again.

"It sure as hell is," Kane agreed, annoyance in his voice. "Looks like I'm gonna need a room for the night if you've got one to let."

"Yeah, I can see that you do. It wouldn't do to let that bunch look at this pretty little thing too long. They'd get all kinds of ideas." The bartender tapped his fingers thoughtfully on the bar. After a moment, he nodded his head.

"I'll get Meg's room cleaned out for you, clean sheets and such. She's that older whore sittin' over there by herself. She don't get took to her room much anymore. I ought to retire her to the kitchen," he added, more to himself than to Kane and D'lise.

D'lise looked at the woman, and compassion for the used-up whore swept through her. Another victim of men,

43

she thought sourly. She looked back at the pleasant-faced bartender. "I wouldn't want to turn her out of her room. Don't you have anything else?"

"No, there's nothin' else. Sometimes a trapper gets too drunk to go home, but he always sleeps on a pile of hay out in the shed with the horses. I wouldn't advise that for you, though. The roof leaks a bit."

Kane could feel the half-drunken patrons inching closer and closer behind him. What was wrong with the foolish girl, objectin' to takin' over a whore's room? he thought impatiently. She must be soft in the head.

Afraid that D'lise might decide on the second option, he pressed, "Can you kinda hurry up the room? These vultures behind me are breathin' down my neck."

While D'lise was still insisting that it wasn't right to take the woman's bed, their host turned and disappeared into the kitchen. A minute later, he returned, a gangly youth following him.

"My son," he explained to Kane and D'lise as the teenager walked around the end of the bar, his arms full of bed linens. As he disappeared down a dimly lit hall leading from the tavern, Kane said what was expected of him.

"He's a fine-lookin' lad."

By the time the son returned and, without a word, walked back into the kitchen, a soiled sheet and pillowcase over his arm, the hill men were only about a foot behind Kane and D'lise.

Kane was wondering if he would have to kill some of them, or be killed himself, when the bartender said, "The room is ready, and just in time, from the looks of it."

His hand firmly on D'lise's arm, his grip so tight she was hard put not to cry out, Kane turned around slowly.

44

This time his other hand was on the handle of the pistol shoved in its holster. He would save the knife for hand-to-hand fighting, if it came to that.

The men, in a semi-circle now, didn't budge as they stared hungrily at D'lise's fresh beauty. With a nerve ticking in his jaw, Kane prepared himself to fight not only for D'lise's honor, but for his very life.

But when one man lifted a hand to her, a leer on his ugly face, Kane received help from a source he hadn't expected. Scrag let out such an unearthly scream, it shook him to the core of his being. And though everyone was startled, none was as surprised as the man who received the full force of the enraged feline that threw itself at him.

A yowl of pain rose to the rafters as the unwary man's face was raked with sharp claws. With loud oaths, the other men scrambled to get out of the way of the furious cat. Within moments there was ample space around Kane and D'lise.

"Come on, let's get the girl to your room before the men recover from their scare," the tall proprietor said quietly.

Kane breathed a sigh of thanksgiving as he and D'lise followed the tall man down the tunnel-like hall, a still angry and upset tomcat walking beside his mistress. Kane had never come any closer to death in the war than he had back there in the tavern. And all for a woman who would never mean anything to him. He was too wise to let that happen. He knew for a fact that beautiful women were bad medicine.

The proprietor, who had introduced himself as Slim, opened a door at the end of the narrow hall and stepped aside so that D'lise and Kane could enter. The room was small, holding only a rickety table with a burning candle on it, a narrow cot-like bed, and a piece of mirror over a short shelf. Meg's clothing hung from pegs driven into the chinking between the log walls.

Slim walked over to the bed and bounced on the straw mattress a couple of times. "It's probably the best bed in the whole place." He grinned. "Like I said before, it don't get much use anymore." He straightened up and gave Kane a sly wink. "It don't seem to squeak much either. It won't give away to anyone what you two might get up to in here."

D'lise blushed a fiery red. She well understood what the man was alluding to. God knew she had heard enough bed-squeaking in the past ten years.

She was hit with a thought that made her fingers clench into fists. *Did* Kane Devlin plan on sharing that narrow bed with her?

Not if I can help it. Her eyes snapped as they flew around the room, looking for a window she could escape through if necessary. There was none. Only solid walls met her searching gaze. Her eyes ranged the room again, looking for a weapon of some kind she could use to fight the trapper off, should it come to that. There was nothing. Not even a chair.

Chapter Three

If Kane saw the uneasy alarm that jumped into D'lise's eyes, he didn't let on. He was too busy wondering how to deny the thinly veiled assumption that he would be making love to D'lise tonight. That wasn't the case, and he didn't want anyone thinking it.

The appearance of Slim's son carrying a tray of steaming food kept him from remarking on the issue for the time being. "Put Miss Alexander's share here, kid." He stepped aside, clearing the path to the table. "I'll have mine at the bar later."

A plate of thickly sliced venison roast, potatoes, and turnips was placed on the table, followed by flatware and a square of corn bread. D'lise's stomach rumbled, her hunger as great as her dread of what the night might bring.

When father and son were gone, closing the door behind them, D'lise edged toward the bed. Scrag was curled up in its center, his green eyes watching Kane. Could a cat be sicced on a person the same as a dog? she wondered.

She gave a startled jump when Kane said, ''Sit down and eat while it's hot. Then I'd advise you to get into bed. It's cold and damp in here.''

D'lise felt a sickening in the pit of her stomach. The time she dreaded was almost upon her. He would let her eat, then have his way with her on the rude little bed.

With her ankle swollen and throbbing, unable to bear her weight, D'lise felt tears gathering behind her eyes. She couldn't even run if she managed to get through the door. Her only hope was the doubtful help of Scrag.

She almost fainted from relief when Kane walked to the door and lifted the latch, saying, ''Bar the door behind me.''

Kane's lips twisted wryly as he stood outside the door waiting to hear D'lise drop the bar across the door. He had seen the fear on her face and knew that it came from believing that he meant to share her bed. She should know how very safe she was now, he thought with a thin smile.

When he heard the thump of the bar being put in place, he made his way back to the tavern room. He found a spot at the end of the bar and the bartender ambled over to him.

''I didn't expect to see you in here for a while.'' He gave Kane a sly smile. ''I thought you'd probably try out the bed, see if it's to your likin', so to speak.''

Although irritated at the sly innuendo, Kane ignored it. ''I'm sure the bed is fine,'' he said coolly. ''But right now I'm more interested in eatin' than I am in sleepin'.''

If the proprietor intended to continue the conversation in the same vein, the warning look in Kane's cold eyes changed his mind. When his son placed a plate of meat and vegetables in front of Kane, Slim moved to the end of the bar.

The kid's cooking wasn't too bad, Kane thought after swallowing a couple of bites. Of course, anything would taste good after army grub.

When he had taken the edge off his hunger, Kane ate more slowly, letting his gaze wander over the whores, who stared at him boldly. He decided that after he tended to Snowy and Hound, he would finish off the night with the redhead.

Though the women were not very attractive, having plied their trade for quite a few years, he imagined she was the least comely of the lot. To make up for her lack of good looks, the whore was more vivacious than the others who moved about, coaxing men to accompany them to their rooms. Besides, it had always been his experience that women with red hair had more stamina than their sisters.

Kane's gray eyes shone wickedly. Whatever woman accommodated him tonight would need plenty of that. He'd been a long time without a woman.

His thoughts turned to the fresh young body at the end of the hall, and his manhood jumped and quivered. He swore under his breath and forced D'lise from his mind. He would have nothing to do with a beautiful woman. He hadn't gone soft in the head yet. Besides, his size would split that delicate little body of hers in two.

Kane had wiped his plate clean with the last piece of bread when Slim moved down the bar and took it away. When he had replaced it with a bottle of corn whiskey and a glass, he leaned an elbow on the bar and said in low tones, "I saw you eyein' Della. How can you possibly be interested in an ugly worn-out whore when you have that little beauty in your room?"

49

Kane's face darkened. It was none of the man's business who he slept with, but it was a logical question. It didn't make a bit of sense that he would prefer a whore over a young woman who was most likely a virgin. He tilted the bottle over the glass and filled it with the raw liquor, then looked up at Slim.

"The girl is my ward, you might say. I'm takin' care of her is all. You got any objections to that?"

"Not at all; I'm glad to hear it. Only thing is, you ought to pretend she's your woman. It'll look mighty strange if you don't spend some time with her. One of the men might get it into his head to go talk to Rufus, try to strike a deal for the girl's hand in marriage. You'd have a real fight on your hands then."

What Slim said made sense, Kane knew after mulling his words over. There was no doubt in his mind that Rufus would agree to most anything just to get back at the man who had crippled him.

He stared down into the glass of whiskey. Although he had no use for beautiful women, there was something about D'lise Alexander that made him feel protective toward her. Maybe it was because she reminded him of Hound in her helplessness to protect herself against her brutal uncle. And her life would be no better married to some dirty, ignorant hill man.

Slim's lips twitched in a slight smile of satisfaction when Kane left the bar and walked down the dark hall.

D'lise was sitting on the bed watching Scrag eat the part of her supper she had held back for him. She had a slight stomachache. It was not used to red meat, and so much of it. She yawned. It had been a long, grief-filled day, and the eruption of Kane Devlin into her life didn't help. The events of this day would normally span at least a year.

What lay in her future? she wondered. She couldn't just live with the trapper the rest of her life. Common sense told her that. But what was a penniless female without relatives to do? She reasoned that marriage was a natural answer, but she had no intention of resorting to that. She'd go into the woods and starve to death first.

Even the foolish thought of becoming a trapper entered her mind as she stood up and turned back the bed covers. Her lips twisted ruefully. Her brain was too muddled to think straight anymore. Maybe tomorrow, after a night of rest, she could come up with an answer that made sense.

D'lise had just gathered up the hem of her dress, ready to pull it over her head, when the rap of knuckles on her door made her heart jump. Who was out there? Her eyes fastened on the heavy bar across the door. Would it hold? It looked sturdy enough.

"We'll just ignore it," she told Scrag. She picked up the cat and held him to her chest as though for protection. "Maybe they'll go away."

The cat was squirming to get out of her arms when the knock came again, this time louder and accompanied by Kane's voice. "D'lise, let me in."

"What does he want?" She spoke the thought out loud as Scrag jumped from her arms onto the bed. Deciding she couldn't ignore *him,* she walked over to the door and reluctantly lifted the bar. "I was just getting ready to go to bed," she said sharply, standing in the door, barring his entry.

"You can sleep later." Kane brushed her out of his path and walked inside the room. "I've got to spend some time with you." He sat down on the bed.

"Why?" D'lise closed the door and leaned against it, her eyes narrowed and watchful.

"Because if I don't, those vultures out there are gonna

think that you aren't my woman and one or more of them will get it in his head to make you his. I could fight half of them off, but there's no way I could take on the whole bunch and win.''

D'lise's face paled. The thought of belonging to one of those dirty hill men made her stomach roll. Still, she eyed Kane suspiciously. Was he telling her the truth? Did he really fear that some of the men would break down her door, or was he telling her that to frighten her, to get into her bed himself?

She knew the trapper well enough by now to know that he wouldn't stoop to subterfuge to get what he wanted. He'd come right out and ask—or demand.

''How long will you have to stay?'' D'lise walked over to the bed and sat down on its very edge.

Humor lifted the corners of Kane's lips. ''Only as long as those yahoos in the tavern think it will take me to perform. Five or ten minutes by their reckonin', I'd say. But we'll play it safe. I'll stick around for half an hour or so.''

Her face fiery red, D'lise made no response. She knew what he was talking about, though. If the men in the other room were anything like Rufus, they'd pounce on a woman, work their hips a couple of times, then roll over. With Rufus there was a difference, however. He had always continued to ram his body against Auntie just to hurt her, to wear her out.

''Tell me about yourself.'' Kane's voice brought a welcome break in her unhappy thoughts.

She gazed at him for a moment, then shrugged and said, ''There's not much to tell about me. I've lived with Auntie and Rufus since I was eight years old. The only thing I've known for the last ten years is work. Other than that, I don't know what to talk about.''

"No beaus to talk about? Most girls are married by eighteen, maybe even with a couple children."

D'lise gave a contemptuous laugh. "Beaus? A couple of men did come around once but Rufus shot at them . . . which was foolish of him. Marriage has no appeal for me."

"Maybe you'll change your mind someday," Kane suggested. "All men aren't like Rufus Enger." He remembered his uncle Buck and what he'd said when Kane had had his first introduction into the world of sex.

"Never be mean to a woman, Kane," the big man had advised him. "They are weaker than us men and should be handled gently." He had grinned then and ruffled his nephew's hair. "You treat a female, whore or squaw, gentle-like, and she'll damn near kill herself pleasurin' you."

"Perhaps you're right," D'lise was answering him, "but it would take a lot to convince me."

"I'll introduce you to some of my trapper friends. They'd treat you like a fine piece of china." As D'lise looked at him doubtfully, he stood up. "I reckon everyone will be satisfied with my time spent in here. I think I'll go sit in on a poker game that's goin' on in the tavern. I feel lucky tonight." He kept to himself that if he didn't get away from D'lise, he'd be confirming her opinion of men. The warmth and clean scent of her body had seeped into him, firing his blood, bringing an ache to his loins. Never had he wanted a woman so badly.

Suddenly angry at himself for letting a beautiful woman affect him so, something that had never happened before, he left the room abruptly, not even saying goodnight.

The crowd in the barroom had thinned out considerably when Kane walked back into it. And as he stood at the bar having a glass of whiskey, more of the men began to brave the weather and head for home. Shortly the only sounds in the room were the slap of cards as the four men left continued their poker game, and the drunken snores of a man passed out on the floor. Kane swallowed the balance of his whiskey and looked over at the corner where the whores stood, eyeing him coyly. The men would think nothing of him spending the rest of the night with a whore. He didn't doubt for a minute that such a practice was normal for these hill men.

He nodded goodnight to Slim and walked over to the redhead. She thrust her sagging breasts at him and said in what she thought were seductive tones, "You want Della to show you a good time, big man?"

"I'm dependin' on it." Kane flipped her a coin, which from long practice she snatched out of the air. Then, to the disappointment of the other women, he followed the whore down the hall. Surprisingly, he felt a twinge of guilt when Della opened a door next to D'lise's. *Cut it out,* he growled to himself, following the woman inside. D'lise Alexander wouldn't care in the least if he slept with a dozen whores. She'd probably expect it of him.

As he shucked his clothes that thought saddened him somehow.

D'lise awakened, curled on her side. Scrag purring loudly in the curve of her body. She rolled over on her back, then with a small cry quickly returned to her side. She had evidently opened more of the gashes on her back than she had realized.

For a moment she thought she was still back at the shack, and raised herself up on one elbow to look. Had she overslept? Surely not. It was still dark, and besides, Rufus wasn't standing over her with his belt. In a flash then, everything that had happened yesterday came back to her—Aunt Anna's burial, Rufus's attempt to rape her, and the stranger who had taken her away.

She remembered that she'd had a hard time falling asleep last night. Her ankle had throbbed painfully, and her nerves had been as tight as the bowstrings on a fiddle. And if that wasn't enough, she could hear through the thin walls the thumping of bed springs as some whore entertained a man.

D'lise gave a bitter laugh as a burst of hilarity reached down the hall and into her room. There were no female voices raised in laughter and song. Men were the only ones who had anything to laugh and sing about. Certainly the women who catered to the men's lust didn't.

And her life wouldn't have been any different if Kane Devlin hadn't come along, she told herself, then frowned in the darkness. Who was to say her future would be any better than her past? She didn't know what the trapper had in mind for her. He was young, still in his early thirties, she thought. Beyond a doubt he wanted a woman often.

"I'd better stop feeling sorry for those tavern women and start thinking about myself," she muttered.

D'lise felt so wide awake that she began to wonder if she *had* overslept. She slid out of bed and limped to the door. When she cracked it open, she blinked in surprise. An outside door, only feet from her own, stood open, and bright sunshine beamed through it.

"Oh, heavens," she exclaimed under her breath. "Kane is probably champing at the bit to get on the trail." She left the door partly open so that she could find her dress spread over the end-rail of the bed. She pulled it over her head and buttoned up the bodice. Then, combing her fingers through her black curls, she picked up her pet, muttering, "Come on, Scrag, we're late."

Half a dozen men looked up when D'lise walked into

55

the tavern. She stopped short, shy and afraid. A quick glance showed that Kane wasn't among them. Her nose twitched at the stale odor of whiskey, rum, ale, and tobacco smoke. As she stood there, undecided what to do, a mouse skittered through the sawdust on the floor, and with a bound, Scrag was out of her arms and chasing after it. She called to him, ordering him back, but the tom was too intent on his prey.

Slim, scrubbing down the bar, gave her a friendly smile. "He don't even hear you, girl. He wants that little brown critter for his breakfast."

"Yes, I suppose so." D'lise returned his smile nervously, aware that the men lolling before the dying fire in the fireplace had turned their chairs to stare at her. She lowered her lids and moved to the bar, pretending not to notice how their hot eyes raked over her.

"I don't see Kane around," she said timidly to Slim. "I imagine he's saddling the horses."

The bartender glanced up at her, then looked away. Her straight gaze disconcerted him. He gave a troubled sigh and said evasively, "I couldn't say, girl. I've been busy cleanin' the kitchen and bar."

"Maybe I'd better go look for him," D'lise said, half to herself, anxiety clouding her eyes. "I know he wanted to get an early start this morning."

Slim shook his head warningly at the loutish hill man who had left his seat and was approaching D'lise. The man ignored him and placed himself beside her. His breath reeked of whiskey and bad teeth as he said, "He'll be along after a while, little lady. He got a late start last night."

D'lise stared into the dirty, whiskered face. "He got a late start at what?" she asked coolly. "Playing cards?"

"Naw." Mean little eyes bored into hers. "Puttin' it to

56

ole Della. And that one can't never get enough. She's probably wore your man all out.''

D'lise held his gaze, her eyes carefully blank, hiding the fact that his words had made an impact on her and that she was astonished that they had. What did she care whom he slept with? Kane Devlin was nothing to her.

''I'll wait for him in my room then,'' she said calmly and turned toward the narrow hall. When Kane was finished with his whore, he could come for her.

She took three steps, and the hill man, with animal swiftness, caught hold of her wrist and swung her around. ''I'll go with you, keep you company.'' He grinned wolfishly.

''Let go of me!'' D'lise gasped, struggling to free her arm. Her heart raced with fear. Her tormentor had that awful look Rufus used to get, and she gathered herself to feel the lash of his fist. ''I've changed my mind. I'll wait for Kane in here.''

''You'll be waitin' a long time, little purty. He's still rustlin' the mattress with Della.'' He tugged at her arm. ''Come on down to her door. You can hear him poundin' away at her.''

D'lise dug in her heels and strained against the pull of strong fingers. She didn't want to hear. She knew all too well the sound of a man pounding his body against that of a woman—the grunts, the oaths that spilled out of his mouth. And strangely, she didn't want to hear Kane making those animal-like noises.

''I believe you,'' she panted, trying to pry loose the biting fingers. ''I just want to go sit down over there and wait for Kane.''

''Naw, I think we'll go to your room. Me and you can have the same kind of fun your man and ole Della is havin'.''

He was picking her up when she screamed and called Slim's name.

Kane gave one last thrust of his hips, groaned his release, then slumped down on the whore. When his breathing returned to normal, he moved off her flaccid body and rolled over on his back.

With an arm flung across his eyes, he thought back over the night just spent in this bed. He had lost count of how many times he had mounted the woman lying beside him, how many times she had serviced him before he had fallen asleep, wondering why he didn't feel fulfilled. Even now, just after emptying his loins he longed for . . . longed for what?

He didn't know, but he did know that something was missing.

"Maybe you long for the one asleep next door," a voice inside him spoke. "She is the one you really wish was sharing your bed, not the one with the stink of other men on her."

Kane raised his head to look at the female body sprawled beside him. Sober now, and in the light of day, he wondered how he could have lain with the whore. Although she probably wasn't that old, she looked to be in her mid-forties, worn-out from the demands of the men who paid for her services.

Kane suddenly sat up as the words "light of day" returned to him. Good Lord, according to the sunshine pouring through the dirty window, it must be past nine o'clock! D'lise probably thought he had gone off and left her. He swore softly, sitting on the edge of the sagging bed and drawing on his buckskins. What if she had left the post? He jerked the doeskin shirt over his head, leaving the thin leather thongs unlaced in his hurry. He remembered the four men who were still playing cards when he'd left with Della, and his fingers became all thumbs as he tugged on his knee-high moccasins. What if they had got hold of D'lise while he wallowed around with the whore?

He was rushing for the door when he heard D'lise scream, then call out to Slim. He tore open the door and dashed down the hall, coming to a skidding halt just inside the barroom. A scalding rage burst inside him. D'lise struggled with a hill man, her face contorted with fear. He noted for a fleeting second that Slim, a club in his hand, was hurrying across the floor to help her.

In that moment before he leapt at the man, Kane felt shame—shame that he hadn't been waiting for the girl when she woke up, shame that he hadn't needed, nor really wanted, that last romp with the whore. By making a hog of himself, he had endangered the girl's welfare.

He also knew a jab of hurt that D'lise had called out to another man for help. It was proof she had little faith in his ability to take care of her.

The room grew deathly quiet, and the hill man took his attention from D'lise and turned his head to look in the direction everyone else was looking. His face blanched, the black stubble of whiskers on his face glaring against the whiteness. In the next instant, he dropped D'lise and bolted for the door. Kane went after him, grabbed him, and spun him around. With lightning speed his fist lashed out, landing between the mean little eyes. Blood spurted from a smashed nose as the man staggered back, caught himself for a moment, then folded senseless to the floor.

Kane wheeled, putting his back to the bar, his fists clenched, ready to do battle if anyone wanted to take up the hill man's fight. A long minute passed in which nobody moved. The threat in the cold eyes, the speed of the hard fist warned them not to mess with the stranger. Kane looked at D'lise then, apology in his gaze.

"Did he hurt you?" he asked.

She smiled weakly. "I think I twisted my ankle again, and my wrists hurt a little." She shivered. "Mostly I was afraid."

Kane started to walk toward her, to examine the red welts on her flesh, then stopped abruptly. Her delicate nostrils were quivering as though she smelled something bad. *Dammit to hell.* He silently berated himself. *I meant to wash the whore smell off me before seeing her today.*

He was still castigating himself when Della brushed past him, a knowing smirk directed at D'lise. When humiliation appeared in D'lise's eyes and she bent her head to stare at the floor, he glared after the whore. He had never hit a woman in his life, but he wanted to smash this one, right in her sneering lips. When she would have sashayed into the kitchen, he caught her by the arm, hauling her back.

"Go wash the stink off you," he ordered coldly, "then serve Miss Alexander some breakfast." He narrowed his eyes on her sullen face and added, "And don't have the kid do it. You serve her, real nice-like."

The threat of violence in his eyes sent Della scurrying to the kitchen with Slim's laughter following her. Kane turned his gaze back to D'lise and said to the top of her head, "I'll be back shortly. I want to check on Snowy and Hound."

When D'lise only nodded, he turned around, and one foot came down on Scrag's tail. The cat let out a screech that made everyone jump. Amusement twitching her lips, D'lise picked up the insulted cat, and scratching his ears soothingly, she sat down at the table and waited for her breakfast.

She knew a sense of satisfaction sitting there, watching Della make her breakfast. Although Kane had slept with the woman, his command said that he held respect for D'lise Alexander. She looked up when Slim's tall figure loomed over her.

"You feelin' all right now?" he asked with a friendly smile.

"I'm fine." She returned the smile. "Thank you for your intention of coming to my rescue."

The bartender dismissed her words with a wave of his hand. "I've wanted an excuse to club that one over the head for a long time. He's always causin' trouble one way or the other." He paused. "I've heated a kettle of water. Would you like to come into the kitchen and wash your face and hands before you eat?"

"Yes, I would, thank you." D'lise stood up, sliding the cat off her lap. As she limped after Slim, she thought it was just as well she was barefoot. She couldn't have worn a shoe on the swollen foot if she'd had one. She sat down on a kitchen chair and said, "If it's not too much trouble, I think I should bathe my ankle in some cold water. The swelling doesn't seem to be coming down."

"Let me take a look at it." Slim knelt beside her and carefully lifted her foot. "You've got a bad sprain there, missy," he said after a moment. "You need to have it bound up real tight." Then, gazing at a spot somewhere above her head, he blushed and stammered, "There's a— a necessary buildin' back of the post if—if you need to use it. When you come back, I'll take care of your ankle."

How had Slim known that her bladder was about to burst? D'lise wondered as she thanked the thoughtful man.

Della didn't look up from the fire as D'lise limped past her and out the back door. By the time she'd used the rude facility and washed up in the water Slim poured into a basin, the sullen whore had ham, eggs, and biscuits waiting. When she walked back into the barroom, Slim chuckled. ''I guess the trapper put the fear of God into her. She's usually full of sass.''

Kane didn't go to check on his animals as he had claimed he was going to do, but rather walked the short distance to the river. He stood on its bank, took off his clothes and moccasins, then dove into the water. It was icy cold when he surfaced. He lost no time reaching down to the river bed and coming up with a handful of sand. He began to scrub himself with it, repeating the action until his whole body, including his head, felt clean and tingly, completely free of Della's stink. He combed his fingers through his heavy, dripping beard. It was time he shaved it off. Maybe the girl wouldn't be so wary of him if he didn't look so much like a buffalo.

He waded out onto the bank and sat down on a large rock, letting the sun warm and dry his body and hair. A three-point deer watched him from the shallows across the river, but he was unaware of its presence. His mind was on D'lise.

He didn't like the way she was beginning to affect him, like his planning to shave off his beard to make her look more kindly on him. He had never cared before if a woman minded his beard, nor had he cared how he looked wearing it. But this slip of a girl with the lonesome-looking eyes had his mind all in a muddle.

What was he to do with this badly treated young woman he had taken under his care? He hadn't given that a thought when he took her away from her brutal uncle. It hadn't entered his mind that taking care of a young female would not be as simple as taking care of the hound he'd adopted. All he'd known was that a young girl was being abused, and that he should take her away from her abuser.

Hound pretty much took care of himself, needing only a pat on the head occasionally. Kane smiled wryly. If he tried to pat D'lise Alexander on the head, he might draw his hand back missing a finger!

Not that he wanted to pat her on the head, or any other place, he told himself.

There was only one thing to do, he decided. When he got home tomorrow, he'd pick up his old life as usual. He'd have his women just like before, come and go as he pleased. What the beautiful one would think about it, he didn't care. In time she would get over her fear of men and he'd be able to marry her off, get her off his hands.

The deer had grown tired of watching the silent, naked man, and with a flick of its tail, it splashed out of the water and bounded into the forest. "You'd make some mighty fine eatin'," Kane murmured as he came back to the present and began donning his clothes.

Headed back to the post a moment later, Kane's stomach rumbled, reminding him that it was well past breakfast time. He hurried along, his brow furrowed in concentration. There was much to do before he and D'lise could get on the trail. First in order, after he had eaten, was purchasing enough grub for one more night out. Thanks to his lust, they were getting too late a start to get to his place before nightfall. Also he wanted to buy D'lise her own mount. She was too uneasy sharing the stallion with him.

Slim's son was pouring D'lise a cup of coffee when Kane stepped through the kitchen door. He sat down across from her and, eyeing her empty plate, teased, "You didn't leave anything for me."

D'lise's eyes widened and she began to stammer, "I didn't—know I—was supposed to share with you. I—I'm sorry."

Kane saw the fear that came in the dark blue eyes and fought the urge to take her into his arms, press her head against his chest. How sad, he thought, that there had never been any levity in her life, no laughter or frivolity that would now tell her that he was having fun with her.

He smiled at her and said gently, "D'lise, I was only teasin' you. The kid will fix me a plate." He then sought for something to say that would ease the tension that had sprung up between them. He started to ask if she had slept well, then thought better of it. She might ask him the same question in return. He'd be hard put to look into those blue eyes and lie.

He asked instead, "Are you ready to hit the trail?"

"Yes," D'lise answered, giving him a smile that made his pulse leap.

"Fine," he said on a sharply caught breath. "We'll be on our way as soon as I eat, buy some grub, and look over Slim's horses. I want to get you your own mount. You'll be more comfortable ridin' alone."

D'lise made no response, but he could see the relief that jumped into her eyes, and his pride was hurt that she didn't like being so close to him. He picked up his fork and dug into the ham and eggs Slim's son placed before him.

D'lise watched Kane eat as she sipped her coffee. He ate quietly, not like Rufus, who stuffed his food in, then chewed with his mouth open.

She was beginning to discover that Rufus and this man differed in many ways. Where her uncle was sneaky, the trapper spoke and acted what was on his mind. Where Rufus was brutal, Kane Devlin was merely strong. Where

Rufus would kick a man who was down, the physically fit Kane had left the hill man alone once he was defeated.

But he's still a man, D'lise reminded herself, and maybe no better than Rufus when gripped by lust. She dragged her thoughts away from that. She didn't want to think of Kane and lust together.

She was thankful when Slim walked into the kitchen and looked down at her. "Have you taken care of your ankle yet?" he asked.

Before she could answer, Kane was out of his chair and had her foot in his hand. "Damn," he muttered, "that looks like hell. Does it hurt a lot?" He looked up at D'lise, a frown pulling his eyebrows together.

"Not too badly unless I try to put my weight on it."

"Which you've been doin' all mornin'," Kane said darkly, mad at himself for not remembering her injury. "Why didn't you say somethin'?"

"I did." D'lise sent him a wary look, afraid from his tone that he was impatient with her, that he thought she was going to be a hindrance on the trail. "I told Slim and he's going to bind it up. I'll be fine then," she added anxiously.

Kane heard the undertone of near panic in her voice and wondered whether she was afraid of him, or maybe afraid that he would go away, leaving her behind. He stroked his palm over the swollen area and said gently, "Of course you will."

He sensed the relief that moved through her body and silently cursed the man who had put such fear and distrust in this young, helpless girl.

Slim set a pail half full of water at D'lise's feet. "I just brought this in from the spring," he said. "It's icy cold and will take a lot of the swelling down."

Kane, still holding her foot, lowered it into the pail,

and she gasped at the shock of the frigid water moving up past her ankle. Kane chuckled. "You sit there and soak while I go visit the storeroom, then look over Slim's horses."

He stood up and patted her back, then frowned when she flinched away from him. Dammit! he thought. Wasn't he to touch her body in any manner? She hadn't seemed to mind his fingers on her ankle. There was resentment in his eyes when he followed Slim out of the kitchen.

As was expected by both men, price was argued over the trim black mare Kane finally chose from the seven horses milling around in the split-rail pen. A bargain was struck when the proprietor agreed to throw in a saddle. It didn't take long then to purchase salt pork, coffee, and hardtack.

"I want to thank you for lookin' out for D'lise this mornin'." Kane held out his hand, which was gripped firmly.

"I didn't do much," Slim said. "You got there before I could hit the bastard." A hardness came over his lean face. "I've always felt sorry for that little girl and her aunt. Rufus Enger never fooled me like he has everyone else around here. If ever I've seen a downtrodden woman, it was Anna Enger. It always struck me as strange that he was so fat and the rest of them were so thin. I've wondered many times if the people in that shack of his got enough to eat."

"Let me tell you the truth about that man," Kane said grimly, "and you can pass it on to his neighbors. He mistreated his wife so much that she killed herself, threw herself off a bluff."

"The hell you say?" the tall man exclaimed in shock and anger. "The bastard put out the word that she slipped and accidently went over that bluff." His lips curled unpleasantly. "He's gonna find a different reception in these hills from now on. It wouldn't surprise me if he leaves this area."

Kane was tempted to tell Slim what he had done to Enger, then decided against it. The fat man would let it be known soon enough. By now the doctor knew. He pushed away from the counter and picked up the sack of supplies.

"I'll go bind up D'lise's ankle; then we gotta get goin'. It must be near noon."

He found D'lise where he had left her, her foot still in the pail of water. She looked up and smiled at him shyly, then indicated the strip of cloth in her lap. "Curtis cut this from a sheet. It's to bind my ankle with." She transferred her smile to the gangly youth.

"It was an old one." Curtis blushed and ducked his head.

Kane hid an amused smile as he squatted down and lifted D'lise foot out of the water. The kid was quite taken with D'lise, he thought, drying off her ankle, then binding it with the strip of cloth. D'lise watched him wind the cloth around her sprain, marveling that a man so hard and tough-looking had a touch so gentle.

"How does that feel?" Kane looked up at her after tying the binding. "Is it too tight?"

"It feels fine." D'lise ran her palm over the cloth-bound ankle. She reached down and picked up a pair of moccasins from the floor. "Curtis gave me these." She smiled at the teenager, making him blush all the more. "Wasn't that kind of him? My feet were beginning to feel the cold, especially at night."

Damn, Kane muttered to himself. Why hadn't he thought about those bare, slender feet, realized how cold they must have been? The silent question made him take stock of himself. Why had a kid, still wet behind the ears, seen things that he could not? Had he become that self-centered over the years, thinking only of himself?

He looked at her worn, patched dress. That, and possibly a petticoat, were her only covering against the chilly nights. "Curtis." He looked up at the boy who sat staring at D'lise. "Would you have an extra jacket I could buy off you?"

"No, I don't." Curtis pulled his gaze from D'lise and looked at Kane. "But my Pa has some in the storeroom. An old squaw and her daughter make them for him."

Kane fished in his pocket and brought out some currency. He pressed it into Curtis's hand. "Go pick out a warm one for D'lise." He turned back to D'lise and took the moccasins from her and slipped them on her feet. She smiled as she wiggled her toes in their warmth. They had a softness she wasn't used to. The shoes she and Auntie wore in the winter were so hard and stiff they could hardly bend their ankles in them.

"Well, I guess we're about ready to go." Kane broke in on her contemplation of her new footwear. She nodded, picked up Scrag from beside her chair, and rose to her feet. Kane took her arm and helped her to limp outside.

Slim stood between Kane's stallion and the mare, holding their reins. He gave D'lise a wide smile. "How do you like this little mare Kane picked out? Ain't she a beauty?"

"Oh my, yes." D'lise approached the sleek mount and grasped the mare's bridle with both hands. She stared into the animal's soft brown eyes. "She is indeed a beauty," she said softly, "and that will be her name." She looked shyly at Kane. "Thank you. I will give her the best of care."

As usual, every time the dark blue eyes were turned on

him, Kane's pulse became erratic, the breath catching in his throat. And as usual, it angered him. "I know you will," he managed gruffly as Curtis ran up with the promised jacket.

Kane took the garment from him and ran his palm over the doeskin. It was soft as silk, with long fringe running down the sleeves and along the hem. The fancy beadwork on each side of the front panels said clearly that it had been made with a woman in mind.

He handed it to D'lise. "Try it on, see if it fits."

"Oh, Curtis, it's beautiful." D'lise's eyes glimmered with tears as the boy leapt to help her into the jacket. "I've never had anything so lovely before."

Dammit, Kane swore silently for the second time within fifteen minutes. Why hadn't he helped her on with the jacket instead of just shoving it at her?

Kane promised himself that he would learn all those nice little things a man did for a lady, and began by placing his hands on her small waist and boosting her into the saddle. From her arms, Scrag spit and hissed at him. D'lise's musical laughter rang out when he hissed back at the tom.

Slim came and stood at the mare's head. "It's been a pleasure finally meeting you, D'lise. If you're ever around these parts again, make sure you stop in and visit awhile."

"I surely will, Slim." D'lise smiled down at the tall, thin man, hoping in her heart that she would never again be in this area. "And I thank you for being so kind to me. And the same goes to you, Curtis. I'll never forget your kindness."

To cover his son's acute embarrassment, Slim said, "Travel safely, and take good care of this little girl. She's a treasure."

"I'll watch over her real good," Kane answered, and

69

swinging into the saddle, he turned the stallion's head westward. D'lise clicked her tongue at the mare and it obediently fell in behind Snowy. Just before the wilderness swallowed her and Kane, she turned and waved to the father and son who stood watching them.

Chapter Four

It was as though last night's rain had bathed the whole world, D'lise mused, following two horse-lengths behind Kane. She breathed in the fresh, fragrant odor of pine and cedar as though it were a tonic.

Kane reined in the stallion at the top of a hill and waited for her to catch up with him. When the two mounts stood side by side, he pointed downward. "That's the Ohio River trail. We'll follow it most of the way home."

D'lise looked down at the broad, yellow river that could be seen for miles as it wound around low hills, disappearing into depressions, reappearing again, finally vanishing altogether in the distance.

"It's beautiful," she said in some awe. "It looks so calm and serene, slipping along."

"Don't you believe it," Kane said with a short laugh. "It's anything but calm. It's wild and deep, with a muddy bottom that's dangerously uneven and filled with deep holes that can suck a man to his death. And when it's in flood, it's a real killer.''

D'lise gave him a shy smile. ''Even so, you sound like you have a fondness for it.''

Kane grinned and ducked his head. ''Yeah, I reckon I do. But I also have a healthy respect for it. I learned early on not to fight it.''

''Does your cabin sit beside the river?'' D'lise asked hopefully, entranced with the murmuring water.

''Hardly,'' Kane said and squashed her desire to live on the Ohio's banks. ''The cabin would have floated away with the first hard rain. The river sometimes floods its banks half a mile inland.''

He saw the disappointment on D'lise's face and hurried to add, ''You can see it from the cabin though. I built high on a hill where the water never reaches, but I can still see the river. Also, a couple yards behind is a tributary that flows into the Ohio. It never floods.''

''Oh.'' D'lise's face brightened.

Exhausting the topic of the river and at a loss to discuss anything else, Kane started the stallion down the other side of the hill. D'lise lifted the reins and the mare fell in behind him.

They had traveled another quarter mile or so when Scrag leapt from the saddle and ran off through the forest to relieve himself. He kept pace with the mounts then, spraying tree trunks and bushes, putting his scent on everything in his path. D'lise had been watching him with amusement when suddenly her eyes widened in alarm.

Kane's hound was running down the trail behind them, panting, his tongue lolling out of his mouth. It took him only seconds to spot Scrag and come to a bristling stop, his hackles raised.

''Oh dear,'' D'lise whispered, her hand going to her

mouth as the big dog began to stalk her pet. Scrag stood
with his ears laid back, his tail twice its normal size, and
his mouth open and hissing. When Hound was a yard
away from him, Scrag let out an unearthly scream and
sprang at the snarling dog. He landed on its broad back,
his claws digging into the fur, still hissing and screaming.
The stunned dog ran around in circles, trying to shake the
angry Scrag off his back.

"Dammit, do somethin', D'lise!" Kane shouted, bringing the stallion to a rearing halt. "That damn cat is gonna
scratch his eyes out!"

D'lise whacked the mare with her heel and sent her
through the trees to where the hound yelped and the cat
yowled. Coming up to them, she reached down and
grabbed Scrag by the scruff of the neck. As she hauled
him onto her lap, Kane leapt to the ground and ran to his
panting dog. Going down on his haunches he ran explor-
atory fingers over his pet's head and down his sides.

"Scrag didn't hurt him," D'lise defended her pet. "He
only scared the hound." There was a hint of scorn in her
tone.

Kane gave her a dark look, not liking at all that a small
cat could frighten such a large dog. "Just keep that animal
away from him from now on, that's all," he said, his
voice clipped.

"Scrag won't bother him if he keeps his distance,"
D'lise shot back, equally short. "I told you he could take
care of himself."

Kane said nothing more, but he gave Scrag a very un-
friendly look as he swung back into the saddle and headed
down the trail, Hound trotting along in front of him.

D'lise followed, a proud smile for Scrag on her face.
"Size doesn't mean anything, does it, boy?" She

scratched behind the sharp-pointed ears, bringing forth loud purrs.

The mare, Beauty, had an easy gait and D'lise scarcely noted the passing miles as the sun moved ever westward. D'lise and Kane had ridden mostly in silence, and she knew he was still smarting that a cat had shamed his dog. D'lise grinned to herself. He wouldn't admit that deep down he felt that she, a woman, had gotten the better of *him*.

Kane broke his silence when they stopped at a cave where a spring bubbled up from the earth. "It's cold," Kane told D'lise when they had dismounted. He took down a long-handled cured gourd from a tree and handed it to her. When she knelt to catch the clear water he thought, *Now why didn't I fill the dipper and hand it to her? Damn, every time I turn around I act like a big dumb lout.*

D'lise lifted the gourd to her lips and gasped as its iciness hit her teeth. "I warned you." Kane laughed as she clapped a hand to her mouth. "You have to sip at it like you do hot coffee. See how the mounts snuffle their nostrils over it." He pointed to where a pool had formed a few yards away. "They're drinkin' real careful-like."

"As are Hound and Scrag." D'lise nodded at their pets lapping water. Hound had joined the horses, and Scrag was at the mouth of the cave; they were keeping their distance from each other. Kane watched them a moment, then allowed that the two pets would probably get along together. "I expect so," D'lise agreed, making sure she hid her amused grin as they swung back into the saddles.

Farther along the trail, they stopped again to watch two Indians hollowing out a tree trunk about forty feet long. Kane spoke to them briefly in their language, then urged the stallion on. "What are they doing?" D'lise asked when they were out of hearing distance.

When Kane answered that they were making a canoe, she asked, "Why would they want one so long? One that long could surely transport at least twenty people."

"There could be a couple reasons," Kane answered thoughtfully, his brow drawn into a frown. "They could be plannin' on movin' their people farther down the river for the winter, or they could be preparin' to paddle upriver and attack cabins along the way."

"But I thought the Indians were peaceful now." D'lise looked nervously over her shoulder and took a relieved breath when she saw the two men still working on their craft, not creeping up behind her and Kane with drawn arrows.

"At the moment the Indians are peaceful," Kane agreed, "but resentment of the white man's intrusion on their land is deep. An Indian never forgets. It will be a long, long time, years probably, before they will truly live peaceably among us."

D'lise shivered at the dire prediction. "Where we're going, will we be safe from them if they decide to go to war?"

Kane heard the uneasy tremor in her voice. "You don't have to worry about that," he assured her. "The Indians and I get along just fine. I respect them and they respect me."

"That is good," D'lise said. "Respect is a fine thing to give, and to receive." If only Rufus had respected Aunt Anna, she thought, he wouldn't have treated her so badly, even if he didn't love her.

The horses clomped on at an easy walk, and along the way D'lise spotted three different cabins, each sitting on a hill, well away from the river. "How many neighbors are there?" she asked.

"There are five white families settled along here. My cabin is the last one in the string," Kane answered. "Beyond that is unbroken wilderness, with only the narrow trails of trappers, and animal runs."

"Is there a village?"

"Sort of. There's a fur post on the order of Slim's, and a mill where the folks bring their corn and wheat to be ground." Kane gave a wry laugh. "Just before I went off to war, the women had nagged their husbands to build a schoolhouse. When it was finished, they couldn't find anyone smart enough to teach their young'uns. They probably still haven't found anyone. I doubt if there are any teachers who'd want to come into these hills."

"Does the village have a name?"

"Yeah, we dubbed it Piney Ridge."

Dusk was coming on when Kane turned the stallion off the beaten trail they had followed all day, and onto a path that was barely visible as it wound through the forest. They were within five miles of his cabin, Kane knew, but there would only be a quarter moon tonight, and the sky was cloudy. Besides, during the time he had been gone, there could be any number of windfalls across the narrow trail. It was best they made camp before much longer.

Fifteen minutes later Kane settled on a small natural clearing surrounded by tall pines on three sides, and the Ohio on the fourth. He stepped out of the saddle and dropped the reins a few feet from the muddy flowing river.

"We'll make camp here," he said, this time not forgetting to help D'lise dismount. "You go sit down while I build a fire and rustle us up some supper."

"Can I help with anything?" D'lise placed her hands on her waist and carefully stretched her stiff back.

Kane's eyes were drawn to her firm breasts pushing

proudly against the worn material of her dress, and a stirring began in his loins that quickly grew into a deep ache. He wanted to unbutton her bodice, pull it down to her waist, baring the white mounds. And after he got his fill of just looking at them, he'd place his lips . . . he broke off the thought when D'lise said his name questioningly.

"No, there's nothin' you can do," he answered huskily and walked away from her so that she wouldn't see the hard ridge of his maleness threatening to break through the fly of his buckskins. He walked along the riverbank, collecting wide, flat stones, telling himself to get such notions about the girl out of his mind.

By the time Kane walked off the desire that had gripped him like a vise, he had a good-sized pile of rocks amassed. He knelt on the riverbank and, using his hands, scooped out a circular pit in the fine gravel, which he then lined with the rocks he had gathered. That finished, he rose and walked into the forest, returning shortly with an armful of dry twigs and good-sized pieces of tree limbs he'd found on the forest floor. Kneeling beside the fire pit he'd constructed, he laid the wood on the ground, took a piece of rag from a small pouch, and spilled some gunpowder on it. He placed the treated rag in the bottom of the pit, then placed the twigs and smaller pieces of wood on top of it. He reached into the pouch again and brought out flint and steel and struck the two pieces together until sparks flew, igniting the cloth. When flames shot up, he carefully crossed larger chunks of wood over them.

In a short time the fire was burning to his satisfaction, and Kane took a coffeepot from his gear and scooped it full of water from the river. When he had added coffee grounds to the battered vessel and placed it on a bed of coals, he turned to D'lise, who had perched herself on a large rock and sat watching him.

"Before I start supper, I'm gonna bring in some more wood for the night. If I'm gone awhile, don't get nervous. I may have to go pretty far back in the woods to find some hardwood. Pine and cedar is good for cookin', but it burns up too fast to last the night."

D'lise nodded and moved to sit on a rock closer to the fire. She held her hands out to the flames, thankful for their heat. The sun was down and the chill air was moving in. When the water in the pot began to simmer, and the odor of coffee hung in the air, she sniffed deeply of its aroma. She loved coffee, but seldom got to drink it. In the Enger household, only Rufus had the bracing taste of it. Occasionally, Auntie had been able to slip D'lise half a cup, but it always came from the bottom of the pot, where the coffee was thick with grounds.

D'lise's thoughts remained on her aunt. She missed her dreadfully, but she wasn't selfish enough to wish her back into the hell that had been her life. She thought of David and Johnny. Somehow she thought that their life was going to be a little easier, thanks to the man who now approached the fire with a load of hard maple that his arms could barely reach around. If not for Kane Devlin, she was sure she would now be occupying her aunt's place in Rufus's bed. Just the idea of it made a shiver run down her spine.

But as Kane sliced the salt pork he'd purchased from Slim and laid the strips in the skillet he'd placed on the fire, she vowed she'd never look back again. She would look to the future in the hope that it would be better than her past. When Kane asked, "Will you watch the meat while I go cut some cedar twigs for our beds?" she nodded and went to kneel before the fire and the sizzling meat.

By the time Kane made two trips into the forest, each

time returning with a large mound of soft, fragrant boughs, supper was ready. Kane divided the meat between them, filled two tin cups with coffee, then passed the hard-tack to D'lise.

She was relishing the crisp meat and hard bread, washed down with satisfying swallows of coffee, when she gave a startled jerk, almost choking on a mouthful of food. Off in the distance wolves had begun to howl. Kane looked at her terror-stricken face with surprise, then remembered that though the yowl of wolves was a familiar sound to him—a part of his everyday existence—to D'lise it could be a terrifying sound as she sat in the dark, in the middle of a wilderness.

"Don't be frightened," he said, moving a little closer to her as though to offer comfort. "They won't come near the fire, and I intend to keep it goin' all night."

D'lise relaxed, unaware yet of how much trust she put in this big man.

The meal was soon eaten, but they sat on before the fire, each with his own thoughts as darkness swallowed them. The night hushed to silence; even the wolves grew silent. The hound lay on his side, his paws extended to the fire, while Scrag perched in a tree, his green eyes never leaving the dog.

D'lise broke the silence. "Do Indians believe in God?"

Kane grinned in the darkness. She was thinking of their conversation about Indians going on the warpath. "I don't know if they believe in the same God we do," he answered, "but they believe strongly in a hereafter. The Supreme Being of the Shawnee is Maneto. It means he who rules the universe."

D'lise nodded and murmured, "Same God, I expect." The fire died down to a dim orange bed of coals, and she yawned.

"It's time we got to bed." Kane rose and laid more wood on the fire. "While I make up our beds you can . . ." He looked suggestively to the edge of the forest. "Take Hound with you."

D'lise stood up, called the dog, and limped into the encroaching trees, stepping behind the first big one she came to. When she returned to the fire, her bed of cedar tips had been covered with her thin blanket, and Kane had added a heavier one, which was turned back, waiting for her to slip beneath it. A few feet away, an identical mound of cedar, although longer, waited to be occupied also.

She could see Kane's silhouette leading the mounts to the river for a drink of water. She hurriedly shrugged out of her jacket, kicked off her moccasins, then whipped the dress over her head. She suppressed a cry of pain as the material stuck to the scabs of one or more belt lashes. When she spread the garment on the ground she saw a dark patch of blood on its back. As she carefully lay down on her side and pulled the blanket up to her chin, she felt the warm oozing of something on her back. More blood? she wondered.

Tears stung her eyes. Always before Auntie had smoothed salve on her cuts, drawing away the smarting pain, helping the wounds to heal. A tear rolled down her cheek. She felt so alone and miserable. Auntie was gone now, and there was no one in the world who cared for her, loved her.

When Scrag leapt from the tree and wormed his way under the blanket, D'lise curled her arms around him, and after a while fell asleep to the comforting sound of his loud purring.

It was around midnight when Kane was jerked awake by whimpering cries coming from D'lise's bed. He sat up, wondering if she was having a bad dream. Should he go awaken her? he wondered. When she began to plead, "No! No more! Don't hit me again!" he flung back the blanket, and, bare-chested, he crossed the short distance to her cedar pallet and knelt down beside her.

D'lise had pushed the covering down to her waist, and her body was writhing as though she was in great pain. The night air was cold, but when Kane pulled the blanket up and started to tuck it around her shoulders, her skin felt as if it were on fire.

"My God, she's burning up with fever," he whispered, his voice shaken. He picked up her delicate wrist to feel her pulse and found it racing. He gave a start when her eyes flew open, wild and filled with delirium. "Get away from me, you devil!" she spat at him. "If you ever beat me again, I'll kill you!" While Kane stared at her in amazement, she closed her eyes and rolled over on her side.

It was then he saw the yellowish-red streaks on her petticoat. How had she hurt herself? he wondered. Had one of the cedar boughs stabbed her? "But that wouldn't bring on a fever," he muttered. "I'd better take a closer look at her back."

He eased the wide straps of her undergarment over her arms, then pulled it down to her waist. He gasped, his eyes widening in disbelief.

The thin, narrow back, with its protruding shoulder blades, was criss-crossed with lash marks, some very old, faded to white lines, some showing yellowish bruises, and some put there recently. Two, longer and deeper, only days old, were infected and full of pus. He burned to get his hands around Rufus's fat neck and squeeze the life out of him. But for now he had to do something for the seriously ill girl.

"We'll clean her wounds first," he spoke to Scrag, who

was sitting quietly at D'lise's head, for once not spitting and hissing at Kane as he sat watching, waiting for him to help his mistress.

The leather canteen was still half-full of spring water, put there when they had stopped at the small cave. Kane gave silent thanks that he hadn't used his handkerchief to wipe his face during the day as he put the clean folded cloth on the infected area, then dribbled water onto it until it was drenched. He gently patted his fingers over the area a moment, then lifted the handkerchief off. The long lashes on the white skin still ran with the yellow poison.

The next hour was like a nightmare to Kane as he tried to bring her fever down. He had torn a strip off her petticoat and bathed her face and throat and chest, but her skin remained hot and dry, and D'lise continued to beg and plead in her delirium. The only way he had been able to help her at all was when he held a cup of water to her parched lips. Each time she drank greedily.

But now his water supply was running low, and he hesitated to give her the muddy river water. Never in his life had he felt so helpless. He was not a religious man, but he firmly believed that there was a higher Being that one day everyone had to account to. He dropped his head in his hands and, closing his eyes, earnestly prayed for the young woman who had touched his heart.

Kane was dribbling the last of the spring water between D'lise's lips when Hound gave a low growl and Scrag arched his back. He dropped the cup and jumped to his feet, cursing the fact that his knife and gun lay on his pallet. When the lean figure of a man came trotting out of the forest, he relaxed with a ragged sigh.

"Big Beaver!" he exclaimed to his long-time Indian friend. "Am I glad to see you."

The brave's stoic features were softened by a wide

smile. "My white brother speaks like a woman. What is it about me that excites you so? Is it men you like now?" He lifted a teasing eyebrow.

"I wouldn't pick an ugly-looking one like you if that was the case." Kane smiled back, shaking the hand offered to him. "Aside from being glad to see you after so long a time, I have a very sick woman on my hands. I'm at my wit's end what to do for her."

He stepped aside so that Big Beaver could see D'lise's inert body. The Indian squatted down beside her and removed the handkerchief Kane had kept wet all night. He studied the yellow pus and black blood on the cloth, then the lashes that still seeped with poison.

He looked up at Kane with searching eyes. "Since when have you started beating your women, friend?" His tone was sharp.

"Dammit, Big Beaver, I didn't do that." Kane gave his friend a hard look. "And I resent the fact that you would think such a thing of me. That's the work of her uncle."

The Indian ran a long finger down D'lise's side as though counting the ribs. "This woman of yours is a skinny thing," he said, "but her face has a beauty that will make men fight over her." At the closed look that came over Kane's face, he said, "I think maybe you have already fought over this one."

"Only to protect her honor," Kane said stiffly, "and she's not my woman. I'm . . . like her guardian."

Big Beaver didn't look convinced. "Then you won't mind when your trapper friends start showing up at your cabin wanting to court her."

"Look," Kane said, a black look on his face, "can you help her or not?"

The brave left off teasing and gazed thoughtfully at D'lise's back. "Those two lashes are badly infected." He gently skimmed a finger along the red, swollen cuts. "They must be drained before the poison enters her blood."

"But how?" Kane ran frustrated fingers through his hair. "The only thing I have, or had, was spring water and she just drank the last of it."

Big Beaver stood up. "Do you have any salt pork in your grub sack?" When Kane nodded, he instructed, "Slice several pieces thin and place them on the sores. It will help the inflammation until I can get something stronger." He looked off through the forest where the trees were beginning to take shape in the gray dawn. "I won't be gone long," he said and trotted off through the trees.

Relieved to finally be doing something constructive, Kane sliced the salt-cured meat. When he had several thin slices, he rushed to D'lise's side. He knelt down, then paused. She had rolled over on her back, and the beauty of her breasts was revealed to him. But other than thinking they were beautiful, he wasn't affected physically. He thought only of making her well again.

He laid the meat down on the blanket, then gently turned her back onto her stomach. She whimpered a bit, then grew quiet as Kane transferred the briny meat to her back.

Around fifteen minutes had passed, and Kane hadn't stirred from D'lise's side when Big Bear came loping back. In one hand he carried some woods plants, in the other roots and barks. He placed them all on the rock where D'lise had sat the night before, then grabbed the coffee pot and walked to the river. Kane watched him scrub it thoroughly with sand before he returned to the fire. He then pulled the stopper from his own water bag and poured a good amount into the pot. He placed it on the hot coals, then looked up at Kane.

"When this boils I'll add snakeroot and penny-royal leaves to it," he said, "then let it steep awhile. There's nothing better to bring down a fever." He picked up a third plant. "This is called poke. I will boil it also. You must use it to bathe her wounds."

A few minutes later Kane stood over his friend, watching him drop the leaves into the simmering water. Big Beaver looked up at him with a crooked grin. "Don't stand there like a dumb buffalo. Go wash me a cup."

The normally graceful trapper tripped over his own feet as he ran to the river, a cup in his hand. Big Beaver's smile turned into a tickled grin. Never had he seen his tough friend so rattled.

Five minutes later, Kane watched the Indian lift D'lise's head and press the cup against her lips. Though she tried to move her mouth away from the bitter-tasting liquid, Big Beaver persisted until she had drunk the last drop. By the time he heated more water and brewed the poke leaves, she was resting quietly, her body bathed in sweat.

Kane looked at the red man, his eyes glistening with gratitude. "Thank you, friend. You have saved her life."

Big Beaver shook his head. "Nature's medicine saved her life. I only prepared it. Let's take the salt pork off her back now, and later you can start bathing her with the poke water."

The tall Indian grunted his satisfaction when Kane carefully lifted the meat and turned it over. The underneath was black from the seepage of the ugly wounds. Most of the swelling was gone and the belt lashes didn't look quite so raw. He tossed the pork into the fire where it sizzled and crackled. Big Beaver handed Kane the coffee pot of poke juices. "Bathe the area often, and by this afternoon you can be back on the trail."

"So soon?" Kane looked his surprise. "Won't she be awfully weak?"

"She will," the Indian agreed, "but not so weak she can't ride. You're not far from home. Shoot a squirrel as you ride along and make some broth from it when you get home. That will strengthen her." He reached into the pouch and brought out a small root shaped like a little man. "This is ginseng root. Have her chew on it as you ride along. It's bitter, but it works quickly to help one regain strength."

Kane took the dry, shriveled root from him, and without another word, Big Beaver lifted a hand, then took off through the forest. Kane wasn't shocked by the abrupt leave-taking. It was the Indian's way. Unlike the white man, he never wasted time in saying goodbye. He might not see his friend again for months; then one day, unexpectedly, he'd drop by and invite him to go hunting.

But Kane knew that if ever he had need of his friend, all he had to do was put out the word and the Indian would come to him. And he would do the same for this special friend.

As he tore another strip off D'lise's petticoat and began to bathe her back, he recalled how his friendship with Big Beaver had begun.

It had been this time of year six years ago, a warm day, Indian summer having its last fling. He was out scouting new territory to lay his trapline when he came to an animal trail and decided to follow it. He was nearing the edge of the forest when he heard the first gunshot, then voices. He instinctively drew back into the thick foliage of a clump of cedar. A man couldn't be too careful in the wilderness.

As Kane waited, another shot rang out, followed by coarse laughter. When he heard the words, "Scream, you bastard,'' he stepped back onto the trail. Some white men must have come upon a lone Indian and were torturing him.

His feet making no noise on the needle-strewn forest floor, Kane trotted in the direction of the gunshots. He had covered but a short distance when, through the straight, tall trunks of pine, he saw two white men with pistols drawn and an Indian lying on the ground. Blood ran from both muscular thighs.

''You bastards,'' he growled under his breath, ''takin' shots at a man just to hear him yell.''

But the stoic brave didn't utter a sound, only looked at the men with contempt. And what was more, Kane knew, no sound would pass his lips if he was shot a dozen times.

Kane drew his own pistol and waited, his eyes skimming the area to make sure the two men were alone. It was then that he saw the woman's body. She lay limply on the ground, much like a cloth doll dropped by a child. She lay so still he knew she was dead.

As though he had witnessed it, he knew what had happened. One of the men had shot the Indian in the thigh, rendering him helpless to defend his woman. And while the poor fellow looked on, they had raped her before killing her. Now the bloody bastards were having sport with her husband before they killed him.

When one of the men raised his pistol and took aim at the Indian's shoulder, Kane brought up his gun and squeezed the trigger. A round, black hole appeared between the gunman's eyes almost before the shot was heard. As the man folded to the ground, his companion spun around, staring wildly. Kane holstered the pistol and drew the sharp hunting knife from its sheath.

The fight didn't last long. Kane's ability with a knife was equal to his skill with a gun. He was agile where his combatant was awkward. They circled each other a couple of times; then with the swiftness of a striking snake, Kane stepped in close to the man and plunged the knife into his heart.

The hill man glared hatred at him. "You have killed two white men over a dirty Indian," he rasped hoarsely, then fell to the ground. He lay there, flat on his back, the sun shining on his wide-open, staring eyes. As Kane bent over him to retrieve his knife, he said, "I didn't kill two white men; I killed two pieces of river scum to save the life of a real man." Wiping the bloody knife on the man's trousers, he shoved it back in its sheath, then walked over to the wounded Indian.

An hour passed in which Kane worked feverishly to keep the brave from bleeding to death. A fire was built, water boiled in the tin cup he carried, the bullets dug out of the red-bronze thighs. Through it all not an exclamation of pain escaped the Indian's lips. Not even when Kane cauterized the wounds with the red-hot blade of his knife. He kept his eyes on his dead wife as though drawing strength from her.

Kane recalled walking over to the woman and kneeling beside her as he straightened her legs, pulled her shift down to her knees, and arranged her arms at her sides. After he took a handkerchief from his pocket and drapped it across her throat where a knife had ended her life, he took off his jacket and spread it lengthwise over her body.

It was then the Indian finally spoke. "Big Beaver gives you his thanks."

"I only wish I had arrived in time to save your woman's life," Kane answered. Then after a thoughtful pause, he said, "I don't know how I'm gonna get you and your wife home. Is your village nearby?"

A bitter look flickered in the black eyes. "It is less than

two miles away. Another hour and we'd have been home.''

"How safe is it for me to go to your village and send someone after you?''

"I don't think it would be wise for you to go with the news you must carry. If you will add some green wood to your fire, and leave your undershirt with me, I can send up a smoke signal. The young braves will come quickly.''

Kane cut small limbs off a maple tree, knowing that they would smoke heavily. When he had arranged them on the fire, he peeled off his buckskin shirt, then the gray woolen undershirt beneath it. Dropping it into the Indian's lap, he pulled the buckskin back on.

"I'll be goin' now,'' he said, "I have a far piece to walk and I want to get home before dark.''

"What are you called?'' Big Beaver asked.

"Devlin. Kane Devlin.''

"Ah, yes.'' The black head nodded. "I have heard of you, trapper. My people speak of you around their camp-fires. They say that you are an honorable and brave white man.''

Embarrassed by the respect in the deep voice, Kane made no response. Then, in the manner in which Indians took their leave, he wheeled abruptly and walked back in the direction from which he'd come.

One evening, two months later, when the first light snow had arrived, a knock had sounded at Kane's door. When he opened it he looked into Big Beaver's face. They gazed at each other a moment, both remembering how it had been the day they met.

"Come in, Big Beaver,'' Kane spoke, opening the door wider and stepping aside for him to enter. "I was just about to have my supper. Will you eat with me?'' The brave stepped inside and Kane noticed that he limped slightly, favoring his right leg, the one that had received the deeper wound.

Before they sat down at the table where a pot of steaming stew waited, Big Beaver took a folded piece of material from inside his fur-lined jacket and handed it to Kane. "My mother made you this in exchange for the one I ruined in sending up smoke signals for help that day."

Kane was about to say, "That wasn't necessary," but remembered in time that the proud Indian would feel insulted if he uttered such words. He unfolded the garment made from finely woven wool and held it up. "Thank your mother for me," he said, his eyes admiring the handiwork. "It is much finer than the one it is replacing."

The softening of his features showed that the brave was pleased with the praise of the undergarment, although he didn't say so. Only a woman would do that.

The stew was eaten in silence. But when their pipes were lit and they sat before the fire, they began a lasting friendship as they discussed hunting, fishing, trapping, and even women.

Big Beaver stayed with Kane for four days. On the fifth day, when Kane rose at dawn to run his traps, the Indian was gone. And so it had continued ever since, his new friend showing up at his door at intervals of weeks, sometimes months. He would spend a few days, then leave, most times not saying goodbye.

Kane came back to the present and left off bathing D'lise when she shivered and goose bumps rose on her flesh. Of course, he thought, now that the fever had left her, the morning air would be cold on her flesh.

He spread the cloth on her wounds and pulled the blanket up, tucking it around her shoulders. He smoothed the sweat-dampened curls from around her face, letting his hand linger on the black hair as he continued to gaze at her delicate face. There grew inside him a protectiveness toward her. He silently swore that as long as he lived, this fragile girl would never again suffer at another man's hand. He would be her father, her brother, her protector.

He ignored the small voice that asked cynically, "And nothing more?"

According to the position of the sun, it was around noon when D'lise stirred and opened her eyes. Where was she? she asked herself. When her gaze shifted and she saw Kane sitting nearby, smoking his pipe, she remembered where she was and why. *Drat!* she thought. *I've overslept again.* Why hadn't he awakened her? She started to throw off the blanket, then realized that she was bare to the waist. How could that be? How could the trapper have partially disrobed her without her being aware of it?

Her eyes were flashing indignantly when Kane rose and walked over to her. "Well." He smiled, hunkering down beside the pallet. "How are you feelin'?"

"What do you mean, how am I feeling?" she retorted sharply. "I feel fine. Why shouldn't I?" She clutched the blanket to her chin.

"Because, young lady, you had a raging fever all last night," Kane said quietly. "A couple of the belt lashes on you back had become infected. If an Indian friend of mine hadn't come along and treated you, I think that by now you would be dead. Why didn't you tell me that fat bastard was in the habit of beatin' you, that you had cuts on you that could only be a few days old?"

A shamed red flushed over D'lise's face and she lowered her lids. "I didn't see any reason to tell you. You were taking me away from him, and that was good enough for me. I didn't know they were becoming infected." She forced herself to look up at Kane. "I would like to thank your friend."

"He's gone. He left as soon as your fever broke."

"Then I must thank you for taking care of me." She gazed at the tired look on his face, his red-rimmed eyes. "You haven't slept all night, have you?"

"I dozed a while back. I don't need much sleep." He looked closely at D'lise. "Now, seriously, how do you really feel?"

"I truly do feel all right, only a little weak. And I can't tell you how good it feels not to have my back hurting."

"Big Beaver, my friend, made up a concoction for me to bathe your cuts with and they're coming along fine. They'll be all healed in a couple days."

D'lise blushed, wondering how much of her body Kane had seen as he tended her. Had he seen her breasts? *Of course he did, you ninny,* she answered herself, her face becoming redder.

Scrag chose that moment to jump from a tree and land on her bed. She pulled him into her arms and buried her face in his fur. Kane suspected what was going on in her mind and said matter-of-factly, "Do you think you're up to riding? We're only about five miles from my cabin. I want to get you home, make you some soup, and get you settled in as soon as possible."

"I'm sure I can." D'lise raised her head from Scrag, more at ease at Kane's practical tone. A woman's breasts probably didn't mean a thing to him. She was sure he had seen dozens of them.

"Turn your back so I can get dressed," she ordered when Kane continued to hunker beside her.

"Oh, sorry." Kane grinned, amused at her imperious tone. This little one could become a dictator if he didn't watch her. He rose and went to saddle the horses.

Kane kept the stallion at a walk, the mare following him. He didn't want D'lise tiring more than necessary. He didn't think he could go through another night like last night should her fever return.

They had ridden a mile or so when they climbed a hill and saw a cabin in the distance. It was a sturdy, neat little place, with curtains at the windows and fall flowers blooming around it. D'lise's pulse leapt with delight.

"Is this your place?" She turned bright eyes on him.

Kane laughed and shook his head. "No, this homestead belongs to Sarah and David Patton. They have three sons and two daughters. They're real nice folk. You're gonna like them."

"Are we stopping here now?" D'lise combed her fingers through her tangled curls as Kane turned the stallion toward the cabin. "I'm a sight." She smoothed her palms over the deep wrinkles in her skirt.

"You look fine," Kane said carelessly. "Nobody will expect you to look spic-and-span after spendin' time on the trail."

They reached the front yard as he talked, and a bright-eyed woman in her early forties stepped out onto the porch. "Kane Devlin!" she exclaimed, coming down the two porch steps. "You're back from the war safe and sound."

So he's been to war, D'lise thought, watching Kane dismount and give the pleasant-looking woman a warm hug.

"Safe and sound, Sarah, and eager to get back to my old life."

"Your old life?" Kane's neighbor pulled away from him and looked at D'lise. "Will the young lady like that, do you think? She may want to change some of your wild ways."

Kane threw back his head and laughed. "You're thinkin' wrong, Sarah. D'lise is not my wife, she's ... an old friend's daughter. Before he died, he asked me to take care of her."

D'lise blinked at the bold-faced lie, but was grateful for it. It would bruise her pride to have this nice woman know why she was really with Kane. She'd rather his friends thought she was playing his whore than to have them pity her because of the abuse she'd suffered at her uncle's hands.

"That's too bad." Sarah looked at D'lise with sympathy in her eyes. "Have you been ailin', child? You look kinda peaked."

Before D'lise could answer, Kane broke in, "She's been sick with the same fever that took her Pa." He grinned at D'lise. "I've got to get some meat on her bones." He looked back at Sarah. "And I'd like to get started doin' that by buyin' one of your cows if you've got one to spare. Fresh milk will fatten her up real fast."

"Well," Sarah said thoughtfully, patting her lips with a finger. "I do have a heifer that freshened for the first time this spring. She ain't much to look at, her legs are too long, but she does give rich milk. I guess I could let you have her."

"Good." Kane nodded, then after a slight pause, "Do you think you could spare half a dozen layin' hens? Eggs would be good for her too."

"I swear to goodness, Kane Devlin, next you'll be wantin' to buy one of my boys." Sarah laughed good-naturedly.

"God forbid I'd want one of them hellions." Kane's eyes twinkled teasingly at his neighbor. "I'll settle for a cow and some hens."

"All right, I'll let you have six or seven. Two old

broody hens hatched out a clutch of chicks this summer, so I'll have new ones comin' along. But you've got to build them warm quarters with a covered pen before you take them home. The wild critters will get them otherwise.''

Kane glanced at D'lise and saw by her pale face that she was beginning to tire. ''Let's get the cow then. I think it's time I get D'lise home.''

''You sure you won't come in and sit a spell, have some coffee?'' When Kane repeated it was best he got D'lise home, Sarah said, ''Wait a minute,'' and hurried inside her cabin. She returned shortly, holding a pewter cup in her hand.

''It's buttermilk.'' She handed the cup up to D'lise.

''Thank you, Sarah.'' D'lise lifted the cold milk with tiny flecks of butter in it to her lips. ''It's delicious,'' she said as the milk hit her empty stomach.

It took less than fifteen minutes to lead the long-legged cow from the pasture and tie her to the mare. Goodbyes were said then, with Sarah inviting D'lise to come visit when she was feeling better. ''I will,'' D'lise promised and followed Kane as he led the way.

As the mounts climbed one hill after the other, D'lise spotted another cabin. It, like the first, looked well kept, with flowers blooming in the yard. She was becoming more and more excited to see her new home, a neat little place like the ones they had passed.

Her eyes were glowing with expectation when they reached the top of a long slope and entered a wild clearing. It was bright with yellow blooming goldenrods and red-orange sumac bushes.

In the center of the splendor stood a tiny shed-like cabin.

Her heart dropped to her feet when Kane said proudly, ''There it is, built by my own hands.''

Chapter Five

Disappointed tears stung the back of D'lise's eyes as her dream of a neat, sturdy cabin faded away. This shedlike building sitting in a weed-choked yard was no better than the one she had fled from. At least Rufus's old shack had two rooms.

She knew that Kane was watching her, waiting for her to say something, to admire his creation. She could not turn her head and look at him. Not yet, at least. First she must let go of her dream, reconcile herself to the fact that she would probably never have a tight, snug place that would keep out the winter winds and the summer heat.

She gave thanks that at least she was free of Rufus. That counted more than having the fanciest cabin in the world.

Gradually she accepted what she could not change. She was at the point of looking at Kane and saying something that would please him when she saw smoke coming from the wood-and-wattle chimney.

"Did you give someone permission to live in your cabin while you were gone?" she asked.

"Not likely. Why do you ask that?"

"Take a look at your chimney."

An angry scowl came over Kane's face, and he kneed the stallion into a loping run. "I'll soon find out who the varmint is and pitch him out on his rear end," he growled.

They thundered up to the cabin just as the door was flung open and an Indian woman rushed outside. "Raven!" Kane exclaimed, his face all smiles now as he swung to the ground and hurried to meet the woman.

When she threw herself into Kane's arms, D'lise felt a prickle of hostility move through her, and was at a loss to say why. She didn't even know the woman, for goodness' sake.

She waited for the trapper to kiss the one he called Raven, but it didn't happen. He only put his arms around her in much the same fashion he had Sarah—well, not exactly, D'lise corrected her thought. He hadn't put a hand on his neighbor's rear.

D'lise sniffed and curled her lips. He had a different feeling for this one. She had probably been his squaw before he went off to war. She turned her head away from the couple but listened intently to what they had to say to each other.

"How did you know I'd arrive today?" Kane spoke first.

"Remember the men you saw making the canoe? One was my cousin. He told me last night. I came early this morning to welcome you."

"Well it's sure good to see you." Kane released Raven and turned to D'lise. "D'lise, I want you to meet an old friend of mine."

D'lise looked into a flat, broad, pock-marked face whose black eyes looked at her with suspicion and hostility. Her greeting smile died a swift death. This woman would be her enemy.

When D'lise and Raven only stared coolly at each other, Kane stirred uneasily, at a loss how to break the tension that had sprung up. Finally, he lifted D'lise and Scrag from the mare's back. Taking her arm, he said, "Let's go inside. You look beat."

D'lise was tired, dead tired, and though she tried to put a bounce in her steps as they moved toward the cabin, she wobbled a bit on her sprained ankle. Kane quickly put a supporting arm around her waist and Raven's lips curled in a sneer. Her black eyes practically shouted, *Weak white woman!*

D'lise ignored the look of contempt as Kane ushered her through the door. She would deal with that one another day.

The dimness in the small room assaulted her eyes, making her blink rapidly before focusing on the burning fireplace. A soft sigh of relief eased through her lips as Kane sat her down in a cushionless rocker. She had carefully leaned back and was beginning to relax when Raven asked with a pout, "Are you finished with Raven now, Devlin? Will you cast her out like an old worn-out moccasin?"

D'lise slid Kane a look from beneath lowered lids, curious to hear his response, to see his reaction to the question.

"Have I told you to go?" His lips twisted in amusement, knowing that Raven was jealous of the woman he had brought home.

"No," Raven answered sullenly, "but . . ." She looked at D'lise meaningfully.

"But nothin'." Kane took her arm and led her toward the door. "Come help me put the animals in the barn."

D'lise pretended not to see the sly, triumphant smile the Indian gave her just before the door closed behind her. She gazed into the flames. Did Kane intend for that woman to live with them in this small room? Was she to sleep on the floor then? That she wouldn't mind, but it would be embarrassing to hear what would go on in the bed at night.

I'll get used to it, she thought. *Better Raven takes care of his needs than me.*

D'lise busied herself looking over the room. The first thing to catch her attention was the chinks between the walls. Some spaces were more than a foot long. She shook her head. Not only would snow seep through in the winter, snakes could slither between the cracks in the summer.

She looked down at the hard-packed earthen floor. Scattered about were cured furs of bear and panther, disarrayed by careless feet. Once smoothed out, they would probably cover the entire floor of the cabin, she imagined. That at least was on the positive side. They wouldn't freeze their feet in the winter.

D'lise lifted her gaze to the one small window in the place, its closed shutters blocking out the daylight. Her eyes accustomed to the dimness now, she looked at the scanty furnishings. Beneath the window was a table with a rough-hewn plank top, a split-log bench on either side of it. In a corner next to the fireplace was a bed made from poles, its frame laced with strips of rawhide. A cotton mattress filled with straw lay on the bed, half propped up against the wall, a pillow carelessly tossed beside it. A few feet away from her was another rocker.

Did Kane own any bed linens? she wondered, her eyes drifting to the leather-bound trunk at the foot of the rudely constructed bed. Her gaze swung back to the window where miscellaneous items had been hung. There was a shelf right next to it, a small mirror above, and four wooden pegs below. For towels and such, she assumed. Her eyes moved on to a long-handled skillet, an iron spider, and two pots hanging on pegs affixed to the wall. She switched her attention back to the other side of the window where another shelf held a stack of pewter plates and cups and some flatware.

D'lise looked back at the fireplace, where an oven had been built inside the hearth. Well, Kane Devlin, she thought wryly, your place doesn't look like much, but it seems to have everything that's required for housekeeping. At least what D'lise was used to. Tomorrow, when she was feeling better, she'd straighten the place up. Maybe it would look a little better.

Her stomach rumbled, reminding her that the only substance that had passed her lips today was the cup of buttermilk Sarah Patton had given her. On top of that discomfort, the sores on her back were beginning to sting again. She hoped that when Kane returned, he'd have her bag of meager clothing with him. She longed to get into something clean.

If he ever gets here, she thought, her eyes clouded with irritation. He and Raven had been gone close to half an hour. Her lips curled contemptuously, imagining what was keeping the pair in the barn.

That thought started a strange fluttering in her chest, almost a pain. But before she could dwell on the sensation or determine its cause, Scrag was scratching on the door.

"Do you have to go out right now?" she complained, not wanting to disturb her back. The cat scratched more forcefully, looking back at her entreatingly. "Oh, all right," she sighed, and started to ease out of the chair.

She found she didn't need to rise after all. The latch was suddenly lifted and Kane walked inside, Raven close behind him. Giving her a wide smile, Kane held up two dressed-out rabbits. "Big Beaver said I should give you squirrel, but I think rabbit will do as well. How do you feel about havin' rabbit stew for supper?"

"My stomach says it will be wonderful." D'lise returned him a smile that made Raven scowl. "But I didn't hear any gunshots. Don't tell me you ran them down," she teased.

"Devlin no need gun," Raven said coldly, tossing D'lise's bag of clothes at her feet. "He split their heads with his knife." She looked at Kane with admiration.

D'lise thought that was quite an accomplishment, too, realizing also that she had been wrong thinking what she had thought about Kane and Raven. Kane had been out hunting, not lying in the barn with the Indian woman.

Then Raven bent to lay another log on the fire and she saw pieces of hay in her braids and on her back. She had been right all along. It was confirmed when Kane remarked dismissively, "The little critters were only a few feet from the barn. I couldn't have missed them."

He handed the carcasses to Raven. "Get the stew goin' and put in a lot of herbs. You know where I keep them." Concern etched his face when he looked down at D'lise's pale face. "Are you hurtin'? Is your back botherin' you?"

"Some. I wish I could have a bath and get into some clean clothes. I feel sticky and grimy."

"I can take care of that right away." Kane strode over to the bed and dragged a wooden tub from beneath it. "It'll just take a few minutes to heat some water," he said, carrying the big vessel over to the fire and placing it in front of the hearth. "I'll go fetch some water from the spring," he said, grabbing a couple of pails.

101

As soon as the door closed behind him, Raven looked up from the meat she was hacking into small pieces. Angrily tossing the chunks of rabbit into a pot, she said disparagingly, "An Indian woman would do such things for herself. She would never expect her brave to prepare her bath water."

"Look, Raven," D'lise flared indignantly, "let's get a few things straight right now. Number one, I am not an Indian woman, number two, it's none of your business what the trapper does for me, and number three, he is not my brave."

"It is good that you know Devlin is not yours." Raven lifted the lid off a cured gourd and took some dried leaves from it. "He has been mine for a long time, and I will allow no woman to take him away from me." She gave a flip of her wrist and the hunting knife she had been using buried its point in the tabletop. "Do you understand?"

"I understand that you are trying to scare me," D'lise retorted contemptuously, "but you're failing to do so. Right now you see a weak woman before you, but that will change. When I get my strength back, you'd better walk softly around me. Also, know this. Even though Devlin is not my man, if I should ask him to send you away, he will do so."

She quickly looked away from the irate woman. She wasn't as confident as she sounded. She seriously doubted that Kane would ask his lover to leave, but maybe she could bluff the hateful woman into believing it.

No more was said when Kane entered the cabin with the pails of water. He filled the big black cast-iron kettle sitting on the hearth and placed it on a bed of red, glowing coals. Then, picking up the other pail, he emptied it into the tub.

102

"It'll take about ten minutes for the water to heat." He sat down in the other rocker and made himself comfortable. "After you've bathed, I'll put some salve on your back. I have some balm of Gilead. It's real healing stuff."

D'lise nodded, and he asked, "Well, what do you think of my little nest?"

Nest is right, D'lise thought—boar's nest. Of course she couldn't say that to him, nor could she bring herself to praise the dark little hovel. The words would stick in her throat. After a moment she said, "I've been looking at the fur pelts on the floor. They must be beautiful when they're all smoothed out. And of course when the shutters are opened, the room will be nice and bright."

It didn't pass Kane's notice that D'lise's words were hardly complimentary. In fact, she hadn't mentioned the cabin at all. He looked around the room, and suddenly saw it through her eyes. It looked like hell, he thought, eyeing the furs kicked carelessly about, the ashes that had spilled onto the hearth. And dammit, he never had gotten around to putting glass panes in the window. He'd have to see to that right away. With winter coming on, it would be as dark as a dungeon in here. It wasn't right to expect a woman to live in the dark all the time. Raven and the other squaws who shared the cabin with him occasionally hadn't minded because they were used to living in wigwams, but a man couldn't ask a white woman to live like a mole.

He smiled at D'lise and said, "Do whatever you want to do to the place, D'lise. I won't fuss you. This is your home. When you're feelin' better, we'll ride over to the post and you can buy whatever you need to to fix things up. Being a rough old bachelor, I didn't fancy up the place much, I guess."

"Thank you, Kane." D'lise smiled gently at the big

bearded man, knowing that she had hurt his feelings. "It really doesn't need much done to it; just a little straightening up and it will be nice and cozy."

She breathed a little sigh of relief when Kane's face brightened at her lie, and she added shyly, "And you're not old."

"Compared to you, I am." Kane gazed into the fire, thinking of all the things he'd seen, the things he'd done, things that would curl this innocent's toes were she to know about them.

He choked back a sigh, regretting for the first time all the wasted years spent with whores and squaws. Because of those years of debauchery, he wasn't fit to even think about taking this fresh, lovely girl to bed, let alone do it.

Anyway, he reminded himself, even if he had always led a life free of depravity, he'd stay clear of becoming involved with D'lise in that way. He knew better than to get tangled up with a beautiful woman. Raven interrupted Kane's gloomy thoughts when she stamped over to the fireplace, picked up the steaming kettle, and emptied half its contents into the pot she had slammed the rabbit into. "Hey, don't use that water," Kane ordered. "It's for D'lise's bath. Why didn't you use the water from the pail sittin' on the table?"

"Hot water make stew cook faster," Raven grunted as she flounced back to the table.

Kane turned around in the rocker and gave her a black look. "Bring that pail over here and replace what you took."

Raven's back stiffened, and it was several seconds before she sullenly obeyed the command. When she straightened from refilling the kettle, Kane said, frowning in annoyance, "And take that look off your face. I won't put up with it, you know that."

So, Miss Raven, D'lise smiled secretly to herself as the woman meekly turned away, *you're not as settled in Kane's life as you would have me believe. In fact, you're scared to death I might oust you in his affections.*

The big black kettle steamed again, and Kane lifted it from the fire and emptied its hot contents into the tub of water. He walked to the shelf next to the window and returned with a bar of yellow, dried-up soap. He dropped it into the tub, then lifted the lid of the large trunk and took out a towel of fustian and a wash cloth of tanned hide.

He grinned down at D'lise. "You can hop in whenever you're ready. Raven can call me when you've finished."

"Thank you, Kane." D'lise stood up, relieved. She had wondered if he intended to remain in the cabin while she bathed.

D'lise didn't linger at her bath. She was too conscious of Raven's black eyes on her body, the scorn for her thinness that must lie in them. She had carefully kept her back from the woman, so at least she couldn't see the condition it was in and think that Kane had beaten her.

When D'lise had toweled herself dry and pulled on a fresh petticoat, she said to Raven, "You can call Kane in now." Her lips twisted wryly at the heated look Raven shot her way as she stalked to the door, jerked it open, and called out to Kane.

"Everything is comin' along fine," Kane said with satisfaction a short time later as he finished dabbing salve on the two remaining open cuts. "Another couple days and you'll be completely healed."

He gently pulled the petticoat straps back to D'lise's shoulders, then lifted her heavy black curls to hang down her back. D'lise thought for a moment that his hands had trembled, then asked herself why they should. It must all have been in her imagination.

By the time Kane emptied the bath water into the yard, shoved the tub back under the bed, and D'lise had donned a clean dress, Raven announced that the stew was on the table.

D'lise didn't know if the stew was as good as she thought it was or if she was so hungry that wood chips would have served as well. At any rate, she felt that she was certainly eating her share of the meal. She caught Kane grinning once and, unabashed, she grinned back and said, "I was starving."

"Hey, it's all right." His grin widened. "I like to see you eat. It means you're healthy. Tomorrow I'll go huntin' and bag a deer." His eyes twinkled mischievously. "I'll have Raven roast a whole haunch just for you. You can eat until you pop."

D'lise laughed, the throaty peal filling the small room. Kane's body grew still. Her laugh was a beautiful, sensuous sound. He wanted to pull her into his arms and devour the red lips that curved so sweetly. *And scare her to death*, a small voice whispered.

To take his mind off what he longed to do, Kane asked D'lise, "What about a cup of coffee?"

"I'd love it." D'lise couldn't get used to the idea that she could have that invigorating brew anytime she wanted it.

"I'm afraid we haven't any milk," Kane said, bringing the coffee pot to the table.

"Of course we have milk." D'lise laughed. "Are you forgetting our long-legged cow?"

"Of course!" Kane remembered. "That's why that heifer is bawlin' so. I thought she was homesick for Sarah."

"Ha!" D'lise snorted. "The poor thing is probably in

pain from a full udder. Do you know how to milk her?''

"Good heavens, no.'' Kane looked insulted. He looked at the silent Raven. "Do you know how?''

She shook her head. "Indians don't own cows.'' There was a slight sneer in her voice.

"Well.'' D'lise stood up. "It looks like I'm elected. I've milked many a cow in my day.''

"But are you up to it?'' Kane rose also, a concerned frown on his face.

"I can give it a try. I feel fine after that good stew.'' D'lise smiled at Raven in an attempt to bridge the hostility between them, to bring about some kind of harmony, if only to halt the cutting exchanges between them.

When Raven ignored her praise, only staring down into her cup of coffee, D'lise shrugged her shoulders. So be it. They would continue to snap and snarl at each other.

Night was slipping over the timbered hills as D'lise and Kane walked toward the small barn that was, surprisingly, sturdier than the cabin. The grass was wet with dew, and a heavy fog hung in the still, cool air. D'lise was saying, "What a beautiful evening,'' when Kane stopped suddenly, his hand catching her arm as he stared to the right of them. She followed his gaze and gasped.

Only a few yards away, a bear was lumbering across the clearing, heading for the forest. "Will he attack us?'' D'lise choked out in breathless alarm.

"Shhh,'' Kane whispered. "Stand real still. Bears have poor eyesight, and chances are he won't see us. Luckily we're upwind of him and he won't smell us. They can catch a scent half a mile away.''

With breath held, they watched the bear move heavily and clumsily along, his big head swaying back and forth. When he finally disappeared into the woods, D'lise let out her breath and asked anxiously, "Do they come around often?"

"Not too often. Snowy attracts them, and now, of course, your mare and the cow will. But don't worry, they'd never get through the heavy doors I put on the barn and cabin. And they could never claw their way through the logs."

He nodded toward the big expanse of timberland the bear had entered. "There's where they live mostly—along with wolves and panthers. Don't ever go in there alone."

D'lise shuddered. "I won't go near it."

They were at the barn then, and Kane was unlocking a padlock attached to a heavy chain that held the split-log door closed. D'lise gave an awed gasp when he pointed to the deep scratches on the door. Most were old ones, but along the frame fresh pieces of bark had been torn away from the logs. She didn't need Kane to tell her that the bear they had just seen was the culprit.

The barn was dry and warm, smelling faintly of old hay and manure. By the dim, gray light coming through a small window high on a wall, D'lise could make out the three animals, each in its own space. Not surprisingly, all three were in a nervous state, thanks to the bear. She took the wooden pail from Kane and entered the cow's stall. She spent a few minutes soothing the animal, scratching the backs of her rough ears and running her fingers gently down the wide space between the brown eyes.

"I shall call you Spider because of your long legs," she said softly. Two stalls down, Kane, calming the horses, grinned. What a name to give to a cow, he thought.

When Spider had settled down somewhat, D'lise knelt beside her and started coaxing milk from her plump teats into the pail. As the cow's udder was relieved of its load, her pain was relieved as well. D'lise smiled when Spider began to contentedly chew her cud.

When the stallion and mare had calmed down, Kane walked over to Spider's stall. A crack of laughter exploded from his throat when he saw D'lise squirting milk into Scrag's open mouth. "That cat beats all," he said when D'lise stood up, a good gallon of milk in the pail.

D'lise looked at her pet and smiled gently. "He's been doing that since he was a kitten. Rufus would never have allowed me to put some in a pan for him. As far as he knew, none of us ever drank his precious milk. It was taken to the post and sold."

Kane remarked with a teasing grin, "I bet you managed to get some though."

"The boys and I usually had a dipperful every day," D'lise answered, leading the way out of the barn.

Raven had lit a candle in their absence, and after Kane found a clean dish towel, D'lise used it to strain the milk into a large glazed crock. After placing a plate over it, she looked up at Kane with a smile. "In the morning I'll skim off most of the cream that will have risen overnight, and in a few days I'll have enough to churn some butter."

Kane almost smacked his lips. He couldn't remember the last time he'd had that golden goodness spread on a slice of fresh, warm bread. He looked at D'lise to say so, then noticed the weary droop to her shoulders. He musn't keep her up any longer.

"I think it's time you went to bed, young lady. We don't want you havin' a relapse."

When D'lise didn't argue, he went to the trunk and, lifting the lid again, rummaged around inside it. When he straightened up, his arms were full of bed linens. He

109

handed them to Raven. ''Make up the bed, but keep back the heavy blanket.''

D'lise watched Raven pull the mattress into place and spread the sheet over it, then the blanket. When the case was pulled over the pillow, she blinked rapidly in surprise when Kane said, ''Drop the bar behind us, D'lise.'' And while she looked at him in confusion, he picked up the blanket and, with Raven close behind him, walked to the door. Just before he stepped out into the night, he looked over his shoulder at her.

''Have a good restful sleep,'' he said, ''and don't worry about anything botherin' you. We'll be in the barn.''

D'lise stared at the closed door. Raven was staying the night? Did that mean the Indian woman was going to live with them? She had expected that she would be around often, but not on a regular basis.

There was a dejected curve to her mouth when she moved across the floor and dropped the heavy bar into its slot, then pulled her dress over her head. She hung the garment on a peg, kicked off her moccasins, and crawled into bed. Scrag jumped up behind her and wiggled his way under the covers until he could snuggle up beside her.

D'lise's cheeks were wet with unexplained tears when finally her eyes drifted shut.

Chapter Six

The sun had just begun to shine through the barn window when Kane came awake. He pushed Raven's drawn-up leg off him and with a grimace sat up, running his fingers through his long hair and dislodging pieces of hay and straw. Raven had given him release three times last night, but that deep-down satisfaction had eluded him. Something had been missing.

He drew up his knees and started to rest his chin on them, then jerked his head away. He smelled something awful—a mixture of sweat, spilled passion, and the bear grease Raven used on her hair. There was no way he'd go around D'lise smelling like this. He'd done that once, and her straight little nose had wrinkled with distaste.

He stood up, gathered up his clothes, and left the sleeping woman.

The air was crisp and the sky clear as Kane made his way to the back of the barn where a branch of the Ohio flowed. He gasped a little when he stepped into the cold water, but waded on until he came to its center, which reached mid-thigh. Gritting his teeth, he eased himself down into the stream. When his body became accustomed to its biting chill, he scooped up a handful of sand and began to scrub himself.

When he was satisfied that only a clean masculine odor clung to him, he stepped shivering onto the grassy bank. Using his palms, he rubbed what water he could off his body, then struggled into his buckskins and moccasins. He'd dry his hair when he reached the cabin.

Coming upon the building, Kane tested its door to see if D'lise had remembered to bar it. It held fast, and he walked to the window. He reached down behind a large rock and brought up the broken blade of a hunting knife. It had rested there since the cabin was constructed, its prime purpose being to slide under and lift the latch that kept the two sides of the shutter together.

The piece of steel did its job, and folding back the wooden slats, Kane swung one long leg over the window sill. He straddled it a moment, looking to see if D'lise had awakened. When the slight mound under the covers didn't stir, he brought his other leg through the opening and quietly walked to the shelf beneath the mirror. Looking at his image, he rubbed his brown, curly beard a minute, then picked up a pair of scissors lying beside a razor and shaving mug.

The snip of the blades was loud in the silence of the room; even the accumulation of beard falling on the floor seemed to make a noise.

When only a stubble remained on his jaw and chin, Kane moved quickly to the fireplace and removed the tea kettle. Lifting the lid, he found that the water was quite warm. He carried it to the mirror and poured a small amount into the mug, then wet the round bar of soap in its bottom and emptied the rest of the water into a basin. He picked up the brush, and after working up a thick lather, spread it over his face.

With the razor in his hand, he hesitated a moment before taking the first swipe of it down his jaw. He'd worn the beard for four years and had become quite attached to it.

His eyes moved often to D'lise's sleeping form as he wielded the sharp blade. She lay so still, her hands folded beneath her chin, her black curls spread out on the pillow. She looked like a painting, he thought.

Kane gave a final swipe of the razor, then bent over the basin and rinsed away the remains of the lather. When he had rubbed his face and hair dry with a coarse towel, he walked over to the bed.

As he leaned over D'lise, wondering if he should awaken her, Scrag opened one eye and hissed at him. Startled, Kane paused a moment, then lightly touched D'lise's shoulder. She stirred, rolled over onto her back, and opened her eyes.

A cry of alarm escaped her throat as she gazed up at the stranger standing over her. "Who are you?" she squeaked. "How did you get in here?" She recognized the twinkling slate-gray eyes then and exclaimed, "Kane! You've shaved off your beard!"

"Yeah." Kane self-consciously ran a hand over his smooth chin. "I feel as naked as a bay blue jay."

D'lise raised herself up on an elbow to peer more closely at him. "That may be," she said, "but you look ten years younger with that brush gone." She studied the wholly masculine features, the strong lines and hard planes. "And a very nice face was hiding there. Even handsome," she teased. "How old are you?"

113

Kane felt himself blushing at her compliment. He affected a careless shrug and drawled, "You think that because it's so dark in here and you can't see good. I'm thirty-one."

He quickly turned the conversation away from himself. "Do you feel like ridin' to the post this mornin'?"

"Yes, I do," D'lise answered at once. "I slept straight through the night and I'm feeling fine this morning."

"Shall we get an early start then?" Kane didn't add that he preferred to get away before Raven was up and about. She would want to go with them, and it would shame D'lise to have his Indian lover with them. Piney Ridge was a small community, its female population prone to gossip. There was no telling what conclusions they might come to.

D'lise scooted off the bed and hurried to the dress hanging on the wall. "As soon as we eat a bite and I milk Spider, we'll go." She didn't want Raven with them either. It would be nice to ride alone with Kane again and not have the Indian woman's sour face setting her teeth on edge.

She turned around, the dress over her arm. "Would you mind stirring up the fire while I slice some salt pork?"

Kane was incapable of answering for a moment. His throat had gone dry as his eyes fastened on her breasts, the dark areolas plainly visible through the threadbare material of her petticoat. He swallowed; then, his voice husky with arousal, he managed to croak out, "I'll get right to it."

Within twenty minutes, the skimpy breakfast had been eaten and Kane and D'lise were walking into the barn. D'lise kept her eyes averted from the deeply asleep Raven scrunched down in a pile of hay. To look would make

114

her imagine Kane lying beside the woman, and that was repulsive to her.

As the milk streamed into the pail, she could hear Kane quietly saddling their mounts. A few minutes later she wondered at the sound of a shovel being used in Snowy's stall.

She stripped the last of the milk from Spider, leaving her udder almost collapsed. She stood up just as Kane led out the stallion and mare and looked curiously at the dirt-covered tin box he carried under one arm. When they were outside and the heavy door closed behind them, Kane explained, "I had just sold my winter's catch of furs before I went off to the war. I put the money in this box and buried it in Snowy's stall."

"I wondered what the digging was about," D'lise remarked. "Don't you trust your neighbors?"

"Most of them I do, but there's a couple I'm not too sure of. Anyway, some renegade Indian could have set fire to the cabin just for the hell of it, and my whole season's work would have gone up in flames."

"You're a smart fellow, aren't you?" D'lise's eyes sparkled mischievously.

"Not always," Kane answered. "Sometimes I do things that even an idiot would know better than to do." *Like thinking it wouldn't bother me to have you around all the time,* he thought.

A short time later, with the milk strained and Scrag shut up in the cabin, Kane boosted D'lise onto the mare's back and swung himself into his own saddle. As they rode along a narrow trail, D'lise feasted her eyes on the vast sweep of forest-clad hills and valleys. Occasionally she caught glimpses of the Ohio, where white mists curled ghost-like above its serenely moving water.

The sun was bright and warm when Kane and D'lise

arrived at the crude frontier post. Kane pulled up the stallion and stared. Piney Ridge had grown in his absence. Where before there had only been the post, the hurriedly thrown together whorehouse, the school off to itself, and a few shacks inhabited by bachelor trappers, there were now several new additions.

Across from the post was a large building constructed from rough planks with good-sized windows on each side of the door, the sign proclaiming in big black letters, *Samuel Majors Emporium.* Kane's gaze moved down the dusty, rutted street to the next new building sporting a shingle reading *Dr. Jacob Ashley.* A few yards farther his eyes encountered what must have been a church, considering the cross on its roof peak.

Kane's attention was caught by the sound of hammering. Another new building going up, he assumed. "I wonder what that's gonna be," he muttered, not sure he liked all these changes.

Nor was he positive about all the new cabins sprinkled about on the hillside in back of the village. Judging by the new dwellings, Piney Ridge's population had increased considerably in his absence.

"I didn't realize that Piney Ridge was such a thriving little village," D'lise said as she urged Beauty to follow the stallion.

"It didn't used to be," Kane remarked grumpily, swinging out of the saddle, then helping D'lise to dismount. "I hope some of my friends are still around," He tied the mounts to a well-worn hitching rack. He took D'lise's arm then, and stepping up on the post's wide porch, he led her through the open door.

Kane and D'lise stood just inside the room a moment, letting their eyes get used to the dim interior. D'lise started when several voices called out surprised greetings to Kane.

"Kane, you old son-of-a-gun, when did you get back?"

"Hey, Devlin, it's good to see you!"

Long-time friends whom Kane had drunk with, brawled with, and whored with surrounded them. Amid all the hand shaking and back slapping, D'lise came in for her share of interest. Kane noted each look given her and thought to himself, *Look all you want to, men, but don't so much as lay a finger on her.*

Everyone moved to the bar, and the bartender, also the owner of the post, stuck out a ham-sized hand. "Things have been quiet around here with you gone, Devlin. I guess I'll have to bring my club out of retirement."

"I can't believe that this bunch of troublemakers haven't been givin' you any trouble, Buck," Kane said, shaking hands.

The big man laughed. "I'll never live to see the day this bunch behave themselves." He brought up a bottle from under the bar. Uncorking it, he said, "Belly up, men, the drinks are on me."

There was a scramble of buckskin-covered bodies as the trappers pushed and shoved each other, trying for a spot next to D'lise. Kane spoke, half in amusement, half in irritation. "Men, meet D'lise Alexander."

The trappers pushed forward, pressing D'lise up against the bar. She gave a frightened squeak, and Kane placed a hand on either side of her, covering her slight frame with his large body. "Take it easy, you men," he growled, "she's been sick, and you're gonna trample her to death."

The men in front hurriedly stepped back, tramping on the toes of those behind them, who let out muted sounds of curses and grunts of pain. The mumbled, "Sorry, ma-'am," was hardly heard.

As Buck placed a tin cup of sarsaparilla in front of D'lise, then began to pour whiskey for the men, a coarse, heavy-featured man who had been drinking alone made his way down the bar to where the others were lined up.

"So, you're back, Devlin," he said in a whiskey-slurred voice when he stopped beside Kane. "Big hero returns with a purty little gal." His reddened eyes skimmed over D'lise's face, then fastened insolently on her breasts. "I thought you only went to bed with ugly bitches," he leered.

Kane pushed away from the bar, a muscle jerking angrily in his jaw. "You got somethin' on your mind, Bracken?"

"Yeah. There's somethin' I'm wonderin' about. You think you're man enough to bed Raven and this little purty too? We all know that you're hung like a horse, but—"

The rest of Albert Bracken's sneering words died on his tongue. With one swift motion, Kane's fist swept up and hit his jaw with a jarring blow. The man's head snapped back; then he was lying motionless on the floor.

A loud sigh left the onlookers in unison. Bracken was lucky it was only a fist he had felt. It could very well have been the touch of a cold, sharp blade.

But each man there got the message that it was hands off where the little beauty was concerned.

"What's got him all riled up?" Kane studied his bruised knuckle. "We were never close friends, but we were always civil to each other."

It looked for a while as if no one was going to answer him as the trappers became very interested in their drinks. Finally, Buck, scratching his balding head and avoiding D'lise's wide eyes, mumbled, "Raven's been his squaw while you was gone. I guess he reckons she'll go back to you now."

A dull red washed over Kane's face. His eyes flickered briefly to D'lise and found her pink-cheeked. Damn! What was she thinking? That he would brawl over an Indian whore? What could he say to her? If he told her he'd hit the drunk because he was enraged at the way he had looked at her, had coupled her with Raven, would she believe him?

He mentally shook his head. It was a useless thought. She would naturally think that the blow had been struck in defense of the woman he had slept with last night.

He lifted the cup of whiskey to his mouth, took a deep swallow, then coolly changed the subject. "The village sure has grown while I was away."

"It sure has," Buck said as a couple of men dragged the unconscious Bracken outside. "We gotta regular store now, across the street. Run by a widower from Boston with two young'uns. Then there's Doctor Ashley's office buildin'. It's real good to have him here. Relieved the womenfolk a lot when he arrived. And we got a church now with our own preacher, no more waitin' for a travelin' one to come through. And that buildin' that's goin' up now is gonna be a hardware store."

"I see there's several new cabins too," Kane said.

"Yes, there are. Six new families have come in the past two years." He winked at Kane and said in an aside for his ears only, "Got three new whores too."

Kane began to note that he and Buck were doing all the talking. He slid a curious glance at his usually loquacious friends and found them all gawking at D'lise. From the look on her downcast face, she was very uncomfortable being stared at.

And why shouldn't she be, he thought, with eight pairs of eyes staring at her like those of hungry wolves? Pushing his empty cup away, he said, "I've come in for some supplies, Buck. My larder is bare as a bone. Will you fill me an order?''

"Sure thing. Course I only got the usual staples. The new store carries more of a variety. Majors has things like raisins, dried fruit, crackers and cheese, and such. The women tell me that he's got all sorts of gee-gaws for them to buy. Gets them in from Boston when the weather's good.''

"What sort of fellow is he?''

"He's nice enough. Fancy talker, proper English and all that. Real educated, I guess. Lost his wife a while back.'' Buck grinned. "A fine-lookin' feller. You ought to see how the single girls shine up to him. He don't seem interested though. Probably still grievin' for his wife.''

Buck walked from behind the bar and motioned for Kane and D'lise to follow him into the storeroom. "Come on, we'll gather up your supplies.''

It took close to an hour for Kane to think of everything he needed, and for Buck to weigh and place the wrapped items on the counter. "D'lise wants to look at some dress lengths,'' Kane said, making D'lise look at him in surprise. She blushed in shame. He *had* noticed her worn-out clothing.

"You'll have to go to the new store for that,'' Buck answered. "Majors carries such fancy yard goods I stopped handlin' it. Miss Alexander can find most anything she wants there.''

Kane eyed the amount of purchases he'd have to get home. "I'll have to make a couple trips before I get this all to the cabin,'' he muttered.

"If it wouldn't cost too much, why don't you buy a pack animal?'' D'lise said timorously, thinking of the garden she'd like to make next spring. Anyway, she doubted that either of their spirited mounts would take kindly to being loaded down with bags and bundles. Certainly they wouldn't like being hitched to a plow.

"Yeah, I could," Kane said after a thoughtful pause. "A pack animal would come in handy when I run my traps too." He looked at Buck. "You got such around?"

"I've got a little jackass. He's young and strong. He belonged to a homesteader who got bit by a copperhead and died."

"How much do you want for him?" Kane's hand went to his shirt pocket where he had put his money from the tin box.

"Considerin' he ain't mine, just pay me for the feed he's been eatin' since I had him."

"After you've totaled everything up, will you have someone load all this on the jackass? I'm gonna take D'lise to that store and get her fixed up for the cold weather that's trampin' at our heels."

When Kane pushed open the door to Samuel Majors's Emporium, a small bell attached to its top jingled cheerily. A drape parted behind a varnished counter and a man in his late thirties, dressed in blue plaid trousers and white shirt, stepped through it. Childish voices and laughter that had sounded behind him were muted when the heavy drape fell back in place.

"Good morning, folks." He smiled genially. "Welcome to my establishment. How can I serve you?"

Although the question was probably asked of Kane, it was D'lise who received the impact of the salesman's warm brown eyes. A scowl came over Kane's face. It had amused him when his friends seemed overwhelmed at the girl's beauty, but the gleam in this man's eyes made him feel threatened. The storekeeper would have smooth ways about him, would know exactly how to seduce a young innocent.

He curled possessive fingers around D'lise's arm and said gruffly, "She'd like to look at some dress goods, and all the other finery women are interested in."

"Yes, certainly." The slender, attractive man pulled his attention from D'lise and stepped from behind the counter. "If you'll come this way?"

Kane followed him, his hand still on D'lise's arm. She let out a small cry of delight when Majors stopped beside a table stacked with dress goods. There were colors and prints she never knew existed in homespuns, fustians, calicos, and twills. Her mouth practically watered when her glance fell on a table of silks, satins, velvets, thin muslins, and lawns. The colors were so vibrant she was reminded of a flower garden.

"Get whatever you want, D'lise," Kane said seeing the yearning in her eyes.

"Oh, I don't need much, Kane," D'lise answered running a palm over a roll of blue calico. "Just enough yardage for a couple of dresses and . . . and what goes under them."

Kane hid his amusement at her shyness and said firmly, "You pick out at least four dress lengths and everything else that—that goes under them. And don't forget needles and thread and such. There's nothin' like that at the cabin."

He thrust a handful of bills into her hand. "There's some nice-lookin' coats over there, and don't forget shoes and a pair of heavy boots for the cold weather." His warm fingers closed over her small one clutching the money. "I don't want you handin' me back any change. Do you understand?"

D'lise could only nod her head as she wondered how much she was supposed to purchase. She had never before held as much as a coin in her hand, and she had no idea what anything cost. With a helpless lift of her shoulders she began her selection of material.

She had chosen two homespun pieces in colorful prints and was trying to decide what color would suit her best in calico when the little bell over the door tinkled, and Sarah Patton and two teenage girls entered the store. The girls were Sarah's daughters, she assumed, since the three looked so much alike, all blond and blue-eyed and on the plump side.

The two girls spotted Kane immediately standing before a gun rack, admiring a Kentucky rifle. As the attractive females converged on him, D'lise realized that the new man in the village wasn't the only male in Piney Ridge the womenfolk made up to. Kane Devlin was very much a favorite with these two.

Confusion swept over D'lise, and her hand paused on the calico. Why did she suddenly care that those two silly girls were fawning over Kane? She wasn't interested in him in that way.

Her fingers gripped the material under her hand as a chilling thought came to her. What if Kane should get married? D'lise Alexander would lose his protection for one thing, also her home.

It didn't bear thinking about. For the first time in her life, as far as she could remember, and not counting Auntie, someone was treating her as a worthwhile human being, a person with the right to speak her mind and not fear a beating because of it. She knew at that moment that she would dislike intensely anyone who threatened to take all that away from her.

Sarah saw her then and called out a friendly greeting as she left off examining a slatted bonnet and walked toward her. "Samuel has some real pretty yard goods, don't he? I bought a couple lengths for the girls last week."

"They're lovely colors," D'lise agreed, running her hand over the calico. "I hardly know what to choose."

"Come and meet my daughters." Sarah took D'lise's arm and led her toward Kane and the two girls. "They were out huntin' greens when you and Kane stopped by our place."

D'lise didn't receive the warmest welcome from eighteen-year-old Milly and sixteen-year-old Becky. "I'm pleased to meet you," they said politely, but coolly. "I guess we won't be seein' that Raven person slinkin' round your cabin anymore," Milly added caustically to Kane.

Kane only grinned at her thinly veiled hostility. Raven's presence at his place had always been a sore spot for the Piney Ridge womenfolk. Wouldn't the tongues wag when they discovered that Raven would still be *slinkin' round* his cabin. All sorts of stories would make the rounds. They'd have him sleeping with both women, and God knew what else.

A frown creased his forehead a moment later. He realized that he didn't want unsavory things being said about D'lise. He wanted his neighbors and friends to like and respect her, to accept her in the community, to visit her, to invite her to call on them.

Kane brought up the subject of how the village had grown, and after he and the girls' mother had discussed it, he said, "Sarah, I'd be mighty pleased if you'd kinda take D'lise under your wing, so to speak, and introduce her to the other ladies. She just lost her father, a close friend of mine. He asked me to look after her when he was gone. As you probably know, I don't know much about raisin' a young female."

Sympathy jumped into Sarah Patton's eyes, and relief appeared on the daughters' faces. "Of course I will,

Kane.'' Sarah almost gushed. "And let me say that it's real Christian of you to take the girl in and give her a home. You just leave it up to me and my girls. We'll make your little ward known to all the ladies."

D'lise wished she was close enough to Kane to give him a sharp kick in the shin. She looked at his solemn face then and wanted to giggle at the amused glitter in his slate-gray eyes. What an ornery fellow he was. It tickled him no end to bamboozle these three women.

A sigh of relief eased through her lips when mother and daughters turned their attention on the storekeeper. Kane went back to the gun rack and she continued choosing material.

D'lise was momentarily distracted when Mrs. Patton said, "Ain't it a shame about Tilda Jessup dyin', leavin' all them young'uns behind."

"I hadn't heard," Samuel Majors said in his cultured voice. "I believe the lady was in a delicate condition."

It took Sarah a moment to figure out what Samuel meant by "delicate condition." "Yes," Sarah said finally, "she was. That's how she died, tryin' to give birth to her thirteenth baby. The poor thing hemorrhaged to death, Dr. Ashley said. Tight-fisted Elijah waited too long to come get him, he told me."

"It's a shame." Majors shook his head. "There are several children in the Jessup household, I understand."

"There's eight of them," Sarah said with a disapproving snap to her voice. "Tilda was only thirteen when Elijah married her and got her bigged right off. She lost that one and the two more that followed. Then two caught, then the next one didn't. She had eight then, one right after the other, hardly nine months between them."

She paused to catch her breath, then went on. "Someone should have castrated Elijah Jessup five or six years ago. Poor Tilda had no relations to look after her, lay down the law to that ruttin' no-good.''

Kane and Samuel caught each other's eye, a pained look on their faces. Kane broke in on Sarah's tirade. ''When are they gonna wake Tilda?''

''Tonight,'' Sarah answered. ''Are you comin'?''

''Yes, we'll be there. D'lise will fix a dish to bring along.''

D'lise turned her attention back to the material, ashamed that she could feel so happy at the dead woman's expense. But Kane's coupling their names had sent such a happy feeling of belonging through her, a sensation she'd never felt before. Rufus had always let it be known that he resented her presence in his home, that he begrudged her the meager food she ate, the straw pallet she slept on.

The Patton women left shortly after that, inviting D'lise to come visit them. Kane promised that he would bring her, and D'lise carried the bolts of material she had selected to the counter. Samuel measured out the dress lengths, and after she added a spool of thread and a packet of needles, he remarked:

''I have some very pretty dress patterns if you'd like to look at them.''

D'lise looked at Kane, as if for his opinion, and when he nodded that she should, she looked back at Samuel. ''I'd like to look at them.''

As she pored over the styles shown on the covers of the thin packets, Kane went about the store picking up ribbons and lace and some bone buttons that were dyed the same color as the dress material lying on the counter. He came to a stack of paper-wrapped, scented soap and added two bars to the other items he laid down out of D'lise's sight. He had a feeling that she would hesitate to spend his money on trimmings for her dresses. He moved over to the table then that held the fancy dress goods. After looking them all over, he picked up a length of bright red satin. The color would look beautiful with her black hair.

Placing it next to what D'lise had chosen, he ordered, "Cut her a piece off this one too."

"Kane," D'lise laughed, "what would I do with a fancy satin dress? I can just see myself wearing it while I make meals, wash clothes, or milk the cow."

Samuel cleared his throat. "She's right, you know. The—ah, ladies at the end of the street buy these flashy materials and colors."

Kane thought a minute, and when the word *whore* flashed through his mind, he said, "Oh," and returned the satin to its spot.

D'lise found that when her purchases were added up she had spent all but a few coins of the money Kane had given her. It was then she spotted the big box of yarn. All the colors in the rainbow, she thought, eyeing the skeins longingly. If only she had seen them before she bought the material to make curtains for the window.

"Pretty colors, huh?" Kane stood at her elbow. "I sure like that red."

"You do like red, don't you?" D'lise chuckled, promising herself that someday she would make him a red shirt. "My favorite color is blue."

"Blue is pretty too," Kane agreed, then looked at the storekeeper. "Place the price of glass sheeting on that list you just totaled up."

"Do you have your measurements?" Samuel asked, coming from behind the counter. "I keep the glass in racks in the store room." Kane nodded that he had the measurements and followed the man from Boston.

127

Left alone, D'lise walked over to one of the windows and looked out. There was a happy fluttering in her stomach as she paraded in her mind the treasures Kane had bought for her—the pretty dress goods, the warm coat, the shiny black shoes with thin cotton laces. She hadn't had new shoes in over three years, and those had been heavy, cumbersome things with wide rawhide laces.

Kane and Samuel returned, carefully, carrying a sheet of glass, and she hurried to open the door for them. Buck was waiting outside for them, holding the reins of a little jackass. The new purchases were added to the packages and bags already strapped to his sturdy back. Buck led him across the street to where the two mounts switched their tails at the flies settling on their rumps. Kane helped D'lise to mount, then climbed on Snowy's back. With a wave of his hand to Buck, he kneed the stallion into motion.

He led at a leisurely pace to accommodate the heavily laden jackass and to ensure that the glass didn't slip its bindings and fall to the ground and break. It was very important to him that D'lise have daylight pouring through the window in the wintertime.

They had ridden along for some minutes when D'lise broke the silence. "How come you've never married?" she asked. "The way those two Patton girls hung round you, either one would jump at the chance to be your wife."

"You think so?" Kane grinned at her when she urged the mare alongside the stallion. When she nodded, her eyes serious, he said, "Marriage has never been in the cards for me. I guess I'm too wild. No woman would put up with my ways for very long. She'd try to change me, tame me, and I couldn't abide that. I'd probably leave her."

"You don't seem all that wild to me."

"You think not?" Kane looked at D'lise, half amused, half serious.

D'lise shook her head. "You're maybe a little rough in your ways, but I guess most men are," she said with a small smile, then let the mare fall back behind the stallion.

He's such a handsome man, she thought, and wondered why, with his good looks, he didn't choose a more attractive woman to spend his nights with. Raven was downright ugly.

I guess a woman's face doesn't matter to him, she decided, and fell to thinking about the new dresses she would sew.

An hour later, D'lise made a grimace of displeasure as she and Kane rode up the hill to where the shabby little cabin sat. Raven sat on a rock, waiting for them, a scowl on her broad face.

Chapter Seven

Other than waving his hand at Raven as he and D'lise
rode past her, Kane ignored the Indian woman. Apparently it made no difference to him that she was in a pout.

"Do you think you could bake a pie to take to the
Jessups' tonight?" he asked as they began to unload the
little pack animal and carry the supplies inside.

"I could make one out of those dried apples you
bought," D'lise answered, laying her treasures on the bed.
"In fact, I'll make two. One for the Jessups and one for
us."

She started to turn around, then paused to sniff the air.
She stooped to examine her bed. The blanket she had
smoothed out so carefully on rising that morning was now
wrinkled and in disarray, and the pillow held the imprint
of a head. Raven had been lolling around on her bed, and
now it stank of bear grease.

"What's wrong?" Kane asked as he saw temper flare across her face.

"Nothing," she answered shortly, starting to walk past him to put the supplies away.

"Come on now, tell me." Kane grabbed her arm and swung her around to face him. "What makes you look like you're ready to bust a gut?"

D'lise looked up at him through her dark lashes. "You'll think it's mean of me."

"No, I won't. You couldn't be mean if you tried." He gave her a small shake. "What's botherin' you?"

"Raven's been lying on my bed and now—now it stinks like bear grease."

Kane knew a mixture of anger and amusement as he gazed down at the lovely face, its full lips drawn into a thin line, the fine brows pulled into a vexed frown. D'lise hadn't been around Indians before; she hadn't yet grown accustomed to the fact that they dressed their hair in bear grease. But Raven had purposely lain on D'lise's bed, messed it up with the full knowledge that it would annoy the white woman.

"Don't fret about it." He unconsciously stroked her arm. "There are more clean bed linens in the trunk. And I'll see to it that she stays off your bed from now on."

"I don't want to make trouble between the two of you." D'lise's eyes were worried.

"Don't go frettin' about that." The fine lines around Kane's eyes deepened in a smile. "There won't be any trouble. Now come show me where you want the supplies to go."

When Kane walked back outside for another load, D'lise looked around the small room. She didn't have much choice where to stow anything. When he returned, a sack of beans on his shoulder, she pointed to the corner next to the fireplace. "Put everything there where it's dry and warm."

Sacks of flour, cornmeal, coffee, sugar, and salt were added as Kane finished unloading the little animal. Small items, such as vinegar, molasses, baking soda, lard, and spices, were arranged neatly in the center of the table.

The bag of dried apples were in the last batch Kane brought in. He tossed it to D'lise. "Here are the apples for your pies." He looked into the empty woodbox. "I'll bring in some wood and get a good fire goin', heat up the oven for you."

With a nod of her head, D'lise took off her jacket, then measured four cups of apples into a pan and poured water over them so they would soak and plump up while she made the pie dough.

Twenty minutes later she stood looking helplessly at the smooth, round ball of dough lying on a floured towel. She had no rolling pin. She looked up at the mantel clock Kane had finally started. It was almost four o'clock and nearing time to milk the cow. When Kane entered the cabin a few minutes later, she was near tears.

"What's wrong?" he asked in concern at the woeful look on her face.

She motioned to the ball of dough. "I can't find a rolling pin to flatten this out."

"I never thought of that," Kane said helplessly. "I reckon you'll find a lot of things like that missin' round here. You're gonna have to keep track of all the things you need and we'll pick them up the next time we go to the village." An embarrassed grimace stirred his lips. "You'll have to add pie tins to your list too. I just remembered we don't have any of those either."

When they continued to stare down at the round piece

of dough, as though they would find the answer in it, Kane suggested, "What if you made a cobbler? There's a pan I bake corn bread in. That would work, wouldn't it?"

D'lise face cleared with a bright smile. "You've come up with the perfect solution. I can flatten the dough with my hands for that. Get me the pan," she ordered, already pressing and pulling at the flour and lard mixture.

Kane grinned at her bossing him about as he lifted the battered tin off its wooden peg. He wondered if this was just the beginning of his taking orders from the delicate little miss whose slender neck he could snap with a twist of his wrist.

He placed the pan on the table and walked outside, his lips still curved in a small smile. However, as he walked past Raven, still sitting on the rock, his features became stern and he growled, "Keep off D'lise's bed in the future."

Raven made no response, but her black eyes glittered with resentment. She turned her gaze to the cabin, revenge in her narrowed eyes. Some day, somehow, she would get rid of the white woman who was drawing the trapper away from her.

Unaware of Raven's dark thoughts, D'lise finally had the dough stretched enough to cover the bottom and the sides of Kane's corn bread pan. The apple filling was ready and the small oven was hot. A few minutes later she slid the pastry onto the rack inside the stone cubicle and closed its door.

As she straightened up, she heard Spider bawl her distress. She picked up the milk pail, and with Scrag pacing alongside her, she headed toward the barn. Her lips curved in a grin when they passed Raven and Scrag paused to arch his back and hiss at the Indian woman.

Kane, chopping more wood, for the evenings were

quite cool now, noted the cat's action and wondered with some amusement if D'lise was able to communicate her dislike of Raven to her pet.

Twenty minutes later, when he and D'lise walked into the cabin, his arms full of wood and she carrying a pail of milk, and a discontented Raven trailing behind them, the cabin was filled with the spicy aroma of apples.

"Boy!" Kane took a deep breath. "This place has never known that smell before. I've a mind not to take the cobbler to the Jessups."

"We've got to take it," D'lise scolded. "We've nothing else." She gave him a consoling smile. "I'll bake one for us tomorrow."

Raven threw herself into one of the rockers. "Why do you go to the Jessups' cabin?" She looked at Kane.

"Mrs. Jessup died last night," Kane answered, "We're goin' to her wake."

Raven set the rocker in motion and stared. "Raven go with you."

Kane sent her a look that said, "You know better than that." Raven's black eyes defied him a moment, then looked away as he stared her down.

That's a relief, D'lise thought, peeling potatoes and slicing them into a skillet. I wouldn't go if Kane allowed her to go with us.

And she wanted to go. She wanted to meet and get to know her new neighbors. She and Auntie had never been allowed to associate with the women who lived in her old neighborhood. They knew them only to speak a greeting, and nothing else. She had no idea what they thought about different things. She often wondered if they were God-fearing, if they worked as hard as she and Auntie did. Were their husbands as mean as Rufus was to his wife?

D'lise continued to muse about the women she would

meet tonight as the evening meal progressed. By the time she had supper on the table, dusk was coming on. She lit a candle, then called out that it was time to eat.

She watched Kane's face as he took a seat and ranged his eyes over the platter of sugar-cured ham, the fried potatoes, stewed turnips, and a round of quick bread.

She relaxed when he looked up at her and smiled. "Like I said before about the cobbler, this table has never before held such a tasty-lookin' meal."

D'lise murmured, "Thank you," and sat down across from him, hiding a smile. Raven had almost knocked the table over in her hurry to sit next to Kane.

Her wry amusement turned into disgust. Raven's eating habits were atrocious. Using her fingers, she stuffed her mouth full of food, then, like Rufus, chewed it with her mouth open. It turned D'lise's stomach each time the woman wiped her greasy fingers down the front of her tunic, and she pushed her plate away long before her companions did. D'lise suffered through the chomping and grinding until finally, with a loud belch, Raven signaled that her hunger was sated.

The well-stuffed woman stood up then, and when she would have left the table, Kane said, "Since D'lise cooked the meal, you can do the cleanin' up." He ignored her scowl as he rose and said to D'lise, "We can get started to the Jessups' whenever you're ready."

True darkness had arrived as D'lise and Kane rode toward the east, along the Ohio River branch. A full moon had risen, clearly marking the trail that would lead them up a hill, down across a hollow, then up another hill to where the Jessup cabin sat. D'lise, keeping the cloth-covered pan of cobbler balanced in her lap, wished that she'd had time to sew a dress from one of the pretty pieces waiting back at the cabin. What would the women think

135

of her drab, worn homespun?

She consoled herself that her dress was clean and turned her thoughts to which piece of material she'd start on tomorrow. Before long, an old decrepit shack loomed before them eerily in the shadows.

It looked much like the one she had lived in most of her life, and D'lise wouldn't have been surprised had Rufus stepped out onto its rotting porch.

"Looks like all the woods people have come to the 'sittin' up,' " Kane said as he dismounted and caught her under the arms as she slid off the mare.

"How did everyone hear about Mrs. Jessup's death so quickly?" D'lise asked as Kane tied the mounts to a tree. "Some of them live quite a distance away, don't they?"

"Yes, some as far as fifteen miles. You see, whenever someone dies a bell is tolled in a particular way that announces a death in the community. Then the bell is tolled real slow, the number of years of the person's age. That way everyone can figure out who the dead person is. Everybody stops whatever they're doin' at the time and starts off to do what they can for the bereaved family."

"What kind of things do they do for the family?" D'lise asked. No one had come to help her and Rufus when Auntie killed herself.

"Oh, you know, all the things that have to be done. The men dig the grave and make a coffin, the women wash the body, if it's a woman who died, then dress her. The clothes have to be put on a corpse before rigor mortis sets in. It's hard to get them dressed when the body gets stiff."

D'lise shivered. She knew all about that. It had been left up to her to wash Auntie, then struggle a clean dress over her poor, broken body. She still dreamed about that.

Kane saw her shiver, and taking her arm, ushered her

onto the porch. "The nights are gettin' cold, huh?" he said, opening the door and nudging her through it.

Everyone looked up when D'lise and Kane entered the room, which was dimly lit by a sole candle. Miserly bastard, Kane thought of Elijah Jessup as he peered at the faces turned toward him and D'lise.

His gaze picked out the Jessup children, ranging in ages from nine to less than a year. Those old enough to understand the finality of death wore grief and uncertainty on their thin features; on the younger ones was only confusion.

It was Sarah Patton who came to greet Kane and D'lise and walk with them up to the pine casket.

"Me and Ellen Travis, the pretty one sittin' next to my Milly, washed and dressed Tilda," Sarah whispered. "Poor thing didn't have a decent dress to meet her maker in, so Ellen went home and got one of hers.

"She looks real nice, don't you think?" she said as Kane and D'lise looked down at the wasted body of the still young woman.

Bad memories came back to D'lise. Auntie hadn't had a decent dress to be buried in either. Had she been ashamed when she stood before God in her faded dress and scuffed shoes? She glanced up at the stern-faced man sitting beside the fire. Had he, like Rufus, beaten this thin little woman? Her body shuddered with a sudden abhorrence of all men. She grimly promised herself that she would never put herself at the mercy of one.

As though he knew what was running through her mind, Kane bent his head and whispered close to her ear, "Although Jessup was cruel to his wife in many ways, he never brutalized her."

D'lise was not sure as she gazed at the thin hands in which someone had placed a bouquet of goldenrods. She had noted that when the children occasionally glanced at their father, it was with guarded looks, as though they didn't want to call attention to themselves. Even the youngest one, riding her eldest sister's hip, made no sound. And the neighbor women here, although they displayed genuine sympathy for the children, didn't seem to extend that emotion to the father. They seemed to shun him, never looking directly at him. Didn't that say something?

Kane was taking her arm then, leading her away from the casket. "I want you to meet the rest of your neighbors," he said.

D'lise couldn't keep up with the names of all those she met in the next few minutes, but she would remember their faces, she told herself, and in time match both together.

When she had been introduced to everyone, Kane led her to a seat next to the woman who had donated the dress for Tilda Jessup to be buried in. "Welcome to Piney Ridge, D'lise," Ellen Travis said with a smile. "I'm sorry we've met under such unhappy circumstances." She gave her attention to Kane then. "It's good to see you've made it back in one piece, Kane. We were all worried that you would try to win the war all by yourself." The curve of her lips was teasing.

Kane laughed softly. "I'm not quite that crazy, Ellen. I knew I'd need a little help." He laid a hand on D'lise's shoulder. "I'm gonna go talk to the men while you and Ellen chat."

"He's a fine man," Ellen said, watching the big trapper walk to the other side of the room where the men were gathered. "I hardly recognized him with his beard shaved off." After a pause, she said, "I understand he's taken you under his wing, so to speak."

"Yes, he's given me a home," D'lise answered, but

divulged no more information. She couldn't lie as readily as Kane could. "Which of those men belongs to you, Ellen?" She asked to change the subject, looking at the knot of males talking quietly together.

"None." There was a sad note in Ellen Travis's voice. "I've been a widow for four years. My husband was killed at the grist mill we owned at the foot of the village. He slipped and fell into the river one day when no one was around. Because he couldn't swim, he was caught in the current and drowned."

"I'm sorry to hear that," D'lise said, then asked, "Was he a good husband?"

"Yes, he was." Ellen gave her a curious look.

"He never beat you, then?"

"Of course not, D'lise. What makes you think that he did?"

D'lise shrugged. "It seems that most men do."

"Oh, but you are so mistaken," Ellen exclaimed. "Most men *don't* beat their wives. Take Kane for instance. I'd bet my life he's never laid a hand on a woman in anger."

D'lise mused on Ellen's words. She hadn't seen Kane strike Raven, although the woman had angered him a couple of times. She told herself she'd wait and see before coming to a conclusion.

She and Ellen looked up when Samuel Majors stood in front of them. "May I join you ladies?" He smiled down at them.

"Certainly." Ellen, pink-cheeked, moved over on the bench so that he could sit between her and D'lise.

"So, D'lise." Samuel crossed an ankle over his knee. "I don't suppose you've had time to get started on any of the material you bought today." His smile was wide and genial.

139

D'lise shook her head. "Not yet, but I plan to get a dress cut out tomorrow."

The storekeeper turned to Ellen. "Have you finished reading those books I lent you?"

"Yes, just today I finished the last one, *Walk into the Wilderness.*"

"Oh, did you like it?" D'lise leaned across Samuel and looked at Ellen with sparkling eyes. "I loved it. I've read it twice."

Samuel and Ellen looked at her with some surprise. "So you can read, D'lise?" Samuel said.

"Of course I can," D'lise answered, slightly insulted. "My aunt was a schoolteacher before she got married and she taught me everything she could."

"I did notice that you use good grammar," Ellen said, then looked at Samuel, a silent query in her eyes. When he nodded, she said to D'lise, "I think you're an answer to our prayers. Would you consent to being our new teacher?"

"Me? A teacher?" D'lise almost gasped. She shook her head vehemently. "I would not have the patience for it." She didn't add that she knew nothing about children, that she would be unable to communicate with them, let alone teach them anything.

"Well, at least think about it," Ellen urged; then the three of them fell to discussing books they had read, their eyes sparkling, their voices animated as they voiced different opinions on certain books.

Across the room, Kane pretended to take part in the conversation going on around him, but barely took his attention from the trio after Samuel had joined D'lise and Ellen.

As he watched D'lise glow and come alive in a manner she'd never displayed before, there grew in him an unyielding resentment. He ignored the sharp pang in his heart and let his anger grow. He should have known she would flirt and carry on with an attractive man. She was beautiful, wasn't she? And all beautiful women were shallow, interested only in drawing men into their nets. He thanked God she hadn't wormed herself under his skin. He wouldn't be left bleeding when she abandoned him for the fancy, educated storekeeper. She could take her book-learning and go to him anytime she pleased. They could read books and discuss them all day.

"And what about the nights?" a small voice whispered.

That question brought Kane to his feet and across the floor to stand in front of D'lise. He nodded coolly to Samuel, then took D'lise by the arm and lifted her to her feet, saying gruffly, "Let's go see what the neighbor women have put on the table over there."

Ellen and Samuel looked at each other, then grinned at Kane's feeble excuse to take D'lise away from them. "I wonder if he's aware that he's finally fallen in love—and with a beautiful woman," Ellen murmured.

"What's unusual about him falling for a beautiful woman?" Samuel asked in surprise. "I would imagine beautiful women throw themselves at him all the time."

"They do, but for some reason none of us can figure out, he always picks the most unattractive female he can find. It will be interesting to see what happens there."

D'lise wondered at the hard coldness in Kane's voice, the almost painful grip he had on her arm as they viewed pots of beans with chunks of ham in them, pans of cornbread, a loaf of light bread, a venison roast, and her apple cobbler. It was almost as though he was angry with her, but she couldn't imagine why.

When they left the table, Kane led D'lise to where three older women, including Sarah Patton, sat on a bench.

141

"We was just talkin' 'bout them poor young'uns, won-derin' what was to become of them," Sarah said as she moved over, making room for D'lise to sit down. "I guess we could parcel them out amongst us." She looked up at Kane leaning against the wall next to where D'lise sat. "What about you and D'lise takin' a couple?"

"No." Kane's answer came so swiftly, so positively, that the women gave him a startled look. "Our place is too small," he added. "Besides, D'lise hasn't been feelin' well."

His lips twisted wryly. "Anyway, give Elijah a couple weeks and he'll have them young'uns a new mama."

"Pooh," Claudie Jacobs, a tall, thin woman with gray-ing hair pulled back into a tight knot, snorted. "There ain't a woman in Piney Ridge who'd marry that randy old goat."

"What's to keep him from goin' out of the area and talkin' some poor unsuspecting woman into marryin' him?"

"Well, there is that." Claudie sniffed. "One way or the other, men always find a way to vent their lust. I guess we'll hold off on the children for a while, see what hap-pens."

D'lise slid a glance at the middle-aged woman sitting on the other side of Sarah. Claudie Jacobs sounded as sour on men as she did herself. Was the woman married to a man like Rufus Enger?

Her attention was diverted from the sharp-faced neigh-bor when Sarah said to Kane, "Will you be bringin' D'lise to the corn huskin' Saturday night at our place? I'm sure she would enjoy it. She'd get to meet all the young people in the neighborhood."

"We'll see," Kane answered shortly. "Like I said, she hasn't been feelin' well lately."

D'lise was about to protest, to say that she felt fine, when she happened to glance up at Kane and changed her mind. There was a dark broodiness about him, a look of displeasure. What had put him in such a mood? When he said it was time they headed home, she stood up with no demur.

"Are you comin' to the burial tomorrow mornin'?" Sarah asked.

Kane nodded. "We'll be there." Without further words, he took D'lise's arm again and led her to the door, giving her no opportunity to say goodbye to Ellen and Samuel.

As he helped her to mount, D'lise grumbled, "You didn't give me time to say goodbye to Ellen. She'll think me awfully rude."

"Are you sure you aren't disappointed you didn't get to say goodbye to the fancy storekeeper?" Kane almost snarled the words as he jerked the mare's reins from the tree and handed them to her.

"What are you talking about?" D'lise began, then closed her mouth when the door opened and Sarah Patton stood in the opening.

"When are you comin' for your hens, Kane? They're layin' right good. It's a shame you ain't enjoyin' their eggs."

"I'll start fixin' a place for them tomorrow, Sarah," he answered, swinging onto Snowy's back and turning his head in the direction of home.

At first D'lise was going to pursue the question Sarah had interrupted, but decided against it. Kane's broad, stiff back didn't encourage further questioning. If she angered him further, he might even strike her.

No, she told herself, Ellen was right. This big man would never use his strength against a woman. She didn't know why, but she was sure of it.

The plaintive call of a whippoorwill floated across the hollow as they entered it, and another answered as they climbed the hill to the cabin. Kane drew rein at the sagging porch and reached over to steady D'lise's arm as she dismounted. As she brushed down her dress he took hold of Beauty's bridle and led her along as he steered the stallion to the barn.

D'lise watched him a moment, then, with a sigh, pushed open the cabin door. Raven, sitting in front of the fire, turned her head as the door creaked, then wordlessly looked back at the fire when she saw only D'lise. "And hello to you too," D'lise muttered to herself and walked over to the bed where her package of material lay.

She was struggling with a knot in the twine holding the heavy paper together when Kane entered the cabin. He watched her a moment, then drew his knife, and with a swipe of the sharp blade the wrapping unfolded.

D'lise gave a gasp of pure delight. Lying on top of the folded material, the soap and ribbons and laces, were several skeins of yarn, a cream color and two shades of blue. "Oh, Kane!" she exclaimed, and impulsively reached up to kiss his cheek.

But her lips didn't land where she intended them to. Kane had made a swift move of his head and her lips met his fully. Too stunned to move, she allowed her body to be swept up against his. As his lips moved hungrily over hers, she could feel his heart beating violently against her breasts.

It wasn't until he made a muffled groaning sound that she was stirred into action. Bracing her hands against his chest, she shoved hard as she jerked her mouth away from the devouring lips.

Kane stared blankly at her a moment as he was

snatched away from a rapture such as he had never known before. D'lise's slender body, although thin, had felt so soft and good, fitting perfectly to his, her feminine mound nestled against his rising masculinity. Awareness came into his eyes then and he realized what he had done.

Full of remorse, he said hoarsely, "I'm sorry, D'lise. I don't know what came over me. Do you forgive me?"

D'lise did not look at him, staring down at the floor and twisting her hands together.

"I promise it won't happen again," Kane said softly, then persisted gently, "Do you forgive me?"

He didn't hurt you, D'lise reminded herself. Actually he had only startled her. And if, as he promised, he never did it again, there was really no reason she shouldn't forgive him. After all, it was partly her fault. Knowing how men were, she should have never tried to kiss his cheek.

She looked up at him with a shy smile. "I forgive you."

Neither paid any attention to Raven's angry snort as they smiled at each other with warm eyes. "So," Kane said, "I take it you like the yarn."

"Oh, yes! I've never had new yarn to work with before, and such a pretty color. Rufus only allowed Auntie to spin yarn from the culls he sheared from the sheep. He always sold the prime wool."

"What are you gonna knit?"

"A nice warm afghan for the winter." She picked up the knitting needles that lay hidden beneath the yarn. "How did you know what size to buy?"

Kane grimaced. "Mr. Fancy Majors told me the size you'd need."

"Don't call him that," D'lise scolded with a smile. "He's a very nice man."

The warmness left Kane's eyes. He walked over to the

fireplace, added a log to the fire, then said gruffly to Raven, "Come on, it's bedtime."

D'lise stared at the door that had snapped shut with a slight bang. Kane hadn't even said good night. What had set him off again? She sighed and started preparing for bed. These swinging moods of his were very upsetting.

Sleep eluded her for some time as she relived Kane's embrace and kiss. It was true she had been startled by his action, but in all truth his lips had felt good on hers, soft and warm and demanding. She had felt a little tingling in the pit of her stomach just before she pushed him away.

When she fell asleep, at last, she dreamed of hungry lips on hers.

D'lise was jerked awake by an ungentle hand shaking her shoulder. She blinked up at a very angry Kane.

"Why did you leave your door unbarred last night?" he fairly yelled at her. "Don't you realize that a man, or a bear, could have entered the cabin? God knows what I'd have found this mornin'."

In her anxiety to calm Kane, D'lise blurted out the truth of why she had forgotten to bar the door. "I'm sorry, Kane. I was troubled that you hadn't said good night, and I forgot to bar the door."

Kane's face lightened like the sun rising in the early morning. "It bothered you that I didn't say goodnight?"

"Yes, it did. I couldn't figure out why you were suddenly mad at me."

Kane lifted a hand and stroked her tumbled curls. "If I promise that from now on I'll always say goodnight, will you remember to bar the door?"

D'lise nodded and gave him a warm smile.

"Get up then. We've only got an hour to make it to the buryin'. While you put on a pot of coffee I'll go saddle up."

As D'lise hurried to get dressed, she remembered with a frown that she had forgotten to ask Kane what had made him angry last night.

It was blustery, gray, and dismal when D'lise and Kane left for Tilda Jessup's funeral. The clouds hung so low and so heavy that when they topped a hill they were swallowed up in fog.

"It's an awful day to bury a person, isn't it?" Kane said as they tied their mounts with the others already tied up outside the cabin.

The same people who had been at the wake were in attendance, with the exception of one new face. "That's Reverend House, the new preacher," Kane whispered to D'lise. "I met him the other day." He grinned ruefully. "I'm afraid he doesn't think much of me."

When everyone had found seats, the preacher, a lanky, cadaverous-looking individual, rose and walked to stand at the head of the casket. He cleared his throat and began to read from a worn Bible. The older children wept softly as his voice droned on, and sympathetic tears for them glistened in most of the women's eyes.

The preacher closed his Bible and stepped back so the hill people could pass single-file past the coffin for a last look at their neighbor. The family came last, and tears that had been held back ran freely when the toddler, riding his sister's hip, held out his arms for his dead mother to take him.

When everyone had gathered outside, Reverend House nodded to the man who had remained inside. He picked up a hammer that had lain beside him during the service, and after placing a flat lid on the pine box, he nailed it shut.

When the sound of hammering stopped, three of the men waiting outside stepped back into the cabin and Tilda

Jessup's remains were carried out and carefully placed on the Jessups' rickety wagon. Then, with the bony old mule leading the way, everyone walked slowly behind the wagon to the cemetery on the next hill.

Tears ran down D'lise cheeks as she remembered another funeral such a short time ago. Walking beside her, Kane saw her wet face and reached into his breast pocket and handed her a handkerchief. She gave him a wet smile and mopped at her eyes.

The wind died down, and the sun burst through the clouds as Tilda Jessup was lowered into her grave. A low murmur went up from among those gathered around, and a woman standing next to D'lise whispered, "It's God welcomin' her into Heaven."

The grave was filled and mounded, and a few women placed bouquets of fall asters on it. The wind came up again and the sun went behind a cloud. D'lise wondered if Tilda had arrived in Heaven as Kane took her arm and they followed the others back down the hill.

Chapter Eight

The hammer came down with force on Kane's thumb. He swore heartily and stuck the injured digit in his mouth. Dammit, he was a trapper, not a carpenter, he muttered to himself.

For two days now he had been working at partitioning off a narrow portion of the barn for the blasted hens Sarah Patton kept nagging at him to come get. He hoped to add on a heavy wire pen for the fowl today and have done with it. He was anxious to get the glass pane installed in the cabin, to be able, after all these years, to open up the shutters and let the sun shine in.

His plans were to get D'lise out of the house for a while and surprise her with the finished job. Maybe he'd take her with him to pick up the hens. He'd leave her to visit with Sarah and the girls while he hurried back to install the glass.

Kane stepped back to see if the four nest boxes were

149

level and stepped on Raven's foot. She had silently entered the barn and come up behind him. Irritation clouded his face. Every time he turned around, she was underfoot. He didn't ask himself why this suddenly irked him. Raven had always followed him about.

He did know, however, why he couldn't sleep with her anymore. Every time he tried to, D'lise's face came between him and Raven and his arousal went limp. It had been three days now, and he was edgy and short-tempered. He hoped that some night, out of pure necessity, he would succumb to Raven's stroking fingers.

He forced a calmness to his tone when he said, "I wish you wouldn't sneak up on me like that, Raven."

Raven ran a palm down the front of his buskskins. "Raven did not sneak. You too busy swearing at your thumb. Why you do this?" She waved a contemptuous hand at all the work he'd done the past three days. "You great trapper, great warrior. The white woman in the cabin has brought you to this."

"I wouldn't be doin' this if I didn't want to, Raven," Kane retorted, annoyed. "I bought six hens and I need a place to put them."

"But you bought them for *her*." Raven's fingers were now on the lacings of his fly. "You do all these things for a woman who will not sleep with you."

"How do you know she won't?" Kane knocked Raven's hand away. "I haven't asked her to."

"She would say no, and we both know it. The skinny one is afraid of men." She reached for him again. "She is not for you. She could never give you the hard ride that Raven can."

Before Kane could answer Raven's charge, D'lise called his name from the open barn door. He hissed to Raven to go sit down on a pile of hay, and she gave him

150

a dark look, muttering, "Fool," before she did as she was bid.

"Over here, D'lise," Kane called out. "I'm just finishing up with the egg nests."

"Oh, I didn't mean to interrupt your work," D'lise exclaimed. "I only wanted to show you my new dress. I just finished it." She stood in the path of the sunlight pouring through the door, and when Kane stepped out of the shadows she turned around slowly so that he could take in every detail.

She's gained weight since I brought her here, Kane thought, his eyes fastening on the ripe breasts filling the bodice. He felt a deep satisfaction that he had furnished her that nourishment. His eyes lingered a moment longer on the bared swell of her breasts that rose just a bit above the lace trimming on the square neckline. When he felt himself swelling, he dropped his gaze to the narrow waist and gently flaring hips. But that only worsened his condition when he remembered that beneath her skirt was the soft mound that had so excited him the day he kissed her.

Kane made himself look up at D'lise's face and forced a smile to his lips. "You're quite a seamstress, D'lise. The dress is the prettiest I've ever seen. Its blue color matches your eyes."

"Thank you, Kane." D'lise smiled shyly, then looked past him. "You're doing a fine job fixing a place for my hens. When do you think we can bring them home?"

"Maybe tomorrow if I can get the pen ready today. Would you like to come with me, visit Sarah and her daughters awhile?"

D'lise's eyes sparkled. "I'd like that. I enjoy Sarah and her daughters' company. They are all so jolly and fun-loving."

They stood looking at each other a moment; then D'lise

151

said, "I'll be getting back to the cabin now. I'm going to bake an apple cobbler for supper."

"Hey, that sounds great, D'lise, and to show my appreciation I promise to get the chicken pen finished today."

With a happy little laugh, D'lise left the barn, unaware that Raven sat in the shadows glaring at her.

Raven watched D'lise and Kane ride away the next day, her eyes boring hatred into D'lise's slender back. Another night had passed without Kane touching her. It was as if the white bitch had taken away his manhood.

Well, she decided, she knew of one man who was always ready for her. She calculated that Kane would be gone at least an hour, giving her plenty of time to visit Albert Bracken, get from him the release that Kane wouldn't give her.

She gave a bitter laugh. She could be gone all day and the trapper wouldn't even notice it. She might just stay with Bracken all day, she thought defiantly, striking off for the cabin two hills away.

Snowy didn't at all like the sack of squawking chickens slung across his back. He tossed his head, rattling the rein buckles. Kane sympathized with him. "We're almost home, fellow." He patted the white neck. "I don't like their infernal noise either, but their eggs sure will taste good for breakfast."

A quarter of an hour later, Kane was releasing the chickens into their new home. Before he and D'lise had left to go fetch them, D'lise had put out a pan of cracked corn and a pan of water for them, and they headed for the water right away. Then, clucking a contented sound, they started pecking at the corn.

Kane watched them for a while, then went to the cabin and pulled the sheet of glass from beneath D'lise's bed where it had lain all the time.

Back at the Patton cabin, D'lise sat at their kitchen table, eating cookies and enjoying her first friendly visit with her own sex. "Make sure Kane brings you to the corn huskin' Saturday night," Milly Patton said, reaching for her fifth cookie.

"Yeah, do that, D'lise. Milly's hopin' he'll find a red ear and that he'll pick her to kiss," sixteen-year-old Becky teased her sister.

"I do not," the eighteen-year-old denied, her face a bright red.

"Oh yes, you do," Becky insisted. "All you talk about is Kane Devlin—how handsome he is, how broad his shoulders are."

"Ma! Will you tell Becky to stop it!" Milly was near tears.

"Hush up, Becky," Sarah ordered. "I see you peekin' looks at Kane all the time too." She shook her head as if mystified. "I don't understand Kane," she said. "He's past the marryin' age and still he keeps Indian women and whores. And if that's not bad enough, he picks the ugliest ones he can find." She looked at D'lise. "I hope he's dropped that squaw, Raven."

D'lise hesitated to answer Sarah's question. She hated to talk about Kane in a derogatory manner, but she found that more and more, she dreaded bedtime when Kane would take the Indian woman to the barn. She was afraid that someday all her bitter feelings would burst loose and she would say something that would anger Kane, make him send her away.

She lifted her eyes to the waiting Pattons. "I'm afraid Raven is still with us," she said quietly.

153

Shock came over the three faces. "You mean to tell me that he lies with her, the three of you in the same room?" Sarah's eyes were outraged.

"Oh, no!" D'lise hastened to say. "They sleep in the barn."

"With the rest of the animals." Sarah's lips curled contemptuously.

"What is this red ear of corn you're talking about?" D'lise asked, steering the conversation away from Kane.

Sarah's face showed that she was reluctant to let the subject go, but she said no more on the matter when Milly began explaining the meaning of a man finding a red ear of corn.

"When it's corn huskin' time in the fall, the farmer slips some red Indian corn in with the yellow. When a man finds a red ear, he gets to kiss any woman there that he wants to." There was a slight pause before she added, "Kane never attends the get-togethers. That's why we're hopin' you can get him to bring you."

"Yeah, half the women in Piney Ridge want to kiss Kane," Becky quipped.

"It sounds like a lot of fun," D'lise said weakly, remembering the hungry kiss Kane had given her.

"Oh, it is," Milly said with sparkling eyes. "So are the box suppers we hold at church."

"And what are those?" D'lise asked.

"My goodness, child," Sarah said, "what did you do for entertainment where you lived before?"

D'lise felt the embarrassed flush that spread over her face. She couldn't tell these new friends of hers that she had been allowed to associate with no one but her aunt and two bound-boys. They would never understand it, probably wouldn't even believe her.

"My father was sickly and I mostly stayed home with

him,'' she said and hoped she wouldn't be questioned further.

"That's a shame," Sarah said with genuine sympathy, then explained the box supper to D'lise. "We have those often, mostly in the winter when there's nothin' else to do. The young single girls make up a light supper and put it in a box. Most of them fry a chicken, and all of them bake a pie or cookies for dessert. At the church the preacher holds the boxes up, one at a time, and the single men bid on them. The money goes to support Reverend House's family."

"And sometimes there's a lot of it," Becky put in. "Sometimes a couple of men will bid against each other if they both like the same girl and they know which box is hers. Remember, Ma, that time them two trappers kept biddin' on that trashy Rosy Davis's box? The one who finally got it had to hand over five dollars."

"I remember." Sarah nodded. "It was the highest price anybody had ever paid at one of the socials. And didn't Rosy put on airs about it."

"Hah!" Milly snorted. "Everybody knew it wasn't the box supper bein' bet on. It was what came with it. Remember how the trapper took her outside to eat? You know dang good and well that box was never opened."

"You mean . . ." D'lise looked questioningly at Milly.

"That's what I mean. Them three Davis girls ain't nothin' but sluts. The only difference between them and the whores in Piney Ridge is they don't take money from the men."

The three Patton women gaped at D'lise when she snapped, "They're fools then."

"Well, maybe," Sarah finally agreed weakly. "I guess they think that by not chargin' the men they ain't whores."

"Well, that's silly thinking." D'lise tone was sharp. "They don't receive any more respect from their neighbors than the whores, do they?"

"Yes, that's true," Sarah said lamely. "Ain't no man in the area that would ask one of the girls to marry him." She looked up with relief when Kane opened the door and stepped inside. D'lise Alexander had a strange way of thinking, even if she did make sense. She was awfully old for her age to think so straight.

"Did you ladies have a nice visit?" Kane asked of everyone in general.

"Speaking for myself, I certainly have," D'lise answered at once.

When Sarah and her daughters echoed her sentiments, a pleased look came over Kane's face. "Sarah, you and the girls will have to come visit D'lise."

"We intend to," Sarah replied. "Milly and Becky can't wait to see D'lise's dress patterns. Your little ward sure is handy with a needle and thread. I've never seen a prettier dress than the one she's wearin'."

Pride was in the eyes Kane turned on D'lise. "She's a fine little cook too. And speaking of which, we'd better get home, D'lise. My stomach is beginnin' to say it's hungry."

"Yes, I expect it's getting that time." D'lise stood up. "I want to take a look at my chickens before I start cooking, though."

The Pattons followed D'lise and Kane outside and stood waving until they were hidden on the other side of the hill. "What do you think, Ma?" Milly asked. "Is Kane fonder of D'lise than he lets on?"

"It's hard to say. He's a deep one. The girl ain't his usual choice of woman, and besides, she's decent. Kane's an honorable man for all his wild ways. He'd never use her like he does the others.'' Sarah's lips firmed in displeasure. ''And he's still got that red squaw with him. I don't think he'd have her around if he was interested in D'lise.''

''That's true, but he has a tenderness in his eyes when he looks at her,'' Milly said, chewing thoughtfully on her bottom lip.

''Well, we'll just have to wait and see.'' Sarah walked back into the cabin, saying, ''You girls do your chores while I get supper started.''

The sun had swung well westward as Kane and D'lise rode along, neither speaking much. D'lise's mind was still back in the Patton cabin, going over the things they had talked about.

Milly was much like her mother, serious and practical, while Becky was fun-loving, with a teasing nature. Milly had a strong yen for Kane, but D'lise could tell he didn't return the girl's sentiment. When she found herself feeling glad about that, she snatched her mind away from the Pattons and gave her attention to her surroundings.

The maple trees were flushed with pink and yellow around their edges from the heavy frosts they'd had three mornings in a row. Winter wasn't far off, she thought, and Kane's cabin wasn't any better weatherproofed than Rufus's had been. She sighed softly, recalling how she used to dread those cold dark days of winter. One was never completely warm.

As though in tune with D'lise's thoughts, Kane remarked, ''I can't believe that November is only a week away. I've got a bunch of work ahead of me preparin' for it.''

''And what is that?'' D'lise asked, riding up beside him as they came to a wide stretch in the trail.

"For one thing I've got to chop a mountain of wood. It gets damn cold in these hills in the winter. Then, there's my traps. I've got to dig them out of the barn and grease them up. I figure I can start layin' my traps in another two or three weeks. Course, I can do the greasing in the evenin's sittin' in front of the fire."

Where it's warm, D'lise mused with a wry smile. *But what about when you take your squaw to the barn? You're going to freeze that appendage she seems so fond of.*

And how was she going to pass the cold days shut up in that dark little room with Raven always underfoot? Could she tolerate the woman's sullen face and rancid odor?

When they began to climb the hill to their cabin, D'lise glanced at the top to see if Raven sat on her usual rock waiting for their return. Something up there winked back at her, and squinting her eyes, she peered up at the distant building.

"What do you make of that, Kane?" she asked. "What could the sun be reflecting off?"

Kane made a disgruntled sound, then growled, "Dammit, D'lise, the sun has gone and ruined my surprise."

"What surprise?" D'lise thumped the mare with her heels, hurrying her up the hill. A couple yards from the cabin, D'lise reined her in, a glad light in her eyes.

"Oh, Kane," she cried, "you've installed glass in the window! What a difference it's going to make this winter."

"It does brighten up the place." Kane's pleased smile at her delight threatened to split his face. He was also glad that she was mounted and wouldn't be able to throw herself at him and kiss him again. For as sure as the sun came up in the east, he'd grab her again.

They drew rein in front of the cabin and D'lise sat and

gazed at the clean, clear glass for several minutes. The place even looked better, more welcoming.

"Why don't you go on in and I'll take care of the mounts." Kane took her arm, steadying her as she slid to the ground.

D'lise pushed open the door, hoping that Raven wasn't inside, that she hadn't got to see the window before she did. She smiled. The cabin was empty. She turned around slowly in the small area. Every corner was now brought out of the darkness by the red glare of the setting sun. A frown creased her forehead. The sunlight was cruel to the room. It brought into stark relief its shabbiness, the total lack of anything homey or attractive.

For a moment she felt like running to the window and slamming the shutters.

"The place could use some fixin' up, huh?" Kane had quietly entered the cabin.

D'lise could only nod her head. She was too near tears to speak.

"I could clean out the corners some." Kane looked around at the accumulation of broken traps, pieces of raveling rope, scraps of animal pelts, old moccasins, and worn-out buckskins that for some reason he'd never thrown away. When D'lise only nodded her head again, he began picking through the rubbish, tossing anything that would burn into the fireplace. When the only things left were the pieces of traps, he gathered them up and carried them outside.

"My goodness, the place looks so much larger with the corners cleared out," D'lise murmured. She began to take more interest in the room, seeing some possibilities for it. If Kane would make her some more shelves she could get all the cookware off the floor, along with the supplies stacked by the fireplace. That would neaten up the cabin considerably. And there was the yellow-flowered calico she had bought for curtains and a matching tablecloth.

It was with a much lighter heart that D'lise started supper. She even had a smile for Kane when he returned to the cabin, a wooden mallet in one hand, a bunch of wooden pegs in the other.

"I'm gonna fasten down these furs," he explained. "I'm tired of havin' them bunching up under my feet all the time."

D'lise hid an amused smile. How many years had it taken him to realize what a hindrance they were?

By the time she had supper on the table, Kane had pegged down the furs that reached to each corner. D'lise was amazed at the difference the stretched pelts brought to the room. It was beginning to look cozy. She was about to bring up the subject of shelves when Raven entered the cabin.

"Where'd you get off to today, Raven?" Kane asked, taking his place at the table and reaching for the bowl of mashed potatoes.

Raven didn't answer; her attention was on the window. Her lips curled in displeasure. "More cold air will enter the cabin this winter," she grunted. "Indian never do anything so foolish."

"But I'm not an Indian," D'lise said, passing Kane a platter of fried steak. "The lack of sunshine bothers me."

Raven muttered some inaudible word and sat down next to Kane. As she piled her plate with meat and potatoes and baked squash, she waited for Kane to ask her again where she had been. When the question wasn't repeated, her lips drooped in her usual pout.

Later, as D'lise and Kane sat before the fire, she working on another dress, he smoking his pipe, their ears were assaulted by the noise Raven made as she angrily slammed pots and pans and pewter ware.

Kane tolerated the din for a while, then turned his head to look at her and growled, "You're giving me a headache, Raven."

The Indian woman lifted a belligerent chin, but the noise of washing up diminished considerably. She knew she had pushed him far enough.

When everything was washed and dried and put away, and the dishwater thrown out, Raven sat down on the hearth and waited for Kane to take her to the barn.

The clock struck seven, then eight, then nine, and still Kane sat on. He was reluctant to leave the lovely girl sitting quietly beside him, taking tiny stitches in the material spread out on her lap. There was a serenity about her that soothed him in a way he had never known before. He glanced often at the neatly made-up bed, wishing that he could share it with her.

But as he watched her beautiful face bent over its task, another face, equally comely, floated before him. The memory of what that woman had done to his uncle made him jump to his feet and say harshly, "It's time for bed, Raven."

D'lise watched them leave with an unexplained tightness around her heart. She hurriedly dropped her lids against the sly, gloating look Raven sent her just before closing the door behind them. She folded the unfinished dress and laid it in the basket she had found in the barn, trying to tell herself that she was glad it was Raven and not she who would receive Kane's lust. Certainly she had no intention of ever letting a man touch her in such a manner. She remembered too well how demeaning the act was to a woman.

Nevertheless, she was a long time falling asleep. She

blamed the moonlight coming through the window, the cat purring loudly in her ears. She blamed everything but the image of Kane and Raven together for keeping her wide awake.

Chapter Nine

October arrived with cool days and cooler nights. Kane shivered slightly as he stood in the barn door, lacing up his buckskins, an angry scowl on his face as Raven's irate words still rang in his ears.

"The white woman has taken away your maleness," she had accused him when he repulsed her stroking fingers.

"You're crazy in the head," he'd retorted. "I just don't feel like doin' anything."

"You no feel like doing anything ever since the skinny girl come here," Raven shouted. "Maybe when Raven sleeps you sneak back to cabin and climb between her legs."

It had been all he could do not to slap the sullen face when she looked at him closely and sneered, "Can she make you groan louder than Raven does?"

"You open your mouth about her again and you're

163

gonna groan from the effect of my hand against it,'' he'd ground out. He turned around and walked back to where Raven still lay sprawled in the bed of hay. ''I've been thinkin','' he said, not unkindly, ''that maybe it's time you went back to your people. As you just pointed out, things aren't the same between us anymore.''

The taunting look immediately left Raven's eyes as she sat up, staring at Kane. ''You don't mean that,'' she whispered, her voice suddenly weak. ''Winter will be here soon, and you know well that hunger is ever present in my village. I doubt that anyone would take me into their lodge.''

She spoke the truth. Kane heaved a troubled sigh. Rations were scant in Indian villages during the winter. Big Beaver had spoken of it often. And he had been quite satisfied with Raven until D'lise came into his life, which was no fault of Raven's.

He raised his gaze from the barn floor and looked at the anxious-faced squaw who waited to hear whether she would go or stay. The relaxing of her body was visible as he said, ''Let me think on it for a while. In the meantime, take your blankets to the other side of the barn. We will no longer share the same pile of hay.''

Raven readily agreed, jumping to her feet and grabbing her blanket. But as Kane passed through the barn door, a look of triumph glittered in her black eyes. He would be hers again. All she had to do was get rid of the pale-faced beauty who—for the moment—had the big trapper acting like a moon-struck buffalo.

Smoke curled from the chimney, and through the new window Kane watched D'lise moving about, preparing breakfast. He stood where he was for a minute, enjoying the graceful way she moved between the table and the fireplace, the way the rising sun shot sparks off her black curls, giving them the sheen of a blackbird's wing.

She reached up to take something from a shelf, emphasizing the thrust of her breasts, making his manhood rise and throb against his buckskins. Damn! He rubbed the hard ridge through the soft leather of his trousers. Why couldn't he get stiff like this when he lay with Raven?

He took off for the cabin, cursing the fact that the Indian woman could no longer stir an interest in that part of him, while just to look at D'lise made him as randy as a buffalo. Maybe he should make a trip to the village, spend some time with a whore. Maybe he was only growing tired of Raven.

Kane walked into the cabin and D'lise greeted him with her usual bright smile, and for the time being he forgot about visiting the whorehouse. It seemed that lately everything flew from his mind when he was with his lovely little ward.

D'lise served him bacon and eggs and fried potatoes on the yellow tablecloth she had stitched to match the curtains at the window. The sun shone on their heads and reflected off the bright patchwork quilt Kane had purchased from Sarah Patton.

When the meal was eaten, and they were sitting over coffee, Kane said, "I've been promisin' to take you to see the army fort. How would you like to go today? If we put it off much longer the snows will be here and we'll have to wait for spring."

"I'd love to go today, Kane." D'lise's eyes sparkled. Then a second later she looked out the window and frowned. "There are some dark clouds building up in the north. Do you think we might get some rain?"

"I don't believe so. Why, are you afraid you'll melt if you get wet?" he teased.

Her laugh rang out. "It's never happened before," she said.

"All right then, let's get started. The fort is a far piece."

"How far?" D'lise asked, rising from the table and gathering up the dishes they had used.

"It's about five miles of woods-runnin', but we'll be goin' by river, which is almost double the distance because of all its twists and turns."

"Oh, that will be fun. I've always wanted to ride the Ohio. As soon as I feed Scrag and Hound we can leave."

She gave the cat a portion of the scraps left over from breakfast, then handed the larger part to Kane to take outside to the dog. The cat and dog still weren't the best of friends, but they were learning to tolerate each other, which was good. When the snows came and the weather dropped below zero, it would be too cold to keep Hound outside all the time.

When D'lise and Kane struck out toward the river where he had a boat stashed, the wind came up, cold and blustery. D'lise took a scarf from her pocket and tied it around her head as her long legs easily kept up with the pace Kane set.

"I hope the wind won't whip up waves on this ornery old river," Kane said as he helped D'lise into the deep-bottomed boat.

"Do you think we should postpone the trip?" D'lise asked worriedly.

"Naw, I've paddled this river in a canoe when it was in full flood." He smiled reassuringly at her as he picked up the oars. "You're in safe hands, lady."

"I trust you completely, Kane." D'lise smiled back, and knew suddenly that it was true. She did trust him, in all ways.

166

A strong push sent the boat into the river, and Kane began paddling upstream, closely hugging the shore to escape the full strength of the current. D'lise settled back, listening to the *swish-click, swish-click* of the oars.

In most places the forest grew right down to the river, and the time flew as she watched deer darting among the trees, wolves slinking along, and once a great black bear swiping at fish across the river. She also looked often at Kane's broad back, fascinated by the sight of his muscles rippling beneath his buckskin jacket.

She looked up in surprise when Kane said, "There she is."

The fort sat on a spit of land jutting out into the Ohio River. It was smaller than D'lise had anticipated, but was nonetheless impressive looking. Kane backed the boat ashore, jumped out, pulled it out of the water, and lifted D'lise over its side.

D'lise pulled the scarf off her head as she and Kane passed through the garrison gates, her eyes full of curiosity as they scanned troops of soldiers practicing formations, cavalrymen putting their mounts through their paces, and others just walking around. She and Kane were soon spotted, and greetings were called to Kane. She soon became aware that he knew many of the soldiers, and that he was popular with them, had probably fought with them.

"Devlin! You son of a gun, how've you been?" A red-headed giant of a man came to meet them, a dozen or so others quickly following him. Kane's back was slapped, but most of the attention was given to D'lise.

"Did you go and get married after all, Devlin?" a man with sergeant's stripes on his sleeve asked.

Kane put a possessive arm around D'lise's shoulders. Neither denying nor affirming the question, he said, "Fellows, meet D'lise."

The women-hungry men gathered round her, hands coming from all directions to shake hers. Just to touch her was all some asked, but there was a look in other eyes that said a handshake wouldn't be enough.

Kane was proud of the way D'lise's beauty affected his friends, but his eyes were a little anxious as they roamed the fort looking for a commanding officer who could step in if the men got out of order. He had been a damn fool to bring her here. He sighed his relief when he sighted a portly general.

Kane's marksmanship with rifle and knife was well known by the soldiers, and it wasn't long before he was challenged to a shooting match. He was tempted to show off before D'lise but didn't trust some of the men not to get familiar with her while his attention was on the target.

He shook his head. "Some other time," he promised. "I think it's time we head up the river for home now. It looks like it might start raining anytime."

He was cajoled into staying a little longer with assurances that the rain would hold off until nightfall. "We'll come another time," Kane said, taking D'lise's arm and leading her back toward the river, his friends following them. When he pushed the boat into the water, half a dozen men tripped over each other in their rush to be the one to help D'lise into the craft.

"You damn fools, you're gonna knock her into the river." Kane's angry voice rang out, stopping the soldiers in their tracks. These men also knew how handy Kane was with his fists, having seen him in many a rough-and-tumble fight.

They stepped back and watched enviously as he swept D'lise up and placed her in the boat. He climbed in behind her and picked up the oars. "It was good seein' you men again." He grinned and dipped the oars into the water.

No one paid any attention to him. All eyes were on D'lise.

"I hope those yahoos didn't frighten you with all their attention," Kane said several yards down the river. "It's just that they haven't seen a white woman in a long time."

"They didn't scare me, just made me a little nervous with their staring."

"You gotta get used to that, D'lise. You're somethin' to stare at," he said softly, making her blush.

The overcast sky grew darker with each passing minute. Kane lifted and dipped the oars a little faster, anxious to get off the river before dark, before the rain came. The Ohio was treacherous during a storm.

They had been on the river about an hour when a beating rain started, accompanied by thunder and lightning. The boat began to fill with water and Kane cursed himself for a fool for setting out without a bailing pail. In this deluge, the boat would swiftly fill and sink to the bottom of the river. Could D'lise swim? He hesitated to ask her at this time. She was probably scared enough without him hinting that the boat might disappear from under her.

Putting his strength into each swipe of the oars and peering through the blinding slash of rain, Kane turned the boat toward the shore. He had to get them off the river for more reasons than one. Lightning was striking the water all around them, and the river was rising, whipped into a fury by the raging wind.

The boat grated on gravel and Kane scrambled over its sides and turned quickly to D'lise sitting in the prow, her feet in three inches of water. He lifted her out and stood her on the bank where she stood shivering.

"I'll get you out of the rain in just a minute," he said, grabbing hold of the boat and dragging it toward the forest about a yard away. "We'll use the boat for shelter," he said.

The only answer he heard from D'lise was the chattering of her teeth and her hefty pushes of the vessel to help him along.

What a mate she would make for a man, Kane thought as the clumsy craft was pushed and pulled into a large stand of oak. She was no whining miss who would drag a man down. She was courageous and would always stand beside him, ready to lend her strength in any manner.

Although the rain fell steadily through the leaves, at least Kane could see what he was doing as he turned the boat over and leaned it against a big tree trunk. When he motioned D'lise to crawl beneath it, he followed her and took her shivering body into his arms. As the lightning continued to flash and the thunder to roll, he massaged her back and arms, trying to warm her, to get her blood pumping.

He didn't know when his fingers stopped rubbing and began stroking. All he knew was that suddenly he was very much aware of her slender body held close to his. His pulse leapt and his body felt as if it were on fire. He withheld a groan when D'lise pressed closer to him, drawn by the heat of his body.

I'm a bastard for doing this, he thought, but nevertheless his hand moved to her bodice, where his fingers expertly undid the small buttons.

On its own, D'lise's bone-chilled body pressed closer and closer to Kane's heat. When hot lips covered her cold ones she clung to them, willing them to warm hers also. Even the tongue that slipped through her teeth was a source of wonderful warmth, and she automatically wrapped her own tongue around it. She welcomed the warm palms on her breasts, the hot fingers that gently caressed the nipples. A glowing warmth was beginning to grow inside her, building higher and higher in her lower regions.

She became conscious of a hard ridge of heat pressing against the apex of her thighs at the same time that a heated mouth took possession of a swollen nipple and drew on it hungrily. She gave a start and raised her head to gaze down on Kane's head lying between her breasts, his mouth working over one of them.

For a moment, exquisite pleasure rushed through her body as the gentle lips caused sensations she'd never known before. Then, although she'd had no idea men did this to women, she knew what would follow. Lust would come upon Kane and he would grow ugly and begin to beat her even as he drove himself inside her.

Tears were suddenly running down her cheeks. She didn't want him to become like Rufus. She wanted him to remain the same man who treated her kindly, who watched over her with such care.

"Kane," she sobbed, "please stop."

Lost in the bliss of doing what he had wanted to do so often, Kane did not hear D'lise's whispered plea. It wasn't until she was crying almost hysterically that he realized he had a very unwilling woman in his arms. He raised his head and shook it, willing the passion and desire to leave his body. Never in his life had he come so close to making love only to be sharply cut off. He found it to be a very painful experience.

At the same time he understood that it must be. He shouldn't have touched her in a carnal way. He knew her fear of men, her belief that when a man took a woman it was in a brutal way.

"Forgive me, D'lise." He gently wiped her face with the heel of his palm. "I got carried away, with the storm and all." He gently smoothed her wet hair behind her

171

ears. "It will never happen again . . . if you don't want it to. Do you forgive me?" He trailed a finger down her cheek. "Will you be my friend again?"

How can I say no when he's sorry for losing his control? D'lise asked herself. She gave him a small smile and answered, "Of course I will. I know men are lustful."

Kane rolled over on his back and she regretted the loss of his warm body. "D'lise," he said quietly, "men aren't always lustful, or depraved. True, any woman will do for a man, if lust is all he feels. But sexual desire is something entirely different when a man cares for a woman. When he makes love to her out of desire, he never abuses her or strikes her. She is never forced, but comes to him willingly."

"Are you sure?" D'lise gazed up at him, doubt in her blue eyes as she remembered her aunt's cries of pain after Rufus jerked her into the bedroom. "Why would any woman want to be hurt that way?"

Kane laughed softly at her ignorance. "They're not always hurt, D'lise. Sometimes they get as much satisfaction as the man does." He raised himself up to look out into the forest and found that the rain had dwindled to a drizzle, and that the thunder and lightning had ceased.

"We can go home now," he said, giving the boat a hard push that turned it over on its bottom.

Neither had much to say once they were back on the river, but both had much on their minds. Kane knew he couldn't trust himself around D'lise and that someday his control would slip and he would seduce the girl. And it wouldn't be all that hard to do. Even though she was afraid of the act, he had felt the passion her slender body was capable of. He could light a flame in her that would burn him to a cinder.

But if that should ever come to pass, he would have to

marry her. D'lise Alexander wasn't the sort that a man could have only once and be satisfied. Nor was she a woman a man could only use. Yes, he had to be doubly careful around her from now on. He would not make the same mistake his uncle had.

D'lise's feelings were so tangled she couldn't begin to sort them out. How much of what Kane had said could she believe? Was it true that all men weren't alike in their treatment of women? Did some women really enjoy going to bed with them? She suspected that last might be true. She'd had such a good feeling when Kane's lips had drawn at her breast.

The boat swept around a bend in the river, and the small cabin appeared on the hill above them. Home, D'lise thought, anxious to get inside its cozy warmth and put some dry clothes on.

Her elation waned as Kane helped her out of the boat. Raven, as usual, sat on her rock, waiting for them. The Indian woman was the fly in her ointment. She would really be content in these beautiful hills if the squaw would go away.

Frost was sparkling on the meadows and the October twilight was cool when Kane and D'lise lifted the reins and headed their mounts toward the Patton farm. D'lise appreciated the warmth of her jacket, the first article of clothing Kane had bought her.

She was gripped with excitement, although at the same time a little apprehensive. The corn husking party would be her first social event. She chewed at her lower lip. She hoped that Ellen Travis would be there. She had felt that the young widow had genuinely liked her when they met at Tilda Jessup's wake. She found herself worrying that Kane might go off and leave her on her own, then angrily chastised herself for thinking that she would need his constant presence. It would be impossible at any rate. The young females would swarm around him like bees on a honey pot.

And this thing of the men finding a red ear of corn. Would any of them want to kiss her? D'lise shivered. She hoped not. And which young woman would Kane kiss if he found a red corn? Probably Milly Patton.

The two mounts lunged to the crest of a long rise and the Patton farm stood before them, the buildings shrouded in mist. Light from several lanterns in the barn opened a long lane in the darkness. Carrying on the soft air was the sound of women's laughter, the loud guffaws of men, and the yelling of children as they darted about the barn in some game or other.

Kane didn't show it as they pulled in the mounts alongside others tied to a tree, but he was as nervous as D'lise. Every single man-jack in there would want to kiss D'lise when they found an Indian ear of corn. That thought didn't sit well with him at all but there wasn't a damn thing he could do about it without setting tongues to wagging.

As Kane helped D'lise to dismount, she heard feminine giggling coming from under a tree a short distance from the barn. When she peered in that direction, Kane explained in some amusement, "That's the Davis sisters. They're waiting for the party to be over and the men to come out. They'll have their own little party then."

"But why don't they go inside and wait? It's cold out here."

"They'd get cold shrift from the womenfolk and they know it."

D'lise remembered then the gossip she'd heard at the wake about the Davis girls and said no more.

The husking was already in progress as Kane and D'lise stepped inside the hay-scented barn. They were welcomed warmly and places were made for them in the circle formed around a huge mound of corn still in its husks. D'lise found herself sitting between Kane and thirteen-year-old Josie Bellows.

D'lise watched with interest as shuck-free ears of corn went sailing into a large bin sitting nearby. She gave a start when everyone laughed and cried out. Samuel Majors had found a red ear. Nervous giggling sounded round the circle as the young women waited to see who the handsome storekeeper would choose to kiss.

D'lise felt Kane stiffen beside her. Samuel had risen and was coming straight toward them. Oh, dear, she thought in some panic, he's going to kiss me.

She wasn't sure whose sigh of relief was louder, hers or Kane's, when Samuel bent over and kissed young Josie on the cheek. Everyone laughed and teased the red-faced girl about her new beau.

Two more red ears were found, both times by married men who dutifully kissed their wives. Then a big, strapping trapper let out a shout and jumped to his feet, a red ear in his hand. He made straight for D'lise, and it was comical the way he suddenly came to an uncertain stop. Only he had seen the cold warning in Kane's steel-gray eyes. He wavered but a split second as his mind raced. He could ignore the silent threat and feel the weight of hard fists later on outside, or he could kiss another woman and save himself a black eye. Angry and disconcerted, and to everyone's mirth, he kissed the woman closest to him. Claudie Bellows. Surprised looks followed him when he stamped out of the barn.

The pile of corn was about depleted when Kane found a red ear. D'lise's heart gave a lurch when he leaned in her direction. But her fear that he was about to kiss her was groundless as instead he leaned past her and Josie received her second kiss from another very attractive man.

The last ear of corn was shucked shortly after that and food and coffee were laid out on three rough planks, a barrel supporting each end. There was hard cider for the men and sweet cider for the ladies.

As D'lise stood with Ellen Travis sipping her drink from a tin cup, her eyes glowed with happiness. To her the evening had been a huge success. She had never had a more enjoyable time. She was a little disappointed when families began to leave and Kane said that they should be getting home also.

Kane strode to the woodpile and picked up the ax stuck in a tree trunk. His arms rose and fell, the sharp blade biting into a heavy limb of a fallen tree. Sweat broke out on his body, drenching his already damp clothes as he sought to work out the desire that pained his loins, clouded his brain.

"Well, my friend, I see you're reduced to doing a woman's work," an amused voice said behind Kane.

"Big Beaver," he exclaimed, dropping the ax and extending his hand. "Where'd you come from?"

"I have been hunting and decided I'd stop by your cabin and see if you'd like to go with me . . . also to see how the skinny little white woman is doing."

"She's doin' right fine, and she's not so skinny anymore."

Big Beaver frowned when he saw Raven slouching along toward them. "I see you still have that one hanging around. I'd hoped you'd have gotten rid of her by now and had taken the little one to your bed. That Raven is an evil woman and will bring you grief someday."

176

"I've been thinkin' about sendin' her packin'. She and D'lise don't get along. But I have no intention of takin' D'lise to bed," he hurriedly added.

"Why not? That one has spirit and courage, or she'd never have endured the beatings she received."

Kane shook his head. "A man just doesn't take a woman like D'lise to bed. He'd have to marry her first."

"So? You should have taken a wife a long time ago."

Kane grinned wryly. "That may be, but I'm not ready to be tied down yet."

Big Beaver's wise eyes studied Kane from beneath his lowered lids a moment; then he said slyly, "I expect you have an eye out for a proper husband for the one you call D'lise?"

Kane turned his profile to the Indian and muttered, "I haven't gotten around to it yet. There's no great hurry. She's afraid of men in the carnal sense. It will take some time before she's ready to be a wife, to sleep with a man."

Hiding his amusement, Big Beaver brought the subject back to hunting. "Well, are you going to go hunting with me? Winter is approaching. All the men in my village are out hunting deer and buffalo. You should be doing the same thing. Once you start running your traps there won't be time for you to hunt."

Kane grinned at his friend. "You don't have to invent reasons for me to go with you, Big Beaver. As you well know I get most of my meat from the farmers around here. As for fresh meat, I can shoot a deer any day of the week as I run my traps." He paused, then asked, "How long would we be gone? I wouldn't want to leave D'lise alone too long. She's not used to the wilderness."

"Two days, no more. You can leave your dog with her."

Kane nodded. "Come on in the cabin and say hello to

177

her. I know she would like to meet the man who saved her life.''

Hatred shone in Raven's eyes as they bored into Big Beaver's back when he and Kane walked toward the cabin. He had scorned her once when she had tried to make up to him. He had spat at her feet and called her a whore, adding that he was ashamed she was of his tribe.

D'lise was taking a tin sheet of cookies from the brick oven when the door opened and Kane and Big Beaver walked in. She immediately recognized the face that had looked at her so gravely the night she had floated in and out of delirium. She placed the cookies on the table and turned expectantly to the two men, a smile curving her lips.

"D'lise, this is someone you should know," Kane said, placing his hand on his friend's broad shoulder.

"I know who he is." D'lise offered her hand to the handsome brave. "Big Beaver who tended my back, then made me drink some foul-tasting liquid."

Both men laughed; then Kane said, "He saved your life that night. The infection from your wounds was near to gettin' in your blood when he come along."

D'lise knew intuitively not to voice her thanks, but nonetheless her gratitude shone in her eyes as her hand was gripped by the strong red one. "Won't you sit down and have some cookies and coffee?" she urged.

Big Beaver looked longingly at the spicy-smelling treats, but Kane knew that he was anxious to get on with his hunting. There were only a few hours of daylight left.

"Maybe you can put some in a cloth and we'll eat them as we walk along," he said. At the query in D'lise's eyes, he explained, "I'm goin' huntin' with Big Beaver."

D'lise took a clean towel from a shelf and placed half the cookies on top of it. "About what time should I have supper ready?'' she asked, gathering up the ends of the cloth and tying them together before handing it to Kane.

''You and Raven eat whenever you want to. We'll be gone a couple of days,'' Kane answered, taking his rifle from over the mantel. At her startled look, he said gently, ''You'll be all right. I'm leaving Hound with you. Just don't go into the woods.''

D'lise wasn't all that confident of her safety, but she didn't let her face show her uneasiness as she followed the men outside. As Big Beaver walked on ahead, Kane looked down at the lovely face whose lips trembled slightly. ''Don't let Raven bother you while I'm gone.'' He smoothed a wisp of hair behind her ear and grinned as he said, ''Just sic Scrag on her if she gets out of hand.'' D'lise smiled weakly, choking back the desire to plead with him not to leave her.

That thought, and everything else, left her mind when suddenly Kane snatched her to him and kissed her fiercely on the lips. Her mind was reeling and her lips were tingling as she watched him hurry to catch up with Big Beaver. It took her a moment to realize that Raven had walked up beside her.

''My bed will be cold tonight,'' she said, looking slyly at D'lise, who was holding tightly on to Hound.

''Just pile more hay on yourself,'' D'lise snapped and dragged the dog into the cabin, wishing fervently that the woman would go away. She hurried to the window to watch Kane's broad shoulders disappear into the forest, her fingers still on her tingling lips. Although his kiss had been hard and demanding, it hadn't frightened her this time. Actually, she had liked it.

''Don't be daft, woman,'' she muttered to herself. ''You know where his kisses would lead.'' She walked briskly to her basket of yarn and carried it to one of the

179

rockers in front of the fire. For the next three hours, until close to sunset, the knitting needles clicked away on the afghan. Then, folding the garment back into the basket until later, she stood up. It was time to feed her hens and milk the cow.

The heavy shade of near twilight was deepening when D'lise left the barn, two eggs in one hand, a pail of milk in the other. She was partway to the cabin when she saw the grizzly lumbering toward the forest. Her heart slamming against her ribs she sprinted the last few yards to the cabin. She jerked open the door, then slammed it behind her and dropped the bar in place. She stood with held breath, listening for the approach of the huge bear. There was only silence.

D'lise jumped and gave a squeak when, from the fireplace, Raven sneered, "Are you running from your shadow?"

"There's a bear out there." She swung around to look at the Indian woman. "A big one. Kane and I have seen him before."

"Let's hope he doesn't come through the window while you sleep," Raven said, watching D'lise's face closely as she added, "They often break into cabins that way."

D'lise hoped that Raven was trying to scare her, but at the same time she thought it quite possible for such a large animal to break through a window if he so wished.

She made herself answer nonchalantly, "Well then, I must try to deter him." She walked to the window and fastened the shutters.

"When we eat supper?" Raven demanded when D'lise sat down and picked up her knitting. "I'm hungry."

"There's cold roast beef and biscuits on the table. Help yourself," D'lise said shortly, the needles flying in her fingers as she wondered how much trouble she was going to have with the surly woman. Kane wasn't here to control her and she could say or do anything she wanted to.

Raven carried a plate of meat and bread to the fireplace and sat down in the other rocker. It seemed to D'lise that she made more noise than usual as she stuffed her mouth and chomped away. She suspected that it was done on purpose.

She managed to knit on, to keep her dark thoughts off her face.

Finally the Indian woman's hunger was sated, and after giving her usual loud belch, she looked at D'lise and asked, "You ever feel an ache for a man? Do you sometimes wish the trapper sleep with you instead of with Raven?"

"Certainly not!" D'lise's face flamed crimson. "Such a thought never entered my mind."

"I think you lie. I think you lie in bed every night wishing that he was between your legs."

"You're crazy!" D'lise gripped the knitting needles so hard her knuckles turned white. "All women aren't like you. They don't think about men all the time."

"Then *they* are crazy. A man's pleasure stick is the most important thing a woman can think about." Raven looked at D'lise with sly, calculating eyes. "Is it possible that you can think of other things because you have not had a man yet? It is hard for me to believe that while on the trail the very randy trapper did not crawl between your white legs."

"Believe what you want." D'lise jumped to her feet, her knitting falling to the floor, the ball of yarn rolling across the skins with Scrag scampering after it. "I think it's time you went to bed. I'm sure Kane won't like the way you've been talking to me."

181

Raven's face paled beneath its bronze. Maybe she had gone too far in her tormenting of the white woman. Kane would be very angry if he found out. He might even send her away. She rose and left the cabin.

D'lise hurried to bar the door, but opened it a crack first to see if Raven was indeed retiring. Her brow knitted in a frown when Raven walked past the barn and took a path that led down into the next hollow. Where was she going?

"I hope she never comes back," she muttered, then looked down at Hound when he came and nudged her hand. She patted his head and opened the door wider. "Go on and do your business, then hurry back," she said. "There's a bear out there somewhere." Scrag shot past her just as she was closing the door. He, too, had the desire to find a bush.

Ten minutes later, both pets were back in the cabin and D'lise had folded away her knitting for the night. She shoveled ashes onto the fire, banking it, then changed into the flannel gown she had finished making two days ago. As she lay in the darkness, she heard the rising sigh of the wind in the cedars in back of the cabin and wondered if it was going to rain again.

When she drifted off to sleep, she found herself hoping that it would rain, pour down in buckets. Kane would come home then.

Chapter Ten

It didn't rain during the night, nor did Kane come home. Raven, too, was still gone, D'lise discovered when she went to the barn to milk Spider. Had the woman gone back to her village for good? She prayed this was true. She didn't know how much longer she could put up with her.

Back in the cabin again, she strained the milk, then fried some bacon and one of the eggs she had collected yesterday. When she finished breakfast, she divided what cold roast Raven hadn't eaten between the dog and the cat. After she made up her bed, she washed up the plate, flatware, and skillet she'd used cooking her morning meal.

Now she was at a loss how to spend her time. If Kane were here, she'd be planning what to make for lunch and supper, carrying him out a cup of coffee as he chopped wood and corded it between the trees that stood around the cabin.

She picked up her knitting, but soon laid it down again. She was too restless to sit still.

It was just past ten o'clock when she heard the sound of trotting horse hooves and the whirring of buggy wheels. She hurried to the window and peered out from the side of the curtain. Her lips spread in a wide smile. Samuel Majors was helping Ellen Travis to the ground. Her first company! She smoothed a hand over her hair, then down the front of her bodice, and hurried to open the door.

"Good morning, D'lise," Ellen called, walking toward her with a smile. "I hope you don't mind a little company."

"Not at all. I'm very pleased to see you." D'lise smiled back. "How are you, Samuel?" she asked the handsome storekeeper.

"I'm just fine, D'lise. When Ellen suggested we come visit you, I brought these along." He handed her two books. "I hope you haven't read them."

D'lise eagerly took the volumes from him and looked at the titles. She lifted glowing eyes to him. "I've read Shakespeare, but not these two plays. Thank you so much, Samuel. They'll give me many hours of pleasure, and rest assured that I will take good care of them."

She wheeled on the barking Hound, commanding him to be quiet. The hound gave a few more yips, then trotted off behind the cabin.

Samuel laughed. "I see he likes to get in the last word."

"Yes," D'lise agreed, "but he's a very good watchdog. I feel quite safe when I'm alone in the cabin. Come on in and we'll have some refreshments."

"Are you alone today?" Samuel asked, following Ellen inside.

"Yes, I am. Also last night. Kane is off hunting with his friend, Big Beaver. He should be back sometime tomorrow."

"You mean you spent the night alone here?" Ellen looked at her in concern as she took off her hat and laid it on the bench beside her. "Weren't you afraid?"

"I was," D'lise admitted, placing cookies on the table, along with three cups missing their saucers. "Just at dusk I saw a big bear at the edge of the forest, and Raven had me believing that he might come through the window while I was asleep. I'm afraid I slept with one eye open all night. I know I had nightmares of the animal breaking through the glass and coming after me."

"That was a cruel thing for that woman to do," Ellen said angrily. "I hope you tell Kane about it."

D'lise didn't know what to answer, for she hadn't made up her mind yet what to do about Raven. Samuel saved her, saying, "The bear won't come through your window, D'lise. They do occasionally break into a home, but only when they're hungry and they smell food. Right now they're finding plenty of berries, wild grapes, and persimmons. In another few weeks, they will go into hibernation and you won't lay eyes on one until spring.

"And that, by the way, is when you have to keep your cabin tightly locked up, with no food lying around to tempt them. They come out of their long sleep skinny and starving. In the early spring there's not much for them to eat."

"I'm glad to hear that," D'lise said. "It rests my mind a lot." She gave Samuel a teasing smile. "How does a city man know so much about wild animals?"

A sadness came into the storekeeper's eyes. "I wasn't always a city fellow. I was raised on a farm back in the Boston area. My wife's father owned the farm next to ours. Jeannie and I grew up together. Neither one of us cared much for farming, and when we got married we moved to Boston and opened a store.''

There was silence in the small room for a moment; then D'lise said softly, ''May I ask how you lost your wife, Samuel?''

Samuel nodded, swallowed, then said quietly, ''She was crossing the street one day and was run over by a team and wagon that was going much too fast on such a busy thoroughfare.''

''I am so sorry, Samuel.'' Ellen reached across the table and laid her hand on his.

''Thank you, Ellen.'' Samuel turned his hand over and clasped her fingers with his. When D'lise filled their cups with steaming coffee, the pair were still holding hands. D'lise smiled to herself. Was there a romance building between them? She hoped so. They were perfect for each other. Both were educated, Samuel a gentleman, Ellen a lady. She would make the perfect mother for Samuel's two young daughters.

The conversation became light then, with much teasing and laughter between them. It was after one burst of hilarity that Ellen wiped her eyes and asked, ''Are you coming to the box supper tomorrow night, D'lise?''

''I'd love to, but I don't know if Kane will get home in time to take me, or for that matter if he'd want to go.''

''That's no problem,'' Samuel said. ''I'll come get you, then pick Ellen up on the way back to the village.''

''Yes, D'lise, please come,'' Ellen urged. ''You'll have lots of fun. There'll be dancing, and the men will bid their pockets empty to get the chance to eat with you.''

''Oh, I don't know about that.'' D'lise blushed. ''What should I bring?'' She remembered that one of the Pattons had mentioned bringing fried chicken, and she hurried to say, "I can't bring fried chicken. I only have six and they're all laying."

Ellen and Samuel laughed at her solemn little face. "No," Ellen said, patting her arm, "you mustn't kill one of your laying hens. When I make up my box, I'll make up one for you."

"I couldn't let you do that, Ellen," D'lise objected. "It's too much trouble."

"It's no trouble at all. You just be ready when Samuel comes to pick you up."

"Well, if you're sure. It's awfully kind of you. I'll do something for you someday."

"Now you've got the right idea," Ellen said with a wide smile. "That's how we do things here in Piney Ridge. We help each other."

D'lise hugged her arms as she watched the buggy roll out of sight half an hour later. She'd had her first visitors and everything had gone fine. They had laughed and talked, and Samuel had claimed that her cookies were the best he'd ever tasted. She had promised to bring him a batch the next time she came to the store, and he had answered that his daughters would be grateful, since his culinary arts didn't extend to cookies and such.

And tomorrow night she was going to her second social. A sadness slipped into D'lise's eyes. If only Auntie could have been here today. D'lise had always known that the gentle woman missed the feminine company she had once enjoyed.

Her steps were light as she turned back into the cabin, going over in her mind the two new dresses she had made. Which one would she wear to the affair? The blue one, she concluded, the one that matched her eyes.

D'lise wandered about the small room, not knowing what to do with herself. She missed Kane, his coming in and out of the cabin, the ring of his axe as he cut a stock-pile of wood against the cold winter months.

Her face brightened. She would go cord the wood he had tossed into a huge pile. That would keep her busy until sundown.

The last rays of the sun were disappearing behind the western treeline when D'lise dusted off her hands and arms and looked at the rows of firewood stacked between the standing trees. Her eyes moved to the pile of back-logs, their trunks as big around as Kane's body. Each one would burn for a full day and part of a night. The big dog looked up and thumped his tail when she said, "It's time I milk the cow, then make us some supper, Hound."

She walked into the cabin and placed a small log on the fire that was about to go out, then picked up the milk pail. Spider freely let down her milk and D'lise was shortly back in the cabin.

Hound watched eagerly, and Scrag wound his body around her legs as she lifted the lid from the hanging pot of beans and ham that had been simmering all afternoon. She ladled a liberal amount into each of two pans, ex-plaining to the pets, "I'm sorry, but this is all I have for you until Kane gets home with some fresh meat." She filled herself a plate then, placing it on the table and light-ing a candle. She next closed the shutters and barred them, wondering if Raven would show up for the evening meal. The woman hadn't been around since Kane left.

"I hope she stays away," she thought, attacking the beans and ham with a ravenous appetite.

After the kitchen area was set to rights, D'lise picked up the ball of blue yarn and worked on her afghan until the clock struck eight. She would wait up for Raven no longer. If she showed up now, she could just go to bed hungry.

It took her a while to fall asleep. She was gripped with excitement. Tomorrow night was the box supper affair, and sometime tomorrow Kane should be home. When she did fall asleep, the image of his handsome face was in the back of her eyes.

White mists curled ghost-like along the Ohio, and a blue haze of smoke lifted from Kane and Big Beaver's campfire. High in a maple tree, well out of reach of marauding animals, were two deer carcasses lashed to a sturdy limb. The Indian had shot one the day before, and Kane had brought down the other today.

Big Beaver tossed the stripped bone of a roasted rabbit into the fire, then looked out at the gathering twilight. "I always miss my people at this hour," he said quietly. "Our evening meal has been eaten by now and the men will be sitting around a huge campfire discussing the day's events." He grinned in amusement. "After a while the old braves will take over, telling about the battles of their youth, bragging loudly of their bravery, arguing among themselves who had taken the most scalps, stolen the most horses."

Kane laughed softly, then turned serious. "I guess when you grow old, memories are all that you have. Toward the end, my uncle reminisced a lot—especially when he was drunk."

"I still miss my wife too." Big Beaver stared into the flames.

"Do you think you'll ever marry again?" Kane asked. "After all, you're still a young man and must want sons."

Big Beaver grinned and poked at the fire. "I took a new wife two years ago, and I have a son who is one year old."

"Why in the hell didn't you tell me?" Kane demanded,

189

half angry. "Did you think I wouldn't be interested?"

Big Beaver shrugged his shoulders. "An Indian man's second marriage is seldom of importance. The second wife is taken because of the need in his loins. Green Leaf pleasures me amply in bed. She was but fifteen when the words were spoken over us, and I have trained her in the ways that give me most pleasure. She is very biddable, and I am content."

Kane thought of D'lise's innocence and said without thinking, "I've heard that it hurts a virgin the first time she is entered by a man. Have you found that to be true?"

"Yes, that is true. She bleeds some when that thin barrier is broken. Green Leaf, being so young, yelped with her pain."

"So you had to stop? How long did it take before you could enter her again?"

Big Beaver looked at Kane as though he were dim-witted. "I didn't stop. She was my wife and knew it was her duty to bring me pleasure. I took her three times that night."

Kane gazed into the firelogs. He could never use D'lise that callously. If she cried out in pain, he would stop immediately.

As though he read Kane's mind, Big Beaver said with amusement, "I am not an animal, friend. It only hurts the woman that one time. After the initial opening, most women receive the same pleasure a man does. Remember that when you get up the nerve to bed the pretty little one."

"You're crazy." Kane glowered at the grinning Indian. "I have no intention of bedding D'lise."

Big Beaver's grin widened when Kane abruptly changed the subject. Just talking about the young woman who lived with him had made a bulge grow in his friend's buckskins. He said no more, however, and shortly they were both rolled up in their blankets beside the fire.

Big Beaver was soon snoring, but Kane lay awake, listening to a pack of wolves running prey and wishing that he could start for home at daybreak tomorrow. But to prove to his sly friend that he wasn't anxious to get home to D'lise, he would hunt all day and give no hint how much he missed her.

D'lise awakened and stretched just as the clock was striking eight. It popped into her mind immediately that Kane would be home sometime today, and excitement rippled through her. She would make him an apple pie and bake a ham. They were his two favorite foods. Besides, by now he would be tired of eating wild game.

She lay a moment longer, wondering if he'd get home in time to take her to the social at the church. She had received the distinct impression the day they met that Kane hadn't liked the storekeeper, and she was a little nervous about accepting a ride from Samuel. It might anger Kane.

D'lise decided that she would choose her own friends and dismissed her worries from her mind.

She had slept later than usual, as if subconsciously she knew that with Kane gone there was no reason to start the day early. She grimaced wryly as she swung her feet to the floor. She could hear the hens fussing for their breakfast and Spider lowing to be milked. They cared not a whit if Kane never came home.

When she had put on a pot of coffee to brew, D'lise headed for the barn, Hound and Scrag trotting along behind her. The air was cold and she shivered in Kane's shirt, which she had shrugged on as she hurried across the yard, the frosted grass crunching under her feet.

Inside the barn, she hurried to where the chickens were confined, glancing at the pile of hay where Kane and Raven slept. There was no sign of the Indian and her hopes were raised higher that her enemy was gone for good.

The day passed swiftly for D'lise as she made the pie and tended to the ham baking slowly in the small oven. Around four o'clock, she tugged the wooden tub off the wall and poured a kettle of hot water into it, then tempered its heat with cold water from the water pail. Dropping a piece of flannel, and the treasured, scented soap Kane had bought her into the tub, she disrobed and started her bath.

She began with her hair, giving it great attention, making sure all the soap was rinsed out before piling it on top of her head and fastening it there with two long, shiny thorns she had broken off a honey locust for just such an occasion. She and her aunt had often been forced to use shorter ones in place of buttons.

It was close to five, and the sun was going down when D'lise finished bathing. She seated herself in front of the fire and began drying her curls. The pie sat cooling on the table, and she had allowed the oven to cool off. The room was filled with delicious odors when she began to get dressed.

As she buttoned up her bodice she looked out the window, hoping to see Kane approaching the cabin in his easy, lithe walk. She sighed when she saw only a mother racoon and her two young ones moving along the edge of the yard. Samuel would be here soon, and she had so wanted to at least see Kane before she left.

D'lise had just finished brushing her hair and tying a small ribbon over each ear when she heard Samuel arriving. She opened the door and stepped out on the porch and Samuel ran an appreciative eye over her. "My, but don't you look pretty!'' he said. ''I wonder how many fights you will start tonight.''

''None, I hope.'' D'lise looked scandalized, then grinned when she saw the teasing in Samuel's eyes. ''I'll be ready to leave just as soon as I leave Kane a note.''

In her hurry, she merely wrote, ''Have gone to a box supper at the church. D'lise.'' A minute later, as Samuel helped her into the buggy, her spirits dropped. From the corner of her eye she saw Raven walk from behind the barn. Kane's lover had returned.

Kane felt like hauling off and knocking his friend on his rear end. Big Beaver was purposely tormenting him by continuing to hunt, even though the sun would be down in a couple of hours. The wily Indian knew that he was anxious to get home to D'lise, and the deer that each of them carried on their shoulders was more than enough for one hunt.

Well, Big Beaver's silent harassment wasn't going to work. He'd stay with the brave until twilight arrived; then he was heading home. It was close to that time when the Indian shot the head off a wild turkey and reluctantly said he guessed it was time to head for home.

Kane did not let his relief show. If he did, he'd be in for good-humored gibes until they parted company. Big Beaver was an expert when it came to taunting a person: a gentle jabbing for a friend, a vicious slicing of the tongue for an enemy.

They soon came to where the trail branched. They paused there to take leave of each other. ''I have enjoyed your company, friend,'' Big Beaver said, then added with a grin, ''Hurry on home to your little dove.''

''And the same to you, you ornery cuss,'' Kane answered and walked on.

A gray gloaming hung over the cabin as Kane approached it. Night was only minutes away. He frowned when he saw Raven sitting on her rock, waiting for him. He hadn't given the woman a thought in his absence, had actually forgotten that she more or less still lived with him.

His eyes went past her to the cabin, surprised that no candlelight shone in the window.

"Why is the cabin in darkness?" he asked Raven, not bothering to greet her first.

Although Raven raged inside at the slight, her stoic features didn't give away the fact. She shrugged indifferently. "I have not lit the candles yet."

There was a sudden uneasiness about Kane. Had Raven driven D'lise away? He took a step toward her. "What do you mean, *you* haven't lit the candles yet? Where is D'lise?"

"The white woman is not here," Raven answered, then watched him closely as she tacked on, "She go away with storekeeper from the village."

Kane's heart lurched and beat painfully against his ribs. D'lise had left him. She had gone off with the educated man with whom she had more in common. Why would she stay with a crude, ignorant trapper? He lifted bleak eyes to his shabby little cabin, realizing that it wasn't much better than a cave. Why had he thought that she would be content in it?

But she had seemed content, he told himself, a dejected droop to his shoulders as he walked on to the barn, the slain deer riding his shoulders. She smiled a lot, even burst into song sometimes as she went about cooking their meals or feeding her hens or milking the cow.

An hour later, when Kane pushed open the cabin door, Hound bounded across the floor to greet him, licking his hands and wagging his tail wildly. Then a feline hiss from the rafters overhead sent a wave of relief over him. D'lise wasn't gone for good. She would never go off and leave her beloved pet.

Picking up a flaming twig from the fireplace, Kane lit the candle in the middle of the table and saw the note D'lise had propped up against a bouquet of goldenrods placed in a tin of water.

It took but a glance to read the single sentence and his relief turned to anger. D'lise hadn't left him yet, but Samuel Majors was working on it. The minute his back was turned, the man had come sniffing around.

His eyes fell on the two books D'lise had placed in her yarn basket. He picked up the top one and opened it to the fly page. It was hard not to toss it into the fire when he saw the storekeeper's name boldly written across the page. He placed the book back on top of the yarn, and as he stared unseeing into the fire he realized with a suddenness that took his breath away that desire wasn't all he felt for D'lise Alexander. He had fallen in love with her. That tender feeling had started from the moment he'd seen her bravely trying to fight the obese Rufus off her thin body. He had loved her the night he had tended to the belt lashes on her back, scared to his soul that she would die from the fever that burned her skin.

It had all been in vain, the reasons he'd given himself that she would never mean any more to him than any of the other young women of his acquaintance. He had even gone so far as keeping Raven with him, a buffer against the beautiful girl with the dark blue eyes. Like all the rest, that had backfired on him also. The Indian woman could no longer rouse him.

"Samuel Majors," Kane muttered, taking clean buckskins from a peg next to one that held a dress of D'lise's,

195

"you're in for one hell of a fight if you think you're gonna take her away from me." He grabbed a towel and a bar of soap and left the cabin.

As he strode swiftly toward the small stream, Raven hurried after him. "I will bathe with you," she panted, keeping up with his long strides.

"Do as you please," Kane growled back at her, "but you're wastin' your time if you think anything else is gonna happen."

Her face flushed and her eyes shooting sparks, Raven grabbed his arm and spun him around to face her. "You go after the white woman, huh?"

"Yes, I go after the white woman."

"You are a fool, trapper. She wants storekeeper. She all smiles and laughter when they rode away."

Kane tore himself free of her clutching fingers and hurried on, telling himself that D'lise shared smiles and laughter with him also. His inner voice whispered, *Ah, but would she want to share the rest of her life with you? Share your bed?*

Share his bed, he thought as he stripped away his sweat-stained clothing and stepped into the stream. Therein lay the problem. Would he ever be able to erase the deep fear D'lise had of men? She knew only of the pain and degradation that had always been visited on her aunt in the marriage bed. She had no idea that there were few men like Rufus Enger.

Raven wheeled around and walked off as he sat down in the deepest part of the river branch and began soaping his hair. Scrubbing his long fingers through the thick, blond-streaked growth, he determined that if it took a life's work he would teach D'lise to trust and love him, to derive pleasure instead of pain from his body.

Back in the cabin again, Kane quickly shaved, nicking

his jaw in his hurry. After pulling a comb through his damp hair a few times, he left the small room and went to saddle Snowy. Raven watched him mount the stallion a moment later and ride off in the direction of the village.

The desire for revenge burned in her eyes.

Chapter Eleven

Kane pulled the stallion to a halt in the shadow of a heavily branched cedar, well out of the light spilling from the church. Dismounting, he walked to the window and looked in. His eyes went unerringly to D'lise, and he swore savagely under his breath. There were so many men, trappers and farmers, gathered round her, he marveled that she hadn't been crushed.

And she had never looked more beautiful, more desirable. Her face glowed, her red lips smiled, and her black curls tumbled around her shoulders. A picture of another woman surrounded by eager men floated before him. She had looked the same way, all excited by the male attention, her eyes promising them heaven.

For a moment, Kane's intention of making D'lise his own wavered. Would she do to him what Uncle Buck's wife had done to him? Would she cheat on him, rip him apart inside?

No, by God, she wouldn't. His hands clenched into fists. He would be strong where his uncle had been weak. He'd beat the living hell out of any man who even looked at D'lise with desire in his eyes.

His gaze was drawn to the preacher standing in front of the room, holding up a box with a red ribbon on it. The men were bidding on it, and from all the shouting going on around D'lise, he knew it was her box supper that was causing so much excitement.

"I'll put a stop to that right now," he muttered, and strode through the open door just as Reverend House was calling excitedly, "Seven dollars, do I hear eight?"

Not slowing his pace as he made for the group of men around D'lise, he called sharply and clearly, "I bid ten dollars." All eyes swung to him. The cold fire gleaming in his eyes dared any man to over-bid him.

The room grew so quiet the plaintive call of a whippoorwill was heard clearly in the night air. Ignoring the simmering tension, Kane reached into his shirt pocket and handed over the money to cover his bid. Then, to D'lise's incredulous surprise, he caught her by the arm and steered her through the staring people and on out the door.

"Kane Devlin," she cried, "what do you think you're doing?" She struggled to free herself from his steel grip, but his fingers didn't loosen their hold until Kane had transferred both hands under her arms and lifted her onto Snowy's back. Before she could catch her breath, he was up behind her, an arm clamped across her waist. With a whack of his heel on the stallion, they were galloping away.

D'lise burned with anger and embarrassment, but knew it would be useless to try to express herself over the noise of thundering hooves and the whistling wind they created.

"But just wait until we get home," she silently told herself.

To add to her anger and irritation, the first thing D'lise saw as they approached the cabin was Raven sitting on her damned rock. The woman reminded her of a scavenger, sitting around waiting to pick her bones.

Kane drew rein in front of the cabin, and before he could assist her out of the saddle, D'lise slid to the ground and ran inside. She paced back and forth, barely able to contain herself as she waited for Kane to stable the stallion and return to the cabin.

He had no right to take her home as if she were a youngster who had disobeyed a parent! She was an adult, for heaven's sake, able to make up her own mind about what she wanted to do.

And she had been having such a good time. She paused in her pacing to stare down into the flames of the fireplace. It was true that the young unmarried women had only been coolly polite, but the older married ones had been nice and friendly. She had been invited to a corn husking party, two quilting bees, and to join the women's little group that met every Friday at the church.

It had all been so wonderful; then *he* had to come along and spoil it.

D'lise had worked herself into a fine rage by the time Kane walked into the cabin and slammed the door behind him. For a moment, they glared at each other like two wild animals ready to go for each other's throats. Hound crawled under the bed and Scrag leapt up on a rafter, spitting and hissing at Kane.

Without warning, D'lise slammed her fist on the table. "Why did you jerk me away from the social like I was a misbehaving child?"

Kane's stormy, slate-colored eyes narrowed, and the

flecks of gray in them were like chips of ice. "Because you were acting like one. Flauntin' yourself, ruinin' your reputation."

"I did not flaunt myself! I acted like all the other single girls did. Better than some of them, but I didn't see them jerked home by angry fathers."

"It's different in your case," Kane shot back. "You're prettier than they are and people will gossip about you." Lowering his tone a bit, he said, "I don't want you ever goin' anywhere again without me. I must protect your reputation."

"What about some things that I want?" D'lise leaned across the table, her eyes flashing.

"What in the hell is it you want?" Kane glared back at her. "I've given you everything you've asked for and will continue to do so."

"I want Raven away from here. Away from the cabin, away from the barn. I'm sick to death of smelling her stench in the cabin, in the barn—and on you!" By the time she was finished with her wants, D'lise was practically yelling.

"Now just a damn minute," Kane yelled back. "You've never smelled her on me—I made sure of that."

D'lise's only answer was a toss of her head, although she knew what Kane said was true. He always smelled of good clean outdoors, but she was too angry to admit it.

Slowly it sank into Kane's mind what D'lise had demanded. His pulse raced. By all that was holy, could she be jealous of Raven? It sure as hell sounded like it.

His face softened, and the lines of strain disappeared. Then, his breathing quick and ragged, he asked, "How long have you wanted her gone, D'lise?"

Unaware of how closely he watched her, how important

her answer was to him, D'lise answered what was in her heart. "Almost from the first time I saw her. She watches me all the time with her black eyes, as if she knows something that I don't know, something that will be harmful to me." After a slight pause, she added with her head bent, "And I don't like staying alone in the cabin at night."

Kane's spirits soared. Was she saying that she wanted him with her? *But not necessarily in her bed*, his inner voice cautioned. *Maybe she is only frightened of being alone at night*.

Kane ignored the warning. He preferred to think that she wanted him with her because she was beginning to care for him. "We must talk," he said softly, "but first can I have something to eat? I'm about starved."

Amusement quirked D'lise's lips as she took a plate off the shelf and walked over to the fireplace. "You should have taken the box supper you paid so dearly for. It had fried chicken in it."

Kane looked at her in disbelief as she placed beans and ham before him. "Are you tellin' me that you killed one of your hens?"

"Of course not." D'lise looked at him as if he were stupid. "Ellen made up my supper." She sat down at the table. "Wasn't that nice of her?"

"How did that come about?" Kane asked after swallowing a hearty mouthful of his supper.

"The day after you went hunting, she and Samuel came to visit. . . ." In a few sentences D'lise had told him what had led up to her going to the social.

Kane said no more as he cleaned his plate, but a lot of dark thoughts were running through his mind. Samuel Majors had lost no time moving in on D'lise, and there would be others beating a path to his cabin.

Well, he'd put a stop to that before it started.

When Kane had finished off his supper with a piece of pie and was drinking a cup of coffee, he said quietly, "I'll go talk to Raven in a minute. I'm going to send her away."

When relief glowed in D'lise's eyes, he held up a hand. "There's more." When D'lise looked at him questioningly, he continued. "You do realize that with her gone, our neighbors are gonna gossip about us livin' here together, both of us single. You'll probably lose the women's respect." He looked away from her as he told his lie.

Surprise, concern, then disappointment chased across D'lise's face. She lifted troubled eyes to Kane. "Must she stay then?"

"No. There is a solution if you'll go for it."

"Oh, I'm sure I will," D'lise answered hopefully. "What is it?"

"We can get married."

Kane wondered how much bigger the blue eyes could get as D'lise stared at him. What was she thinking?

She was thinking, in a bewildered way, of many things. She did not want to lose her new home, no matter that it was one room with a dirt floor. It was hers to rule without any interference from anyone. Kane gave her free rein to do as she pleased.

But marriage? She had sworn never to get trapped in that institution. Just thinking of going to bed with a man made her shake as if with the ague. Could she make herself bear it? Kane did seem to be a kind man. He had never so much as raised his voice to her—well, tonight he had for some reason. For her own good, she imagined. But she had seen evidence of the violence that lay beneath the surface—the way he had driven his knife into Rufus's shoulder without a blink of the eye.

203

But certainly she could no longer tolerate having Raven a part of their life. She felt a jabbing around her heart every time the two of them went off to the barn at night. She could not even let herself think of what went on between them.

D'lise lifted her eyes from her clenched hands, and while Kane held his breath, she said in a voice so low he could barely hear her, "If marriage is the only alternative, I guess we'd better get married."

"You'll never regret it, D'lise." Kane let his breath out and stroked a hand down her cheek. He let it drop when she sat back, out of his reach. He was going to have one hell of a time coaxing her into making love with him, he thought wryly.

He would take one step at a time, he told himself, and the first step was to get them safely married as soon as possible. He stood up. "I'll talk to Reverend House tomorrow, set the date for next Saturday. If that's all right with you."

Next Saturday, D'lise thought in near panic. That was only seven days away. Seven more nights of sleeping alone, and after that she would be sharing her bed with a husband . . . for the rest of her days. She commanded her pulse to slow down, to show Kane a calm face, devoid of dread.

"Saturday will be fine," she said, a slight quaver in her voice.

Kane nodded. "I'll send Raven on her way now." At the door he turned and gave her a boyish smile. "Can I roll up in my blankets here by the fire tonight? It's gettin' a little cool in the barn."

D'lise couldn't resist smiling back at him. "You may, if you can make Hound move over. He's pretty much taken over the hearth."

Kane didn't find Raven waiting for him in the barn as he had expected. He didn't know that she had lurked around the window, listening to his conversation with D'lise, her face growing ugly with the hatred she felt for the white woman. She had known this was coming, had sensed it from the beginning.

When inside the cabin the talk turned to marriage, she had clutched her blanket tighter around her shoulders and taken the path that led to the valley and to a man who would welcome her.

"But you have not seen the last of me, white bitch," she muttered darkly as she hurried along, laying her plans.

When Kane couldn't find Raven anywhere, he decided to walk around a bit, to think and savor his victory. It hadn't been all that hard to convince D'lise to marry him. Maybe it wouldn't be as hard as he thought to make love to her. He knew that although his kiss had frightened her, it had also aroused her. If he went slowly with her, had patience, that lovely body would be his.

Maybe he could at least get a goodnight kiss from her, he thought. He hurried to the barn, picked up his blanket, and walked quickly to the cabin.

His hopes for a kiss were dashed. D'lise had already retired and Scrag looked as if he would spring on Kane if he went near the bed.

D'lise heard the cabin door open quietly and didn't know whether to be glad or to hold on to her suspicion that Kane had bedded Raven before sending her away. He had been gone close to an hour. How long did it take to tell the woman he was through with her?

A tear ran down her cheek as she heard Kane remove his clothes, then the rustle of the blankets as he made his bed. Just because he had sent his lover away didn't mean that he wouldn't see her. There were a dozen ways that could be accomplished—in the barn in the early evenings, in the woods at any time of the day.

It will be up to you to see that he doesn't need the woman anymore, her inner voice whispered.

But I don't know the first thing about pleasing a man, she silently whispered back.

You will learn, she was consoled.

D'lise finally fell asleep, but only for a short time. Startled awake, at first she thought she was dreaming about the breaking glass and the rattling shutters. But when Hound began raising a ruckus and Kane began swearing, she knew immediately what was happening. The big bear had returned and was trying to break into the cabin.

She sat up in bed, gripped with a terror that rendered her speechless. The great animal would kill her and Kane. But when Kane's gun spat sparks, its report filling the cabin with a deafening noise, her screams split the air.

Kane dropped the rifle and hurried to D'lise. Murmuring softly to her, as one would to a child, he slid an arm across her back and lifted her to his bare chest.

At first he thought only to soothe her as he held her tight and stroked her hair, trying to calm her shaking body. It took but a few minutes, however, for him to become aware of the two breasts pushed against his chest, burning him with their soft heat. He didn't stop to think that he might frighten her as his stroking hand moved over her breasts, his palm gently fitting itself over one of the firm mounds. He was beyond thinking clearly; he knew only that his blood was on fire to possess the warm body curled into his.

Kane let his hand lie still; then, when several seconds passed and D'lise made no move to dislodge it, his fingers began to slowly massage the roundness, moving ever so slowly toward the sensitive tip.

He had just begun to run a finger around the nipple, which had grown hard and pressed against her gown, when with a gasped, "No!" D'lise's slender fingers grasped his wrist.

"Please, D'lise, let me," Kane whispered hoarsely. "I only want to touch you. I've dreamed about it so often."

She opened her mouth to protest and the words were shut off by his descending lips. She stiffened, but only for a moment as their softness moved against hers, seeking, asking her to return the pressure.

As though she were someone else, D'lise's lips moved to form themselves against his, quickly growing hot with a need she couldn't understand. She had never before felt the sensations that began in the pit of her being and traveled all the way up to where Kane's fingers had resumed the gentle, slow massaging.

Her lips parted in a little sigh and Kane's tongue, as though waiting for the chance, darted into her mouth. She moaned softly, whether in denial or acceptance, Kane didn't know. Not waiting to find out which, he lay back on the bed, pulling her with him. His arm still around her back, his shoulders hanging over her, he lifted a leg across her hips, imprisoning her in his warmth. His tongue continued to move in and out of her mouth in a rhythm as old as time.

When her arms crept up around his neck, he turned her to lie tightly against his body, positioning her so that his rock-hard length rested in the apex of her thighs. With a slow, measured motion, he began to rock his hips against hers.

It was the thrusting of his masculinity against the core of her being that made D'lise stiffen again. In her mind she could see Rufus, his hard, ugly member in his hand, jerking Auntie into the bedroom. The bed would creak as he shoved her onto it; then shortly her smothered, pained cries would filter through the cabin as her niece sat with clenched fists, helpless to stop what was happening in the next room.

She snatched her mouth away from Kane and pressed her hands against his chest. "What's wrong, honey?" His passion-ridden eyes looked down at her in bewilderment. "Surely I haven't hurt you."

D'lise gazed up at him in the moonlight that now shone through the broken window, remnants of her panic still in her eyes. She shook her head. "Of course you didn't hurt me." Her fingers picked nervously at the ribbon tied at her throat. "I just remembered how Auntie would cry when Rufus would shove her into the bedroom." She looked up at him through tear-brightened eyes. "I'm sorry, Kane. Do you still want to marry me?"

"Sure I do," Kane answered, trying to keep the relief out of his voice. He'd had the terrible thought that *she* would change her mind. He sat up and helped her back under the covers. "We'll lick this fear of yours." He brushed the tumbled curls off her forehead. "But you must trust me, let me show you how beautiful it can be between us. Will you do that?"

D'lise's lips curled in a small, shy smile. "I'll try, Kane. I truly will."

"That's all I ask." Kane dropped a kiss on her forehead. "I'm gonna get dressed now and see how much damage our visitor has done."

Is he naked? D'lise wondered, then saw that he was as he lit the candle on the table. She ducked her head under the covers. She had never thought a man's body could be almost beautiful, she mused, listening to Kane pull on his trousers, then stamp on his moccasins.

She fell asleep listening to the sound of the broom sweeping up glass.

When Kane finally got back to his blankets, after checking to see if his bullet had killed the bear, he lay a long time, wide awake with unappeased hunger gnawing at his loins. He wanted D'lise so badly, he felt like howling at the moon. When at last he fell asleep he was cursing Rufus Enger to the depths of hell.

Chapter Twelve

Kane left his blanket just as the rising sun shone its light into the cabin. He drew on his clothes, washed up as quietly as possible, and went to saddle Snowy. There was an urgency inside him, something telling him to push his marriage forward with all haste. D'lise was like a wary, unbroken colt, and could change her mind about marrying him at any minute.

An hour later, a disgruntled Reverend House was answering Kane's firm knock at the door. "Kane Devlin," he grumbled, "what in the blue blazes do you want at this early hour?"

Kane bit back a grin. The preacher looked like a scarecrow, his long, scrawny body clad only in his long johns, his sparse hair standing on end all over his head. When he stated his business, the man of the cloth stared at him, his mouth agape.

After his Adam's apple bobbed a couple of times, he

croaked, "What poor unfortunate female has agreed to be your wife? Did you lie to her, promise to give up your whores and squaws?"

"Look, Reverend, that's none of your business." Kane's voice was dangerously cold. "All I want to know is will you marry me to Miss D'lise Alexander this coming Saturday?"

The answer was so long in coming Kane was sure it would be no. His mind was racing as he wondered where he could find another preacher when House spoke.

"I'll marry you for that innocent girl's sake. God would never forgive me if I let her live in sin. Be here at two o'clock Saturday afternoon."

It was by pure willpower that Kane didn't wrap his fingers around the self-righteous man's long neck. Not trusting himself to speak, he turned and walked to where he had tied the stallion to the white picket fence enclosing the preacher's yard. A smile of satisfaction curved his lips as he swung into the saddle. The stallion had cropped the heads off half the blooming flowers lining the fence.

He turned the mount in the direction of the Patton farm. He had a big favor to ask of Sarah. He wanted to surprise D'lise with a fine wedding dress, and he hoped that Sarah would make it.

At the Patton place he was again greeted with surprise. "Kane!" Sarah exclaimed when she opened the door to him. "Is anything wrong at your place? Is D'lise sick?"

"No and yes, Sarah." Kane stepped inside the warm kitchen. "I'm gettin' married, and I want you to do somethin' for me."

Sarah was so staggered by his announcement she had to sit down. "Oh, Kane," she gasped, "please don't tell me you're gonna marry that Raven."

"Oh, for heaven's sake, Sarah," Kane snapped impatiently. "Why in the world would I want to marry that one?"

"Well, who then?"

Her face wore the same expression that Reverend House's had when Kane said quietly, "D'lise has agreed to marry me." The half-wild trapper standing before her, his eyes shining with a quiet happiness, had shunned beautiful women all his life, and he was going to marry the most comely girl she'd ever seen.

"D'lise is not your usual taste in women, Kane, but I wish you both all the happiness in the world." She stood up and brought the coffee pot to the table. "Sit down, Kane, and have some breakfast while you tell me what it is I can do for you."

"Thanks, Sarah, but I've got a lot of things to do. A bear broke our window last night and I've got to pick up a new piece of glass." A gleam of gratification shone in his eyes as he added, "I want to see what kind of wedding rings Majors carries too." It was going to give him great pleasure to let the fancy storekeeper know that he had been wasting his time shining up to D'lise.

"You haven't told me what the favor is you want of me." Sarah placed a cup of coffee in front of him.

"I want to surprise D'lise with a weddin' dress. Will you make it for her?"

"I'd be happy to." Sarah's face glowed at his request. Pouring a generous amount of milk into her own coffee, she said, "You'll want it to be white, of course. It's plain that she's never known a man before."

Kane hoped that Sarah wouldn't notice the guilty red flush spreading over his face. D'lise had very nearly known a man last night. "White, of course," he answered. "A nice material."

"I'll pick out a soft muslin," Sarah mused aloud,

mostly to herself, already planning what pattern she would use. "Maybe Samuel will have some veils in his store too. D'lise would look lovely wearing a veil."

Kane started to ask Sarah if she would stand up with D'lise, then realized it was up to D'lise to choose that important person. It struck him then that he, too, would need someone to stand with him. His mind ran over his friends and he wished he could have them all stand beside him. For if he chose one over the others there would be hurt feelings. An idea came to him and he turned hopeful eyes on Sarah.

"Do you think David would stand up with me in front of the preacher?"

Sarah didn't hesitate to answer for her husband. "He'd be proud to do it, Kane."

Kane finished his coffee, the first he'd had this morning, and with Sarah's assurance that the wedding gown would be ready on time, he left to tie up the last threads in his preparation for his wedding.

Arriving at the village, he went straight to Samuel's store, anticipating with much glee the storekeeper's disappointment when he was told of his marriage to D'lise. However, when, with a hint of crowing in his voice, he announced that he wanted to look at wedding bands, that he and D'lise were going to get married, there was only a flicker of interest in the man's eyes as he smiled and stuck out his hand to shake Kane's in congratulations.

"You're a lucky man, Devlin." He smiled. "D'lise is a lovely young woman."

Kane frowned. This wasn't the reaction he had expected. As he shook the offered hand, he told himself that this man was a master at hiding his true feelings.

"Kane, let me offer my best wishes also," a feminine

voice spoke behind him. "You're getting the best little wife these hills could offer. D'lise is the sweetest, most caring young woman I've ever met. Maybe you can take the sadness out of her eyes."

"Thank you, Ellen." Kane turned and smiled at the attractive widow. "We're gettin' married next Saturday at two o'clock. I hope you can come. I know that D'lise would like for you to be there."

"Oh, we'll be there." Ellen smiled at Samuel as he placed a tray of gold wedding bands on the counter.

Kane gazed down at the plain gold bands laid out on a black shiny material. They were all the same, he had only to choose the size. D'lise had long slender fingers and he dithered between two rings.

"Perhaps I can help you, Kane." Ellen moved to stand beside him. "I think D'lise and I take the same size."

"I need some help all right," Kane said and pushed the tray toward her.

The smallest ring winking in the sunlight slid smoothly along Ellen's wedding finger. "I think this will fit her perfectly, Kane," she said quietly, a slight sadness in her tone. She removed the wide band and handed it to Samuel. "Who has D'lise chosen to stand beside her?"

"I don't know, actually. We haven't talked much about our wedding yet. We only decided last night to get married."

As Ellen and Kane talked, Samuel put the golden circle into a small box. Kane fished his money out of his shirt pocket, then remembered the glass.

"You want the same size, I expect," Samuel asked, leading the way to the storage room.

"Yes, but I'm not sure of the dimensions. I forgot to measure the window."

"That's all right. I've got it written down. Windows

214

are always getting broken around here for some reason or other.'' He walked over to a piece of paper pinned to the wall and ran a finger down a list of names until he came to Kane's.

The glass was soon cut, and Kane was carrying it back through the store to lash onto the stallion's back. He nodded at Ellen and stepped outside.

''He's a surly one,'' Samuel said, watching Kane through the window. ''He and D'lise are an unlikely pair. He's so big and rough, and she's so delicate and ladylike. Do you think he will treat her kindly?''

''He loves her very much,'' Ellen said with firm belief. ''They'll be fine together. He'll treasure her, and she'll adore him.''

While Kane ran his errands, D'lise sat in front of the fire, trying to decide if she was happy or scared half to death. Her soul-searching revealed two things. She loved Kane Devlin. But it was a love she must never let him know about. For he did not return that love. This marriage was only to save her reputation. She felt sure that he would never treat her harshly, but was Raven really out of his life?

One question in particular troubled her. Could she bring herself to consummate their marriage on the wedding night? Could she overcome the fear that she knew would come? Scripture said that she must, but her mind still screamed, ''No!''

Kane's image floated before her, his strong body, his hard, clean-cut features, his cold eyes—but eyes that grew soft when he looked at her. She came out of her reverie when the door opened and Kane walked inside, carrying the glass.

Her face flamed as memories of last night merged with

reality. Kane pretended not to see her embarrassment, and sniffed the air.

"Did you leave any bacon for me?" he teased.

D'lise relaxed. Last night wasn't going to be brought up. She smiled, rose, and lifted the lid off the skillet of ham and potatoes keeping warm on the hearth. "I haven't eaten yet. I've been waiting for you." She looked at him as if to say, "Where were you?"

"I had some things to see to, the glass and all," Kane answered, dipping water into the wash basin. "And I wanted to see the Reverend House."

D'lise waited until he dried his face and sat down at the table before asking, "Is everything set?"

Kane beamed her a wide smile. "Everything is goin' along real smooth. Next Saturday by this time you will be Mrs. Kane Devlin." He frowned when D'lise's face paled. Was the thought of marriage that abhorrent to her, or was it just that she was marrying him?

He laid his fork down and said quietly, "D'lise, if you have any doubts about this marriage, of spending the rest of your life with me, you'd better examine them real close and come to a firm decision before tomorrow afternoon. Once we stand in front of the preacher and he binds us together, it will be too late to change your mind."

"Oh, no, Kane." D'lise reached across the table and laid her hand on his. "I have no doubts about us having a good marriage. I'll be the best wife I know how." She removed her hand and lowered her lids. "I'm concerned about my wifely duty in bed. I know I can't be what you're used to."

A smile tilted Kane's lips. He took her chin and tilted it up so that he could gaze into her eyes. "What does such an innocent girl know about what I'm used to?" He stroked a finger across her bottom lip. "Maybe I'm tired of what I'm *used* to. I've got a feelin' that you're gonna suit me just fine. I've wanted you from the moment I saw you fightin' off that fat Rufus.''

Elation jumped in D'lise breast at his words, then slowly died. Kane had only said that he had wanted her. He had made no mention of love. She worried a piece of bread between her fingers. Did happy marriages exist where only one partner loved? She knew there were many marriages where neither mate loved, and they were easy to spot. Both parties wore long, sour faces, neither ever speaking to the other more than necessary, or hurling insults between them from the time they got out of bed.

D'lise mentally shook her head. Strangely enough, such couples seemed to have the most children. Was it possible the only thing they had in common was the coupling of their bodies, to forget for a while the bleakness of the trap they were caught in?

''Please, dear Lord,'' she prayed silently, ''don't let this happen to Kane and me.''

Kane ran his finger over her lip again. ''Don't worry about the marriage bed.'' His eyes were warm and understanding. ''Everything will be fine, you'll see.''

He sounded so sure that some of the doubt left D'lise. On her wedding night she would try to relax and put herself in his hands.

The clock struck eleven as Kane and D'lise pushed away from their late breakfast. As D'lise began to clear the table, Kane walked toward the door. ''If you have the time,'' D'lise called after him, ''would you please ride with me to Ellen's cabin? I want to ask her to be my witness.''

''Whenever you're ready. I was only gonna dig out my traps and start greasin' them up.''

* * *

Word of Kane and D'lise's marriage spread through Piney Ridge and the outlying areas like a fire burning out of control. The news was received with surprise, disbelief, and no little disappointment. Kane's friends cursed the luck that the little beauty was to be taken out of circulation before they could court her. They discussed their disbelief among themselves that the perennial bachlor was giving up his freedom, settling down to the mundane routine of marriage.

It was voiced among them that the newness of a wife and home fire would wear off and that Kane would be carousing with them as usual. And it was agreed that the delicate Miss Alexander could not long please their friend. There would be no riding her as he was used to doing with squaws and whores.

And while the area wives made preparation for the big event, bustling around, baking pies and cakes, roasting hams and great pieces of venison, their daughters privately either shed tears or gnashed their teeth. There wasn't a single girl in the hills who hadn't wanted Kane for herself.

From the number of wagons and mounts tied to trees, everyone living in Piney Ridge was inside the church, Kane thought as he and D'lise approached the small log building. He looked at his soon-to-be bride and was filled with pride. How beautiful she looked in the white dress Sarah had made for her. He was glad that Sarah hadn't been able to find a veil, although he knew that D'lise would love to have one to hide behind. She was nervous, he knew. Her white-knuckled grip on the reins gave her away.

He was nervous too, Kane admitted to himself. Niggling doubts had jabbed him a few times in the past couple of days, especially an hour ago when he was donning a new pair of butter-soft buckskins, preparing for that time he'd stand before Reverend House. After today he'd be giving up that freedom he'd sworn he never would, and if that wasn't enough, he was tying himself to a woman of extraordinary good looks, the sort of woman he had shunned all his life.

Lottie, his uncle's wife, had come to mind many times in the past twenty-four hours.

Although D'lise was shy and retiring around men now, how might she become once he had taught her the many pleasures of the marriage bed? What if her eyes and attention should begin to wander to those men who would always want her, watch for the chance to take her away from him?

It's too late to mull that over now, Kane told himself as he swung out of the saddle and tied the two mounts beneath a maple whose fall colors had deepened from each succeeding frost. He smiled up at D'lise. "You ready?" When she nodded, he lifted her to the ground, helped her to smooth down the gown's full skirt, then led her into the church.

There was a stir of bodies; then everyone was turning around and watching them walk slowly toward the preacher standing before the pulpit, flanked by Ellen Travis and David Patton. The men's eyes kindled, and a murmuring sigh went up from feminine throats as all eyes looked at D'lise. *I might as well not be here,* Kane thought wryly, *for all the attention I'm getting.*

They were in front of Reverend House now, and the two witnesses were taking their places. It grew quiet as the tall, angular man opened his Bible and began to read from it.

"We are met here today to join this man and woman in holy wedlock."

The sonorous voice receded to a dim murmur as near panic gripped D'lise. Was she making the biggest mistake of her life? Was her neighbors' good opinion so important that she would marry a man who didn't love her? Would their approval of her marrying Kane keep her warm and content through long, loveless years?

She came back to the present with a jolt when Ellen secretly nudged her into awareness. The ceremony was coming to an end. She gripped the bouquet of fall asters that Sarah had sent along with the dress and gave her full attention to the preacher. It was too late to do otherwise.

"Do you, Kane Devlin, take this woman to be your lawful wedded wife in the eyes of God? Do you promise to love and cherish her in sickness and in health, for better or worse, until death do you part?"

Kane's "I do" came loud and clear.

"Do you, D'lise Alexander, take this man to be your wedded husband? Do you promise to love and cherish him, to honor and obey him, in sickness and in health, for better or worse, until death do you part?"

D'lise's "I do" was spoken in such a low tone the preacher had to lean forward to hear her.

He nodded and said the words that united them. "By the power vested in me, I pronounce you man and wife." He gave Kane a doubtful look. "If you have a ring, Devlin, place it on your wife's finger."

You old goat, Kane thought angrily, bringing the gold band from his breast pocket. Did the preacher think he was so uncivilized he didn't know he needed a ring for his wife?

As Kane slid the ring on D'lise's finger, he saw by the look on her face that she, too, was surprised that he had thought of a wedding band. Damn, he thought, keeping his face calm, didn't anybody have any kind of faith in him?

"You may kiss the bride now," the preacher said as though reluctant to say the words.

Kane slipped his arm around D'lise's waist and pulled her to him. The kiss he dropped on her lips was warm and gentle and respectfully short. As he led her back up the narrow aisle he heard male voices whispering something about a shivaree. Well, he thought with dry humor, his friends were going to be in for a big disappointment. There would be no serenade of rattling pots and pans, no long blowing of horns. He and D'lise weren't spending their wedding night at the cabin. When it came time for them to slip away, they would go to Ellen Travis's cabin down by the mill.

The thoughtful young widow had suggested it, knowing that D'lise would be nervous enough without a bunch of crude trappers racketing around.

Out in the church yard, everyone gathered around the newlyweds, the men shaking Kane's hand and slapping him on the back, sometimes unnecessarily hard. Ribald jokes were passed, making D'lise blush to the roots of her hair.

"Don't you pay any attention to them ignorant jackasses," Sarah said, giving the trappers a scolding look. "They ain't never had no manners."

Kane saw that the men were trying to gather the nerve to kiss the bride. The cold warning look he directed at them made them flush and move on toward the tavern where the food, a fiddle, and a banjo awaited the wedding party. Kane placed D'lise's arm in his, and together they followed them.

One end of the bar practically sagged with the food

placed upon it. In the mundane lives of the hill people, a wedding was a big event and everyone took part in it. Wives had brought roasts of pork, beef, and venison, and someone had brought a large platter piled high with fried chicken. Next to the meats were bowls of every vegetable imaginable, as well as a large basin of late-maturing corn on the cob. Taking their own place were at least a dozen cakes and pies.

There was no evidence of spirits. It was a firm rule that no alcohol was to be served at any celebration. When rowdy trappers drank too much, there were always fights.

D'lise couldn't believe how fast the food disappeared. She was reminded of a wave of locusts swarming over a garden patch so quickly that everything was consumed in seconds. She wondered how the men managed to dance when the fiddle and banjo struck up a tune.

But the wooden floor bounced and creaked as, with much hopping and jumping, men swung their partners around the room. She and Kane decided that they wouldn't join the dancers. Once they did, every single man and woman would converge on them, wanting their turn with the bride and groom. By the time the festivities were over, they would be worn to a frazzle. Kane thought privately that he didn't want a tired bride on his hands when he took her to bed. He preferred to wear her out himself.

D'lise watched the merry-makers but didn't really see them. Her mind was on what was going to happen later, in Ellen's bedroom. Could she bring herself to do what was expected of her?

An hour later, her nerves tightened when Kane leaned over and whispered, "It's ten o'clock. Let's slip away while everyone is dancin'."

She wanted to pull back when Kane closed his fingers

around her arm and brought her to her feet. But even as the thought crossed her mind, he whisked her outside and they were running for their mounts. Kane swept her into the saddle and climbed onto the stallion; then they were galloping away. No one but Sarah and Ellen noticed their hasty departure. They smiled at each other, each remembering fondly her own wedding night, neither aware of D'lise's unnatural fear.

D'lise forgot for a moment what lay ahead of her when Kane opened the door and she walked into Ellen's pretty parlor. A cozy fire and two lit candles on a small table welcomed them.

"Isn't this a lovely room, Kane?" D'lise asked in awe. "I've never seen anything lovelier." Her hand stroked the surface of a highly polished table as her other hand started a thickly padded rocker in motion. She walked over to the mantel and gazed up at the porcelain figurines there.

"Have you ever seen anything so beautiful?"

Kane didn't hear her question. He was thinking of the rough quarters he had asked D'lise to share with him. There was no beauty there for a woman to gaze on. Suddenly he wanted to change that, was determined that he would.

He joined D'lise at the fireplace and, putting an arm around her waist, said, "It's too late in the season now—snow will be falling before we know it—but come spring I'm gonna build the nicest and largest cabin in these parts. You can have all the little gee-gaws you want to fancy it up."

"That will be nice." D'lise gave him a small smile, but Kane knew by her tone that she didn't believe him. She'd have to believe the evidence of her eyes when he started building, he told himself. He took her hand, and with anticipation and apprehension, he led her to a door that had to be a bedroom.

It was a very feminine room, the kind that Ellen Travis would have, D'lise mused, looking around. The comforter on the bed was bright green, its frilly white dust ruffle matching the curtains at the window. There were no clothes hanging from pegs on these walls. She imagined they hung in the large piece of furniture with two long doors. She walked over to a narrow table with a gilt-framed mirror hanging over it. It must be what Auntie had described as a dressing table, she thought, gazing down at a comb and brush, a matching receptacle holding wire hairpins. There were three small jars with lids capping them.

She was about to unscrew one when Kane moved up behind her and put his arms around her waist. "Let's go to bed," he murmured, his hands sliding to her rib cage.

With a tightening of nerves, D'lise felt his hands cup her breasts, and she closed her eyes against the image of them in the mirror.

"Come along, honey," he whispered, his voice rough and unsteady. "I've waited a long time for this night."

When he released her and took her hand, D'lise allowed him to lead her to the bed. A pretty night-gown of sheer muslin had been laid across the foot of the bed, a gift from Ellen. She reached for it as Kane turned down the covers, but he caught her hand.

"Leave it, D'lise. I want nothin' between us. I want to feel every inch of your soft, bare body against mine."

"But, Kane." D'lise shrank from the idea of his seeing her naked.

"But nothin', wife." Kane's fingers were already working at the small buttons of her bodice. "Didn't you promise the preacher that you'd obey me?" He quirked a teasing eyebrow at her. "Are you goin' to disobey my first order?"

She wanted to—God, how she wanted to. Everything within her cried out her desire. But she knew she would only be prolonging the inevitable, so she might as well swallow her reluctance and get it over with.

She stood quietly, her eyes closed, too embarrassed to look at Kane as he slowly pushed her dress down past her hips to settle around her feet. She felt the tug of the ribbon tied around her waist, then the slide of the petticoat joining the dress.

She gave a small gasp when her knee-length, lace-trimmed pantaloons followed the path of her other clothes. There remained only her camisole. The unheated air wafted over her, making her nipples pucker and push against the material. The twin peaks did not escape Kane's notice. With a low groan, he whipped the last remaining cover over her head and the warmth of his mouth closed over one uptilted breast.

At first, D'lise tried to push his face away. Then, without warning, her pulse quickened and she let her hand drop. She grew as weak as water when waves of pleasure flooded through her as Kane suckled first one and then the other breast. Her hand cupped the back of his head, pressing him closer to her. A low moan of satisfaction sounded in his throat.

He ran a palm down the smoothness of her stomach, coming to rest on the tight black curls between her thighs. When he felt a moistness there, he placed one arm across her back and the other behind her knees, lifting her effortlessly and laying her on the bed.

As D'lise lay there, her blue eyes limpid with desire, a sensation she'd never known before making her seem to float, Kane shed his own clothes, never taking his eyes off her silken body.

In her craving for his body to join hers, there was no shyness or shock as D'lise ran her gaze over the first full view she had ever seen of a man completely bare. Her husband's body was magnificent, his shoulders broad, his chest lightly furred, his midriff lean, his hips narrow.

A flicker of uneasiness washed across her face when her inspection encountered the object that had pressed against her bottom a few minutes ago. She had thought then that even through their clothes he was large, but freed of all constraint, stiff with erection, it looked fearsome to her. There was no way in the world her body could accept it.

She looked up at Kane, her eyes large and reflecting her thoughts. He came down on the bed beside her, a gentle smile curving his lips. ''I'll fit inside you,'' he whispered, stretching out beside her and drawing her into his arms.

''Oh, Kane, please, I don't think it's possible.'' D'lise drew back her head and looked at him imploringly.

''You'll open for me, honey,'' he whispered, and cupping her head with his hands, lowered his lips to hers.

At first Kane only traced her lips with his tongue, teasing, inviting. But when she sighed a protest and pressed closer to him, his lips firmed over hers, forcing them to open, to accept his tongue. When she moaned softly, he moved one hand from her head and caressed it down her throat, stopping to let it lie on her breast. Deepening his kiss, his fingers stroked the rosy nipple that was rigid with the excitement that shuddered through her. Lifting its heaviness in his hand, he left off kissing D'lise and drew the nipple into his mouth.

D'lise's body convulsed with spasms of pleasure as he

suckled her. Her arms went around his shoulders, her fingers threading lovingly through his hair. He raised his head and whispered hoarsely, "Touch me, D'lise."

She gently stroked her finger down his cheek. "No, honey, not there." He took her hand and pushed it down the flat plane of his stomach. "Here," he whispered in a raw voice as he curled her fingers around his arousal. When her hand only held him, stiff and uncertain, he coaxed, "Stroke it, honey, can't you feel what it wants?"

Timidly, still uncertain, D'lise tightened her fingers around him, and cautiously moved her palm up and down. Kane groaned and searched her lips as she felt his life-force pulsating in her hand.

D'lise gave a choked moan of her own when Kane's hand moved down her body and found the little nub of sensitivity hidden in the short curls. His fingers teased and tormented it until she was arching against him, wanting more, but not sure what it was she wanted. But Kane knew, and he continued to stroke her until the soft whisper of his name escaped her lips.

With a ragged sigh of relief, he removed his hand from her and slid a thigh between hers. Another stroke of her hand and he would be erupting inside it.

As he hung over her, the tip of his erection nudging at her virgin opening, D'lise stiffened and gazed up at him, dread in her eyes. Now he would hurt her like Rufus used to do to Auntie.

"What is it, D'lise?" Kane gave her a puzzled look. "You can't stop now. You've got me too worked up."

D'lise lifted a trembling, beseeching hand to his cheek. "Please, Kane, don't hit me too hard."

"Hit you hard?" Kane's puzzlement changed to bewilderment. "I have no intention of hitting you hard or otherwise. What made you think I would hit you?"

"Rufus always hit Aunt Anna." D'lise almost sobbed.

"Ah, honey." Kane kissed her gently on the forehead. "I thought I told you not to compare that bastard to other men. I would never hurt you."

D'lise gave him a tremulous smile. "You promise? Never?"

"Well," Kane hedged. "I will hurt you a little the first time I enter you. It can't be helped. You're a virgin and there's a thin little skin protecting you down there. I have to break through it. But I'm told it doesn't hurt long."

Convinced that Kane didn't lie, D'lise relaxed, and tracing a finger around his lips, teased, "How many women told you that?"

Kane smiled ruefully. "None. You will be my first virgin. Big Beaver told me. So you will have him to thank when I try not to hurt you too badly."

He dropped his head and suckled her until she was again arching her hips to him, then took his hard length in his hand to enter her. Still he hesitated, wondering whether to go slow, or make one plunging drive to break the thin membrane.

When he started to enter her, D'lise took the decision away from him. Her body on fire with the need of him, she brought her legs up around his hips, the pressure forcing him inside her, burying deep, filling her, stretching her. She gave a small cry of pain, but did not loosen the grip her legs had on him.

"Oh, God," Kane gasped, "how good you feel, so hot and tight." Bracing himself on his elbows, he looked down at her and whispered, "Are you in pain?"

D'lise shook her head. "Not now, it's going away."

"Does it feel good?" he asked hopefully.

D'lise blushed and nodded. "I think so."

"You think so?" Kane laughed softly and gave a small thrust of his hips.

"I'm sure," she murmured, copying his motion.

To Kane's embarrassment, that small movement made him lose control. Without warning his body convulsed and he was spilling his seed inside D'lise.

Lord, he thought when his body stopped shuddering, that had never happened to him before. Was it possible that just being inside his wife made him lose all control? If that was the case, how would he ever be able to pleasure her?

D'lise felt Kane's warmth flood her, then felt the slumping of his body on hers and wondered about it. Was this all there was to coupling? She still ached for . . . something. Were women supposed to feel that way?

I'd better not let Kane know, she thought, and forced her body to grow quiet, her pulse to calm down. She didn't want him to think that she was shameless. She was positive that Auntie had not felt the way she was feeling.

She didn't know what to think when Kane whispered softly, "I'm sorry, honey, but you felt so good I couldn't help myself. I promise to wait for you this time."

D'lise felt him swelling inside her, and startled, she looked up at him. Was she expected to feel something after all? It sounded like it. She certainly hoped so, because the rhythmic stroking of Kane's manhood was causing a feeling she couldn't stop.

It felt so good, the slow rocking of his body, and D'lise wished it could go on forever. She felt the straining of his body then, and knew he was striving with all his strength, waiting for her to do something. "Let yourself go, honey," he whispered against her shoulder. "Ride to the top of the mountain with me."

Clutching his shoulders, D'lise let go and felt herself

tumbling, tumbling into a void of unbelievable sensation.

Kane felt the walls of her femininity tightening around him, and when she called his name, he gave one last drive of his hips and shuddered against her, moaning his release into her throat and shoulder.

Breathing fast, his body sweat-slicked, Kane marveled that he would know this mindless bliss the rest of his life. His young wife had given him a pleasure he'd never before known existed.

But D'lise's thoughts as she lay quietly beneath him didn't run in the same vein. She hadn't realized that it would hurt so to know that her husband's need of her was based on lust, not love. That word had not passed between them.

Chapter Thirteen

The first snow fell in late November. In the full sun, it soon melted, but patches lingered on the north slopes of the hills. Kane's trapline was laid and in the dead stillness of every morning before dawn he left the cabin to run his traps.

But first, before rising, he'd draw D'lise's warm body into his arms to stroke and suckle her awake. He'd pull her beneath him and grasp her hips, holding them steady as he moved in and out of her eager body.

D'lise always looked forward to these early mornings of love-making, because with the exception of a good-night kiss, Kane never touched her when they retired at night. In fact, she didn't even see him much anymore. Every night after supper he excused himself and left the cabin for a couple of hours. Where he went he never said, and she was too proud to ask.

One day the wind came out of the north, bringing with

it a heavy rain mixed with sleet. It beat against the cabin, rattling the window. When it died down, winter came in earnest, with flurries of snow falling almost every day for a week. The days grew shorter, the sun paler, giving little warmth as it slanted through the trees. In only a matter of a few hours, it seemed to D'lise, the sun would be replaced by the moon, chill and remote. Many freezing nights, as she lay beside Kane's sleeping form wondering why he hadn't made love to her, she could hear trees splitting with loud, sudden reports.

This night, snuggled up to Kane, fitting spoon-fashion in the curve of his body, her thoughts were on Christmas, a few days away. Would Kane celebrate the holiday? Or would it be just another day? She would like to go to church, and she could if she went without Kane. Ellen and Samuel would take her. There were all kinds of festivities going on in the village, but it wouldn't seem right, her enjoying herself while Kane trudged along in the freezing cold.

But he doesn't think about you, her inner voice whispered. *He knows that you are here alone all day with no one to talk to, yet he goes off every night, leaving you still alone.*

Where did he go? D'lise stared into the darkness. She never saw him ride off on the stallion. Wherever he went, he walked.

A suspicion grew inside her, one she tried to turn away but it persisted stubbornly. Tomorrow she was going to check for footprints around the barn.

D'lise wasn't aware of falling asleep, but as usual, in the first gray light of dawn she awakened to Kane's caressing fingers on her body. He was always so hungry for her at that hour, she mused, stroking her hands over his shoulders, down his back, across his flat stomach and finally down to that part of him that brought her such mindless bliss.

Kane whispered her name as her fingers closed around his hard flesh, and rolled her over on her back. She parted her legs for him and he climbed between them. He hung over her, waiting for her to guide him inside her.

As usual, like the first time he'd made love to her, Kane's release came fast. D'lise was used to this and didn't mind. It meant that in their second union Kane would take all the time in the world, moving with a leisurely lift and thrust of his hips. And when their climax came, it would be so strong, so overpowering, they would be too weak to move for several minutes.

His heart and pulse slowing to a normal rate, Kane sat up and gazed down at his wife's lovely face, still flushed from the blood that had pumped through her veins so furiously. *I can never get enough of her,* he thought, smoothing the tangled curls that framed her delicate face. *Never was a man so blessed.*

"I gotta get goin'," he said reluctantly, dropping a kiss on her nose. When D'lise would have risen also, he pushed her back down. "It's too cold this morning." He brushed a ripple of snow off the foot of the bed where it had sifted through a crack he had missed caulking. "I'll build up the fire and get the coffee goin'."

D'lise pulled the covers up to her chin and watched her husband's naked body move to the fireplace, the muscles rippling on his shoulders and arms as he raked the dead ashes off the red coals beneath them, then added small pieces of wood. When they caught, he laid short, split logs on the flames, then rose and walked to the table where she put the coffee pot every night after scrubbing it out. He poured water into it from a water pail sitting next to it and measured in the coffee she had ground the night before. When he had set the pot on the fire, he walked toward the bed to pull on his buckskins.

D'lise, who had been watching his every move, grinned as she watched him pull on the buckskin trousers and fasten the laces of his fly, adjusting the bulge there until everything lay where it belonged. She sighed. She would not have him to herself again until this time tomorrow morning.

Kane lit a candle, then filled the pockets of his rabbit-fur jacket with parched kernels of corn and strips of pemmican. The coffee had brewed by now, and after swiftly drinking two cups of the steaming liquid, he flipped the jacket's hood over his head, pulled on his mittens, and picked up his rifle.

"I'm off now, D'lise." He smiled at her. "Don't forget to bar the door behind me." She sat up, the covers falling to her waist, her bare breasts a picture he would carry with him all day, he thought, closing the door behind him.

Her flesh all goose bumps from the many drafts in the room, D'lise reached for her flannel gown and hurriedly jerked it over her head. Swinging her feet to the floor she fumbled them into the fur-lined moccasins she wore in the house. She hurried to the fire. As she sipped her first cup of coffee of the day, she stared into the flames, wondering how she was to pass another lonely day.

One day continued to run into the next, with nothing for D'lise to occupy her time with. She even found herself looking forward to washday, a chore she ordinarily didn't care for at all. She had baked pies, cakes, and cookies until they couldn't eat any more.

The only time the monotony of a day was broken was when Ellen and Samuel came for a visit.

The first time the couple braved the cold and snowdrifts was to invite her and Kane to Ellen's for Thanksgiving dinner. But since Kane naturally couldn't go, she had refused to attend without him.

But now Christmas was only a few days away, and she wanted to go to church. Two days earlier, when Ellen and Samuel had dropped by, Ellen had spoken of how prettily the wives of Piney Ridge had decorated the church. "They have even trimmed a tree," she'd finished, then began urging D'lise to attend services Christmas day. "We know that Kane has to run his traps every day, but there's no reason Samuel and I can't pick you up and take you to church."

She had finally agreed, although she hadn't mentioned it to Kane yet. For some reason he didn't like the friendly storekeeper, and it upset him when he and Ellen came to visit her. He did like Ellen, though, for which she was thankful. She and Ellen had become very good friends, and she didn't want anything to interfere with that friendship.

There was to be a little get-together after the service, Ellen had said. The preacher's wife would be serving tea and cake. She had laughed then and said, "The tea will be weak, and the cake tasteless, but we can have a good time catching up on what everyone has been doing these house-bound days." She giggled. "Everyone knows what Elijah Jessup has been up to."

Tilda Jessup had been buried but a month when Elijah left the area for a week and returned with a new wife. The girl was young and awkward, looking to be around sixteen. Within a month, she was with child.

As D'lise prepared to go to the barn to tend the stock, she wondered why she wasn't in a family way yet. God knew Kane had spilled enough of his seed inside her. Was she one of those women who couldn't conceive, she wondered, and would Kane care if she never made him a father?

These questions nagged at her mind as she changed her moccasins for her heavy shoes and shrugged into a jacket like Kane's. As she pushed open the heavy door, Hound slid past her and ran ahead to the barn. The trodden snow scrunched under her feet as she followed the dog. When the first true snowfall had finally stopped it had taken Kane half the day to shovel a path to the barn. After that, each new layer of snow that came along had been easily tramped down by their coming and going between cabin and out-buildings.

D'lise had to tug hard at the heavy, ice-encrusted door to open it wide enough for her to squeeze through. She was greeted with whinnies, lowing, and squawking chickens.

"So, everybody is hungry, eh?" she called out cheerfully, grabbing a pitchfork and lifting hay into the troughs of each stall. She noted that the watering pails were empty; in fact Snowy had turned his over on its side in his quest to quench his thirst. As soon as she fed the hens, she would scoop up a pail of snow for each animal.

D'lise was so occupied with feeding the stock that she didn't hear the soft sound of stealthy feet. It took Hound's deep snarl to make her spin around. Her stomach clenched in a knot, and the blood drummed in her ears. A fierce-eyed Indian was coming toward her, his fringed buckskins rustling.

I'm going to be raped by this savage, she thought in terror, taking a frantic step backward. But when, with a wild yell, the Indian jerked a scalping knife from his belt and came at her, her heart skipped a beat. He didn't mean to rape her—he meant to kill her!

But as she stood frozen in place, her eyes horror-stricken, a long, furry body sprang from her feet straight at the Indian's throat. In one furious snap of his teeth, Hound tore open the man's throat. Blood gushed out and, unable to move or speak, D'lise watched the dying Indian sink slowly to the floor, the broad-bladed knife slipping from his fingers.

Released from her near-hypnotic spell, D'lise raced out of the barn, the dog at her heels. She slammed the door shut and dropped the bar in place. Hound jumped around at her feet, his tail wagging, plainly looking for praise. She leaned over him, started to pat his head and say, "Good boy"—and almost retched. His mouth was rimmed with the Indian's blood. She hurriedly placed a basin of water on the floor for the faithful animal to drink and wash away the bright red stain.

While Hound lapped at the water, D'lise threw herself on the bed, and for over an hour shuddering sobs racked her body. Why had the Indian wanted to kill her? She could understand if he had rape in mind. It wasn't uncommon for a white woman to be assaulted by an Indian, the same as the white man raped the Indian woman, but except in times of war, she'd never heard of an Indian intentionally murdering a woman.

Could he be an enemy of Kane's? She didn't think so. Kane got along well with the Indians. Big Beaver was his best friend.

She finally rose from bed and somehow got through the day, even managing to get a pot of stew cooking. It plagued her mind that the barn animals hadn't been watered, but she couldn't bring herself to return to the place where the dead Indian lay.

At last dusk darkened the cabin, and D'lise was lighting the candles when she glanced out the window and saw Kane trudging home, as usual burdened down with pelts.

When she heard him scraping the snow off his feet on the small porch, she flung open the door and launched herself at him. The tears she'd thought were dried returned full force.

"D'lise, what is it? What's wrong?" Kane pulled her arms from around his neck. He looked worriedly into her face. "Have you had an accident? Are you hurt?"

"No, no," she choked out, waving her hands toward the barn. "The Indian, he tried to—he wanted to kill me."

"Let me get a lantern; I'll track him down." Kane led her back inside.

"No, Kane, he's in the barn. Hound killed him!"

"Are you sure?" Kane asked, doubt in his voice. "Maybe he just chewed him up a little."

"No, he's dead. You'll see."

"All right, calm down. Let me light the lantern and I'll go take a look.

"By God, she's right," Kane muttered a few minutes later as he stared down at the lifeless face of the brave, his staring eyes still full of his terror as the huge dog had sprung for his throat. He studied the red face, thinking that he looked familiar, but he couldn't place him.

"Well, you bastard, I'm glad you're dead, whoever you are," Kane muttered, grabbing the Indian under the arms and hefting him over his shoulder. There was a ravine about a hundred yards behind the cabin. He'd dump the body there. When it was found, it would be assumed that a wolf had killed him.

And it must be kept a secret that D'lise had been involved in the brave's death. His relatives might think that she was lying about being attacked, that she had sicced the dog onto him out of hatred of the red man.

As he returned to the cabin, he carefully smoothed out his footprints. "I was getting worried about you, Kane,"

D'lise said as he stepped through the cabin door and shrugged out of his jacket. "What kept you so long?" She carried the black kettle of water from the fireplace and filled the washbasin for him.

"I was gettin' rid of the body." Kane picked up the bar of lye soap and, working up a lather in his hands, began to scrub his face and arms. D'lise put a towel in his groping hands after he had rinsed off, splattering water on the floor. He used it and hung it back on its nail. "Don't say a word to anybody about this, D'lise. I pitched him into the ravine in back of the cabin. I'm hoping the black clouds in the north will bring more snow tonight, hiding the fact that wolves didn't do him in."

"Do you know who he was?" D'lise began dishing up the stew when Kane sat down at the table. "Do you think he's from around here?"

"I know I've seen him somewhere, but I can't remember where."

No more was said as the meal was eaten, D'lise hoping that Kane wouldn't leave her tonight. She was still shaken and needed the comfort of his arms.

But, in his usual custom when Kane finished his coffee, he pulled his jacket back on and left the cabin.

D'lise stared at the closed door, hurt that her husband couldn't have stayed with her tonight. He had to know how upset she was. She tried to push from her mind the persistent suspicion that Kane went to meet Raven somewhere. After all, the woman had been his squaw for a long time, and he must have cared for her.

More than he did for his wife, perhaps. Raven would still be here if she hadn't demanded the woman go.

"And he would never have married me if not to save my reputation," she said to the empty room.

D'lise stared unseeing into her cup of coffee. She

shouldn't blame Kane if he still sought out Raven. A person couldn't help who he loved. She loved Kane, and it was the last thing she wanted to do. It wrung her heart thinking of them together, making love.

But it angered her also. If he still cared for Raven, continued to need her, he should leave his wife alone, not make a whore out of her.

You don't know for a fact that your husband meets the Indian woman, her inner voice cautioned. "You may be working yourself up for nothing. Wait until you have proof."

D'lise rose and walked to the window and stared out. The full moon had escaped the dark clouds for a moment, reflecting its light on the snow, making it appear almost daylight. She gazed at the forest, thinking how gaunt and dreary the hardwoods looked without their leaves.

Her breath misted the glass, and as she wiped the film away with the palm of her hand she gave a start. Cupping a hand to each side of her face to block out the candle and firelight, she peered closely at the forest. She had seen a figure move out from the shadow of the trees and walk toward the barn. Was there yet another Indian come to harm the Devlins?

"Oh no!" she whispered, a desolation such as she'd never known gripping her heart. Just before slipping into the barn, the figure had turned and looked toward the cabin, straight at the window. She knew now that Kane didn't go anywhere to meet Raven. She came to him.

Sick to her soul, D'lise drew the curtain across the window and stumbled to the rocker she had taken as her own. She gazed blindly into the fire, thinking wildly. So much for her inner voice's advice. She'd never listen to it again.

What was she to do? She had no place to go and no money, and the snow was up past her waist in some places. But how could she continue to live with Kane knowing that his affair with Raven had never ceased?

Scrag came and jumped upon her lap, purring loudly as he settled in. *One thing for sure,* she thought, *I'm going with Ellen and Samuel to church on Christmas day.* Not only that, she would stay for the party afterward. In fact she was going to attend any get-together that came along. If she was to live out her life as D'lise Devlin, she must make herself a life apart from her husband.

She lifted the cat to the floor and prepared for bed. She would not sleep, she knew, but she didn't want to be up when Kane came in. She would be unable to look at him without bursting into tears. And what would she answer when he asked her the cause? That she cried because he did not love her? Her pride was deeply crushed, but it wasn't completely dead.

Kane had just finished placing a bucket of snow in each horse's stall and was walking over to the cow's when the barn door creaked open. He jerked around, his hand dropping to the knife at his waist. He dropped it then and watched the woman come toward him.

"Raven," he said quietly in greeting, "what brings you here?"

"Don't look so worried. I am not staying long," Raven answered, stopping in front of him. "I think it's time you know something about your wife that everyone else knows."

"And what is that?" Kane frowned.

"That Samuel Majors's buggy is seen often in front of your cabin while you run your traps."

"I know that. He brings Ellen Travis to visit D'lise."

Raven's lips curled. "Is the widow with him every time he comes?"

241

Before he could question her further, Raven wheeled around and left the barn, leaving him with suspicion building in his mind. Was D'lise seeing Majors behind his back? He would have no way of knowing. He left the cabin at dawn, not returning until dusk. For all he knew, the storekeeper could be riding out here, spending the whole day with her.

His clenched fist lashed out, striking the top board of Snowy's stall and smashing it, making the stallion whinny in protest. *The bitch, the beautiful bitch.* She was just like Lottie, his uncle's wife, after all. One man wasn't enough for her. He had tutored her in the art of love-making, taking away her fear of it, and this was the way she was repaying him. God, he'd like to smash that lovely face of hers.

But later, lying in bed beside D'lise's warm body, smelling the rose scent of her hair, it was all he could do not to draw her into his arms and make love to her until he couldn't move. He sighed tiredly and turned his back to her.

The next morning at dawn, however, he had no resistance against her at all. In their sleep they had turned to each other, and D'lise's head lay on his shoulder, her black curls spreading over his chest.

How innocent she looked, he thought sadly, gazing down at her. Asleep she still looked virginal, as though she had never known a man, let alone two.

D'lise sighed in her sleep and pressed her lips against his throat. Kane swore in self-disgust as his male member stirred and grew hard. Hating himself for needing her so, even though Samuel Majors might be sharing the bed with her later, he drew her unresisting body into his arms and dropped his mouth to hers.

Half asleep, D'lise opened her lips to let the probing

tongue enter her mouth as she pressed closer to his arousal. When rough-textured but gentle fingers stroked her breasts, she trailed a hand down the firm body and closed her fingers around the rock-hard member nudging her leg.

It wasn't until Kane pushed her gown up around her waist and entered her that D'lise came fully awake. *I don't want this,* she cried silently to herself and tried not to respond to the slow, measured strokes of the satin-smooth length thrusting in and out of her.

She might as well have told the sun not to rise. The rhythmic rub against her nub of sensitivity robbed her of all thought. For the moment, she was only aware of the need clamoring for release.

They reached their zenith together, a soft feminine cry and a male groan of satisfaction filling the small confines of the room.

Unlike the aftermath of other mornings, however, there was no cuddling for a few minutes, no lazy stroking of hands as their breathing returned to normal, their heartbeat slowing. Kane withdrew from D'lise even while his heart was still pounding in his ears, and left the bed. As he hated himself for having no will-power where she was concerned, D'lise's whole body burned with shame. Where had her pride gone? Was she like the Davis sisters the women talked about, thinking only of her bodily needs?

No! she denied hotly. With those girls any man would do. She only wanted Kane.

Kane's routine was broken this morning. After he dressed, he built up the fire, then without a look at her he stalked out of the cabin. Silent sobs shook D'lise's body. He wasn't even going to pretend a fondness for her anymore. Why? Was Raven pressuring him to move back in with them?

Chapter Fourteen

Reverend House was finally winding down his fire-and-brimstone sermon, and relief showed on the congregation's faces, especially those of the children who had been squirming on the hard benches for the past half hour. They wanted to examine the Christmas tree and fill their stomachs with the different pastries whose delicious aromas filled the small church.

D'lise, sitting next to Samuel, with Ellen on his other side, was just as eager as the children to view the tree up close, and she managed to keep her features calm and her hands folded in her lap. But it was hard to keep her feet still. She wanted to stamp them against the floor, to start the blood flowing into them to combat the icy coldness that seeped through the wide gaps in the planked floor, up under her skirt and petticoat.

She let her gaze roam over the worshipers, every one bundled up to their chins. She envied the babies wrapped in their warm blankets and held closely to their mothers' breasts.

Still, she wouldn't have missed this occasion for the world. It was Christmas day, and for the first time in her life she was a part of celebrating it. She was a part of the community, liked and welcomed by everyone. A sadness crept into her eyes. If only she had that same sense of belonging in her own home. There was such a coldness, an aloofness between her and Kane now, and she didn't know how much longer she could stand it. There was also the shame and self-loathing she felt at the beginning of each new day. For though she and Kane barely spoke to each other from the time he came home from running his traps until he left the cabin at his usual time in early dawn, each morning before he left the bed, they turned to each other, and as though they couldn't help themselves, they made love.

How much longer could they go on like this? D'lise stared down at her clasped hands. She knew that Raven continued to meet Kane in the barn, for every morning when she went to tend the animals she found the woman's fresh footprints in front of the door. Each time it was like being stabbed in the heart, and she would swear that Kane Devlin would never again know her body.

But even as she made the vow, she knew that when he reached for her in the early mornings she would go into his arms.

D'lise came back to the present when everyone stood up to sing the closing hymn. She could only hum along, having attended church so seldom she'd never learned the verses.

The men filed outside to light their pipes, and the reverend placed a short, makeshift table at the back of the church. Children ran underfoot, chasing each other about as Mrs. House brought out a thin-layered cake and two pots of tea. The men were called in, and within twenty minutes the pots were empty and nothing left of the cake but a few crumbs.

Ellen whispered to D'lise, "Look at the frown on the reverend's face. He's irked that everything has been eaten. It's always been the rule that any food left over from a gathering goes home with him."

D'lise glanced at the tall, thin preacher. He did have a hungry look, although she had noticed he seemed to eat more than anyone else. "Is he so poor he has to depend on leftovers?" she whispered back to Ellen.

"If he is, it's his own fault. He has plenty of time to farm like most of the other men do. He doesn't spend that much time preparing his sermons. Every Sunday he lambasts us with the same threat that we are headed for hell."

D'lise giggled, then straightened her features when Sarah Patton came up to her, followed by three of her neighbors.

"D'lise," Sarah said in her clipped, no-nonsense manner, "I've been tellin' the ladies how educated you are." When D'lise looked surprised, she explained, "Samuel told me, and we all think that it would be selfish of you if you refuse to impart some of your learnin' to our young'uns. You know how desperately we need a teacher."

At first D'lise was too dumbfounded to speak. D'lise Alex—Devlin, a schoolteacher? A young woman who until recently had never been around children, who still did not know how to communicate with them?

"I'm sorry, Sarah, but I wouldn't even know how to begin to teach. Besides, I have no books."

"You could learn our young'uns the same way you learned how to read and write and do figures."

246

"And Samuel has all the books you'll need in his stockroom," Ellen said, slipping an arm through D'lise's. "He sent away to Boston for them right after he moved here. He's anxious for his daughters to continue their education and he feels sure that you can do it."

"Oh, I don't know, Ellen," D'lise began, wondering how Kane would feel about it.

"It would help you spend the time while Kane is running his traps," Ellen pointed out. "I don't know how you can bear it, shut up in the cabin all day with no one to talk to but the cat and dog. I know you have Kane's company in the evenings, but is that truly enough?"

Oh, Ellen, D'lise thought, *if only you knew I don't even have that. That sometimes we don't even exchange a dozen words.*

And that fact was beginning to bother her something fierce. If she didn't have human companionship before long, she didn't know what she'd do. And Kane couldn't care less what she did with her days. He probably wouldn't even be aware of what she was doing. Of course she would tell him.

"Well"—she smiled weakly at the waiting women— "if you think I should, I'm willing to give it a try."

She was almost smothered by the happy women crowding around her, exclaiming their thanks and telling her that she would do just fine. Ellen took her hand and tugged her toward the door. "Come on, you might as well take a look at your classroom right now."

The sturdy one-room schoolhouse was filled with women and children pushing in behind D'lise and Ellen. Her attention was called a dozen different times at once. "See the well-built fireplace." "Look at the big woodbox beside it, already filled with wood." "Look at your desk—the coffinmaker built that." "And see the four

247

long desks, each capable of seating four pupils."

Finally, when she had looked at everything so proudly pointed out to her, Ellen walked to a door she imagined led outside. But when it was unlocked and pushed open, she saw that it led into a large room the width of the building.

"When the schoolhouse was built," Ellen explained, walking inside, "we imagined we'd be getting someone who would need their own quarters, and so we had this room added on and furnished. As you know, no one is interested in coming here to teach."

How cozy it looked, D'lise thought, standing in the doorway, taking in the bed in one corner, a table beneath a window, a bench on either side of it, a fireplace on the west end of the room, and a very used rocker sitting in front of it.

As she turned to follow Ellen back into the schoolroom, she hoped the quarters would be used soon, that someone else would come to take her place. Someone who would know what they were doing.

"I just remembered something, Ellen," D'lise said as they walked back to the church. "I'm not too fond of the idea of making the trip here and back home alone every day. What if I should run into a pack of wolves, or a wildcat?"

"Oh, honey, we wouldn't let you do that." Ellen put her arm around the younger girl's waist. "Have you met old Tom Spears?"

"I'm not sure. Is he the skinny old man with the white beard?"

"That's Tom. He's a queer old fellow and lives alone about a half mile from your place. He rides into the village every day and sits around the post with the other older gentlemen. They talk of old times, how they used to hunt

248

and trap and the Indian fights they've fought. He'll bring you to the village, then take you home.''

An inaudible sigh feathered through D'lise lips. She'd used every excuse she could think of. There was no way she could get out of trying to teach the children of Piney Ridge without appearing to be a very selfish person, unwilling to share her knowledge with a younger generation who might otherwise grow up unable to read or write.

The little party was breaking up. The mothers, including Abbey Davis, whose daughters were the talk of the village, thanked D'lise for agreeing to teach their youngsters.

Dusk was coming on as Samuel helped Ellen and D'lise into the buggy, the air growing colder with the setting of the sun. As the buggy moved away from the village, white puffs of cold air escaped their mouths as Ellen and Samuel talked excitedly about school opening after the holidays.

D'lise tried to capture their enthusiasm, but could not. The closer she got to home, the more she worried about what Kane's attitude would be toward her teaching.

It was full dark when Samuel brought the buggy to a halt in front of the cabin. A pale light flickered through the cabin window and D'lise, suddenly nervous, wondered if Kane was inside the cabin or in the barn with Raven.

Samuel was helping her from the conveyance and Ellen was saying good night when the cabin door was flung open and Kane stood there like an avenging angel.

''Where in the hell have you been?''

Kane's shoulders stooped with weariness as he removed a beaver from his last trap, rebaited it, then headed down the beaten path that would take him the three miles to home. His feet didn't have their usual bounce as he plodded along. The emotional upheaval he'd lived in recently seemed to have drained him of all energy.

His skin crawled with self-loathing that he still loved and desired his wife, even though another man visited her while he was away. The very thing he had scorned his uncle for, he was allowing to happen to him. To make it complete, all he had to do now was to begin drinking, to dull the pain that his wife found another man more to her liking—a man who was educated like herself, one who spoke and acted like a gentleman.

Kane frowned when the cabin came in view. It was dark inside. Why hadn't D'lise lit the candles? He stepped up his pace, apprehension and dread growing inside him. Had another Indian come along? Would he find his wife dead?

He flung open the door to be greeted by the tail-wagging Hound and a hissing Scrag. Other than the pair of pets, the cabin was empty. He spun around and raced to the barn, his heart pounding against his ribs. What would he find there? He found only the animals and hungry, fussing chickens.

It was when he returned to the cabin that he noticed the fresh buggy tracks by the door. The blood drained from his face. D'lise had left him. She had gone off with the fancy storekeeper.

His movements slow and lethargic, he untied the raw-hide strips that held his catch to his back and let it slide to the ground. Entering the cabin he lit a candle, then stirred up the fire and added more wood to it. He continued to kneel by the hearth, staring unseeing into the flames. How was he to get through the days, the years, without her?

The hound's whining at the door made Kane lift his head and listen. He heard the stamping of hooves and the sound of feminine laughter. She was back!

He jumped to his feet, anger growing inside him. Forgotten was his panic and despair of only minutes ago. Samuel had just helped D'lise to the ground when he flung the door open and demanded in ringing tones, "Where in the hell have you been?"

There was an embarrassed silence for a moment; then D'lise said calmly, her chin in the air, "Merry Christmas, Kane. I've been to church."

The startled look that came over Kane's face was comical, and D'lise would have laughed had she not been so angry. What right did he have speaking that way to her, especially in front of her friends?

She turned to her silent, uneasy companions. "Thank you, Ellen and Samuel, for taking me to the service. Wouldn't you like to come in and get warmed before making the trip back to the village?"

"I think we'd better get on back before the wolves start prowling." Samuel smiled down at her, then climbed into the buggy. "Ellen and I will be warm enough under the lap-robe." He nodded to Kane and picked up the reins. Ellen, always the pacifier, smiled and called, "Merry Christmas, Kane," as the buggy rolled away.

D'lise swept into the cabin, her eyes bright with anger. Kane was right behind her, gripped with rage. Before he could release it on her, she swung around, hissing, "You had no right talking to me like that in front of my friends."

"You had no right goin' off and not tellin' me where you were goin'!" Kane was equally loud. "I won't stand for you sneakin' off with that fancy storekeeper, shamin' me in front of everyone."

D'lise stared at him in confusion for a moment. She hadn't sneaked off with Samuel. And he was a fine one to talk about shaming someone. What about his sneaking off to the barn every night to meet Raven? All of Piney Ridge probably knew about it.

She drew herself up proudly, and giving Kane a scathing look, said coldly, "To borrow a phrase from the Bible, before you remove the splinter from your brother's eye, first remove the log from your own." And while he mulled that remark over, she added, "I left you a note telling where I had gone." She looked down at the table. "There it is under the salt cellar where I put it."

In his fear that something had happened to D'lise, Kane had missed seeing the square of paper. He picked up the note, crushed it in his fist, and flung it into the fire.

Ellen Travis was brought along to cover up what was going on between them. His uncle's wife had started out the same way, then gradually got to the point where she hadn't bothered to hide anything from her husband. Well, it wasn't going to happen to him. He was putting a stop to it right here and now. Turning a glowering look on D'lise, he bit out, "I don't want to ever see that bastard's buggy tracks around here again, and I'd better not hear of you bein' with him. You will not bring shame to the Devlin name."

Spots of angry red appeared on D'lise cheeks. "Are you accusing me of—"

"Exactly, lady. There will be no more galavantin' around while I'm at work."

D'lise shot a look at the determined jut of his jaw and lost all self-control. She had planned to tell him quietly about the teaching job, explain how the mothers had more or less shamed her into taking the position, how time dragged so with him gone all day. But she realized now that he couldn't care less how she spent her days. His prime concern was that people would think he was being cuckolded, that his friends would laugh behind his back.

With angry defiance snapping in her eyes, she glared at Kane, her clenched fists on her hips. "You might as well know right now that I have agreed to be Piney Ridge's new schoolteacher. I start January second."

"So!" Kane shouted back, "the pair of you have dreamed up another scheme to see each other. He'll pick you up in the mornin's and bring you home at night. How big a fool do you think I am?"

"I think you're all manner of fool!" D'lise yelled back. "I probably won't see Samuel at all unless I run into him accidentally."

"Hah! Do you expect me to believe that you're crazy enough to make that trip twice a day to Piney Ridge alone?"

"I don't intend to make it alone. Old Tom Spears is going to ride with me. He'll come by in the mornings, ride with me to the village, then return with me at the end of the schoolday."

Kane glared back at her for several seconds then, turning on his heel, left the cabin, slamming the door behind him. "That's it, go to your squaw." D'lise stared at the shuddering door before collapsing into a rocker.

Her head was beginning to ache with a dull throbbing. Scrag came and rubbed against her legs, and Hound laid his head in her lap. She wondered if they were aware of her unhappiness.

The clock struck six and she jumped to her feet. The cow had to be milked. The poor thing was probably in a lot of pain. Supper was going to be a little late also.

Kane was feeding the horses when she entered the barn, but he didn't look up as she walked straight to Spider. No word was spoken between them as she hurriedly coaxed the milk into the pail, then fed the chickens. His back was still turned to her when she left the barn.

As D'lise buried three potatoes in the hot ashes, then covered them with red coals, she wondered how it would all end. How long could they go on with this coldness that had developed between them? How many evenings could she sit alone in the cabin, knowing that her husband was spending his time with his squaw?

Forty-five minutes later, as she placed a platter of steak and a dish of stewed turnips on the table, she still hadn't come up with an answer. For the time being she must live one day at a time, she told herself.

D'lise picked at her supper, her ears alert for the sound of footsteps. Kane had to be starving. When half an hour had passed, and he hadn't returned, she covered the steak and turnips, placed them on the hearth to keep warm, and returned two of the potatoes to the hot ashes. After setting two pans of scraps on the floor for the cat and dog, she undressed and went to bed.

Although she was sure she wouldn't close her eyes all night, the next thing D'lise knew, the sun was pouring through the window. She turned her head and looked at Kane's pillow, and a stab of pain and bitterness jabbed her heart. There was no imprint of his head on the plump pillow. He had not slept with her. He had spent the entire night with Raven.

She sat up in bed and wearily ran her fingers through her curls. Was this his way of telling her that their marriage was over?

A cynical grimace curved her lips. Their marriage had been doomed from the beginning. Wedlock was hard enough when two people loved each other. It never ran smooth when only half of a married couple felt love toward the other. She had known from the start that Kane didn't love her. It was true he took great pleasure in her body, but evidently he found more satisfaction with

Raven. Even in that respect she hadn't been able to hold him.

She swung her legs over the side of the bed, her bare toes fumbling for her moccasins. She had pushed one foot into one when her eyes strayed to the fireplace and widened. There lay Kane's bedroll, all tangled up with Hound asleep on it.

Her pulse sang. He hadn't spent the night with Raven. "Nor did he spend it with you," she muttered, putting on the other moccasin.

Nevertheless, her steps were light as she made up her bed and folded Kane's blankets.

Chapter Fifteen

To her surprise, D'lise began to look forward to each new day. She soon found that she loved teaching her students. There were several of them, ranging in age from six to seventeen. Samuel's little girls, six and eight, were her favorites. They were well-mannered children, eager to learn, and never gave her any trouble.

Of the Bellows children, Josie, thirteen, was well behaved but wasn't too bright. D'lise feared she wouldn't be able to teach the girl a great deal. Her two brothers, James, seven, and Daniel, ten, although bright, were real mischief-makers, always doing something to disrupt the other students.

Then there was Becky Patton, age sixteen, and her three brothers, Josh, fourteen, Raymond, twelve, and Jessie, ten. The boys behaved fairly well, knowing that if they didn't they'd feel the strap at home.

Finally, there were four Jessup children, three girls and

one boy, ranging in age from six to ten. Thinly clad and always looking hungry, they sat in their seats as quietly as mice.

D'lise sighed over her first cup of coffee. There were the two Davis girls, thirteen and fifteen. Lillibeth, the younger, was interested in an education and paid close attention to everything her teacher said. But Amy, the older one, shouldn't have been taking up her time. She was already as man-crazy as her eighteen-year-old sister Rosy and was more interested in Jason Thomas, age seventeen, than she was in learning anything.

Jason was in charge of building a fire in the school's fireplace every morning and keeping the woodbox filled. Most times when she and old Tom arrived at the sturdy little building with its bell hanging from the porch, Amy was with Jason, a smug, contented look on her narrow little face. D'lise often wondered what the two of them got up to, all alone, and what time they arrived at the schoolhouse.

When she mentioned her thoughts to Tom one day, he'd grunted and stated as if it were a fact, "They be buildin' more than one fire."

D'lise grinned and poured herself another cup of coffee. Tom Spears was a cantankerous old man, who had come to the remote, unvisited wilderness years ago and built his cabin. He had lived alone all his life, and some said that he was strange because he didn't invite friendliness from most people. But united in their loneliness, a fast friendship had developed between D'lise and the old gent.

Tom was uneducated, couldn't even write his own name, but he was quite intelligent and thought deeply about many things. One day when they were discussing the women who whored for a living, she had remarked that she somehow felt sorry for those women, having to

257

cater to a man's lust. Tom had agreed, then asked, "You ever look deep in a whore's eyes? They look kind of used-up. Like they've seen too much." She had thought it was a good description of the women's eyes.

The old fellow was racked with rheumatism, unable to run a trapline anymore, and the winter days were long for him. But in the summer, he always planted and tended a large garden that kept him outside under the sun, which eased his aching joints somewhat.

She had heard that he gave away much of what he grew, but that he put a lot away for his winter use. Ever since school started and he rode with her to and from Piney Ridge, he had kept the Devlins supplied with dried stringbeans, which he called leather britches, kernels of sweet corn, dried apples, crocks of sauerkraut, potatoes, dry beans, and the best pickles she'd ever bitten into. The dried vegetables, soaked in water overnight, were almost as good as if freshly picked.

D'lise in turn shared her eggs with him, and kept him in bread, pies, and cookies.

D'lise had just finished her second cup of coffee and was rinsing out the cup when Tom halloed the cabin. She slipped on her fur jacket, picked up the school papers she had been grading, and hurried to the barn. As usual, Tom had Beauty saddled and waiting for her.

As they headed the mounts toward the village, Tom glanced up at the chimney and said, "Look how the smoke is goin' toward the ground. That means it's gonna rain."

"Or maybe snow." D'lise slid him a twinkling look. Sometimes she liked to bait him. "After all, it's still February."

"No." Tom shook his head. "There won't be no more snowin'. March arrives next week, and before long the

258

days will get longer and the sun warmer. I can't hardly wait for to feel the hot sun beatin' down on me again.''

D'lise had her doubts about the rain. The sky was as blue as it could be. She slid Tom another teasing look. ''Do you suppose it will hold off until we get home this afternoon?''

''Yes, more's the pity,'' Tom snapped. ''There's one smart-tongued lady I'd like to see get her rear end soaked.''

''Now who could that be, I wonder?'' D'lise chuckled.

''It's a little smart-ass ridin' half a horse-length behind me,'' the old fellow grumped.

They entered the village then, and riding up beside her elderly friend, D'lise gave him a twisted grin. After a moment, he returned it. They pulled rein in front of the schoolhouse and were greeted by Jason and Amy sitting on the top step to the porch. Both looked as innocent as babes.

''Look at the boy,'' Tom said in an aside as D'lise slipped out of the saddle. ''That little whore has just about wore him out.''

''Tom!'' D'lise whispered the exclamation. ''You don't know that.''

''I know. It's plain to see. He's all droopy and she's full of vinegar. Come lunchtime and you let them out to eat their lunches, them two will run to the woodshed and go to it until the school bell rings.''

''Do you know that for a fact?'' D'lise looked at him wide-eyed.

Old Tom nodded. ''Yep, I do. I've watched them.''

''That wasn't very nice of you to spy on them, Tom,'' D'lise scolded, ''even if they shouldn't have been doing it.''

''I didn't spy on them exactly. The first time I just

259

kinda happened on them when I went to the shed to get an ax. The other times I see them go in there, I just imagine they're doin' the same thing. I'm sure they're not sittin' in there holdin' hands.''

''I hope that foolish girl doesn't find herself pregnant someday,'' D'lise said, still whispering.

The old man's lips twisted in a thin smile. ''That Jason had better pray that she don't. It could belong to any one of a dozen men, but you can bet she'd name him as the father. His daddy, Buck, would peel the hide off him should he have to marry into that riff-raff.''

D'lise gave the teenagers a narrow look as she came up the three steps to the porch, and did not return their smile. Over the coming weekend she'd think of some way to keep the pair apart—at least during the time they were attending school.

As usual on Friday, the children were restless, anxious for school to let out, to enjoy two days away from readers and spellers. D'lise sighed her relief after looking at the school clock and seeing it was three-thirty. Only another half hour to go.

''Who wants to sweep the floor?'' she asked, and every hand in the room except those of the older boys went up. That was female work. She chose Becky Patton. Becky would get all the corners.

The clock struck four, and there was a hurried rush of slates put away. When D'lise gave the word, the children filed out of the room in an orderly fashion, then whooped like a pack of Indians on the war path as they ran off in different directions.

Tom waited for D'lise, holding Beauty's reins. As she came down the steps, he pointed a finger at the northwest sky. ''Take a look at them black clouds buildin' up there,

Missy. I told you it was gonna rain. We might even get wet before we get home.''

"Well, let's get a move on.'' D'lise swung into the saddle and led off. "It won't do your rheumatism any good if you get soaked through by a cold rain.''

An early darkness had descended by the time they reached D'lise's cabin. Old Tom started to take Beauty to the barn to unsaddle her. D'lise took the reins from him. "I'll take care of her,'' she said. "You get on home. You just might make it before those clouds open up.''

"If you don't mind, I think I'll do that,'' Tom said, and lifted his mount into a trot, mindful of the icy condition of the trail.

D'lise turned Beauty into her stall, stripped off the saddle, and pitched her a forkful of hay before sprinting toward the cabin. She pushed the door open just as the first drops of rain began to fall. The hound darted out to lift his leg against a tree, then dashed back to scratch at the door. Scrag lay in her rocker looking smug as Hound shook himself, showering water over the hearth. *He* didn't have to go outside when nature called. Back in a corner was a long pan of dirt for him to use.

D'lise lit some candles and changed into one of her work dresses. She was uncovering the live coals and adding wood to them when the rain began in earnest. Old Tom was going to get wet, she thought, shaking her head worriedly.

As she went about preparing supper, the rain thundered on the roof and sheeted down the window. She glanced often from the potatoes she was peeling, searching the trail Kane always took when running his line. She tried not to feel sorry for him in the cold, drenching wetness.

Nevertheless, she lit another candle and placed it in the window to guide him to the cabin.

261

As she laid out three pork chops to be dredged in flour later, a happy thought came to her. Surely Raven wouldn't come out in this downpour to meet Kane in the barn.

Kane still went to the barn as soon as he finished eating, and she still found Raven's footprints around the barn door. She and Kane lived in a strained atmosphere that was beginning to tell on them both. Only at night did they find a short time of peace, an erasing of the turmoil that was tearing them apart.

Kane had slept on the floor only that one night. Giving no explanation for his change of mind, he had gotten into bed when he returned to the cabin the next night.

Had D'lise questioned him, and had he had a mind to tell her the truth, he'd have answered that he missed waking up in the middle of the night and feeling her soft body curled up against him.

Each had hugged their own side of the bed for several nights before, in the middle of one night, they had rolled toward each other in their sleep, their legs entwining. The touch of their limbs was all that it took. In a flash Kane had D'lise in his arms, his lips moving over hers with raw hunger. D'lise welcomed his kiss eagerly, and deepening the kiss, Kane moved his body to lie on top of hers, and she opened up to him.

With a hoarse groan, he slid inside her and began a deep, rhythmic thrusting. She caught his fevered pace and lifted her hips to capture each inch of him. In no time at all, she reached the crest of no return. At the same time, Kane groaned his scorching release.

He collapsed on top of her, his face buried between her chin and shoulder. Then, even as his heart still raced, he silently rolled off her and moved to his side of the bed. And as D'lise moved toward her side, she wasn't sure she hadn't dreamed it all.

It had become common practice then, that in the middle of the night they would turn to each other. But they never indulged in morning desire anymore, that wonderful time of leisurely lovemaking.

Flames were leaping in the fireplace, and the meat was fried a golden brown when Kane pushed open the cabin door, soaked to the skin. D'lise wanted to cry out her sympathy for him, help him out of his wet jacket. But she knew he wouldn't want her pity, nor her help, so she silently handed him a towel to dry his face and hair. He muttered something, which she took for words of reluctant thanks.

She kept her eyes averted from him as he stripped before the fire, then changed into dry clothes. She thought about that lean body often enough without looking at it. To see the broad shoulders, the narrow hips, and what lay beyond might make her lose control, make her throw herself against his body. It would be too embarrassing if he should repulse her while he was fully awake. For all she knew, when he turned to her in the middle of the night, he could very well be dreaming of Raven.

Supper was eaten in its usual fashion—in silence. Kane drank two cups of coffee, then pulled on a hooded oilskin jacket and, as usual, left the cabin. D'lise's lips trembled. Evidently he was sure that Raven would meet him in the barn, regardless of the downpour.

When she had washed and dried everything used in preparing the meal, she sat in front of the fire correcting her pupils' test papers. She found with satisfaction that most of the children were coming along nicely with her tutoring. It gave her a great sense of accomplishment.

D'lise stretched and yawned, then changed into her nightgown. As she lay curled on her side of the bed, she tried not to think about what was going on in the barn.

"You must stop thinking of them," she chastised herself. Constant fretting had pared down her weight alarmingly. Her breasts and hip bones were becoming almost undiscernible under her clothes. Ellen had remarked on her weight loss a couple of times. She had laughingly brushed it off, claiming that keeping her students in line was keeping her in trim shape. Not for the world would she tell anyone that she was heartsick because Raven was back in Kane's life.

It rained for four days, sometimes only a drizzle, other times a steady beat of rain. D'lise tried to talk old Tom into staying home, telling him that the wet and damp would aggravate his rheumatism and that she would be perfectly safe riding to school alone. But he would have none of it, and every morning when she stepped out of the cabin, he was waiting for her, bundled up to his chin.

In those four days, a change had taken place in the Devlin household. Each day now when Kane returned from running his lines, he brought home some traps. And at night, surprisingly, he spent less time in the barn, less than an hour usually. One night D'lise had still been up, sitting in front of the fire in her nightgown, when he walked into the cabin. A tingling ran through the bottom of her stomach as his hot gaze raked over her, raw desire in his eyes.

It has to be me he wants, she told herself, for he wasn't half asleep now, and there was no way possible he could mistake her for Raven. Hope flared in her breast that tonight when he came to bed he would pull her into his arms and make love to her the way he had when they were first married.

It had not happened that way. Kane was still sitting

before the fire staring broodingly into the flames when she finally fell asleep. Nor had he turned to her later in the night.

D'lise sighed and tried to put her attention to what Tom was talking about: "... so I think the best thing for me to do is tell Buck what Jason is up to these days. It would be too embarrassin' for you to come right out and say that his son is humpin' that Davis girl ever' chance he gets."

It was hard for D'lise to keep a straight face as she answered soberly, "That is true. I doubt if I could say it just like that."

"Yeah, you're too ladylike to lay it on the line so's Buck would know what was goin' on. He wouldn't know what you wuz talkin' about if you wuz to say real prissy-like, 'Mr. Thomas, your son Jason has been seein' far too much of the Davis girl.' Ole Buck would think you meant the girl didn't have on enough clothes."

D'lise grinned, wondering if other people saw her as being prissy-like.

The long rain had washed away every trace of snow, turning paths and trails to ankle-deep mud. The Ohio rose and overflowed its banks, coming within feet of the cabins built lower on the hillsides. But spring had arrived, bringing with it the promise of a new life. The days became longer, the sun warmer, and Kane brought in all his traps. And much to D'lise's delight, he no longer went to the barn after supper. He spent quite a bit of time there in the daytime, though, especially when she returned from school, as though to avoid her.

D'lise was as happy as her students when the last day of school arrived. The older children were needed at home to help put in crops and plant family gardens. She wondered cynically how Kane would manage to shun her, when she was home all day and he had no traps to run. A big part of his time would be spent with Raven, she imagined, blinking at the wetness that sprang into her eyes.

"Tom, you're looking mighty smug about something this morning." D'lise tore her thoughts away from Kane and brought Beauty up to ride alongside the old man. "What have you been up to?"

"Me? I ain't been up to nothin'. Just enjoyin' the sun on my old bones again and thankful that I made it through another winter."

It made sense, but D'lise wasn't satisfied that being alive and taking pleasure in the sun was the only reason for that half smile that twitched his heavy mustache.

She hadn't long to wonder about it. As they rode down the mud-mired street and approached the schoolhouse, she saw several horses and two mules tied up under the maple tree that was just putting on new leaf growth.

Every mother in the area must be here, she thought, recognizing two of the mounts, one belonging to Sarah Patton, the other always ridden by Claudie Bellows. She gave Tom a reproachful look. "You might have warned me."

"And have them wimmen all over me? I ain't that brave. Anyways, it ain't nothin' for you to get all hetted up about. They just want to show you their appreciation for learnin' their young'uns how to read and such."

When D'lise entered the schoolhouse, she was greeted with the aroma of brewing coffee and a dozen voices calling, "Surprise!" Tears sprang into her eyes. Imagine skinny little D'lise Alexander being feted this way. How proud Auntie would have been.

The top of her desk was covered with platters of cookies and small cloth bags. While she wondered what they contained, Sarah Patton broke into a speech, saying how grateful they all were for her putting up with their children, and giving them an education, and they hoped she would return next fall and continue to pound some learnin' in their heads.

"We hope you don't mind," she went on, "that we took it on ourselves to bring some cookies and make a pot of coffee. But first we'd like for you to open the little gifts we've brought you."

Sarah picked up one of the bags, about six inches long and four inches wide, and handed it to D'lise. "You can start with mine."

D'lise swiped at her wet eyes and pulled the drawstring of the bag. She peered inside and gave an exclamation of happy surprise. It was full of mixed flower seeds. How did this practical, no-nonsense woman know how starved she was for some beauty in her life?

"Thank you, Sarah," she said softly, "thank you for your kindness since I came to Piney Ridge." She retied the string, adding, "I can't wait to get them in the ground."

D'lise remembered with bitterness that Kane had once promised that he would build them a new cabin come spring. Of course, that was before everything had gone wrong between them. Naturally he wouldn't do it now. He was more apt to send her packing.

She kept that unhappy thought off her face as, one after another, she untied the other bags. It was clear that the women had gotten together and decided what each woman should bring her. There were no doubles of string beans, butter beans, radishes, peas, corn, squash and pumpkin, lettuce and tomatoes. There was even a sack of tobacco seed for Kane.

Tears were spilling freely down D'lise's cheeks when

all the seed had been exclaimed over and thanked for. The good women of Piney Ridge smiled broadly at her happiness, having no idea that there was also sadness in her tears—sadness at the possibility that she wouldn't have the chance of planting the seeds.

"Well," said practical Sarah, "let's have our refreshments and get on back home. I don't know about you other ladies, but I've got a heap of work to do. If you don't mind, D'lise, I'll take Becky with me. I want to get the garden planted today."

The cookies and coffee weren't wolfed down as expected, considering the work that awaited each woman at home. It wasn't every day the neighbors got together in the middle of the week, and a good half hour was spent in catching up on each other, how they had fared during the cold weather when they were housebound for weeks on end.

And, of course, a great deal of gossiping went on. Elijah Jessup's new wife had lost her baby as had been expected. They had all heard that the oldest Davis girl had finally got herself "bigged," which wasn't surprising, the way she lay down for any man who came along. A lot of the menfolk were uneasy, waiting for her to point a finger. And Amy Davis was going to turn up the same way, she was so man-crazy.

D'lise grew uneasy at those last words and decided she would urge Tom to speak to Jason's father today. Jason was bright and could make something of himself if he didn't have a wife and child on his young shoulders—a child that might not even be his.

The ladies were gone then, taking their children with them for the same reason that Sarah took Becky. It would be a busy time for the home-steaders until the snow arrived again.

D'lise was gathering up the cookies that were left over, putting them in a napkin for Tom to take home with him, when the door opened quietly and Abbey Davis slipped into the room. She approached D'lise shyly, clutching a burlap bag in her hand.

"Hello, Mrs. Davis." D'lise smiled at the woman her daughters had got their good looks from. "You should have come sooner. Your neighbors just left. There's some cookies and coffee left over. Would you like to join me in having some?" She pulled out a bench for Abbey to sit down on. She figured that since she hadn't heard a horse arrive, the woman must have walked here and would be tired.

It was evident that Abbey had walked the three miles in the way a soft sigh of relief feathered through her lips as she sat down. "I ain't hungry, Miz Devlin," she said. "I just et breakfast a short time ago." She held the bag out to D'lise. "I brung this to you for bein' so good to my Lillibeth, teachin' her things. She's smart and wants to learn things—not like Amy, who don't care for nothin' but men—her and Rosy."

She glanced up at D'lise, then quickly looked away. "I guess . . . you heard about my Rosy gettin' herself caught."

"Well, yes, I heard." D'lise decided not to lie about it. It seemed that everybody knew. "I was sorry to hear about it. Has she told the father yet?"

A bleakness came over Abbey Davis's face. "She don't know who the father is. It could be any of a dozen men, and most of them already married. Me and Elton is waitin' for Amy to turn up the same way." The words came out at the end of a heavy sigh. "She's always sneakin' off to meet some man. I used to take a switch to them, but it didn't do any good. They're like their pa in that respect.

269

He's hot-blooded too. But he's a good and kind man,'' she hurried to add. ''Never once has he raised a hand to me, and I don't think he's ever laid around with other wimmen.''

D'lise found herself envying this woman despite the fact she had two daughters who had brought shame to her home. Abbey had a good and loving husband who never looked beyond his wife for carnal pleasure. Did she realize and appreciate how lucky she was in that respect?

''A loving husband is very important, Abbey,'' she said quietly, ''and I'm sure Lillibeth will make you proud of her. As for Rosy and Amy, you've tried your best, so you have nothing to be ashamed of. They're the ones to feel shame. In the meantime, you keep your head up and your chin out, keeping in mind that you're as good as any woman who lives in the area. Maybe even better than some.''

The defeat in Abbey Davis's eyes faded somewhat at D'lise's advice, and unconsciously her shoulders straightened. ''I'll tell Elton that. He's feelin' mighty low right now.'' She gave the burlap bag a push with her foot. ''I think you'll like what I brung you.''

''I'm sure I will, Abbey.'' D'lise bent over and untied the string holding the bag together. ''Abbey!'' she exclaimed. ''A rosebush! My favorite flower.''

Abbey blushed with pleasure. ''It's red, and blooms off and on all summer. Roses like a lot of water and manure. It'll start puttin' out leaves and buds in about a month. It has a real strong scent. I got mine underneath the kitchen window so's I can smell it when I'm washin' the dishes.''

''I'll plant this one under my window too.'' D'lise smiled at the once pretty woman.

Old Tom broke up their visit.

''You about ready to leave, D'lise?'' he called from the

porch. "I wanna get home and start my garden. Half the day is gone already."

Abbey stood up with a smile. "I expect Elton is waitin' for me to get home and give him a hand. As you probably know, we ain't got no sons to help us." D'lise was about to ask what was wrong with the daughters helping out, then decided not to bring it up. Abbey didn't need to be reminded that her two older daughters were lazy as well as morally loose.

She and Abbey walked out onto the porch together, D'lise clutching the bag with the rosebush, along with the seeds she'd tossed in with it. Tom said a pleasant "howdy" to Abbey; then she and D'lise said goodbye, each going off in different directions.

D'lise and Tom were within half a mile of the cabin when, off to their right, there came the ringing sound of an ax biting into wood. D'lise looked at the old man with questioning eyes. "Aren't we on Kane's property?"

"We sure are. I wonder who's choppin' down his trees." He turned his mount's head in the direction of the sound. "Let's go take a look," he said, leading off.

Chapter Sixteen

D'lise pulled Beauty up so sharply, the mare shook her head in protest. "What in the world is Kane up to?"

Bare-chested, her husband gave one last swing of the ax at a tree about eight inches thick. He stepped back as the young oak creaked, tottered, then went crashing to the ground to join the many others that had succumbed to the sharp bit of his steel.

Tom, having reined in beside D'lise, shot a stream of tobacco juice at an unfortunate toad that had stuck its head from behind a tree, and he called, "Hey, Kane, you gettin' a head start on next winter's wood supply?"

Startled, Kane swung around, sweat pouring down his face. He glanced briefly at D'lise, a careful blankness in his eyes, then gave his attention to Tom.

"I promised D'lise that I'd build her a bigger cabin come spring. I decided to get started on it today." He pulled a handkerchief from his pocket and mopped his face.

D'lise could only gape at Kane. She could not believe what she was hearing. She thought that, if anything, Kane would be more apt to send her away than build her a new cabin.

She clamped down on the ridiculous joy strumming madly through her body. *You fool,* she cried silently, *do you think a new cabin is going to keep Raven out of his life? He'll probably move her into the old cabin.*

Tom interrupted D'lise's gloomy musing. "Well, folks, I'm gonna get on over the hill and start my garden. When you're ready to start yours, D'lise, let me know if I can help you." He lifted his hand and rode off.

D'lise turned her attention back to Kane, who, ignoring her, was swinging the ax at another tree. *You can't pretend that I'm not here all day, you arrogant devil,* she thought. She made up her mind to sit there until he acknowledged her presence, if it took all day. She'd make him tell her exactly what was on his mind, once and for all. She couldn't go on like this, putting up with his cold treatment and cheating.

The tree came crashing down, and Kane looked surprised when he turned and saw D'lise sitting on the mare, staring at him grimly. "Why are you still here?" The question was almost a growl.

"I'm still here to get some straight answers to the questions I want to ask you."

"Like what?" Kane narrowed his eyes at her.

"For instance, why are you building this cabin?"

There was a flicker of pain in the slate-colored eyes. Then, his face hard and tight, Kane sank the ax blade into the trunk of the tree he had just felled and said coldly, "I

Norah Hess

can see where this conversation is headin', so let's go to
the cabin and get it over with.'' He jerked the looped reins
off a tree branch and swung onto the stallion's back, sending him into a loping run.

D'lise slim shoulders sagged as she kept a horse-length
behind Kane. In just minutes she was going to hear the
words that would rip her heart apart. At last she was going
to hear the truth, a truth she dreaded hearing with all her
being. Kane was going to tell her that their sham marriage
was over, that they would be living apart once the new
building had gone up.

They arrived at the cabin and Kane was off his mount
and pushing the door open before D'lise had climbed out
of the saddle. When she entered the small room he was
standing at the window, staring outside, his body held
stiffly. After she closed the door, he turned around and
faced her.

"What did you mean, why am I buildin' the cabin?"
He came straight to the point.

"I meant just what I said. The way things have dete-
riorated between us, I can't imagine why you'd go to so
much trouble. It's plain you want nothing more to do with
me—except maybe in the middle of the night when you
can't see who you're making love to, can pretend that I
am Raven—"

D'lise got no further. "That's a scabbin' lie!" Kane
half shouted.

D'lise stared at the flaming anger in his eyes. Why was
he so angry? She'd given him the perfect opportunity to
admit that what she accused him of was true. Why did he
continue to pretend?

Kane took the few steps that separated them. Glaring
down at her, he grated out, "Don't ease your own con-

science by tellin' yourself that *I've* broken my marriage vows too.''

"What do you mean, *too?*" D'lise looked at him in bewilderment. "I've never so much as looked at a man in that way since we married. Come to that, not even before I married you.''

"Hah! Are you tryin' to tell me that nothin' went on between you and Majors all those times he came here, stayin' all day while I was out runnin' my traps?''

"Staying here all day?" D'lise was blazingly angry. "Who's making up excuses for their behavior now? It's true that Samuel came here a few times to take me to a church doing, but he never set foot inside the cabin. And most of the time, Ellen was with him or we'd pick her up later. They—''

"Well, I heard different. Someone saw his buggy in front of the cabin almost every day, and it stayed there until shortly before it was time for me to get home.''

Her eyes snapping, D'lise sneered, "Who is this *someone?* Your ugly-faced Indian lover?''

She saw the truth of her charge in Kane's eyes before he could look away from her. Her heart a heavy weight in her chest, and her legs feeling boneless, D'lise walked toward her rocker to sit down.

She took but one step when her arm was caught and she was spun around. "You haven't said whether it is true or not." There was steel in Kane's eyes.

"Is it true that you've been sleeping with Raven all winter?" she shot back at him.

"I haven't slept with that woman since we got married—even longer than that.''

"That's a lie. I've seen her come out of the forest numerous times and sneak up to the barn. Are you trying to tell me that the two of you were just sitting around chatting? That you went there every night just to hold her hand? You must think I'm really ignorant.''

Kane looked at his shouting wife, puzzlement growing on his face. ''I admit that Raven came to the barn once, but only to tell me about Majors.''

D'lise shook her head in denial. ''I've seen her go to the barn many times. But let's say that your claim is the truth—why would you go sit in a cold barn every night? Is my company so unpleasant?''

''Damn you!'' Kane gritted out, and jerked her toward the door. ''I'm gonna show you what took me to the barn every night.''

His angry strides kept D'lise at a half run in order not to fall to her knees and be dragged along. Surprisingly, when they came to the barn, Kane skirted it, coming up behind the building. ''There!'' He flung her arm away from him. ''That's what I've been doin' with my evenin's these past months.''

D'lise stared at the long side of the log building. There wasn't an inch of it that wasn't covered with pegged-down animal pelts. ''I don't . . . don't understand,'' she finally managed to stammer.

''What did you think happened to my catch every night?'' Kane asked impatiently. ''Did you think I just tossed them into a corner until it was time to sell them? Catching them is only the first step. After you get them home, you spend hours fleshing them out, stretching them on proper-sized boards.''

D'lise gazed mutely at Kane, remorse in her eyes. All this time she had falsely accused him in her mind, created a coldness between them, wasted precious months.

She laid a hand on his arm pleadingly. ''I'm so sorry and ashamed, Kane. Can you ever forgive me?''

Kane gazed down into D'lise's upturned face and thought, *God, she is so beautiful.* But then there came to taunt him another beautiful face, one that had ruined, and finally killed his uncle. He remembered, too, how his lovely wife came alive in Samuel Majors's company, and that she hadn't answered his question about the storekeeper.

Suddenly he didn't want to know. It would be unbearable if he asked her again and she admitted that she loved another man.

With a groan, almost of defeat, he wrapped his arms around her and pulled her into the wall of his chest. "Of course I forgive you," he whispered in her hair. "That bitch Raven was out to cause trouble, and she succeeded."

D'lise hugged her arms around Kane's waist. "We're wise to her now and she'll never fool us again."

Kane tilted her chin and fastened his mouth on hers, as if starving for her. D'lise returned the kiss with equal pressure, straining her body into his. He cupped her small rear end and bucked his immediate arousal against her. She gave a little moan and mimicked his action.

His breath coming in pants, Kane swung an arm under her knees and lifted her in his arms to carry her back to the cabin. Inside, he stood her on her feet and they began to feverishly undress each other.

Clothes lay scattered all over the floor when again Kane picked D'lise up and laid her on the bright quilt. Her bare arms reached for him as he climbed in beside her, settling himself immediately between the legs she opened for him. He entered her fiercely, as a starving man would rush to a table loaded with food. D'lise smiled in sweet memory as, after that one hard drive, he reached a scorching release.

She cradled his body with her own while he regained his breath, controlled the shuddering of his body. Then, whispering her name, he grasped her hips, and holding them steady, he began to pump inside her, slow and steady, never breaking the rhythm. She moved with him, urging him on, her fingers mindlessly threading through the hair at his nape, aware only of a deep need, so strong it obliterated everything around her.

Though each wanted, needed, that release from the ache gripping their bodies, they nevertheless fought it, wanting to stretch time, to anticipate the moment they would tumble together into that chasm where they would experience the little death.

Finally, their sweaty, working bodies would be denied no longer. With a husky sound, almost a shout, Kane gathered D'lise's slender body close to the well of his hips, and as he lengthened his strokes, the bed creaked and groaned as he drove harder and faster inside her.

It took but seconds for their seeds of hot passion to spring forth and mingle as they tumbled over and over into that deep well that caught them and sapped their strength, leaving them weak as babies.

His breathing finally returning to normal, Kane leaned up on his elbows, taking his weight from D'lise. She gazed up at him from slumberous eyes. "It's so good to be with you again . . . like this, I mean."

"I missed you too." Kane ran little kisses down her throat, her shoulder. "I suppose I should get back to fellin' trees," he asked more than stated.

D'lise felt his long length expanding, filling her. She smiled up at him, a teasing in her blue eyes. "There's something inside me that says you'd rather stay here in bed. Something right about here." She bucked her narrow hips, making Kane catch his breath as his manhood again sprang to full arousal.

"You're gonna break my back, woman, you know that?" Kane growled, sliding his hands under her hips and lifting them several inches off the bed. A soft sigh feathered through D'lise's lips as she wrapped her arms around his shoulders, her legs around his hips, as his body rose and fell slowly over her, each long stroke more exquisite than the last.

D'lise's back ached, and there were blisters on her palms. All day, since early in the morning, she had tramped behind the little jackass Kane had got from Buck Thomas. The single-footed plow he pulled turned over dark, rich soil that would produce a lush garden.

She pulled the little animal in when old Tom called her name. "I'm goin' sang-huntin'," he said. "I know where there's a patch full of four-prongers. I get a lot of money from them there doctors back east for four-prongers."

D'lise knew that Tom's *sang* was ginseng, and that it was true that learned doctors set a lot of store in its curative powers. She remembered how Big Beaver had given a root of it to Kane with orders that she chew on the root, that it would help her recover from her bout of fever.

She sat down on a tree stump and wiped her sweating face with a piece of rag she took from her pocket.

"You hadn't oughta plant your garden before you build your fence," Tom said. "A high one, too, one the deers can't hop over and eat every blasted thing that pops up out of the ground."

Two days later, as D'lise dropped seeds into the long furrows of her garden patch, she mused on what Tom had said about the deer eating her vegetables. She had mentioned to Kane the old man's advice, and he had sighed and said, "When in the hell am I goin' to find time to split rails for a fence?" She had suggested they hire Jason Thomas to do the job, and he had agreed readily.

Buck's son had jumped at the chance to earn some money, and she could hear the ring of his ax down by their new homesite. She'd go check on how he was doing after a while, make sure Amy Davis wasn't hanging around him.

Tom had gone to the post and talked to Buck, telling him what had been going on between his son and the hot little Davis girl. According to Tom, Buck had flown into a rage, threatening to geld his son before he'd see him caught by that piece of white trash.

D'lise grinned. She doubted that Buck would be that drastic in handling his son, but she wouldn't put it past him to give young Jason a licking he wouldn't forget in a long time. He loved the boy enough to do that if he thought it would stop him from ruining his life.

Her mind swung back to her old friend and neighbor. He never stopped amazing her, his insight into people, his knowledge of most anything one cared to talk about— like his advising her to plant her garden according to the twelve signs of the zodiac. She had been stunned by the illiterate man's knowledge of the signs. He knew every one, its symbol, its body part, its planet and element.

When she asked him how he knew all this, he had answered, "My pappy learned me, and his pappy learned him."

D'lise remembered with a smile that the old man had even warned Kane last week not to cut down any more trees until the moon was full. "The wood will dry better," he'd said before thumping his horse with a heel and riding away.

Kane had laughed, but he waited the two days for the moon to become full before felling any more trees. "He'll only be over here jawin' at me if I keep on cuttin'." He'd grinned, then put an arm around her waist, adding, "It'll give us time to go fishin'."

She had spent a couple of hours on the Ohio's bank with him, holding on to the long hickory stick, its line drifting in the current of the river. Then Kane's friend, Big Beaver, came paddling down the river, pulling ashore when he saw them. She had soon seen that her company wasn't necessary, as the two men started talking trapping and hunting.

She had left them to go searching for spring greens, commonly called "garden sass," consisting of dock, poke, dandelion, sheep sorrel, and lamb's quarter. How she and Kane had relished their first mess of fresh greens after the long winter! They were like a tonic, bringing fresh, strong blood to their veins.

D'lise glanced down the hill to watch Kane. Today he was laying a solid rock foundation for the cabin. For two days they had scoured the area, collecting rocks, lugging them to the spot they had chosen for the new cabin. They needed a lot of them, for the new place would have three rooms—a family room, bedroom, and kitchen, the kitchen being off to one side, giving the cabin an L-shape.

She hugged her arms. She couldn't wait for the walls to start going up. "Next week," Kane had said as they ate breakfast. He already had the doorsills hewed, ready to be placed on the foundation, and all the logs were notched. She had helped there, wielding a sharp little hatchet, slicing off the smaller limbs on the tree trunks. She and Kane had worked so hard, two nights had passed without their making love.

Watching Kane move about, shaping the twelve-inch

wall, there came the familiar catch to her breath, the increased beat of her heart. She smiled serenely. If she were to join him, give him a sleepy look from beneath her lashes, his gray eyes would turn stormy, and before she knew it he'd have her on her back, her skirt and petticoat up around her waist, his fingers ripping at the laces of his buckskins.

Why not? she thought, rising from the stump and stretching like a cat. So what if they spent the afternoon making love in the woods?

Chapter Seventeen

It had taken Kane two weeks to split two-inch puncheons for the cabin's floor, and another week to split the shingles for the roof. D'lise stood at his shoulder now, surveying all the hard work he had done.

A smile of anticipation curved her lips. Today the cabin would start going up, and she would do her share of the work by helping Kane to lift the logs, to match up their notches. When the walls became too high for either of them to reach, their neighbors would come to help them. The wives would come, too, each bringing a dish of something they had baked or roasted.

A cabin-building, old Tom had told her, was part work, part play-time. It was turned into a kind of party with lots to eat and plenty to drink once all the work was done. The men never drank while working, he'd said. A man had to be alert as he lifted the logs and heaved them into place. If he didn't have his wits about him, he could drop a log and hurt a man, maybe kill him if the log fell on his head.

"Well," Kane said, smiling down at D'lise, "are you ready to get started?" She nodded and they walked over to the stack of logs waiting for them. As they positioned log after log, the sun rose in the sky and grew hot. Sweat ran in rivulets down their faces and soaked the backs of their clothes. When they stopped work for the noon meal, the cabin walls stood about three feet high.

They ate thick sandwiches of cold beef, drank a cup of coffee, then went back to work. The sun was close to the treeline when the structure became too high for D'lise to reach any farther. She rubbed her aching arms. "I guess that's as far as we can go alone."

Kane nodded and took his shirt off a tree branch. "While you make supper, I'll ride over to the Patton farm and tell David that we're ready for some help. He'll pass the word to our other neighbors."

"Oh, I hope they'll come tomorrow," D'lise exclaimed. "I can't wait for the cabin to be finished."

Kane grinned at her, half amused, half indulgent. There were times when she made him feel like a doting father, ready to give her anything she wanted. "I'll tell David you'll go into a decline if he and the men aren't over here tomorrow morning at the crack of dawn."

Her trilling laughter followed him as he made for the opposite hill where their neighbor lived.

Back at the one-room cabin where D'lise had known every emotion—pain, bafflement, love, understanding, trust—she paused a moment to look at her garden before starting their supper. Long rows of tiny green plants were pushing up through the soil. Jason had finished the fence just in time. In this heavy loam, the plants would be a foot high in no time, very tempting to the many deer in the forest.

Oh, Auntie, she thought, *I hope you are aware of how happy I am!*

"I must say, D'lise," Sarah Patton began from her seat on a stump, "Kane sure is buildin' you a fine place. All of Piney Ridge is talkin' about it. Nobody would have thought a year ago that wild wolf would ever marry and settle down, let alone build a cabin practically by himself. Most trappers are lazy when it comes to doin' anything but running their traplines in the winter. In the summer they hang around the tavern, fraternizin' with the whores."

"I think any man would change his ways for D'lise," Ellen Travis said, smiling fondly at D'lise. The other women laughed in a nice way when her face turned red at Ellen's compliment. She was thankful when her friend exclaimed, "Look, the walls are up!" taking the attention away from her.

All that was left to do now was put on the roof, hang the two doors, chink in between the logs, and set the glass in the windows. Mr. Davis, the soon-to-become grandfather, had already built the fireplaces and chimneys.

The last spike was driven into the peak of the cabin, and the men scrambled to the ground. Brown jugs of ale had been chilling in the icy water of the spring in back of the cabin, and they all made a beeline to the small cave from which the clear water flowed. Corks popped and toasts were made to Kane and D'lise's new home. Buck Thomas went to his wagon and returned with a fiddle and a banjo. Waving everyone forward, he led the way into the Devlins' roofless parlor, and handing his son the banjo, he tucked the fiddle under his chin. When a rollicking tune rang out, Jacob Bellows grabbed Claudie around the waist, and much hopping and jumping began. Samuel bowed to Ellen and they joined the dancing. Other husbands and wives took to the floor, and soon everyone was dancing, including the children—everyone but Kane, D'lise, and old Tom.

Kane looked at D'lise, a smiling query in his eyes. She nodded, and he swung her out onto the floor, lifting her so high her skirts swirled past her knees. Tom watched them a minute, then, picking up an empty jug, joined the musicians and began blowing in it to make a tune.

The party-making lasted until the sun was a red ball in the west. The women gathered up their empty pots, pans, and dishes, and herded their youngsters into wagons, while those old enough to ride climbed onto their mounts. D'lise and Kane stood in the doorless doorway waving and calling their thanks as horses and conveyances took off in different directions, the men singing loudly, the women shouting for them to shut their stupid traps.

"You know, Kane, I think the single girls like me, even if I did steal the most handsome bachelor in the hills away from them." D'lise smiled up at Kane as they climbed the few yards to the old cabin.

Kane tightened his arm around her waist and gave her a mischievous grin. "You think so, huh? What if I was tell you that they're only pretendin', that each and every one of them is plannin' your demise."

D'lise jabbed him in the ribs with her elbow. "They are not!"

D'lise had just finished straightening up the cabin and had stepped outside to inspect her rosebush for new growth when old Tom came riding up. "Good morning, Tom," she called, walking up to the mount. "Are you going to the village or have you come to visit?''

Tom shook his head. "Neither. I thought you might like to go with me green-huntin'. They'd taste awful good with beans and ham for supper.'' He pointed to a small pail hanging from the saddle. "Maybe we'll find somethin' for dessert too.''

"I'd like that just fine. I'll go saddle Beauty.''

Twenty minutes later, Tom pulled in his mount and pointed to a long, narrow meadow. "Nature's garden,'' he said. "Here we'll find dandelion, lamb's quarter, cress, wild onions, pepper grass, and wild lettuce. If we're lucky, we might even find some wild strawberries.''

They dismounted and started walking through the wild garden patch. Tom handed D'lise a knife and ordered, "Get busy.''

"But what am I to put the greens in?'' D'lise asked.

"Hell, I never thought of that.'' Tom chewed thoughtfully on the wad of tobacco that formed a bulge in his cheek. Then he looked at D'lise hopefully. "Iffen you don't mind, we could use your petticoat.''

"My petticoat?'' D'lise gave him a wide-eyed stare.

"Sure, why not. Iffen it gets dirty, you can wash it, can't you?''

"Well, yes,'' D'lise answered, if a little reluctantly.

"Well, get it off, girl, and let's get busy. I wouldn't be surprised if we don't get some rain before nightfall.''

Within half an hour D'lise's petticoat held enough greens for both Devlin's and Spears's suppers and they were working their way home. D'lise could see Kane on the roof of the new building, almost finished with the shingling. She turned her head to say to Tom, "Let's stop by the cabin and see how Kane is coming along,'' then snapped her mouth shut with an angry frown.

She had recognized Raven approaching the building,

calling out something to Kane. Kane lifted a hand to her, then a minute later he stood up and walked along the roof to where a ladder leaned against the building and descended it to the ground. Two red spots appeared on D'lise's cheeks when he followed Raven inside the cabin.

What was that woman doing, hanging around Kane again? And how dare he take the woman into their new home? She wished she could stay until Raven left, see how long she remained in the cabin with Kane, but Tom would think it strange if she stood there like a knot on a log, staring at the cabin.

She glanced at the old man from the corner of her eye. Had he seen the Indian woman enter the building with Kane? She saw that he hadn't. He had left her side and was digging under a tree farther on, probably looking for the "sang" he talked about so much. She hurried after him, calling out, "Let's get a move on, Tom. I have to start supper."

Raven, following Kane through the cabin, pretending an interest in the things he pointed out to her, glanced through a window and saw D'lise wheel and walk away. She was ready to leave now. She had accomplished what she had come here for—to raise suspicions in the white woman's mind.

All the while that D'lise went about preparing supper, washing the greens, peeling potatoes, and setting the table, she kept seeing in her mind Kane and Raven entering the cabin. Her cabin. Were they still there? What were they doing?

She tried to ignore the hateful little voice that suggested slyly, *Maybe that's not the only time she's been to see him. There have been plenty of times when Kane has been alone, times when she could come to the cabin.*

"You just hush up." The sharply uttered words made

Scrag and the hound look at her curiously. "Kane gave me his word he'd have nothing more to do with that woman. When he comes home he'll tell me why she was there, how it was all innocent."

Time had never passed so slowly for D'lise as she waited for her husband to come home. Dusk was turning into night and she had lit a candle when Kane walked into the cabin. It was all she could do not to throw herself into his arms, demand why he was so late coming home—and what was Raven doing in their new home.

Instead, she asked with a smile, "Did you finish the roof?"

"That I did." Kane grabbed her to him and planted a hard kiss on her lips. "Tomorrow we start chinking between the logs, and then we'll move in." He released her and she brought the kettle of hot water from the fireplace and filled the basin for him to wash up in.

Move what in? D'lise wondered as she put supper on the table. This table and the two rockers? The bed was attached to the wall and couldn't be moved.

When they were having coffee, D'lise brought up the subject of furniture. "You'll have to build us a new bunk before we can move in."

"Oh, it won't take me long to knock one together," Kane answered. "In the meantime, we can cuddle up on a pallet."

At the wistful look that came into D'lise's eyes, Kane was tempted to tell her of the surprise he'd planned for her—that at this very minute, somewhere on the Ohio was a flatboat carrying furniture all the way from Boston. Ellen Travis had helped him to choose it from a catalog she'd borrowed from Samuel Majors. The pieces would be delivered to his store, then brought to their cabin by wagon when he gave the word.

D'lise suppressed a little sigh. If she had to sleep on the floor for a while, it wouldn't be the first time, and she would have three rooms to move about in, something unheard of as far as she could remember. She only vaguely remembered her father and mother's home.

She looked at Kane from under her lashes. "Did any of our neighbors stop by to give you a hand today?"

"No. I expect they're all busy gettin' in their crops. Of course, my lazy trapper friends give me a wide berth these days." A wry smile curved his lips as he mused on his rough and rowdy friends. They would fight for him to their last breath, but would run a mile to keep from helping to build a cabin. That sort of manual labor was beneath them. He understood that. Only a short while ago, he'd have felt the same way.

He looked at D'lise with loving eyes. The things a man would do when he fell in love.

D'lise missed the tender look. She was staring into her coffee, waiting for him to tell her that Raven had visited him. She had given him the opening, why hadn't he taken it? If he had nothing to hide, why didn't he come right out and say that he'd had one visitor, his old lover?

It became evident that the subject of Raven wasn't going to come up as Kane finished his coffee, then lit the lantern to light his way to the barn. "I'm gonna go bring the stock in from the pasture," he said at the door. "I heard the hungry squall of a cat as I came up the hill before."

Later, in bed, memories of when Kane would take Raven to the barn at night, came to devil D'lise. Although tonight he had as usual drawn her into his arms, he hadn't made love to her. After a quick kiss that had landed under her ear, he had dropped off to sleep. Listening to his steady breathing, she tried to convince herself that he was too tired. But as she finally drifted off to sleep, that aggravating inner voice of hers taunted, *He was never too tired before. Could it be that a certain squaw overworked him before he got home?*

D'lise's sleep was fitful, filled with images of her husband and Raven together. But when the sun began to peek over the hills, the bad dreams were forgotten. She came awake to a hungry pulling on her breast.

Whispering his name with a soft sigh, she stroked her hand down his flat stomach and curled her fingers around an arousal so hard and firm, her lower body leapt in anticipation. What she had been denied last night she would receive double this morning.

The sun was quite high when the Devlins got around to chinking their new home.

Chapter Eighteen

Since daylight, and for the past hour, D'lise had toured
her new home. Her slender body could hardly contain its
happiness as she went from room to room, then did it all
over again.

She had paused half a dozen times in front of the fireplace in the main room to run her hands over the mantel
of polished oak. Elton Davis had done a superb job of
building the fireplace. It was large, built of fieldstone, and
open at both ends. It would be deeply appreciated this
winter when it threw heat in three directions. She planned
that she and Kane would spend many cozy nights before
it, their stockinged feet propped on the wide hearth.

There was a window with shutters in each room, a little
larger than most in the neighborhood. She hugged her
arms contentedly as she moved across the wooden floors.
How good it felt to walk on floor boards again and not

have to worry that snakes might be lurking in corners—
her big fear in the old cabin.

D'lise paused in the doorway of the kitchen and slowly
ran her gaze over the room that was most important to
her. Here she would spend most of her daylight hours.

In a back corner was a trapdoor in the floor, leading
down to a cellar Kane had dug, then lined with rocks. He
had directed the stream from the spring to run beneath the
building before making its way back outside to wend its
way into a deep gully and disappear. He had built shelves
to hold crocks of milk and butter and whatever else she
might want to store on them, and there were bins to hold
vegetables and fruits that would last through the winter
months.

She switched her gaze to the opposite corner, where a
ladder led to the loft above. There she could store things,
hang her strips of green beans to dry from the rafters, dry
off cut corn and sliced apples and mushrooms, as well as
the herbs, barks, and roots she intended to gather from
the forest.

And last, D'lise looked at the small fireplace, built only
for cooking purposes. Kane had placed iron hooks on a
crossbar from which pots and kettles could be swung over
the fire, and on one side was a bricked-in oven. Her lips
spread in a wide smile as she thought of all the delicious
meals she could cook for Kane.

While D'lise was gloating over her new home, Kane
leaned against the railing fronting the cabin, watching for
the wagonload of furniture that should be arriving any
minute. Old Tom had told him privately yesterday that it
had arrived and was sitting in Samuel's store room. He
was on tenterhooks anticipating the surprise on D'lise's
face when it arrived.

Kane started when D'lise walked quietly up beside him and laid a hand on his shoulder. Turning around, he reached an arm around her waist and pulled her to rest between his spread legs. "Is there anything special you would like for the cabin?" he asked, then waited for her to give him a long list of furniture.

She surprised him by saying, "I would like a spinning wheel for making thread and yarn, a loom for weaving cloth and rugs, and a churn for making butter."

He smoothed back the curls a light breeze had blown across her face. He must be the luckiest man in Piney Ridge, he thought. "Will you be content with a kitchen table that has one leg too short, two benches full of splinters, and two wobbly rockin' chairs?"

D'lise shrugged. "I've become used to them. Anyhow, I figure that when you can afford it you'll buy an occasional piece of furniture."

Kane drew her up against his chest, murmuring in her hair, "You're a wonder, D'lise Devlin. I don't deserve you."

He was gripped with guilt. As his wife, D'lise had every right to know their financial situation. He had always made good money trapping furs, and his expenditures had been slight—food, moderate drinking of spirits, a couple of sets of new buckskins every spring. Of course an equal amount of money had gone to the whores whose services he bought on a regular basis.

Still, that had only made a small dent in the monies he had hidden in Snowy's stall. And that was not counting the five bales of furs he'd trapped over the winter and sold to Buck at the fur post. The money from them had paid for the furniture he'd ordered.

There was no better time than now to tell D'lise about their finances, he thought, let her know that she hadn't married a poor man. He held her away from him, opened his mouth to speak, then paused to listen. He grinned at the sound of creaking wagon wheels.

D'lise heard them too. "I wonder who could be up so early in the morning?" She shielded her eyes against the sun's bright rays. "I don't recognize the vehicle, but old Tom is driving the team and—why, that looks like Samuel sitting next to him. Do you suppose they're coming here?"

"I wouldn't be surprised." Kane stood up and, draping an arm across her shoulders, guided her down the two steps just as the wagon rolled to a stop in front of them.

"Good morning, folks." Samuel leapt lightly to the ground and walked toward them.

"Good morning, Samuel," D'lise answered, a smile in her voice. Kane only nodded in the storekeeper's direction. He still didn't trust the good-looking man from Boston. He knew in his heart that, given the chance, the man would take D'lise away from him.

He was quite friendly to Tom, though, and moved close to the wagon so that the old man could lean a hand on his shoulder in his painful climb from the wagon. When he saw a flicker of pain cross the wrinkled face, he asked quietly, "Your rheumatism actin' up today, Tom?"

"Yeah, dad-blast it. I wish this rain that's been threatenin' would come and get it over with. The humidity is sure hard on my bones."

Kane broke off their conversation when D'lise's merry laugh rang out. He glowered at her and Samuel standing on the porch, sharing something that didn't include him. He gave D'lise a cold look when she smiled at him, and after giving him a curious scrutiny, she turned to look at Tom.

"Where are you taking this fine furniture, Tom? Do we

295

have new neighbors I don't know about?''

"Well, not exactly." Tom looked helplessly at Kane. "It is for a new cabin though."

Kane was practically gnashing his teeth. Nothing was going the way he'd planned. Why did Samuel Majors have to come along with Tom, shining up to D'lise in his usual fashion?

His tone was harsh when he muttered, "The furniture is for you, D'lise."

"For me!" D'lise gasped, her hands clasping together at her breasts, her eyes wide as she gazed at her husband. When he only stared back at her, stony-eyed, she smiled nervously. "You shouldn't tease like that, Kane. I almost had a heart attack."

"He's not teasin', girl," old Tom snorted. "Kane ordered the furniture away back. It come all the way from Boston. Cost him a purty nickel too."

"Oh, Kane." D'lise ignored the cold look and threw herself at him. When her arms wrapped themselves around his waist and she planted a warm kiss on his lips, Kane couldn't hold out against her any longer. Besides, if she cared for Majors, she wouldn't be acting this way with him. His arms came around her and he hugged her tightly before releasing her.

Smiling down into her eager face, he said, "Well, woman, get on in the cabin and show us where you want everything put."

The first thing that was lugged in was the large frame for a double bed. It was set up in the corner D'lise pointed out; then Kane and Samuel carried in a straw tick and a feather mattress. Tom carried in two pillows.

D'lise was too choked up to express her joy when a heavy dresser with a mirror, and a tall wardrobe followed.

Never in all her daydreaming had she imagined having anything like this.

But there was more to come. Her eyes almost popped out of her head when two highly polished rocking chairs were carried in, padded and covered with a bright blue flowered material. She could only *oooh* and *ahhh* when Samuel placed a matching table between them, and Kane brought in two deacon benches and set them facing each other on either side of the fireplace.

Tears flowed down her cheeks when a sturdy pine table and four chairs were carried in. When Kane and Samuel carried in a wide china cabinet, she sat down on one of the chairs and, laying her head on the table, sobbed her joy.

"Well," Samuel joked, "I do believe she likes everything, Kane. What do you think?"

"I'd say she's overcome," Kane said softly, pulling D'lise out of the chair and drawing her into his arms.

"I never . . . never expected it," D'lise hiccuped into his shoulder. "I never had . . ."

Outside, the horses moved restlessly in their traces. "We've gotta get goin'," Tom broke in on D'lise. "From the sound of it, she's gonna blubber the rest of the day and I ain't got the time to stand around and listen to it."

The two younger men hid their amusement. They knew how fond the old fellow was of D'lise, and that it bothered him to see her cry. D'lise knew it too, and with a watery chuckle she raised her head from Kane's shoulder.

"I'm all finished, Tom." She fished Kane's handkerchief from his breast pocket and wiped her eyes.

"We gotta go anyway." Tom limped to the kitchen door that led outside. "I've got work waitin' for me at home."

While Kane followed Tom outside and again stood beside the wagon, offering the support of his broad shoulder, Samuel lingered in the doorway having a last few words with D'lise. "Ellen said to tell you that she'd be over tomorrow afternoon to visit. She said you lovebirds would want to be alone today."

Kane looked up in time to see D'lise blush and smile from beneath lowered lids. Jealousy ripped through him. What was that bastard saying to her? Only Tom's clutching fingers on his shoulder as he climbed into the wagon kept him from springing onto the porch and smashing the handsome storekeeper in his smiling face. When Tom finally got settled, Samuel was climbing in beside him. Tom snapped the reins over the team, and the wagon rolled away.

D'lise still stood in the doorway, a happy look on her face. It disappeared when Kane, his face a stormcloud, brushed past her, knocking her against the door frame. What had gotten into him? D'lise chewed her bottom lip worriedly, then followed him inside.

"He just doesn't give up, does he?" Kane spun around to glare at her. "I wonder why? He must get some encouragement from you."

D'lise stared at him aghast. Was he talking about Samuel? Certainly not old Tom, she reasoned. But neither should he mention Samuel in that tone. Samuel was her dear friend and nothing more.

Impatience and anger grew inside her. Resentment sparking in her eyes, she said coolly, "I give Samuel no more encouragement than you do Raven."

"Hah! So you claim." Kane kicked out at one of the new chairs, sending it skittering across the floor to fall on its side.

"You stop kicking my furniture around!" D'lise yelled, hurrying to pick the chair up and put it back in place.

"I'll kick anything I damn well please," Kane shot back, slamming a fist on the table. "I paid for the damn things, and if I want to smash every piece of it, I'll do it."

Fear of Kane washed through D'lise for the first time since knowing him. She backed warily away from the anger in his eyes. Would he smash her next? The sharp memory of the beatings her aunt had endured stabbed her brain.

"Please, God," she prayed silently, "don't let Kane demean himself that way."

Jealousy still drove Kane, prodding him to strike out at D'lise with hurtful words and accusations. But the stinging words never came. The look on her face, the dread in her eyes, stilled his tongue. The one thing he had sworn he would never do had happened. In his rage, he had brought back that scared, haunted look she had worn the time he'd rescued her from Rufus Enger.

He held out a conciliatory hand to her and knew a bitter pain when she cringed away from him. He dropped his hand, only regret inside him now. His wife thought that he was going to strike her. He stood a moment, gazing helplessly at her averted face, willing her to look at him, to see the apology in his eyes. When she continued to look away from him, he turned and left the cabin, closing the door quietly behind him.

A relieved sigh whispered through D'lise's lips. She rushed to the window and watched Kane climb the hill to the old cabin. She frowned when he passed the shabby building and continued on to the barn. Why was he going there? she wondered, then whispered, "Oh, no!"

Kane had ridden his stallion through the wide barn door and was thundering toward the village. Had he left her for good? She stood a minute, tears stinging the backs of

299

her eyes, then turned back to the kitchen, telling herself that he would be back when he cooled down and realized how foolish he was to be jealous of Samuel.

Although all her elation over the unexpected furniture was gone, D'lise began sorting through the crate of dishes and cooking utensils she and Kane had brought to the new cabin. It didn't take long to place the few pewter plates and mugs in the china cabinet, and she thought how lost they looked in the big piece of furniture. It took less time to put away the pots and skillets. The big cast-iron pot she cooked beans, soup, and stew in, she hung from the crane over the fireplace.

The kitchen taken care of, D'lise went next to the bedroom, carrying bed linens over her arm. As she made up the bed, she wondered if her husband would be sharing it with her tonight—or any other night.

For the rest of the day, D'lise moved about the cabin, her face drawn as she stared out any window that gave her a view of the trail leading to the village. Each time she found it empty. There was no big stallion carrying a handsome man home.

When the clock struck four, D'lise started a fire up against the brick oven. She felt sure that Kane would return home in time for supper, and to show him that she wanted to make peace, she would bake him an apple pie.

While the pastry baked, she sliced thick slabs of ham from a smoked hindquarter and peeled a panful of potatoes. She would mash them and make red gravy to go over them. Kane loved red gravy.

The hour hand on the clock was nearing six, the pie was cooling in the open window, and the rest of the meal was ready to be placed on the table. All was in readiness for the man who hadn't come yet. And to add to D'lise flagging spirits, the dark clouds that had been gathering all day had turned black and threatening, bringing on an early dusk. And there was the stock still to be taken care of.

She took the lantern down from the wall and, lifting its chimney, lit the candle inside it. "Come on, Hound," she called to the dog, "let's go do the chores your master should be doing."

The lantern light threw shadows on the ground, leaping and swaying ahead of D'lise as she climbed the hill. A wind had come up and now moaned in the pines, and from away on a ridge there drifted the dismal yowl of a wolf. She stepped up her pace. Never had the wilderness, the loneliness, gripped her so.

In the barn, D'lise made short work of milking Spider, pitching hay to her and to Beauty, and scattering corn for her hens. She didn't take the time to gather any eggs that might have been laid that day.

Nevertheless, for all her hurrying, when she stepped out of the barn she found that night had fallen, dark and starless with lightning zig-zagging across the sky. It was going to storm, and soon. A deafening crash of thunder shook the hills and she broke into a run, arriving at the cabin just as the storm broke in a wild fury.

D'lise slammed the door behind her and Hound, and hurried to close all the shutters as the rain came down in torrents. She sat down in one of the rockers, trying to ignore the almost continuous glare of lightning that that pierced its way through the narrow cracks of the shutters, followed by peals of thunder reverberating through the hills.

Where was Kane? she wondered. No doubt somewhere with Raven, all cozy out of the rain, without a thought of his wife cowering every time the thunder crashed.

A sneaking suspicion had entered D'lise's mind as she

milked the cow. Had Kane deliberately started an argument, giving him an excuse to ride away, to search out Raven? She didn't want to believe that, but the thought wouldn't go away. He couldn't be that jealous of Samuel simply talking to her.

After a couple of hours, the wind died down and the thunder rumbled in the distance; the rain fell gently. The clock struck the quarter hour to ten, and D'lise gave up hope that Kane was coming home. She dropped the bar on both doors, picked up the candle holder, and walked to the bedroom. She stripped to the skin, then pulled a lightweight gown over her head.

I'll never get to sleep, she thought, sinking down into the feather mattress. The welcoming warmth it would give on cold winter nights was smothering in the heat of late June. Tomorrow she would take it off and store it in the loft until cold weather . . . if she was still here.

And just as annoying, a pine branch outside her window tapped and scratched on the glass. Then Scrag, banished from her bed by Kane, came to curl up beside her. His loud purring took away some of the emptiness where Kane should be lying, and her eyes grew heavy with sleep.

The gallop Kane had put the stallion to slowed to a canter, then became a trot. Kane's rage had left him before he left the cabin and now only jealousy and self-contempt remained. He stared moodily ahead, seeing nothing, hearing nothing. He was beginning to learn, to understand the helpless love his uncle had held for his whorish wife. All these years he'd called the man spineless, accused him of having no self-respect, and now his uncle's nephew was following in his footsteps.

Just like his uncle Buck, he had married a woman much

younger than himself, and one of exceptional beauty. All those years when he had deliberately chosen plain, sometimes downright ugly women, had all been for nothing.

"God, I don't want to love her," Kane whispered, his throat constricting, "but I do. She is like a disease that won't let up, always eatin' away at me."

The village came in view and he urged the stallion into a gallop. He wanted to get to Buck's tavern and pour whiskey down his throat until his brain was numb. Maybe then he'd forget the wife whose beauty drew other men to her.

His trapper friends sat on the wide porch that fronted the fur post, lazing away the day, when Kane drew rein and dismounted. "Hey, stranger," someone called as he flipped the reins over a long hitching post. "We ain't seen you in a new moon. The little wife sure is keepin' you home. She got you tied to her apron strings, friend?"

When Kane turned from the stallion and faced the loungers, those who would have taken up the ribbing snapped their mouths shut. Kane's face rivaled the dark clouds building overhead. It was clear he had something on his mind—he was dark and brooding.

"I was only joshin' you, Kane," the man who had spoken hurried to say as he slapped Kane on the back. "It's good to see you again. You got time to have a drink with us?"

"I got all day," Kane growled, and led the way into the tavern end of the post.

"Well, howdy, Kane." Buck Thomas grinned at Kane as he and his friends bellied up to the bar. "What brings you in? Have you finished buildin' that new cabin for D'lise? The last time she was in town, that's all she talked about."

303

Kane's head jerked up, his eyes narrowing. "When was D'lise in here?"

Buck gave him a startled look. "Your wife wasn't in here, man. You oughta know better than that. I ran into her and Ellen Travis comin' out of Majors's store one day. We chatted a while, and I asked her how my kid was doin' on that fence. She said he done a fine job; then she rattled on about the cabin you was buildin' her."

Kane felt foolish, and the red that crept up to his hairline gave the fact away. Of course D'lise would never enter a tavern. He ordered a bottle of whiskey and some glasses for his companions. As he filled his own glass, then pushed the bottle down to be grabbed by the trapper at the end of the bar, he asked himself why D'lise hadn't mentioned seeing Buck. He remembered the day two weeks ago when Ellen came by, inviting D'lise to her home for luncheon, saying that Sarah Patton and Claudie Jacobs would be there also.

His fingers turned white, he gripped the glass so hard. Had it all been a hoax, an excuse for Majors to see D'lise? His heart gave a painful beat. Had his wife been in on the deception also? If not, why hadn't she mentioned seeing Buck? Was it because she hadn't spent all her time at Ellen's, maybe none of it? Had she been with the store-keeper all that time?

Kane downed the whiskey in his glass, then splashed it full again.

The tavern whores, who had been inching closer and closer to the bar, wondering if any of the trappers—especially Kane—could be coaxed across the street to their quarters, decided it was worth trying.

"Hi there, Devlin." One woman sidled up to Kane. "I've missed you all these past months. Did you finally get lonesome for Corrie?"

"How you been, Corrie?" Kane hung a loose arm across the woman's plump shoulders.

"Like I said, I been missin' you." She leaned into his lean frame. "Everyone's been sayin' you're so wrapped up in your bride that we won't be seein' you around anymore." She laid a hand on his hip. "But I knew better. I told the girls that you'd miss your rowdy lovin' and come visit me again."

When Corrie's fingers started inching toward Kane's crotch, he removed his arm and turned his body back to face the bar, dislodging her hand. "Look, Corrie," he said, almost overcome from her body odor and the strong perfume she had liberally patted on her shoulders and between her heavy breasts, "right now I want to visit with my friends. I'll talk with you some more later on, all right?"

"Sure, Devlin," Corrie agreed, reading what she wanted to in his words—a promise to take her to bed later on. "When you're ready, just go across the street and I'll be right behind you." She gave his arm a squeeze, then sat down at a table in a corner and crossed her legs, waiting for Kane to signal that he was ready for her.

The whore grew tired of waiting as the sun started its westward path, and Kane gave no hint of needing her soon. He and his friends had shoved two tables together and now sat talking about trapping as they passed a bottle among them. Corrie noted that Kane drank more than the others, and she frowned.

"A few more drinks and he ain't gonna be worth spit in bed," she complained to the others.

"I don't think he ever had in mind to bed you," one of the whores taunted Corrie. "If he did, he'd have done it by now."

"That's a lie, Maybelle," Corrie snapped indignantly.

"You're just jealous 'cause he never took you to bed."

Maybelle shrugged her shoulders indifferently. "I took that as a compliment, seein' as how he always favored ugly whores."

Corrie jumped to her feet, her fingers curved into claws, ready to go for Maybelle's hair. She caught Buck's cold stare then, and sat back down. The fur post owner allowed no fights between the whores. They either got along with each other or they left. Maybelle rose and sauntered over to the bar and struck up a conversation with the village blacksmith. A few minutes later, he was escorting her outside. Before the door closed behind them, a streak of lightning lit up the sky.

Seeing it, Buck frowned. It was almost as dark as night outside, and before long, rain was going to be pouring down on the hills. He looked at Kane. *Damn, but he's drunk,* he thought. Drunker than Buck had ever seen him. Would he be able to sit the stallion, get home before the deluge that was on its way?

He walked over to the table, hoping that the big trapper wasn't in a quarrelsome mood. D'lise would be worried if he didn't get home soon.

Kane's brain was so numb with drink that he gave Buck no trouble at all. He agreed with a loose grin that he had to get home to his wife, and let Buck lead him outside and help him climb onto Snowy's back.

The stallion knew the way home and, wanting his supper, started out at a fast walk, as if knowing also that his rider would fall off his back if he were to increase his pace. Buck watched them out of sight, shaking his head, wondering what had set Kane off. He doubted that he had come to the village just because he missed his friends.

The reins clasped loosely in his hands, his chin almost on his chest, Kane was only vaguely aware of the lightning and the risen wind. He was completely unaware of the Indian pony that followed him at a distance. He was half asleep when Snowy stopped abruptly and snorted.

He stared owlishly at the barn, the big door the wind had blown open. "Looks like we made it home, huh, fellow," he muttered, more or less falling out of the saddle and fumbling with the belly cinches before finally dragging the saddle off the stallion's back. He dropped it to the ground, then managed to slip the bit from Snowy's mouth. The mount trotted inside the barn, and Kane, leaving the riding gear on the ground, staggered his way to the old cabin. He fell across the bed, wondering where D'lise was.

He didn't hear the cabin door open quietly, the footsteps that approached the bed.

Chapter Nineteen

D'lise came awake to bird song outside her window. Goodness, what time was it? she wondered. She turned her head to see if Kane had overslept also. When she saw the empty space beside her, yesterday's events washed over her like a douse of cold water.

They'd had a terrible row, and Kane had ridden off to the village—or to find Raven.

A pained look came into her eyes. Evidently he had found his Indian lover. She sat up in bed, a flicker of hope in her breast. Maybe he was rolled up in his blankets in the main room.

She stood in the connecting doorway, the light going out of her eyes. There was no long body sleeping there.

With drooping spirits she went into the kitchen, built a fire in the small fireplace, and put a pot of coffee to brewing. She told herself that if she kept to her regular routine, Kane would arrive to eat breakfast with her.

Keeping to her customary procedure, she washed her face in the battered basin, then brought her brush from the bedroom and stepped out on the small kitchen porch to groom her hair.

As she pulled the bristles through her curls, making her scalp tingle, she breathed deeply of the rain-cleaned air. The rain would bring out the wrinkled and pitted morel mushrooms. She would spend the morning looking for them.

When D'lise had brushed all the tangles out of her hair and tied it back with a ribbon, she remained on the porch a while, taking in the beauty of her surroundings. She glanced down at the old cabin and was about to look away when her heart began to beat so hard it took her breath away. Raven, her long black hair unbound and tangled on her shoulders, had just stepped through the cabin door, Kane coming along behind her. The Indian woman stood a moment, saying something to Kane, then climbed onto a pony D'lise hadn't noticed tied to a tree. As she rode away, Kane turned back into the cabin.

D'lise's heartbeat was so painful she couldn't catch her breath for several seconds. In a bitter rush of memory, she recalled the time she'd seen Raven at the half-finished cabin, remembered Kane taking her inside, recalled that he had never mentioned the woman's visit.

Heartsick, she took a pail off the wall. Although she should go milk Spider, she was going to go look for the mushrooms first. Should she run into Kane right now, she might attack him.

She had just called Hound to her when she heard the footsteps on the porch. Her eyes widened in alarm. It was Kane! She ran to the door, but before she could bolt it, the latch clicked.

* * *

Kane awakened with a groan, a hundred little hammers pounding in his head, the hot rays of the sun burning like a fiery torch in his eyes. His lips were dry, his tongue sticking to the roof of his mouth.

He ran a palm over his whiskered jaw and frowned as he realized he'd slept in his buckskins. He turned his head to ask D'lise how that had come about—and froze.

It wasn't his wife's soft, sweet-smelling curls spilling over his chest, but straight, coarse hair, rank with the odor of bear grease. He shot up in bed like a startled deer. What in the hell was Raven doing in his bed, and buck-naked at that?

In that same moment, he became aware that his trousers were unlaced, his flaccid member lying exposed. "Dear God," he muttered, "I must be havin' a nightmare." His gaze ran wildly around the small room. Where was D'lise in this crazy dream?

His throbbing brain finally began to operate, and some of yesterday's events came back to him—his angry ride to the village, the heavy drinking with his friends. He vaguely remembered being put astride the stallion, the reins shoved into his hands. But after that it was all pretty blurry. How he had ended up in the old cabin, and with Raven, he had no idea.

Kane's face turned a pasty gray. Good Lord, had he done more than sleep with her? He looked down at his manhood as if finding the answer there. He hurriedly pulled the buckskins together and laced them tightly. Now to get Raven out of here, and pray God D'lise didn't see her leaving.

His hand wasn't gentle when he shook the Indian awake. When she blinked open her eyes, he demanded harshly, "What in the hell are you doin' in my bed?"

Raven trailed a dirt-rimmed finger down his cheek.

"You know what I'm doing here," she answered. "Don't you remember the good time we had last night?"

"I damn hell don't!" Kane brushed her hand away. "And I sure as hell didn't invite you into my bed," he bluffed, not knowing what had happened during the night.

"That is true." Raven nodded. "But when you found me here, you didn't turn me away. You were eager to know my body again."

"You lie," Kane gritted between his teeth. "Even dead drunk, I wouldn't want you in my bed again."

Raven's face darkened at the insult, and her eyes narrowed to angry slits. "You'll regret those words someday, squaw-man," she hissed vehemently, jumping out of bed and jerking the doe-skin tunic over her head.

Kane was right behind her when she started for the door. "Just what do you mean by that remark?" He grabbed at her arm and missed as Raven eluded him and stepped out onto the porch. "What are you plannin' in that schemin' mind of yours?" he demanded, stepping outside behind her.

"You'll just have to wait and see, won't you?" Raven sneered. Leaving the porch, she climbed onto the spotted pony's back and gave the little animal a hard thump of her heels. He sprang away into the woods.

Kane glanced down the hill at the new cabin, praying that D'lise hadn't seen Raven. His heart dropped to his stomach. His wife stood on the porch, staring up at him. As he called himself all manner of fool, she turned and walked into the cabin.

With a ragged sigh and a pounding head, Kane walked into the cabin, but almost immediately stepped back outside. Squaring his shoulders, he stepped off the porch. He might as well go and get it over with.

As Kane walked down the hill, he was assailed with

doubts. How was he to convince D'lise that he wasn't guilty of sleeping with Raven when he wasn't sure that he hadn't? He lifted the door latch, knowing that he was going to have to talk as he'd never talked before.

The door barely missed hitting D'lise as it opened. She stepped back, her features cold and pinched when Kane walked inside. "Look, D'lise," he began right off, "I know how it must look to you, but I can explain everything."

"Can you now?" D'lise's eyes shot scorn at him. "Even if I hadn't seen that slut leaving you, I can smell her on your body."

Her nose wrinkled and she sniffed the air. "I also smell cheap perfume and the body odor of whores on you." Her eyes ran over him with distaste, and Kane shrank from her scrutiny. He knew how he must look—whisker-stubbled jaw, messed-up hair, wrinkled buckskins—and he must smell like a whorehouse.

There was a tonelessness in D'lise's voice as she said, "Save your explanations. I've believed your lies before, but never again."

"But, D'lise, I have never lied to you," Kane said earnestly. "That damned Raven—"

He closed his mouth. D'lise had walked through the door, slamming it behind her. He banged a fist on the table in frustration and self-contempt. He had brought it all on himself through his jealousy and suspicions.

After Kane drank two cups of coffee, one right after the other, he went into the bedroom to get a change of clean clothes and gather up his shaving paraphernalia. It was no wonder D'lise had curled her nose at him. He couldn't stand his stench either. He'd go down to the branch, and in the process of cleansing his body maybe he could do the same thing with his mind, once and for all wash from his brain the distrust he so often felt for his wife.

He had learned a lesson this morning. Things weren't always as they appeared. In D'lise's eyes, he must look guilty as hell, but in his heart he felt sure nothing had gone on between him and Raven last night.

Kane stood in the bedroom doorway a moment, looking at the bed, the covers that had been thrown aside, the one pillow dented by D'lise's head. He knew it would carry the rose scent he always smelled in her hair. With a ragged sigh, he hurriedly snatched up what he needed, not wanting to smell up the room with his presence.

With Hound at her heels, D'lise walked toward a clump of maple trees, where she felt she could find the tasty morel mushrooms. The tears that had scorched her cheeks since leaving the cabin had eased her pain, but it was still there in a raw niche of her heart.

She guessed it would always be there, for it appeared Raven would always be a part of Kane's life. She wondered bleakly if Raven was the woman he really wished that he had married but hadn't because his friends wouldn't accept her.

A question she had asked herself so many times since entering into this marriage nagged her brain again. What could she do about the unhappy situation? Besides having no money, no place to go, she suspected that she was with child. Four mornings in a row she had lost her breakfast, and her breasts were sore lately.

No solution had come to her when she spotted the first growth of the little tree-shaped mushrooms. Ordering Hound to lie down beneath a tree, afraid his big feet would trample the tender fungi, she knelt down and began gathering the delicacies.

The morels were plentiful, and she soon had enough for supper, as well as plenty to dry in the loft for winter use. They would be delicious dropped into gravy.

She stood up, brushed off the knees of her skirt, and called to the hound. As she headed home, she didn't know whether she wanted Kane to be there or not. A part of her feared that he had moved back into the old cabin where Raven could visit him at will, while another part of her wondered if she could bear continuing to live with him. It would test her fortitude to endure his presence as if nothing had happened.

D'lise's unhappy musings were interrupted when she heard a rapid clip-clop behind her. A searing anger took hold of her when an Indian pony was pulled up beside her and Raven looked down at her, a smug smile on her lips.

"You're out early, Mrs. Devlin," she drawled. "Did you and your husband have a lover's spat?"

Keep walking, don't answer her, D'lise ordered herself. *She's trying to rile you, make you say something so that she can get in more digs.*

She almost broke her angry silence when, keeping pace with her, Raven said, "Perhaps you've noticed I've been gone for the last two months. I went to my village to visit my people." When D'lise made no response, only hurried along with her chin in the air, Raven sent her a sly look. "But I'm back now and ready to take up my life in the white man's world again."

Yes, D'lise thought, one white man's world. Kane Devlin's.

There was such a drumming in her ears that D'lise didn't know when the Indian grew tired of baiting her and ceased following her. The tears she wouldn't let fall burned her throat. Raven had more or less confirmed that she was picking up where she had left off with Kane. It was clear now why he had been so attentive to his wife for a while. His lover had been gone.

Her dark blue eyes turned almost black. God, but she would love to cut Kane's lying tongue out of his mouth! All this time he had pretended a jealousy of Samuel to cover up his feelings for Raven, and now he would use that pretended jealousy as an excuse to remove himself from his wife.

When D'lise arrived back at the cabin, she glanced up the hill at the old one. The glass that Kane had installed looked like an eye gazing at her in amusement, as if saying, "You never belonged here. You weren't really wanted."

She pulled her gaze away from the building, afraid she'd climb the hill and set fire to it. Kane would have to take his squaw somewhere else then. At least she wouldn't have to see them coming and going, see their light at night, see it go out, then lie in her lonely bed imagining Kane making love to Raven the way he had once done to her.

D'lise was about to enter the cabin, when from the corner of the building, she caught sight of a horse's tail swishing at flies. Which of their neighbors did it belong to? She walked alongside the cabin to look, and her mouth flew open as she saw two mounts and recognized them both. She had walked behind them, holding on to a plow, for hundreds of miles. What were Rufus Enger's horse and mule doing here?

She picked up the heavy stick she used for stirring her washing as it boiled over a fire. She was sure her uncle wasn't paying her and Kane a friendly visit. If he made one move toward her, she'd crack his skull.

D'lise hopped up on the porch, stood in the kitchen doorway, and stared. Sitting at the table, looking at her, half scared, half hopeful, sat David and Johnny, the two bound-boys. Kane sat with them, all three drinking coffee.

Chapter Twenty

"Hey, D'lise," the boys said in unison, their thin faces expressing uncertainty as to how she would welcome them. "I guess you're surprised to see us," David added, his grubby fingers gripped tightly around his coffee mug, as she continued to gape at them.

"My goodness, boys, you're the last two people I ever expected to see again." Ignoring Kane, D'lise sat down in the empty chair at the table. "You fellows aren't in trouble of any kind, are you?" She looked from one to the other, a frown worrying her forehead. "You didn't do anything to Rufus before you ran away, did you?"

Young Johnny shook his head vehemently, and David's denial was just as impassioned as he declared, "We didn't lay a hand on him, D'lise, I swear it."

"Then how in the world did you get away from that old devil? Did you steal the horse and mule while he was asleep?"

"Rufus Enger is dead, D'lise," Kane said quietly.

D'lise looked at Kane, noting that he had shaved and taken a bath. She looked back at David. "What happened, did he choke to death on his own venom?"

"Something like that." David grinned. "He got mad at the old mule for some reason and was lashing him somethin' terrible with a whip. Finally, ole Gray had had enough and he kicked Rufus in the head, almost took it off his shoulders."

"You didn't just go off and leave him, did you?" D'lise asked, afraid for them, afraid they might be accused of the brutal man's death.

"Oh no," David answered, while Johnny shook his head. "When I couldn't find any pulse and knew that he was dead, I sent Johnny to get our nearest neighbor, Mr. Sparrow—you remember him. When he got there, he could see that we didn't do it. Old Gray was still tied to the post, all bloody, and his hoofprint was on the side of Rufus's face and head.

"After the old varmint was buried, nobody wanted to take responsibility for us, so Mr. Sparrow told us to take Gray and Roany and just ride away." He ducked his head. "We been lookin' for you for over two weeks."

But after a second, David's head came up proudly. "We don't mean to sponge off you, D'lise." He looked at Kane. "We thought maybe you might need some help around your place. We're good workers."

The boys held their breath as they waited for Kane's answer, and so did D'lise. She couldn't believe what she was hearing when Kane said, "We can always find something for you boys to do. You can live up the hill in that old cabin." He added after a slight pause, "Of course you'll eat your meals with D'lise and me."

While David and Johnny were thanking Kane profusely, D'lise was mulling over his words. His last remarks told her that he would be staying here with her, and that if the boys occupied the old cabin, Raven wouldn't be moving in. Confusion muddled her brain. What was going on in Kane's conniving mind?

She'd have to wait and see, she guessed, standing up and pushing the chair back under the table. "I guess you boys are hungry. Kane can take you up the hill and settle you in while I make us some lunch."

"Thank you, D'lise," David said, looking ready to cry. And Johnny, trying to speak over the tears that choked his throat, finally gave up and threw his arms around her waist, hugging her tightly, his head buried on her chest. She put her arms around his thin shoulders and stroked his blond head. Johnny had been denied affection for a long time, and she knew he needed it desperately.

After a moment she raised his head and said softly, "Before you come back down, would you please milk my cow and feed my hens? And if you find any eggs, we'll have them with bacon tomorrow morning."

"With fried potatoes?" Johnny looked at her hopefully.

"With fried potatoes." D'lise smiled down at him. She looked up in time to see Kane watching her, and thought that she must be mistaken about the softness, the longing, in his eyes.

She gave Johnny a push toward the door. "Off with you, fellows. Lunch will be ready in about an hour."

Kane paused at the door before following the boys outside. When D'lise saw that he was going to speak, she turned and walked out of the kitchen. She didn't want to hear any more of his lies. When she heard him talking to David outside, she returned to the kitchen and started preparing the meal. If her randy husband thought all was forgotten and forgiven, that everything would remain the

319

same as before with them, he'd better think again. He had played her for a fool twice, but he wouldn't do it for the third time.

D'lise fried three times the amount of beef-steaks she usually prepared for her and Kane. David and Johnny were growing boys, and there had never been enough food on the Enger table. Besides, the poor kids had probably been existing on berries and roots on their journey to find her.

When an hour later, on the dot, Johnny and David dug into the meat and potatoes and baked squash, D'lise wished that she had cooked even more. They ate like young, hungry animals that hadn't seen food in several days. At one point she had to caution Johnny to eat more slowly. If he didn't take the time to chew his food, he was going to choke on it.

She wasn't surprised to see Kane watching the boys, sympathy in his eyes. Although he treated her shabbily, going to bed with whores and his squaw, there was a softness in her husband for the young and the mistreated.

When the meat platter and the bowls were empty, D'lise brought out a plate of cookies. She hid her smile when young Johnny sat on his hands in order not to snatch up a handful. Would that bottomless pit of his ever be filled? she wondered.

Finally, when nothing but crumbs was left on the plate, David and Johnny started talking as eagerly as they had eaten. "We looked over your garden, D'lise," Johnny said, "and we're gonna take real good care of it. You won't find one weed in your vegetables."

"And this winter, I'm gonna help Kane run his trap-line," David broke in. "He's gonna learn me all about trappin'."

"Teach you about trapping," D'lise corrected him.

"Yeah, that's what I said," David agreed with a nod of his head. "He's gonna learn me everything about it."

D'lise chose to ignore the amused grin that twitched the corners of Kane's lips.

"I won't be goin' with them, D'lise," Johnny piped up, a look of importance in his soft brown eyes. "Kane said it would be my job to stay with you. Me and Hound will scare the Indians and wolves away from the cabin."

"Hound and I," the schoolteacher came out in D'lise again.

"No, not you and Hound, D'lise," Johnny explained carefully. "Me and Hound will do it."

This time Kane's mirth found release. He threw back his head and roared with laughter. D'lise wanted to laugh with him, but bit her tongue.

The boys gave Kane a curious look, wondering what he was so tickled about. Then David said solemnly, "I guess everyone will look down on me and Johnny just like they did back there with old Enger. Some people acted like we wasn't human, that we didn't have any feelin's because we're bound-boys."

"I gave that some thought while you were up at the old cabin," D'lise said. "I've decided I'm going to introduce you fellows as my cousins—David and Johnny Alexander, who lost their parents to typhoid fever. Can you remember that?"

"Oh, yes," the pair answered together. "We won't ever forget that, D'lise," Johnny said. "Thank you for sharin' your name with us."

"And we won't ever do anything that will bring shame to it," David promised.

"I know you won't, David." D'lise smiled at him. "Now, how about filling the woodbox and bringing me a couple of pails of water from the spring."

When they almost knocked over the table in their eagerness to fill D'lise's request, D'lise said, "While you're doing that, I'll scare up a couple of Kane's shirts to put on after you've bathed in the stream back of the old cabin. Bring your soiled clothing to me, and I'll have them washed and dried for you to put back on in a little while."

It was Kane who brought the boys' threadbare clothing to D'lise half an hour later. "David is too embarrassed for you to see him. My shirt doesn't quite hide his you-know-what." He grinned at D'lise, trying to coax her into laughing with him, to ease the tension between them.

D'lise merely nodded and remarked, "David is tall for his age." Kane looked undecided what to do with himself, and finally dropped the clothes on the floor and walked outside. When, a short time later, she carried a kettle of hot water out onto the porch she was surprised to see him sitting on the top step, smoking his pipe. When she reached up to lift the wooden washtub off its peg in the wall, he jumped to his feet.

"Let me get that," he said. "It's too heavy for you."

D'lise stepped well away from him. She did not want any part of his body touching her. His touch was a danger she must avoid. His slim fingers were magical and had the power to render her mindless. And never again would she surrender herself in such reckless passion.

The old closeness D'lise and Kane had once shared seemed to be gone forever. When D'lise had to talk to Kane, she was polite and to the point. After a week of her cool treatment, a resentment grew in Kane and he stopped trying to cajole her into resuming their old relationship. He was as careful as she that their bodies did not touch in the big bed at night.

But he stuck around the cabin, giving her no cause to

think that he was meeting Raven somewhere. He still hoped that her coolness toward him would wear itself out and that some night she would turn to him.

What David and Johnny thought about the strained atmosphere between D'lise and Kane, they never let on. Chances were they never noticed. Having seen the abuse Rufus had visited on his wife, that Kane didn't beat D'lise was good enough for them. Had Kane used his fists on his wife, the two boys would have been hard to put to choose sides. They practically worshiped the big trapper who had become like a father to them, and they adored the gentle, beautiful D'lise. The two adults had completely changed their world around.

Both boys were beginning to put on weight from the hearty meals D'lise prepared, and there was now life in the eyes that once had been so dull. Every day saw them in the garden looking for any weed that dared raise its head, and every evening at sunset, when the hills had cooled off, they lugged buckets of water from the spring to give every plant a good drink. Every night at the supper table they gave D'lise a glowing report of how well her garden was growing.

A week later, the first day of July, when the boys showed up for breakfast, D'lise and Kane stared at them in alarm. David's face was white with anger, and tears ran down Johnny's cheeks.

"What in the world is wrong?" D'lise put her arms around the boy's shaking shoulders. "What has happened?" She looked at David when Johnny buried his face in her side.

"A damn Indian has ridden his mount over the garden—destroying every bit of it," David answered in red-hot fury.

"What makes you think that it was an Indian, son?"

Kane asked. "Did you see him?"

"No, but the horse didn't wear shoes, so it must have been an Indian."

"It was an Indian, but no man," D'lise said with conviction. "It was Raven. It's just what she would do."

"Aren't you jumpin' to conclusions, D'lise?" Kane frowned. "I can't see her doin' that. She can be ornery sometimes, I know, but she knows how important the raising of food is."

"And that is exactly why she would ruin my garden. She would like nothing better than to see me starve to death." D'lise voice rose as her anger did.

"What did you do to her, D'lise, to make her hate you that much?" David asked.

"She has the mistaken idea that I stole her lover's affection from her," D'lise snapped.

"Who is her lover?" Johnny knuckled the tears from his eyes.

"A confounded trapper," D'lise muttered through her teeth.

"Dammit, D'lise, that just isn't so," Kane began, but D'lise had left the kitchen and was running up the hill to the garden patch. With a sigh, he followed her, David and Johnny at his heels.

D'lise's tears fell as freely as Johnny's had when she looked down on the ruined garden. Not one plant had survived trampling. Big green tomatoes were squashed into the ground, as well as succulent cucumbers. The tall corn plants with their silky tassels were broken, already beginning to wilt. A row of lacy-topped carrots was sheared off, and the pumpkin and squash vines would never bear fruit. All the hard work that had been put into the garden had been demolished in one night.

D'lise knew as well as she stood under the hot rays of

the morning sun that only a jealous, vengeful woman would have caused such destruction. When Kane came and stood beside her, starting to lay a comforting hand on her shoulder, she gave him such a look of scorn, he felt it to his very core.

"Look, D'lise, I'll find out who did this dastardly crime, and whoever it was, man or woman, they'll pay for it." Again he was talking to empty air. D'lise had turned and was walking back to the new cabin.

Kane stared after her, then turned around at the sound of approaching hooves. "What in the hell has happened to your garden, Devlin?" Tom Spears reined in his mount, surveying the ruined garden. "I thought the Indians in the area liked you."

"Evidently not." Kane kicked at a clod of soil. "Whoever he is, when I find him he's gonna pay dearly for this night's work."

After a pause, Tom said, "I saw that squaw ride past my place last night around ten o'clock. My old hound set up a barkin', and I went outside to see what had riled him. He was barkin' at Raven. She was along the edge of the forest like she didn't want to be seen."

Could D'lise be right? Kane asked himself. Was Raven capable of such wanton destruction? He had to find out. If this *had* been her work, what would she do to D'lise next? A cold chill went down his spine. The bitch might do her real harm.

But dammit, how was he to find out for sure? If he went hunting for Raven, it would only make D'lise more suspicious.

"Kane," David interrupted his gloomy musings. "Tom says we can try to raise a late garden, that if we have a late fall it might produce real good."

"I don't know much about gardening, but Tom should

know. We'll start clearin' everything away after we've had breakfast.''

"No need to clear anything," Tom said, "just turn it over with a plow. Green foliage makes real good fertilizer."

Kane nodded, then said, "Come on down to the cabin and have breakfast with us, Tom."

"Thank you, Kane. Don't mind if I do. I'll give you and the boys a hand with the garden then."

Chapter Twenty-one

It was mid-July, scorching hot, with flies biting by day and mosquitoes stinging at night. David and Johnny's new garden was up and looked as if it might do very well if only it would rain and give the plants the deep watering they needed. Although the boys worked tirelessly at fetching water to the tender plants, the hot rays of the sun soon sucked the moisture out of the ground.

D'lise walked out onto the porch and sat down. She hitched her skirt up to her knees, then mopped at her face with a white rag. She had piled her hair on top of her head and tied it there with a piece of ribbon, and had unbuttoned her bodice to a point that was most unladylike, since a large portion of her breasts was visible.

Her breasts were large and heavy these days, for she knew beyond a doubt that she carried Kane's child. She hadn't flowed in two months. "If only it would rain," she said to Scrag, purring beside her.

Scrag was quite content these days. Hound lived mostly with David and Johnny now. The dog was allowed to run free during the day, but at night he was chained outside to alert the boys if anyone came around their garden.

D'lise's gaze moved up the hill to the old place. She could see Kane and the boys sitting under a tree, trying to catch a breeze. She, like all the other women of Piney Ridge, had been cooking outside since the heat wave had started two weeks ago. It was unthinkable to heat the cabin more by building a fire in the fireplace. There was no release at night either, and it had been almost impossible to sleep. She and Kane had been sleeping on a pallet in front of the open kitchen door, sweating and slapping at mosquitoes.

D'lise gazed unseeing at the small cookfire in the shade of a tree. Nothing had changed between her and Kane, and she was beginning to feel the strain of the cool politeness, the never looking directly at each other, never touching. And to her annoyance, she had began to awaken in the middle of the night, desire curling in the lower regions of her body. She desired her husband and hated herself for it.

She heard Kane's deep laugh roll down the hill, and she lifted her head to it. She had watched him with the boys the past weeks, noting the patience he had with them while teaching David how to aim and shoot a rifle, showing Johnny the correct way to toss a horseshoe in order to get a ringer, and she had come to the realization that he would make a wonderful father.

As the humidity grew and dark clouds gathered, D'lise wondered if she should tell Kane he was going to become a father, or if she should wait and let him discover it himself as her belly grew. Would he be pleased? she asked herself. Or would he feel trapped? Would he feel a resentment toward her, a reluctant obligation to remain in the marriage?

As, with a troubled sigh, she rose to stir the stew simmering over the fire, she saw lightning flashing in the valley below. *I'd better take in my washing first,* she thought, and hurried to the clothesline Kane had strung for her.

She had grabbed a sheet and was reaching for a shirt when she felt the first drops of rain. She was snatching the rest of the wash from the line when a slim, brown hand grabbed at a pillowcase at the same time she did.

Both pair of hands grew still as slate-gray eyes gazed into deep blue ones. It was never clear to D'lise who moved first. But she was suddenly in Kane's arms, his lips on hers, his tongue slipping into her mouth. When she accepted it eagerly, she heard his breath quicken. In a need so fierce it obliterated everything around her, her fingers threaded through his hair at his nape.

The kiss went on and on, Kane not releasing her until the rain was pattering on the leaves overhead. Then, laughing like a pair of happy children, they grabbed the rest of the wash and sprinted to the cabin. The laundry was dumped on the table, and D'lise and Kane were reaching for each other when footsteps trampled across the porch floor.

"Whew!" Johnny exclaimed, drawing an arm across his wet face, "we just barely made it. It's beginnin' to come down in buckets." Both boys grinned at them, sure of their welcome. Had they lowered their eyes to the hard bulge in Kane's buckskins, they would have known that he, at least, was wishing them a hundred miles away.

To hide her amusement at Kane's predicament, D'lise walked to the door and stood watching the rain fall. Women were lucky, she thought. When desire gripped them, they could hide it. Unless, of course, one looked too deeply in her eyes, or noticed the pebble-hard nipples pushing against her bodice.

"What are you thinking?" Kane came and stood beside her, curving an arm around her waist.

D'lise heard the husky desire in his voice, and thought, *Blast him.* Every nerve in her body was on edge with the need to have him make love to her. But she hesitated to chance any more mental pain than she had already experienced at his hands.

She knew that she would chance it when Kane's hand moved up to cup her breast, to rub his thumb across the nipple that was already hard. But she would not make it easy for him, she determined. He would squirm and wonder for a while.

"I was thinking," she answered his question, "that if it doesn't stop raining soon we'll be eating a late supper. And maybe a cold one at that. The rain has put out the fire under the stew."

When Kane whispered that he wasn't hungry for supper, she moved away from his arm, saying that she was sure the boys were. She walked back into the kitchen and started folding the sheets dumped on the table. She avoided Kane's probing gray eyes as he lounged in the doorway, afraid that if she looked at him, saw the hunger that she was sure she'd see in his eyes, she just might take him by the hand and lead him into the bedroom, forgetting all about supper and the hungry boys.

"The rain is lettin' up, D'lise," Johnny called from the porch, where he and David had gone to keep Hound company. When the dog got wet he smelled so bad he wasn't allowed inside.

"I'll set the table," D'lise called back, "and when it slacks some more you can bring in the kettle of stew."

When, later, the sun had gone in and only a fine drizzle was falling, D'lise lit the candles and called David in to open all the windows, to catch the flow of cool air that had followed the rain. She knew that she would be on dangerous ground if she left the kitchen. Kane was just waiting to get her alone, to work his magical persuasion on her.

"I think it's still warm enough to eat, D'lise." Johnny grinned at D'lise as he carried in the wet pot of stew and placed it on the table. She lifted off the lid and found that he was correct. The heavy cast iron had kept the meat and vegetables at just the right temperature.

Although David and Johnny ate as though they hadn't had a hearty meal a few hours back, D'lise noted that Kane ate very little. From the smoldering looks he cast her way, she knew where his hunger lay.

But should she feed that hunger? she still wondered. Her mind said absolutely not, but her body argued—no, demanded—"Yes!"

Dessert was eaten and coffee drunk, and the boys were ready to settle in for a couple of hours of talk and laughter with the two people who were the hub of their lives. But Kane was lighting the lantern and saying, "I'm tired tonight, boys. You two go on home and I'll see you in the morning at breakfast."

When Johnny would have expressed his disappointment, David's sharp elbow in his ribs shut him up. Nevertheless, his lips drooped at the corners when he said goodnight and followed David outside.

D'lise couldn't remember ever being so nervous as she cleared the table and washed and dried the dishes. She was acutely aware of Kane's eyes following her every move.

Finally the kitchen was spotless, and she had no reason

331

to linger in it. She was taking off her apron when Kane came up behind her and wrapped his arms around her waist. When her body tensed, he whispered, "Please, D'lise, I can't stand this coldness between us. It's drivin' me mad."

"You should have thought about that before spending the night with Raven." D'lise tried to pry his arms away, to escape the heat of the body that was setting fire to her own.

The arms didn't budge, only tightened, and now she felt the nudge of his hard manhood on her buttocks. "D'lise." Kane nuzzled the side of her neck. "I told you I didn't take that woman to bed. She might have been there when I passed out on the bed, but I wasn't aware of her until I woke up the next morning."

His fingers began undoing the buttons on her bodice. "I drank so much that day I couldn't have made love even to you." He turned her around to face him. "And you know how I love doin' that." He traced a finger around her lips. "Please, honey, let's start all over again. I promise to curb my jealousy of Majors, and you must stop havin' your suspicions about Raven. I swear there is nothin' between us anymore."

"Truly, Kane?" D'lise's blue eyes begged him not to lie to her.

"I swear it on my dead uncle. You're the only woman I'll ever want."

D'lise gazed up at him, so handsome and earnest, and whispered, "I believe you."

Kane made a small groaning sound of relief as his lips, hot and hungry, fastened on hers. She curled her fingers in his hair as her lips parted eagerly under his, and her body began to throb as their tongues sparred and his hand slipped into her bodice.

It was but moments later when Scrag, from his perch on a rafter in the bedroom, watched with curious eyes as his mistress and her husband soared to the heights together. When only a short time later it happened again, he lost interest and fell asleep.

D'lise awakened in the warm cocoon of possessive arms. She smiled tiredly. It had been past midnight before she and Kane sated themselves with each other. She wondered if she could slip out of bed without awakening Kane. She knew how strong his morning desire was and that he'd want to spend at least an hour catering to it; he'd probably still be working that hard body of his over hers when the boys arrived for breakfast, which could be anytime now according to the height of the sun.

She managed to ease out of Kane's arms and slide off the bed without rousing him. She quietly gathered up her clothes and moved through the main room and on into the kitchen. Filling a basin with water from the wooden pail that rested on its own long, narrow table, she dropped soap and a cloth into it and took a hurried sponge bath.

She had just finished dressing and was building a fire when David and Johnny arrived, their hair wet and slicked back. There was no comparing these two boys to the woebegone-looking young men who had appeared at their door in the late spring.

"It's a fine day, D'lise," Johnny said. "It's cool and fresh, just beggin' a fellow to stay outside. Do you think Kane might take us fishin'?"

"He might," D'lise answered, mixing up pancake batter. "Maybe I'll go with you, if you don't mind. I haven't fished but once this year."

"We'd be proud to have you, D'lise," David said gravely, not having Johnny's exuberant nature.

333

"Have her what?" Kane growled from the doorway, giving D'lise an accusing look as he scratched his head.

"D'lise said that she would go with us if you agreed to go fishin' today," Johnny explained with a wide smile. "Will you take us, Kane, will you?" he begged, his eyes shining hopefully.

"Well, I don't know about takin' D'lise with us," Kane grumbled. "She's a sneaky, hard-hearted woman. It doesn't matter to her if her man has a hurt."

An amused light jumped into D'lise's eyes. "Oh, Kane," she said with sham sympathy, "do you have a hurt? Show me where you're hurting and I'll kiss it and make it all well."

A roguish smile played around Kane's lips. "I'll show you later, and hold you to your promise."

D'lise turned her back on Kane when she felt her face redden. Then she had to bite her tongue to keep from roaring with laughter when Johnny innocently said, "It's your leg, huh, Kane? Remember yesterday when you got mad and kicked that big rock? Remember how you yowled and swore like a buffalo hunter?"

Johnny slid a sly look at David. "David's been sayin' them words ever since."

D'lise gave Kane a scorching look, thinking that he'd better not talk that way in front of his son. She remembered then that she still hadn't told him that he was going to become a father. She would tell him while they were fishing, she decided.

She'd turn the event into a picnic. She'd make sandwiches from the piece of ham left over from Sunday's dinner and take along a sack of cookies. When they found some time alone, she would tell him. She wasn't afraid to tell him now. After last night, she truly believed that Kane loved her and would be delighted at the thought of becoming a father.

After breakfast was eaten, Kane reluctantly let Johnny and David drag him off to dig worms. "I'd rather show you my hurt." He looked hopefully at D'lise from the kitchen door, rubbing the pronounced bulge in his buckskins. "It wouldn't take long," he coaxed, his fingers going to the lacing of his trousers.

His hands dropped to his sides when Johnny called from outside, "Are you comin', Kane?"

"I wish I was," Kane said with a whimsical twist of his lips before stepping outside. D'lise laughed softly and began to tidy the kitchen.

The river was smooth, without any current, when four lines were dropped into its water a short time later. Johnny and David held their poles, while Kane shoved his and D'lise into the sandy bank. He unfolded the blanket D'lise had brought along, and sitting down on it, he pulled her down beside him.

"That's the lazy way to fish, accordin' to ole Tom," Johnny informed Kane. "He says a man ain't never gonna catch a fish sittin' on his a—er, rump."

"Old Tom talks a lot of balderdash," Kane said, lying back on the blanket. "We'll see who catches the most fish."

The words were barely out of his mouth when David gave a whoop and whipped a good-sized bass out of the river. "See there, Kane, I told you so," Johnny crowed.

He crowed louder yet when, a moment later, a catfish took his bait. "I'm tellin' you, Kane, you'd better hold your pole in your hand."

"I'd rather let you hold my pole, D'lise," Kane said softly, turning on his side and giving D'lise a look that made her catch her breath at the message in it.

335

"You're the limit, Kane," she whispered. "Now behave yourself before David catches on to what you're hinting at.".

"Do you think he would frown on my kissing you?" Kane came up on an elbow and leaned over her, his hand grasping her waist.

"I don't know, but I wish you wouldn't. You know as well as I do that a kiss wouldn't be enough for you." She raised a hand and lovingly stroked his cheek.

"Let me send the boys farther down the river," he whispered huskily, then gave a grunt of pain and clutched his thigh at the same time the sharp report of a rifle sounded off in the forest.

"Kane!" D'lise jerked erect. "You've been shot!" She stared horrified at the blood already spreading through the rent in his buckskins and running down between his fingers.

When David and Johnny came running up, their faces pale, she said to David, "Run fetch the stallion. We've got to get Kane to the cabin." David had taken but a few running steps when she called after him, "Bring the jackass instead. It will be easier to get Kane on his back."

"The shot came from over there." Johnny pointed a trembling finger to the right. "Look, there's the powder smoke driftin' up through the trees." He knelt down beside Kane and took his hands. "You're gonna be all right, ain't you, Kane?" his young voice quavered.

"Of course he's going to be all right," D'lise said fiercely. "Now I want you to saddle Snowy and ride to the village as fast as you can and bring back Doctor Ashley."

Johnny was on his feet and sprinting away as soon as the words left D'lise's mouth. She turned back to Kane, trying not to wring her hands in her inability to help him.

He looked so vulnerable, this man who never showed a weakness of any kind.

She gently wiped his sweating brow with her handkerchief. "Are you in a lot of pain, Kane?"

"My leg feels like someone is holdin' a flamin' torch to it," he answered hoarsely, his teeth clenched.

"I can't imagine who would want to shoot you. Do you have any enemies that you know of?"

"I'm sure there's some who don't like me, but I can't think of anyone who would want me dead."

D'lise chewed her bottom lip. What was taking David so long? Blood was still seeping through Kane's fingers. Was he going to lie and bleed to death? *Dear Jesus, I'd want to die too,* she whispered silently.

Finally there came the sound of small trotting hooves. A long sigh of relief whistled through D'lise's lips as David pulled the little jackass to a halt only a few feet away from where Kane lay. With Kane helping all he could, D'lise and David got him onto his feet and over to the little animal. He snorted and shook his head at the scent of blood, but when D'lise spoke to him in soothing tones, he allowed Kane to be boosted onto his back.

Although it was less than a mile to the cabin, D'lise felt it was more like five before they arrived and she and David got Kane inside and stretched out on the bed.

D'lise had just cut away the trouser leg, revealing a long, angry-looking gash about six inches long, when Doctor Ashley stepped into the room, Johnny right behind him.

"So, you've been shot, Mr. Devlin?" the slightly built man in his mid-fifties said as he rolled up his sleeves. He smiled at D'lise. "Where can I wash my hands?"

She led him into the kitchen and filled a basin with water and handed the doctor a bar of soap. As he scrubbed his hands, he said, "I'll need a basin of hot water and some strips of white cloth."

D'lise hurried to the fireplace, poked up the fire that was nearly out, then added more wood. When flames shot up, engulfing the tea kettle hanging from the crane, she half ran to the closet where she kept her linens.

Thank God she had washed clothes yesterday, she thought, grabbing a sheet and tearing it into strips. The water in the kettle was steaming now, and filling a basin with it, she rushed back into the bedroom.

"How serious is the wound, Doctor?" she asked in a voice barely above a whisper, the scared look on David's face increasing her fear.

"Actually, it's not serious at all," the doctor answered. "That is, if your husband stays off his feet for at least a week." He looked down at Kane and grinned. "It's painful as hell though, isn't it, Mr. Devlin?" Kane nodded and the doctor added, "The bullet passed through his leg, missing the bone, but tearing through muscles and nerves."

He opened the little black bag he'd carried into the cabin and took from it a bottle marked carbolic acid. He measured some of the liquid into the steaming water; then after swirling a cloth through it, he began to cleanse the wound. Kane flinched at the bite of the acid but made no sound.

It came time then for the stitches. D'lise gripped both of Kane's hands in hers, but looked away when the doctor bent over him with the needle. But she knew each time the needle penetrated Kane's flesh by the tightening of his fingers around hers, and she felt his pain as though it were happening to her.

It was over finally, with Kane's face pale and beaded with sweat. D'lise patted his face dry with the corner of the sheet and stroked his forehead as Dr. Ashley bandaged his leg. She looked up when the doctor spoke.

"He'll probably sleep a while now. Don't let him move that leg when he wakes up." He snapped his bag closed and stood up. "I'll be by tomorrow to check on him."

"Thank you, Dr. Ashley." D'lise rose and walked with him from the room. Out on the porch the man gave her arm a friendly pat. "Don't look so worried," he said. "Your husband is going to be just fine. In fact, he looks better than you do." He studied her face with professional eyes. "Are you with child, by any chance?"

Surprise flickered across D'lise's face. It was a few seconds before she answered, "I think I am. I've missed two menses." She looked at him anxiously. "I haven't told anyone yet, Doctor. Not even Kane."

"Your secret is safe with me, D'lise." Dr. Ashley smiled at her as he climbed into his buggy. He flicked a whip over the horse's back, and the vehicle whirred away.

When D'lise returned to the bedroom, she found Kane asleep, and the boys sitting on each side of him, holding his hands. *How frightened they look,* she thought, pity stirring inside her. They were so afraid of losing this man who had shown them the first kindness they had known in years.

She smiled ruefully. They both thought that Kane could walk on water.

"Maybe we should leave the room," D'lise said softly, closing the shutters to darken the room. "Kane needs rest now."

"But what if he wakes up and wants somethin'?" Johnny asked in a whisper.

"We'll hear him if he does. He'll probably sleep for a couple of hours, and in the meantime you can go back to the river and retrieve our fishing poles and the two fish you caught, and then do your chores.''

The boys agreed, though reluctantly, and left the room with dragging feet. D'lise smoothed the sheet over Kane and dropped a kiss on his cool forehead. A tightness gripped her chest. She could have lost him today. As she left the room, she tried to imagine a world without Kane in it. The thought was unendurable.

D'lise had just started putting a light supper together when the boys returned. David's face was solemn. ''It wasn't an Indian who shot Kane, D'lise. I went over the area where we saw the smoke and I found shod horse prints and boot tracks. It was a white man, but not a trapper. If you've noticed, trappers always wear moccasins.''

In the days that followed, the four of them discussed who could have shot Kane. They came up with no answers, nor did the neighbors who came to visit him. All of Piney Ridge wondered who wanted Kane Devlin dead.

It was the fifth day of Kane's confinement when Raven appeared at the cabin door in the early afternoon. ''I have come to see Devlin,'' she said, and rudely pushed past D'lise, making her way toward the bedroom. D'lise stood staring after the arrogant woman, her mouth fallen open.

Kane's mouth flew open too when Raven swept into the room, her black eyes snapping. His recovery was faster than D'lise's. ''What in the hell are you doin' here?'' He sat up, his mouth firm and forbidding.

''Why should I not come to visit a sick friend?''

''Who are you tryin' to fool, Raven? You're no friend of mine. You're here to cause trouble between me and D'lise.''

''That is not true.'' Raven stepped closer to the bed. ''I come here because I have the right.''

''And what right is that?'' Kane watched her closely.

340

"Because I carry your child."

Kane looked at Raven incredulously. Then, his face and voice harsh, he thundered, "Don't give me that, woman! I was always very careful that would never happen."

"That's right," Raven agreed, "except the night you got drunk and took me to your old cabin. You forgot to spill your seed on the bed that night. You let it come inside me."

Staring blindly at her triumphant face, Kane wished with all his being that he could remember what had happened that night he drank himself senseless in a jealous rage. He'd swear that he hadn't brought Raven to the cabin, but she had been in bed with him the next morning, naked. Could he have made love to her, thinking she was D'lise in his drunken state?

Back in the kitchen, D'lise had sat down, not sure what to do about the woman who had just disappeared into her bedroom with such assurance that she would be welcome. She looked up from her tightly clasped hands when a light tap sounded on the open door.

"I thought I'd drop in and see how Kane is comin' along." Claudie Jacobs stepped into the kitchen, a covered pie tin in her hand. "I brought him an apple pie. I know he's partial to it."

"Why thank you, Claudie." D'lise stood up. "That's kind of you."

"I can't stay long." Claudie set the pie on the table. "I'll just go and say howdy to Kane and then be on my way."

"Well, he—ah, has company right now," D'lise stammered.

Claudie looked at her curiously, then asked abruptly, "Who?"

D'lise looked away from her probing stare. "That Indian woman, Raven."

"What?" Claudie exclaimed, scandalized. "You mean to say you let that red slut come into your home, and worse yet, let her go into your bedroom where your husband is lyin' in bed?"

She grabbed D'lise's arm. "Come on, girl, order her out of there."

"Oh, I don't know if I should, Claudie." D'lise hung back. "Maybe Kane doesn't mind her being there."

"D'lise Devlin, where is your spunk? That woman has no right bein' there, and Kane has no right wantin' her there."

"Now, Claudie, I didn't say for sure he wants her there. I said maybe he does."

"Well, we'll just march in there and see."

They were almost at the bedroom door when they both stopped at once. From inside the room Raven was saying, "You forgot to spill your seed on the bed that night. You let it come inside me."

D'lise heard Claudie gasp, but she was too stunned, too heartsick to make a sound. Even her breathing stopped as she waited for Kane to deny the woman's accusation.

Seconds ticked away to a full minute, and D'lise could stand it no longer. She stepped into the room and wished that she hadn't. Kane sat in the middle of the bed, guilt and confusion on his face. She choked back a sob, but he heard it.

"God, D'lise," he cried, "it's not true. I know the bitch is lyin'. I know she's not carryin' my child."

The blood roared in D'lise's ears. Raven was going to have Kane's baby. In a split second she went from painful shock to cold anger. Her blue eyes like frozen spring water, she said, "Do you, Kane? I don't think you know for sure. The uncertainty is in your eyes.''

"Well, I'm sure," Raven gloated, rubbing her stomach. "His child is growing inside me."

Like an angry, disturbed wasp, Claudie flew across the room and slapped Raven's sneering, complacent face with all her strength. "You red slut," she gritted out, then slapped the woman again.

Before anyone could catch their breath, she had D'lise by the arm, drawing her toward the door. "Come on, honey," she said gently. "It smells in here."

"D'lise, come back!" Kane's frantic voice followed them. "I'll make the bitch tell the truth."

"Don't listen to him, D'lise. All men are liars."

In a deep stupor, D'lise nodded, unable to think for herself. She made no demur when Claudie urged her into the buggy. As they rolled away from the little home where she had thought she would be so happy, she was unaware that Kane had hobbled out onto the porch, calling her name.

Chapter Twenty-two

Dusk was falling as the buggy neared the village, and D'lise had recovered from her numbed state. Only pain gripped her now and she wished that she could crawl into a dark cave until it eased.

And where and how was she to go on with her life? she wondered as her brain functioned again. She refused to be a burden to her friends, and did not want their pity. But she would get pity, she knew. Claudie was a loving, caring woman, but she was the biggest gossip in Piney Ridge. Before the sun set, everyone for miles around would know that D'lise Devlin's husband had gotten his squaw with child.

And what of the child she was carrying? she asked herself. How unfair for it to grow up knowing that it had a half-breed brother or sister. Any child was bound to resent that fact.

D'lise's lips firmed in a straight line. She would remain

in Piney Ridge until her baby was born. Then, with Samuel's help, she would take it and move to Boston. He would give her names and places of business where she could find employment. As for the money to get her there, she would demand it from Kane. He owed her that much at least. She had no doubt that he would give it to her, out of guilt if nothing else.

When the rutted road led into the village, D'lise turned her head and looked at Claudie's grim profile. Neither of them had uttered a word in the two-mile trip. "Where are you taking me, Claudie?"

"Why, to the schoolhouse, of course," the skinny woman answered as if D'lise should have known all along. "Have you forgotten there's two nice rooms attached to it, all furnished, just waiting to be used? When school starts in the fall, you'll be there ready to start teachin' our young'uns again."

D'lise was hard put not to throw her arms around her friend. She had come up with the perfect answer to her dilemma. Why hadn't she thought of it herself?

Claudie pulled up in front of the schoolhouse, and while she looped the reins over a post, D'lise pushed open the heavy door to its living quarters.

This time she paid more attention to the combination kitchen and family room. After all, she was going to be here for some months. She walked into the small bedroom and pressed her hands on the feather mattress. It was thickly filled and would be very comfortable. She glanced at the small table beneath a window, noting the water pitcher and matching basin. A straight-backed chair completed the furnishings. All she needed to purchase was a mirror to hang on the wall.

"I'll get it from Samuel and tell him to put it on Kane's

345

bill,'' she muttered sourly, going back into the other room.

Claudie had let her tour the quarters alone, and D'lise smiled at her neighbor and said, ''I'll never be able to thank you enough, Claudie. I don't know what I'd have done if you hadn't been there when I needed someone so desperately.''

''It pleases me very much to help you, D'lise.''

''I guess good men are few in these hills,'' D'lise said as Claudie prepared to leave. ''I know I'll never take a chance on loving one again.''

''You've got the right idea if you can make it on your own.'' Claudie paused at the door. ''But you can probably make it, what with your education. You can teach until you're an old woman.''

Claudie left then, hurrying down the street to Samuel's store. Within the hour she would have spread the news that D'lise had left her husband and was living in back of the schoolhouse.

Tongues would wag tonight, D'lise thought wryly, closing the door and barring it.

Kane watched the buggy disappear into the forest, despair gripping his heart. This time he had lost D'lise for good. That bitch inside had seen to that.

He splayed a hand over his healing wound. In his rush to catch D'lise, to beg her to stay, some of the stitches had broken and he was bleeding again. His leg was throbbing painfully, and a sweat had broken out on his forehead. Could he make it back to bed? He'd have to. He wasn't about to call the boys to help him. He hadn't the nerve yet to tell them that D'lise had left him, and why. They would look at him so reproachfully.

Moving slowly and carefully, he limped back to the

bedroom. Raven still stood where he had left her. She gave him a furtive glance and stirred uneasily at the angry, erratic pulse in his jawline. She jumped out of his reach when he lunged for her with barely controlled savagery.

"You ugly bitch," he grated, "you've ruined my life. Get out of my sight before I choke the life out of you!"

"But, Devlin," Raven whined, making sure she was out of his reach, "you will need me now that the pale-faced one is gone. Who is going to take care of you? Who will pleasure you at night when you grow hard with need?"

"It sure as hell won't be you." Kane moved toward her, grimacing with pain. "If I can get my hands on you, you'll never pleasure any man again."

Kane's desire to do her harm was a fire in his eyes. Realizing it, Raven wheeled and sped through the bedroom door. She stopped in the main room long enough to taunt furiously, "I at least am able to give you a son. That is more than your delicate flower of a wife can do."

When the cabin door slammed, Kane wearily stretched out on the bed. His lips drew down at the grim mockery of life. He had never trusted beautiful women, had always sought out the unattractive ones to put his trust in. And now, the ugliest of the lot had done him in.

When D'lise awakened the first morning in her new home, she was disoriented. The sun should be coming through the window on her right, and Kane should be lying on her left.

When she put out a hand to touch him and felt only an empty space, everything rushed over her like a black cloud. Kane was no longer a part of her life, would never be again. She laid a hand on her stomach. That was not quite true. There was a part of him with her. But then, he was a part of Raven also.

She buried her face in her pillow and choking sobs shook her slender body until she wept herself dry of tears. "I'll never cry over him again," she promised herself, wiping her eyes with the edge of the pillowcase.

D'lise rolled over on her back and stared at the ceiling. How was she to get her clothes and cat from the cabin? Scrag would be upset, wondering where she was. She hoped he hadn't been left outside all night. He was a tough little scrap, but there were many wild creatures who could kill him.

She sat up and slid off the bed. No doubt Claudie would stop in today. She would ask her to go after her belongings and pet.

D'lise started across the floor, and nausea gripped her. She pulled the chamber pot from under the bed, but only dry heaves twisted her stomach. She wasn't surprised. She'd had no supper, and her stomach was growling for nourishment. And naturally there was no food in her quarters. She had been too upset to think about supplies last night, and Claudie had been in too much of a hurry to spread the news about Kane's infidelity to think of anything else.

With a ragged sigh, D'lise pulled on her dress and combed her fingers through her tumbled curls. According to the position of the sun, it must be around nine o'clock. The store would be open, and there was nothing she could do but go out and brave the questions that would shower her like a barrage of arrows. She had hoped to have a couple days to herself to lick her wounds, and to begin the healing process. But she had to eat, if only for the baby growing beneath her heart.

She took a deep bracing breath, unbarred the door, and

348

stepped out onto the little porch. She went no farther. A small haversack leaned against the wall, a note pinned to it. Her eyes shimmered with tears as she unfolded the paper and read, ''We figured you had no supplies yet, so we have left you a few items for breakfast. Will stop in later to see how we can help you. Love, Ellen and Samuel.''

When D'lise had wiped her wet eyes, she saw the pail of water and stack of wood. Her dear friends had thought of everything. Maybe she had been unwise in her choice of a husband, but she couldn't have picked better friends.

She set the sack of groceries inside the door, then carried in an armful of wood. The small fireplace drew well, and she soon had flames shooting up the chimney. While it burned down to red coals, she sorted through the contents of the sack. She found a bag of coffee beans, a slab of bacon, a dozen eggs in their own cloth bag, a small sack of sugar, a box of salt, and a can of milk. And wrapped in a cloth was a loaf of light bread, no doubt from Ellen's kitchen, she thought with a fond smile.

In a short time, D'lise's new home was experiencing its first aroma of brewing coffee and frying bacon.

D'lise's spirits rose considerably after she had eaten breakfast and drunk two cups of coffee. She was sitting at the table making half-formed plans for her future when she heard the arrival of horses outside. As she rose and went to the door, she heard the unmistakable sound of squawking chickens and the mewling of a distressed cat. She yanked open the door and her eyes widened in surprise and delight. Grinning up at her stood David and Johnny. Johnny held a burlap bag in his arms, snarls and hisses coming from inside it. He shoved it into her hands.

''That's the meanest damn cat I ever seen, D'lise,'' Johnny complained. ''He bit me three times right through the cloth. I'd have whacked him one, but Kane said if I did, he would whack me.''

D'lise's smile died when she looked at David. His face held a mixture of reproach and confusion. She knew that he didn't like it one bit that she had left Kane. She wondered what her husband had told the boys.

She looked away from his solemn face. ''I see you've brought my hens.''

''Yeah, Kane said that you would want them, that they were like pets to you,'' Johnny said. ''We brought your mare and cow too.'' He glanced around the schoolhouse area. ''Hound is around here somewhere. Kane said he could look out for you as good as any man.''

D'lise wanted to make a sharp comment about that remark, but there was a look in David's eyes that kept her silent. She said instead, ''Come on in and see my new home and have a cup of coffee.'' The boys stepped in behind her, and after she untied the bag and set Scrag free, she asked, ''How did you fellows know where to find me?''

''Old Tom came by this mornin' and told us,'' Johnny answered. ''He's still at the cabin, I expect. He was jawin' at Kane somethin' fierce when we left.''

As D'lise poured the coffee, she noted David's eyes roaming around the room and she waited to hear what he would say about her new quarters. When he spoke, however, it was not about the room.

''When are you comin' home, D'lise?'' he asked.

Home, D'lise mused. How good the word sounded. But the cabin halfway up the hill was no longer her home, and she, as well as David and Johnny, might as well get used to the idea. She looked at each of them in turn. ''What explanation did Kane give you two for my leaving?''

"He said that the two of you had had a misunderstanding," David answered.

D'lise stared down into her coffee. Trust Kane to put it that way. There was no misunderstanding. Raven had said it clearly enough. She was carrying his baby, and Kane could not deny her claim with a clear conscience. Her lips curled contemptuously. A fine misunderstanding.

When D'lise didn't affirm or dispute Kane's claim, David said with some asperity, "I always thought misunderstandings could be worked out. I didn't know that one person had to leave home."

D'lise laid a hand on David's clenched fist lying on the table. "I'm sorry to disappoint you, David, but this so-called misunderstanding can't be worked out. I had to leave."

David jerked his hand from beneath hers. "His leg is bleedin' again. He needs you."

D'lise's first instinct was to hurry to Kane, to tend his leg, to look after him. She remembered in time why she was here and not with her husband and hardened her heart against him.

"I'm sorry to hear that, David. Stop by Dr. Ashley's office and ask him to look in on Kane."

His eyes snapping angrily, David stood up. "Come on, Johnny," he said shortly, "it's time we left."

Johnny hung back, reluctant to leave D'lise so soon. He had grown used to her gentleness, her smiles, the hugs she sometimes gave him—something he hadn't had since his mother and father died.

D'lise knew from the longing in his eyes that the youngster needed that contact now, that he was worried about the future. When David stepped outside without a word of goodbye, she gave Johnny a big hug and a kiss on his cheek. "I hope you can come visit me every day. I'm going to miss you."

Johnny swiped at the tears that had escaped his eyes. "I'm gonna miss you too, D'lise, and I'll be here every day even if I have to come by myself."

She walked outside with him, her arm across his shoulders. She looked down at the crate of chickens David had placed next to the porch. "I don't know what I'm going to do with them," she sighed.

"Oh, I forgot to tell you," Johnny said. "Old Tom is comin' over here later to build a pen for them. He said that you can keep the mare and cow at the livery stable." Then, with a wave of his hand, Johnny ran to join a disapproving David.

The boys were barely out of sight, and D'lise was crumbling some bread for the squawking hens, when Tom arrived, his mule clumping along behind him. It carried a load of rough planks and mesh chicken wire. Her old friend looked down at her, a frowning, pensive look on his wrinkled face.

"Are you sure you did the right thing, girl?" he asked. When D'lise nodded, he asked, "Where do you want me to build the chicken coop?"

D'lise skimmed a gaze over the small area of cleared trees. "I think close to the schoolhouse so that I can hear them if any creatures come around at night."

"I'll build it right up against the schoolhouse, then," Tom said and began to unload the mule. D'lise hurried to help him. She wanted to ask about Kane's leg. Had the bleeding stopped? Did the stitches look all right?

The mule was unloaded before she managed to say offhandedly, "The boys said that Kane's wound started bleeding again. Did he say anything to you about it?"

"Not much," Tom answered briefly as drove a wooden

stake into the ground. "He seemed to have somethin' more important on his mind."

"Like Raven carrying his child." D'lise sniffed contemptuously.

"Oh, that's on his mind all right, but only because he thinks the bitch is lyin'. And so do I."

"He *thinks* she's lying, but he's not sure. I saw the look on his face that said it might be true." Tom opened his mouth to speak, but D'lise rushed on. "Claudie Jacobs was there. She saw the guilt on his face too."

"Yeah, and by now that flappin' tongue of hers has spread it all over the hills that Kane's gonna have a half-breed young'un."

"I expect so," D'lise retorted sharply and marched into her two rooms. "Men," she muttered, gathering up the cups her young visitors had used. "No matter what, they always take up for each other."

D'lise was making up her bed when a welcome voice called from the door, "Are you home, D'lise?" She rushed into the main room and straight into Ellen Travis's open arms. The young widow let her cry until only an occasional sob shook her slender shoulders.

"Are you all right now?" Ellen released D'lise and guided her to a chair shoved under the table. She sat down next to her and said quietly, "Like everyone else in Piney Ridge, I've heard about Kane and the Indian woman. It's so hard for me to believe it's true."

"I guess you can believe it, Ellen." D'lise smiled weakly. "When Raven told him, he only half-heartedly denied it." She looked uncomfortably at her hands clasped on top of the table. "That day when Tom and Samuel delivered the new furniture, Kane went into a rage when he saw me and Samuel talking and laughing together. Right after Tom and Samuel left, he rode into the village and didn't come home at night.''

D'lise paused, as if gathering the strength to go on with her story. ''From what I could piece together, Kane really got drunk. At any rate, the next morning I saw him and Raven together at the old cabin. They'd obviously spent the night there.

''I wanted to leave him then, but I had no money, and at the time I didn't remember these rooms, so I didn't think I had anywhere to go. The next thing I knew I was letting him make love to me again.'' She looked up at Ellen, tears forming in her eyes.

''I feel like such a fool. I feel used, no better than the village whores.''

''Now you just hush up such talk,'' Ellen ordered angrily. ''You're a good, honorable woman. If anyone's a fool, it's that husband of yours. He doesn't deserve you.''

She turned D'lise's tear-swollen face toward her. ''However, I sincerely think the big, dumb trapper truly loves you. Didn't you tell him that Samuel and I are getting married this fall?''

''I did not!'' D'lise answered hotly. ''There was nothing wrong with my talking to a friend. I never threw a fit when he joked around with Milly Patton. I trusted him, and I feel he owed me the same respect. What kind of marriage would we have without trust between us?''

''You're absolutely right, honey,'' Ellen soothed. ''It takes some men and women time to realize that, though. And sadly, some never do. Now,'' she added, standing up, ''bathe your face and brush your hair. I'm having a little luncheon for you. I've invited all the ladies so that they can, once and for all, talk about and express their views on what happened. That way you won't be deluged with visitors every day and have to go over and over your separation from Kane. I have found that to be the best policy. Meet unpleasant things head on.''

"Oh, Ellen, I don't know if I'm up to it yet. What if I break down and cry in front of them?''

"You won't. You've got too much pride.''

Ellen had been right, D'lise thought that night as she prepared for bed. She hadn't cried, but it had been hard not to defend Kane against some of the harsher things said about him. A couple of the women had made him sound no better than a rutting buffalo before he met and married her. According to them, he had spent all his time taking a squaw or a whore to bed. That she did not believe. Basically, Kane was a man's man. He enjoyed the other trappers' company and was content when he could hunt all day or fish for hours in the Ohio. She imagined he was no worse and no better than most men when it came to women.

Later, however, curled up in her narrow bed, D'lise had no answer for her husband's seemingly continued interest in the Indian woman.

Chapter Twenty-three

Kane limped across the kitchen floor to gaze out the window. He could see David and Johnny in the garden, filling a basket with vegetables to take to D'lise. Every day they took her something, maybe only a few string beans. Their late garden wasn't going to have time to produce a great deal.

Kane shook his head. And every day he waited impatiently for the boys to return home, hungry to hear any little scrap of information about his wife.

It was a dark day, though, when one of them would mention nonchalantly that Samuel Majors had been visiting with D'lise, that he had brought her something from his store. He wished it was safe for the boys to be out at night. He'd send them to the schoolhouse to see how often the storekeeper visited D'lise after dark.

Kane bent his head in black despair. He hadn't been surprised that Majors would start going around D'lise.

From the very first, there had been an attraction between them. They were both educated, shared a love of books, could talk about things he had no idea of. And the fancy man from Boston could give her a big home, nice clothes, even servants to help her around the house.

He turned his head to look at the plain furniture he had bought for D'lise. She had seemed very pleased with it then, but he imagined it compared badly with what Majors could give her. He had heard the talk of how grand the man's home was. Hell, he even had a piano. And could play it.

Well, by God, there was one thing he didn't have, and that was D'lise. And the bastard would never have her because Kane Devlin would never give her a divorce. She might think she had grounds for one, but time would prove that she didn't. He knew damn well that baby Raven was carrying wasn't his.

"And another thing," he muttered, turning from the window, "I'm goin' to that bastard's store and pay him for everything he's given D'lise. I take care of my own, even if it's not wanted."

Kane got fully dressed for the first time in two weeks. His buckskins didn't fit him as snugly as they once had; he had lost weight. After he shaved a week's stubble off his face, he limped out to the barn. The boys came running up when he led Snowy outside.

"Where are you goin', Kane?" Johnny asked.

"Into the village. I have some business to take care of."

"Do you think you should?" David asked anxiously. "What if your leg starts bleedin' again?"

"The leg is fine, David. I won't be gone long. Meantime, you fellas stick close to the cabin until I get back."

"Are you gonna bring D'lise home?" Johnny asked hopefully.

"I doubt if I will this trip, kid, but she'll come back to us eventually."

Kane found that his leg wasn't as fine as he thought it was. By the time he reached the village, it was throbbing painfully. He was thankful to swing out of the saddle and stretch the muscles that had stiffened from disuse the past three weeks.

As he tied the stallion to the hitching rack in front of Samuel's store and ran through his mind what he would say to the owner, Claudie Jacobs and Sarah Patton came through the door. He smiled at them and started to speak, then didn't. After one cold look at him, the ladies stuck their chins in the air and sailed right past him.

Well, he thought ruefully, staring after them, *it's plain to see whose side they are on.* He stepped up on the porch and walked into the store. Samuel looked up from filling small bags with coffee beans and, after a startled look, smiled at him genially.

"It's good to see you up and around, Devlin. How's the leg?"

Kane stalked over to the counter and, ignoring the inquiry about his leg, said coldly, "I've come to settle up for whatever you've taken over to my wife."

"It's not a great deal." Samuel reached under the counter and brought up a slim ledger. "She's been charging everything to you. It will just take me a minute to total it up."

Primed to have an argument with Majors, to warn him not to give his wife any more gifts, Kane was at a loss what to say now. It appeared there hadn't been any gifts after all.

He knew a warm feeling that D'lise was still depending

358

on him to support her. His spirits lifted for the first time since she left him. He handed over the money requested and limped out of the store without another word.

Twice, as Kane walked to Buck's fur post, he was snubbed by females. First by Claudie Jacobs, then of all people, Abbey Davis. Shy little Abbey, mother of two daughters who weren't everything they should be, seldom looked at anybody, but she cut him cold. His lips twisted in a half smile. What kind of treatment would he get from their husbands? he wondered.

When he walked into the tavern, he was greeted mostly as he'd always been, certainly by his fellow trappers. There was a little coolness from some of the men, but at least they didn't look at him as if he was lower than a snake's belly. Inquiries were made about his leg, but nothing was said about Raven's charge, or about his wife's leaving him because of it. Buck, however, handed him a surprise a little later on.

"You wanna pay up your bill today, Kane?"

Kane gave him a startled look. "Pay my bill? I don't owe you anything."

"You sure as hell do." Buck mopped at the bar. "D'lise has been buyin' some things and chargin' 'em to you." He looked at Kane quzzically. "It's all right I let her, ain't it?"

"Oh, sure," Kane answered promptly. "Give her anything she wants. How much do I owe you?" He reached into his pocket, ready and eager to spend his last dime on his wife.

When he saw the cost of the totaled items, he wondered if that was what D'lise had in mind. She certainly wasn't stinting herself.

But that was fine. Her action told him that all was not lost between them. By now, she'd had time to think over

Raven's charge and remember that the woman was a troublemaker.

As Kane poured himself another whiskey, he cursed the day the Indian woman had come into his life. If ever there was a more vengeful, more conniving bitch, he'd never seen her.

He remembered the day he was putting the roof on the new cabin and Raven had come by. She had wheedled him into showing her the inside of the cabin. He hadn't wanted to take the time, because he was anxious to get the roof finished, to move D'lise in. But for old times and a sense of guilt for pushing her out of his life, he had showed her through the cabin.

It was as they were walking back outside that he saw from the corner of his eye D'lise watching them from across the next hill. Why he hadn't acknowledged her presence, he didn't know. He could have waved to her, called her to join him and Raven. But for some perverse reason he hadn't. Maybe he had thought she was spying on him. Then later, as they ate supper, when D'lise hadn't mentioned Raven, he hadn't either. He had figured that she didn't think it was important.

He had been mistaken, he knew now. That incident had only added to the suspicions D'lise already had.

Kane's elation began to wane, and he felt the strain of being on his healing leg too long. It was time he got home and rested it. Besides, he didn't like leaving the boys alone too long. Johnny had a habit of getting into mischief.

The two lads had become very dear to him and made him want a son of his own. Would that ever happen? he asked himself as he finished his whiskey and set the glass down. It didn't look to be in the cards very soon. He ignored the nasty little voice that sneered, *Don't forget*

Raven. She may give you a son.

Protests were sounded when Kane announced he was leaving. "You can stay out as long as you want to now, Kane," a trapper at the end of the bar said. "Ain't no little woman sittin' up there on your hill to tell you no."

"Much to my sorrow," Kane answered, loud enough for everyone to hear as he limped to the door.

He stepped outside—and straight into D'lise. The weight of his body made her stagger, and his hands went out to steady her. His eyes moved hungrily over her delicately carved features, and he fought the urge to draw her into his arms. It had been so long since he had felt her softness crushed up against him.

D'lise felt the same desire as she gazed back at Kane, noting the fine line fanning out at the corners of his eyes. Had they been so deep the day she left him? She could almost believe that he had been grieving. *Don't be dimwitted,* she told herself and tried to pull away.

Kane didn't release his hold. He continued to gaze at her, his thumbs rubbing the softness of her inner arms. There was a raw sound in his voice when he asked, "How have you been, honey? Are you gettin' along all right? Do you have everything you need?"

Her heart thundering against her ribs, D'lise forced herself to say coolly, "I'm getting along fine." She gave a little jerk of her head over her shoulder. "My friends are looking after me."

Kane lifted his gaze at her gesture, and for the first time saw Samuel Majors and Ellen Travis a few feet behind D'lise. His insides knotted and his body grew rigid in the icy silence that developed. His fingers bit into D'lise's arms a split second before he scornfully pushed her away from him.

"You mean *a* friend is takin' care of your needs?" he

sneered, then turned on his heel and walked away.

D'lise watched Kane limp down the dusty street and wanted to run after him, ask about his wound—had it healed properly, did his leg still hurt him? She remembered then why she didn't know all this first-hand and hardened her heart against her unfaithful husband. When Samuel nudged her arm and asked, "Are you ready to go?" she nodded and they walked on.

Ellen was having her and Samuel over to her home for lunch and to discuss plans for the wedding that was fast approaching. Ellen's wedding gown had arrived last week, the loveliest creation D'lise had ever seen. Piney Ridge would probably never see a lovelier bride.

But D'lise Devlin wouldn't look bad either, D'lise remembered with a pleased smile. She was going to be witness for Ellen, and her friend had ordered her a dress from Boston also. She repressed a giggle. Wait until Kane had to pay that bill. His angry roar would be heard all through the hills.

Her dress was a shade of blue that matched her eyes and it was quite daring in the neckline. It hadn't been designed that way, but due to her pregnancy her breasts had filled out considerably, making them much too large for the dress since it was ordered to her measurements a month ago. Poor Ellen was quite irate at the seamstress in Boston.

"I can't understand it," she'd wailed when they tried on the dresses and D'lise's was so snug in the bodice. "Mine fits perfectly, but your breasts are ready to fall out of your bodice."

D'lise had been afraid the dress wouldn't fit her at all on the day of the wedding two weeks away. Then she discovered that the garment had wide seams and tucks, and if her breasts didn't get too much larger, she would be able to make it fit, with some lace tucked into the low-cut top.

She sighed softly as she walked along. She'd have to tell Ellen and her friends about her approaching motherhood soon. Pregnancy was something you could hide only so long.

What would they say? she wondered. What advice would they give her? And what would Kane's thoughts be on becoming a father—for a second time. Would it anger him, or would it pump up his ego that he had begotten two babies almost within the same month?

Probably the latter, the prowling tomcat.

David and Johnny came loping down the hill to meet Kane. They had made beans and ham hocks for supper, Johnny informed him as they walked alongside the stallion. Puffing a little, he added, "David baked a pan of cornpone, and it ain't bad. I told him how to, though. I used to watch D'lise, and I remembered what she put in it."

Kane knew the youngster was dying to ask him about D'lise, but that most likely David had told him not to. He gazed down at the freckled face lifted to his and said gently, "I saw D'lise, but she won't be comin' back to us for a while."

"Did you go to the schoolhouse and talk to her?" Johnny asked, looking as if he might cry any minute.

"No, I saw her on the street with Mr. Majors and Ellen Travis."

"Heck." Johnny kicked at a rock. "She's always with them."

That bit of news darkened Kane's mood to a point that lasted through the consumption of slightly scorched beans and cornbread burned on the underside. He could have been chewing on wood chips for all the attention he was paying to what was in his mouth. The boys were unaware of what had put him in this sullen mood and were almost glad that he left the cabin as soon as the meal was over.

"I sure wish D'lise would come back, so Kane would laugh and smile again," Johnny said wistfully, watching Kane descend the hill to another empty, lonely night.

Inside the cabin he had shared with D'lise but a short time, Kane took a bottle of whiskey off the mantel and sat down in one of the rocking chairs. He stared into the dead fireplace struggling with the desire to ride back to Piney Ridge, find Samuel Majors, and pound his handsome face into a bloody pulp.

He fought the wild desire, and it slowly died away. With a sigh, he uncorked the bottle and lifted it to his lips. Slowly the whiskey blunted his thoughts and made him sleepy.

Two miles beyond Tom Spears's place, Albert Bracken lay on top of Raven in a one-room shack of a cabin. Bracken, in his mid-thirties, was mostly a loner, not caring overly for his fellow men. He never visited any of his neighbors, nor did he want them coming to pass the time of day with him.

The man hated Kane Devlin and loved his former squaw, Raven. Sometimes he almost choked on the bile he felt for the trapper. Where Kane was tall and muscular, Albert was short and squat. Where Kane was the handsomest man in the hills, Albert's face was deeply pockmarked, with a bulbous nose and small squinty eyes.

Raven had visited Albert off and on, sometimes spending a week or two with him. She had lived with him all the time Kane was away fighting in the war, but on his return she had gone back to her handsome lover. Then

Kane had got married and kicked her out.

Although Albert was happy beyond words to have Raven back, there was a bitterness in his soul. The trapper's wife had left him, and he knew that if Devlin said the word, Raven would go back to him again.

He plunged himself deeper into Raven's writhing body, and at her command moved faster and faster, his belly slapping against hers in time with the loud creaking of the bed attached to the wall. Sweat gathered on his face, back, and shoulders. He had been working over her for at least half an hour, and she still wanted more.

Well, he would give it to her, he told himself. The thing that attracted him to Raven was her ability to keep up with the lust that seemed to ride him constantly. He knew that his great size and stamina were what kept her coming back to him. He felt pretty sure that, in that department, he outshone Kane Devlin—or any other man.

"You'll never have her again, Devlin, you bastard," he whispered to himself, pumping his hips fiercely.

Chapter Twenty-four

Two more weeks passed, and August was only two days away. Kane's leg had almost regained its full strength, helped along by his hunting with the boys a couple of hours each day. Stretching his legs, climbing the hills, had toned up the muscles the bullet had ripped through. It was no hardship to ride anymore, and three or four times a week he rode to the village.

He had grown used to being snubbed by the women-folk, and though it bothered him, it was a small price to pay for the off-chance he might catch a glimpse of D'lise. Maybe he'd get lucky today, he thought, his seat easy in the saddle, his body moving with the ambling gait of the stallion. He had seen D'lise twice, each time going into Majors's store. He had wanted to call out to her, but had dreaded the cold look she would turn on him. Her glacial blue stare froze him to his very heart.

Pulling up in front of the fur post, Kane swung to the

ground and tied Snowy to the hitching post. He stepped up on the porch, but instead of entering the tavern, he sat down in one of the chairs Buck kept there for anyone who wanted to sit and gab with friends, or just watch the people who went about their business.

It was a hot, drowsy afternoon and there weren't many people about. After a half hour had passed, he'd seen only a couple of boys wander down the street, kicking an empty whiskey bottle to each other, and an old hound crawl under a porch across the street.

He had just about given up hope of seeing D'lise—it was probably too hot for her to be out—when he saw her coming down the street. He stopped the rocker and sat forward, his eyes practically eating her. As he silently prayed she wouldn't go into Majors's store, she lifted her skirt a bit and climbed the two steps of the emporium. He ground his teeth together when she disappeared through the door. He took out his pocket watch and noted the time, then sat back and waited for her reappearance.

An hour passed, and then another, and still D'lise hadn't left the store. Images that rocked his soul flashed through Kane's mind—D'lise and Majors in bed together, she making love to the man in the same way she had once done to him—a hundred years ago, it seemed. And the storekeeper would be whispering love words to her, words her husband didn't know how to say, even though his mind screamed them.

Hell, he'd never even been able to say the words ''I love you,'' although he loved her so much it scared him half to death.

Kane was ready to storm the store, find Majors's bedroom, and march D'lise out of it after knocking hell out of the man, when D'lise stepped out onto the porch, Ellen Travis behind her. He hadn't known that Ellen was in there, too, and his whole being lightened. He watched the two women say goodbye to Majors, then walk down the street. There couldn't have been too much going on with Ellen in there too.

"She and the widder had lunch with the storekeeper." Old Tom had quietly come up behind him.

"How come you know that?" Kane asked, his eyes following D'lise as she walked along, watching the sway of her rounded hips, recalling with a twist in his loins how they had felt beneath his body, rising to meet his thrusts.

God, it had been so long.

"D'lise told me yesterday," Tom was saying. "The three of them are thicker than fleas on an old hound dog. They're always havin' lunch together, either at the store or at the widder's cabin."

"What about supper?" Kane growled. "I expect they get together for that too."

"Nope. Majors has them two little girls, and he can't leave them alone at night. His housekeeper goes home around four o'clock, and naturally D'lise and the widder don't go on the streets after dark."

"I guess," Kane agreed, then said, "Tom, you're close to D'lise. Can't you put in a good word for me, tell her I'm innocent of anything to do with Raven? I still think the bitch is lyin'."

"I've done tried, son. Ain't no use. She's hurtin', and she feels betrayed. Your only hope is that when that Indian bitch drops her papoose, it don't look like you. If it's fair with light-colored hair like yourn, I think you can forget about ever gettin' D'lise back."

"Well, by God," Kane shouted, jumping to his feet and sending the chair over backward, "there ain't no other man gonna have her either. You tell her that, tell her to relay the message to that bastard across the street. He's wanted her ever since he laid eyes on her. I'll shoot him in a heartbeat if he ever tries to take her away from me.''

The old trapper looked at him, for a moment seeming about to disagree with Kane's heated announcement. Then, with his gnarled hand covering a tickled grin, he said solemnly, ''I'll tell her, Kane.''

Without further words, Kane left the porch and swung onto Snowy's back. Tom watched him ride away. ''I should have told him about the widder and Majors gettin' married next Saturday,'' he said to himself. ''Put an end to the poor devil's misery.'' But it pleased his odd sense of humor to teach the younger trapper not to be so full of himself. For years, the young buck had gone his careless way, taking his pleasure where he found it. It was time he knew mental pain, learned a little humility. The fiddler wanted to be paid now. He had given Kane Devlin too many years of free music.

His brows drawn together in annoyance, Kane muttered, ''Damn ornery old coot. My misery tickles the hell out of him. Deep down he thinks I'm guilty.''

The stallion climbed the hill and Kane looked across the narrow valley to where the two cabins drowsed in the late afternoon sun. He had known such happiness in both of them. It had been the furthest thing from his mind that it could all be wiped out in just a few minutes.

Kane's first indication of danger was the tightening of Snowy's body, the pricking forward of his ears. He firmed his grip on the reins, but before he could goad the stallion into action a shot rang out, and a bullet splintered the bark of a tree only inches from his head. He flung himself to the ground, his hand snatching his gun from its holster. He rolled over once, came up on one knee, and squeezed the trigger, aiming at a rider disappearing through a thick growth of trees. He gritted out a furious oath. He had missed the sneaking sniper. Nor had he been able to recognize the man in the gloom of the trees.

He stood up, brushed himself off, and climbed back on the stallion. His expression dark and hard, he sent Snowy down the hill. Somebody wanted him dead, and had come damn close to seeing it happen. He rubbed the still tender scar on his leg. He had no doubt it was the same man who had put the mark on his thigh—but what man? As far as he knew, only Samuel Majors would benefit from his death. He would be free to marry D'lise once her husband was out of the way.

Kane shook his head at that thought. As much as he hated the man, the storekeeper wasn't the sort to sneak up on a man and try to kill him. He was still racking his brain for an answer when he rode past the new cabin and continued on up to the old one.

As he neared the one-room shack, he squinted his eyes against the setting sun shining on his face. Was that Big Beaver sitting on the porch with the boys? He hoped so. He could use some of his friend's wise counsel.

The tall brave stood up as Kane swung to the ground and stepped onto the porch. They stood a moment grinning at each other; then Kane said, "Where have you been all summer? I hope you've come to do some huntin'."

"Maybe," Big Beaver answered, his black eyes skimming over Kane's face. When he had noted its thinness, the deep grooves along his cheeks, he said, "It is told around our campfires that much has happened to you since last we hunted together."

"That sure as hell is true," Kane grunted, dropping down on the edge of the porch. "I've been shot at twice, took a bullet in my leg the first time."

"We didn't know you was shot at again, Kane," David exclaimed.

"It just happened on my way home, over on the other hill. He damn near got me this time. Missed my head by inches. I heard the whistle of the bullet."

Big Beaver sat quietly, letting David and Johnny fire questions at Kane, speculating on who the sniper was and why he had shot at Kane. When they finally ran down, he spoke:

"I have heard also that your little flower has left you."

"Yes." Kane looked out over the yard to the encroaching trees.

The Indian chuckled softly. "Maybe she's the one trying to kill you. Does your wife believe Raven's foolish claim?"

Kane's head shot up, and he stared at the tall brave. "Friend, you must be the only person in these hills who thinks the woman is lyin'."

"Thinks she's lying?" Big Beaver grunted. "I know she's lying. The woman cannot get with child."

"Are you sure of this, Big Beaver?" Kane asked, afraid to believe it was so.

"When Raven was thirteen, she was racing her pony down a valley one day. It stepped in a hole, tossed her off its back, then fell on her lower body. The female part of her body was badly damaged."

It seemed to Kane that the weight of the hills had been lifted off his shoulders. Proof—at last he had proof. "Big Beaver," he said earnestly, "you have just given me back a reason for livin'. Will you ride with me to the village, tell my wife that I didn't sleep with that lyin' bitch?"

"Hold on, friend." Big Beaver held up a hand. "I have no proof that you didn't sleep with Raven. I can only prove that she's not carrying your child. It's up to you to convince your woman otherwise.''

"How in the hell do I do that?'' Kane ran agitated fingers through his hair. "If I only knew where Raven is holed up, I'd try to threaten the truth out of her.''

"She's living with your neighbor, Albert Bracken,'' Big Beaver said quietly. "Has been all summer—and while you were away those two years.''

"I forgot about Bracken's yen for her,'' Kane said thoughtfully. "We had a little set-to over her right after I returned home from the war.''

"Didn't it occur to you that he might be the one trying to kill you?'' the Shawnee asked. "With your wife gone, he probably fears that Raven will leave him for you again.''

"I think he's the one to talk to. He'll know better than anyone if you took the squaw in a drunken stupor.'' This last was said with a slightly condemning tone.

Kane gave Big Beaver a reproachful look. "You think I'm guilty. I can hear it in your voice.''

"I don't think you're guilty of any wrongdoing with the woman. I think you're guilty of acting the fool and drinking so much firewater you forgot where you lived.''

Kane let that pass. He had no defense. Now he must try to undo all the damage his pride and jealousy had brought about.

"I'm gonna have one hell of a time tryin' to talk to Bracken,'' Kane said, half to himself. "If he's the one who's been tryin' to kill me, he'll not miss when I come knockin' at his door.''

"That is true,'' Big Beaver agreed. "As you well know, a jealous man acts first, then wonders at his actions. What you must do is watch his cabin. When he leaves it, you follow him, catch up with him. First you calm his worries that you will want his woman back and convince him that you care only for your wife. Only then will he tell you what you want to know.''

Night had fallen as D'lise sat on her small porch, and here and there through the darkness lights began to shine in the windows of Piney Ridge. A screech owl sent up his long, quavering call, and her eyes smarted with tears at the sound.

She and Kane used to sit on the porch of the old cabin after dark, listening to the night sounds as they talked quietly together. She sighed wistfully. She missed him so, missed being aroused in the middle of the night by the feel of his arms wrapped around her.

Kane had been on her mind so much the past four days, ever since she had glimpsed him when she and Ellen left Samuel's store. She had glanced over her shoulder to look at him again, but she saw only his back as he strode away in that careless, arrogant way of his.

With a choked-off sob, she dropped her head on her drawn-up knees. She knew she shouldn't, but she still loved her husband. She had no illusions remaining that he returned that love, for never once had he said that he did.

Yet, for some reason she couldn't understand, he hadn't wanted her to leave him that heart-breaking morning. There was also the fact, according to David and Johnny, that Raven hadn't been around the cabin. That must mean . . .

D'lise raised her head suddenly, a startled look on her face. She had just felt a stirring in her lower stomach, as though a tiny animal had darted across it. Her face broke into a wide smile. Her baby had moved for the first time! She laid her palm over her slightly thickened waist and waited for the movement again. Although she waited for ten minutes, nothing happened.

She did some serious thinking as she sat staring into the darkness. Did she have the right to rob her child of its father? Kane would make a good father—if he wanted to. She came to a hard-thought-out decision. If only for the life growing inside her, tomorrow after Ellen's wedding, she was going to the cabin to tell Kane about the coming baby. His reaction to her news would determine whether she stayed there, giving her marriage another chance, or continued to make plans to go to Boston.

The stallion nibbled at clumps of grass as Kane knelt behind a screening of brush. This was the fourth morning he'd been there, watching the Bracken shack. He had seen both Albert and Raven moving around outside, but the man he wanted to talk to hadn't left the premises.

"He's got to be runnin' out of fresh meat pretty soon," Kane muttered. "In this hot weather when the meat spoils so fast, he should have been out in the woods two days ago."

He stopped talking to himself, his body stiffening. Bracken was leaving the shack, his rifle on his shoulder. Finally, hunger was driving him from Raven's arms for a while.

Kane soon came to the conclusion that the man he followed didn't intend to stay away from Raven any longer than necessary. He really had to stretch his long legs to keep up with the shorter man's hurried pace.

Kane had followed his quarry about half a mile when the stocky man suddenly stepped behind a tree and stared up among its branches. Kane followed Bracken's line of vision and saw the bushy tail of a squirrel sticking out from behind the trunk. The hunter raised his rifle, braced the butt against his shoulder, and waited for the furry little animal to show his head.

In a couple of minutes, the rifle spat, and Albert's supper hit the ground. "There's no better time than now," Kane said under his breath. "Get him before he can reload."

His moccasin-shod feet making no sound on the needle-strewn forest, Kane slipped up behind the man stooping to pick up his kill and spoke his name.

Bracken stiffened in his bent position, the squirrel in his hand. He froze that way for a few minutes, as though listening for the sound of death. "I should put a bullet in your head, you sneakin' polecat," Kane gritted when Bracken, gray-faced with fear, straightened up. "And I may still do it if I don't get some straight answers from you."

His voice harsh with tension, Bracken croaked, "What do you want to know?"

"I want to know why you've been shootin' at me, and if that bitchin' squaw put you up to it."

Kane read in the man's scared face that he intended to lie, to deny that he had shot at him. His black stare dared Bracken to try it.

With a helpless shrug, Bracken said, "Raven doesn't know that I've been shootin' at you. She did ask me once to kill your wife. When I wouldn't do it, she had a cousin of hers try it."

"That bitch!" Kane's face turned as grim as death. "Do you think she'll try to get someone else to do it?"

"I don't think so. Now that she's played that trick on your wife, she seems satisfied."

"What trick is that?" Kane's eyes narrowed dangerously.

"You know. The night she went to your cabin and took off her clothes and climbed in bed with you when you was drunk. She still laughs about it."

Kane's voice trembled with rage. "But we hadn't done anything, had we?"

Bracken gave him a look that said he was short of brains. "As piss-drunk as you was? That thing of yours was so limber I could have tied a knot in it."

"So you were there too?"

"I was outside lookin' through the window. I was makin' sure nothin' was gonna happen between you two."

Kane stared silently at the ground so long that Bracken stirred uneasily. "What are you thinkin' to do with me?" he ventured finally. "I know you won't kill me in cold blood. And if you tell anyone that I admitted shootin' at you, I'll deny it."

"Why, you—" Kane began, then spun around when the brush behind him crackled. His tightly held body relaxed when a half-naked Indian stepped in view. "Big Beaver, I thought you were back to your village by now."

"No, I too have been watching this man with the yellow streak down his back. I thought it best you have a witness to what he might tell you." He grinned at Kane. "It was a good thought, was it not?"

"It was a very good thought, friend. What do we do now?"

"You do as you please about this one. I go now to speak to the woman who shames our village. She will either go to your wife and tell her what evil thing she has done, or I will sell her as a slave to another tribe. There she will do hard labor from sunrise to sunset. She will never again lie with a man."

"No!" Bracken shouted. "Don't do that. I'll take her away from here. She'll never bother anyone again. I swear it. I'll beat her if I have to."

"That is what she needs," Big Beaver grunted, "but

first she will make her confession to my friend's wife.''
He turned and walked off in the direction of Bracken's
shack.

When Bracken would have followed him, Kane drew
his gun and aimed it at his belt buckle. "Sit down and
make yourself comfortable while we give Big Beaver time
to take care of his business.''

Chapter Twenty-five

D'lise had been up since the first pink strips of dawn lightened the eastern sky. At three o'clock this afternoon, Ellen and Samuel would become one.

What a friend Ellen had been to her, she mused, lifting her wet hair so that the warm morning breeze could waft through it. She had washed it the first thing on rising, and for the last hour she had been sitting on a stump in back of the school-house waiting for the thick mass to dry.

For that matter, all her friends had rallied round her, giving her moral support. Even shy little Abbey Davis, who never went anywhere, would slip through the woods at night when she was sure no one else was around to visit with D'lise for an hour or so. Sometimes she drew more courage from that little person's gentle silence than she did from all the others. Abbey never made denouncements against men in general like most of the other women did. She never mentioned men, other than her husband. You could hear the love she felt for him in her voice.

Should the wives of Piney Ridge pity Abbey Davis so? D'lise wondered, rubbing a strand of hair with the towel. It was true the little woman didn't have much in the line of material things and that her daughters shamed her with their carrying on, but she had the wonderful assurance that she was deeply loved by her husband. Nothing could be more important than that in a marriage. She, D'lise Devlin, should know that better than anyone.

Loved or not by her husband, D'lise was holding to the decision she had made last night. Unless Kane made it blatantly clear that he was unhappy that she was expecting, she was ready to resume her loveless marriage.

An unexpected rush of desire swept over her. It would be good to have him make love to her again. They were suitably matched in that department. She had sometimes suspected that very reason was why Kane hadn't wanted to lose her. Maybe he didn't love his wife, but he certainly lusted after her.

I guess that's better than nothing, she thought, rising from the stump and entering her quarters. She gave her nearly dry hair a final brushing, then placed two flatirons on the red coals to heat.

She had to iron shirts and pants for David and Johnny. The boys didn't know it, but they were attending the wedding also. She smiled to herself as she placed thick padding on the table and covered it with a sheet. David would grouse about attending the affair and having to wear his Sunday best. He would complain that the starched collar was too tight and that it scratched, but fun-loving Johnny would be so excited he'd have to make numerous trips to the outhouse.

D'lise brought the basket of clean laundry from her

bedroom. She had insisted that the boys bring their dirty clothes to her every week. If it was left up to Kane, he'd let them wear the same clothes until they fell off them.

No article of Kane's had appeared in the bundle that was delivered to her every Saturday, for which she was thankful. His clothing would carry the familiar scent of tobacco and piney outdoors. She wasn't ready to breathe in his particular scent yet. It would make her cry, she knew.

She wondered if Kane was keeping the cabin clean, or had he let it get in the same shape as she had found the old place when he first brought her to it?

She flinched, picturing in her mind muddy footprints on all the floors and grease splattered all over the kitchen.

But that might not be the case at all, she told herself, spreading David's shirt out on the table. From the way the boys talked, it appeared that Kane took his meals with them in the old cabin. And Johnny had laughed one day about how he had accidentally kicked Kane in the head one night when he'd got up to go outside to relieve himself. He had finished his tale by saying that, after Kane got through swearing, he'd remarked that from now on he'd make sure he didn't spread his blankets too close to the bed anymore. That sounded as though Kane might be living with them.

The sun had been making its way westward for a couple of hours, and Big Beaver sat on in his perch high in a maple tree. His eyes never left the Bracken shack. Raven hadn't answered his knock on the door around noon, and he had gone inside and searched the single room thoroughly in case she had seen him coming and was hiding. When he had made sure she wasn't there, he had gone to the lean-to attached to the shack. Only Bracken's horse was there. There was no sign of the spotted Indian pony Raven rode. He had then climbed the tree to wait for her return.

Big Beaver was beginning to wonder if Raven had seen him after all and had slipped off to their village, which was about ten miles away. The cagey bitch knew that her sly ways had never fooled him, that he could, and would, make her rectify the damage she had done to his friend.

The big Indian was debating if he was wasting his time waiting for Raven to return when he saw her come riding up from behind the shack. He waited until she dismounted and stepped onto the small stoop. When she reached out a hand for the door latch, he slid down the tree and stepped up behind her.

Raven gave a startled screech that could be heard a mile away when her arms were gripped by steel-like fingers. Dread spread over her face when Big Beaver swung her around and she read the dire message in his coal-black eyes.

"What do you want?" she croaked. "I have done nothing to you."

The long fingers tightened cruelly on her arms. "When you hurt my friend, you hurt me. I don't need to tell you how you have hurt him."

Raven looked away from his grim face, muttering, "I don't know what you are talking about."

Tears sprang into her eyes when one hand left her arm and slapped her across the mouth. "You well know what I'm talking about." Big Beaver shoved her off the porch and continued to shove her toward the pony. "Now you're going to D'lise Devlin and tell her about the trick you pulled on her and her husband. You are not to let her know that you are being forced to do this." He boosted her onto the little mount's bare back, adding, "You will pretend that you are filled with remorse for what you've done, that you couldn't rest until you told her the truth.''

Raven's eyes shot hate and defiance at Big Beaver. ''I will not humiliate myself to that pale-faced bitch. She stole my man.''

''Kane Devlin was never your man. In your heart you know that.'' The Indian grabbed the pony's reins when Raven would have sent him sprinting away. His cold tone struck to her heart when he said, ''You can either do as I say, or I'll take you right now across the river and sell you into slavery. You've never had to work like the rest of our women do. You have grown soft from bartering your body to the white man. How long do you think you would last doing hard labor for at least ten hours out of each day, never having a man in your blankets again?''

Raven bent her head in defeat. There were women slaves in her own village, and she knew too well the life they led. They had to obey any order given them or feel the bite of a whip or a clubbing from the village women.

When Big Beaver whistled up his mount and swung onto its back, she obediently followed him as he rode toward Piney Ridge.

It seemed to Kane that he had been pacing for hours before he saw Big Beaver riding up the hill Raven meekly following him. He watched them disappear down the back of the hill, then climbed onto Snowy's back. ''You can go now, Bracken.'' He looked down at the man's anxious face. ''But don't let me see you in these parts again. Take that trouble-causin' squaw and get the hell out of these hills.''

Bracken rose from his seat beneath the tree and, without a word, strode off in the direction of his shack. Kane kicked the stallion's rump with his heels, sending him galloping in the direction of his own cabin. In another two hours the sun would be setting and he had much to do in that time.

It was a beautiful wedding, D'lise thought, standing beside the radiant Ellen as she accepted the good wishes of her friends and neighbors. It had been bittersweet listening to the same words that had been spoken at her own wedding. Foolishly, she had believed every word Kane had spoken, for she had meant every promise she had made in God's house.

She sighed and waited for everyone to leave to go to Ellen's house where a banquet awaited them. She still had to tell Ellen of her decision. Her friend would probably think she was limber-brained for still loving a man who sought out his old lover. But she did love Kane, and if he showed no reluctance to becoming a father twice, maybe the baby's arrival, and time, would make him forget about Raven and make him at least contented with his wife.

When D'lise finally got Ellen alone, she was surprised and relieved at how the new Mrs. Majors took her news. Ellen smiled and gave her a big hug. "I've known all along that you still loved Kane," she said. "And truthfully, Samuel and I have had our doubts about what you and Claudie heard that morning. Oh, I know what you heard," she said when D'lise started to protest, "but I think you heard a lie.

"Your husband adores you, D'lise. It's in his eyes every time he looks at you. Believe me, that Indian woman holds no allure for him."

"Oh, Ellen, wouldn't it be wonderful if you're right." D'lise's eyes glowed with hope.

"I am right." Ellen took her hands and squeezed them gently. "Now, go make peace with your man."

D'lise could only nod, for she was too choked up to speak. After giving her friend a quick kiss on the cheek, she went to change her dress and to find David and Johnny.

Big Beaver drew rein at the edge of the village, grunting to Raven to do the same. The single dusty street that wound its way around tree stumps was empty. He gazed toward its end, where apparently all the village's residents were gathered at the white man's house of worship.

"Some kind of celebration going on," he said. "We'll wait here until we see Kane's woman alone."

Raven made no response, only stared sullenly down the street, her hatred for Kane Devlin and his wife burning like a fire through her body. If not for this meddlesome man sitting beside her, she'd have had complete revenge on both of them.

She looked at Big Beaver when he gave a surprised grunt. He was staring at the trapper she'd been thinking of with such hostility. "I didn't know he planned on coming to the village," Big Beaver said. "I hope he's not looking for his wife."

"Whether he is or not," Raven said nervously, "he's going to see her. She's riding toward him right now."

As Big Beaver watched, undecided what to do, Kane kicked his mount into a gallop, eating up the distance between him and D'lise. There was an uneasy sensation in the pit of his stomach as the mare and stallion came together. He gazed hungrily at D'lise, wondering if Raven had talked to her yet, and if so, if it had made any difference to her. In his hurry to get dressed, he'd almost overlooked a note David had left for him saying that he shouldn't worry if they got home after dark, that D'lise was bringing them home. The question burning in his breast now—was she coming home to stay, or to ask him for her freedom?

D'lise gazed back into the slate-colored eyes, feeling the familiar leap of the blood and pulse every time she saw him. What would he say when she told him she wanted to come back? What would he say about the baby?

"D'lise." Kane urged the stallion up alongside the mare until his and D'lise's knees were touching. "David left me a note sayin' that you were comin' back with them. I've got to know, is it just for a visit, or are you comin' back for good? I've got to tell you, if it's only for a visit, I don't want you there. It would be more than I could bear to watch you ride away again."

He leaned from the saddle and gripped her arms, and she could feel the tension in his fingers. "I'm not as strong as these hills, D'lise. I'm just a mortal man who bleeds when he's cut. You cut me deep when you left me and I bled, woman."

"No more than I did, Kane." D'lise leaned forward and covered his hands with hers. "Can you imagine what it did to me, hearing Raven say she was carrying your baby, and you looking as though it might be true?"

"God, D'lise, I know how you must have felt, but—"

D'lise raised her hand to cover his lips, shutting out the rest of his sentence. "We will let the past go. I am coming back to you, but there is one condition, whether I stay with you or not."

"Anything, D'lise. Just name it. I love you so much I'll agree to anything—except your seeing another man."

D'lise's eyes flew to his face, wide and shimmering with happy tears. "You love me, Kane?"

"Of course I love you, you silly woman. Why do you think I'm so desperate to have you back?"

"You never once said it. How was I to know?"

385

"I know I didn't." Kane shifted about in the saddle. "I'm not good with words, but my body screamed it every time I made love to you. Couldn't you feel it?"

"I thought I did, but I didn't want to mistake it for lust."

"Ah, honey." Kane stroked a finger down her cheek. "I admit that sometimes I lusted after you like a ruttin' buffalo, but I loved you at the same time." He tilted her chin. "Tell the truth now, didn't you lust after me just a little bit?"

D'lise ducked her scarlet, embarrassed face. She had lusted after him—a lot. She forced herself to look back at Kane when he asked, "What was that condition you were talkin' about?"

D'lise's lips curved in a soft, dreamy smile. "I'm going to have your baby, Kane."

With incredulous joy flashing across his face, leaping out of his eyes, Kane lifted D'lise from the saddle and set her in front of him. When he would have kissed her, she braced her hands against his chest, holding him away. They had one more thing to discuss. She had to ask him about the other child he might have fathered, what he planned to do about it if it was true. In all honesty, she was not Christian enough to raise the child as her own, and she felt that Kane should know this from the start.

Back at the edge of the forest, where Big Beaver sat watching Kane and D'lise, it looked to him as if D'lise was pushing Kane away in anger. He turned a stern look on Raven. "Get on down there. It's time you admit your lies to my friend and his wife. Don't forget that I'll be close enough to hear what you say and to see the expression on your face. You know the consequences if one word or look makes a mockery out of your apologies." He gave the pony a slap on the rump, and it broke into a startled run. Raven could only hang on and steer it toward D'lise and Kane and the two boys who had been watching and listening intently to what was going on between the two adults.

"What the hell!" Kane's arms tightened around D'lise protectively as Raven managed to pull the pony to a rearing halt beside them. Where in the hell was Big Beaver? He looked anxiously into the forest. When he didn't see his friend, his hand dropped to the butt of his gun. He'd shoot the bitch if he had to. No way was she going to hurt D'lise again in any manner.

But as Kane glared at the Indian woman, his hard, cold eyes warning her to make no wrong move, say no wrong word, he noted that, though sullenness gripped her features, there was no threat about her. Evidently, Big Beaver had managed to scare the hell out of her.

"What do you want, Raven?" His words were short and clipped.

For a moment hatred for him shone in the black eyes; then Raven was saying the words that would save her from a lifetime of slavery.

"I want to tell your woman that you did not know when I slipped into your bed that night, and that not once did you come out of your drunken stupor." She took a deep breath and continued, "I did it because I wanted to hurt you both. I am not carrying your child."

While D'lise looked on, remorse building in her because she hadn't believed her husband, had had no faith in him, Kane asked, "Whose child are you carryin', Raven?" His eyes bored into her. He wanted no lingering doubts left in D'lise's mind.

"I carry no one's," Raven muttered, avoiding the deep blue eyes that watched her intently. She looked at Kane instead. "I think that you know I can't have children. I think that Big Beaver has told you this.''

"Is that true, Kane?" D'lise asked softly.

"Yes, it's true."

"But why didn't you tell me?"

"I only found out today. But I wouldn't have told you anyway, I don't think.''

"I don't understand.''

Kane's arms tightened around her. "I didn't want your love conditionally, D'lise. I wanted you to love me no matter what. That's how I love you, even when I thought Majors had taken my place in your heart and bed."

"Oh, Kane, I thought you knew that Samuel has been courting Ellen for months. They got married today. The boys and I have just come from their wedding.''

Johnny, who had managed to keep quiet until now, burst out, "Yeah, and there's all kinds of eats at Ellen's house, but D'lise said we couldn't go, that we had to hurry home before dark. I peeked in the window, and there was all kinds of pies and cakes.''

"I'll bake you a cake tomorrow," D'lise consoled the eight-year-old.

Johnny's face brightened. "A spice cake, D'lise? I can't wait for you to make supper tonight. Me and David can't cook worth spit, and Kane ain't much better. He makes awful biscuits. Even Hound won't eat them when he comes to visit.''

"Thanks, you little tadpole," Kane laughed. "I'll remember that. And as for supper tonight, you're gonna have to get along with your own cookin'. D'lise and I are goin' to celebrate tonight, and we don't want any company. Do you get my drift?''

"But why not?" Johnny began. "Me and David have missed—'' The rest of his sentence was jolted out of him as David gave his mount a swat with his hat and the old mule took off like a scared rabbit. He grinned at D'lise and Kane; then jabbing his own mount into action, he overtook the irate Johnny.

"Where's Raven?" D'lise looked around.

"She left five minutes ago," Kane said. "You won't be seein' her anymore."

"It wouldn't bother me if I saw her every day of the year for the rest of my life." D'lise snuggled up against Kane's broad chest. "I don't have to worry anymore whether or not you love me."

"And I've laid my jealousy to rest." Kane turned the stallion around and headed him toward home. "And I've learned that beauty isn't necessarily evil."

"Did you used to think that?" D'lise looked up at him in surprise. "Tell me about it."

As they rode through the thickening dusk of evening, Kane shifted about in the saddle to ease his growing arousal. "I'll tell you about it someday," he said. "There are some trails you hate goin' back over. Right now, all I want to think about is gettin' you home and makin' love to you until I can't move."

D'lise put her arms around his neck. "I think that is a wonderful idea, husband."

Epilogue

The May twilight air was soft and scented with early-blooming wildflowers as Kane sat sidewise in the doorway of the candlelit cabin.

His expression grew soft as he watched his wife nursing their two-month-old daughter. D'lise's face wore a glow of radiant beauty, and he asked himself if there could be anything more lovely than her giving nourishment to her child.

Mary Kate had given her mother a painful, difficult time while entering the world. D'lise had labored close to twenty hours delivering the small, red-faced infant. He and the boys had paced across the yard after Doctor Ashley had banished him from the bedroom, snapping, "I don't have the time or the patience to put up with bothersome expectant fathers."

He had been a bother, Kane knew now, demanding that

Doctor Ashley do something to help D'lise, give her something for her pain.

There had never been a more welcome sound to him than that which came from the cabin a short time later— the angry cry of his child entering the world. He and the boys had looked at each other with relieved, happy eyes, then dashed up on the porch.

Again the doctor barred him from the bedroom. "I'm still tending to mother and daughter," he said, but in a kinder tone than he had used when ordering Kane out of the cabin. "You can come back in about ten or fifteen minutes."

"A little girl, Kane," David whispered almost in awe.

"I have a little sister." Johnny hugged himself, his eyes shining.

"She's not your sister, you lop-head." David poked the younger boy with his elbow, at the same time giving Kane a hopeful look.

Kane had caught the look of longing in the older boy's eyes and, putting an arm across each young shoulder, said quietly, "The little one is very lucky to have two big brothers to look after her."

Kane smiled to himself. He hadn't become father to one that March morning; he had become father to three. David and Johnny spent all their waking hours with him and D'lise, returning to the old cabin only to sleep. But next week he intended to get started on a two-room addition to the new cabin, and then the boys would be a complete part of the family.

The neighbor women had been so kind to D'lise. Kane's thoughts drifted back to that morning two months ago. He had spent less than half an hour with his new baby and her tired mother when they began to call. Each had brought a favorite dish, which they claimed would be healing to her and provide a plentiful supply of milk for the baby. When he said, with tongue in cheek, that probably he'd better not eat anything they had brought, soft laughter greeted his remark, along with a few pink blushes.

Old Tom had arrived at dusk, carefully holding a brown glazed jug. When he had looked at the baby and remarked to D'lise that she had done a pretty good job, considering it was her first time, he tapped the jug with a bent, arthritic finger and ordered, "Drink a glass of this liquid every day for a week. It will heal your insides real fast."

And whatever was in the old man's concoction, it had apparently done its job. Before the week was out, D'lise was up and about, almost her old self.

Kane's attention was caught by D'lise removing the sleeping baby from her breast. He watched her gently lay the little one on her knees, then rebutton her bodice. She had regained her slim, supple figure, and as he ran his gaze over it, desire tugged sharply at his loins. Doctor Ashley had said today that it was all right for him and D'lise to make love again.

He looked at young Johnny sitting at D'lise's feet, then at David sitting on the raised hearth, absently scratching Hound's ears as he stared into the flames. He hated to send the boys off so early, but it had been four long months since he had made love to his wife, and he didn't think he could wait much longer.

Five minutes later he was undressing D'lise, his hands hungrily stroking her shoulders and breasts after he had tossed her camisole to the floor. "I'm sure the boys didn't understand your sending them off so early," D'lise said breathlessly as his hands moved down to her waist and began sliding her petticoat over her hips.

''They'll understand when they're a little older,'' Kane said, his voice hoarse with passion as he scooped her naked body into his arms and carried her to the big bed waiting for them.

Scrag and Hound listened to its soft, rhythmic creaking for a long time.

Spice Cake
Young Johnny's Favorite

Two cups brown sugar
⅓ cup hot water
Two tablespoons butter
One tablespoon salt
Two cups diced dried apples

One teaspoon cinnamon
One teaspoon cloves
Three cups flour
One teaspoon soda

Boil together sugar, water, butter, salt, apples, and spices for ten minutes. When cold, add flour and soda, which has been dissolved in one-fourth cup hot water. Bake forty minutes in a 325°F oven, or until a broom straw stuck in the middle comes out clean.

BESTSELLING AUTHOR OF
BLAZE

Kane Roemer heads up into the Wyoming mountains hell-bent on fulfilling his heart's desire. There the rugged horseman falls in love with a white stallion that has no equal anywhere in the West. But Kane has to use his considerable charms to gentle a beautiful spitfire who claims the animal as her own. Jade Farrow will be damned if she'll give up her beloved horse without a fight. But then a sudden blizzard traps Jade with her sworn enemy, and she discovers that the only way to true bliss is to rope, corral, and brand Kane with her unbridled passion.

___4310-6 $5.99 US/$6.99 CAN

Dorchester Publishing Co., Inc.
P.O. Box 6640
Wayne, PA 19087-8640

Please add $1.75 for shipping and handling for the first book and $.50 for each book thereafter. NY, NYC, and PA residents, please add appropriate sales tax. No cash, stamps, or C.O.D.s. All orders shipped within 6 weeks via postal service book rate. Canadian orders require $2.00 extra postage and must be paid in U.S. dollars through a U.S. banking facility.

Name_____
Address_____
City_____ State_____ Zip_____
I have enclosed $_____ in payment for the checked book(s).
Payment <u>must</u> accompany all orders. ☐ Please send a free catalog.

Storm
NORAH HESS

"Norah Hess not only overwhelms you with characters who seem to be breathing right next to you, she transports you into their world!"
—Romantic Times

Wade Magallen leads the life of a devil-may-care bachelor until Storm Roemer tames his wild heart and calms his hotheaded ways. But a devastating secret makes him send away the most breathtaking girl in Wyoming—and with her, his one chance at happiness.

As gentle as a breeze, yet as strong willed a gale, Storm returns to Laramie after years of trying to forget Wade. One look at the handsome cowboy unleashes a torrent of longing she can't deny, no matter what obstacle stands between them. Storm only has to decide if she'll win Wade back with a love as sweet as summer rain—or a whirlwind of passion that will leave him begging for more.

_3672-X $4.99 US/$5.99 CAN

Fancy

NORAH HESS

After her father's accidental death, it is up to young Fancy Cranson to keep her small family together. But to survive in the pristine woodlands of the Pacific Northwest, she has to use her brains or her body. With no other choice, Fancy vows she'll work herself to the bone before selling herself to any timberman—even one as handsome, virile, and arrogant as Chance Dawson.

From the moment Chance Dawson lays eyes on Fancy, he wants to claim her for himself. But the mighty woodsman has felled forests less stubborn than the beautiful orphan. To win her hand he has to trade his roughhewn ways for tender caresses, and brazen curses for soft words of desire. Only then will he be able to share with her a love that unites them in passionate splendor.

__3783-1 $5.99 US/$6.99 CAN

NORAH HESS *Wildfire*

Bestselling Author Of *Storm*

"A grand and beautiful love story....Never a dull moment! A masterpiece about the American spirit."
—*Affaire de Coeur*

The Yankees killed her sweetheart, imprisoned her brother, and drove her from her home, but beautiful, golden-haired Serena Bain faces the future boldly as the wagon trains roll out. Ahead lie countless dangers. But all the perils in the world won't change her bitter resentment of the darkly handsome Yankee wagon master, Josh Quade.

Soon, however, her heart betrays her will. Serena cannot resist her own mounting desire for the rough trapper from Michigan. His strong, rippling, buckskin-clad body sets her senses on fire. But pride and fate continue to tear them apart as the wagon trains roll west—until one night, in the soft, secret darkness of a bordello, Serena and Josh unleash their wildest passions and open their souls to the sweetest raptures of love.

_51988-7 $4.99 US/$5.99 CAN